# THE
# ART OF
# SCANDAL

## REGINA BLACK

GRAND
CENTRAL

New York  Boston

Copyright © 2023 by Regina Black

Reading group guide copyright © 2024 by Regina Black and Hachette Book Group, Inc.

Cover design by Lila Selle
Cover images from Shutterstock

Cover copyright © 2024 by Hachette Book Group, Inc.

Grand Central Publishing
Hachette Book Group
1290 Avenue of the Americas, New York, NY 10104
grandcentralpublishing.com
twitter.com/grandcentralpub

Originally published in hardcover and ebook by Grand Central Publishing in August 2023.

First Trade Paperback Edition: April 2024

Grand Central Publishing is a division of Hachette Book Group, Inc.
The Grand Central Publishing name and logo is a trademark of Hachette Book Group, Inc.

The publisher is not responsible for websites (or their content) that are not owned by the publisher.

The Hachette Speakers Bureau provides a wide range of authors for speaking events. To find out more, go to hachettespeakersbureau.com or email HachetteSpeakers@hbgusa.com.

Library of Congress Cataloging-in-Publication Data

Names: Black, Regina, author.
Title: The art of scandal / Regina Black.
Description: First edition. | New York, NY : Grand Central Publishing, 2023.
Identifiers: LCCN 2022057936 | ISBN 9781538722770 (hardcover) | ISBN 9781538722794 (ebook)
Subjects: LCGFT: Romance fiction. | Novels.
Classification: LCC PS3602.L3252413 A88 2023 | DDC 813/.6—dc23/eng/20230104
LC record available at https://lccn.loc.gov/2022057936

ISBNs: 978-1-5387-2277-0 (hardcover); 978-1-5387-2278-7 (trade paperback); 978-1-5387-2279-4 (ebook)

Printed in the United States of America

LSC-C

Printing 1, 2024

Praise for
# The Art of Scandal

"As a hopeless romantic, Regina Black's *The Art of Scandal* hit every beat for me. This wildly steamy, utterly heartwarming novel is all about finding transcendent love and passion where you least expect it—and the ways in which art can transform our lives. Rachel and Nathan are incredibly drawn, flawed-but-lovable characters, and their love story will stay with me for ages. Such dreamy escapism!"

—Tia Williams, *New York Times* bestselling
author of *Seven Days in June*

"A seductive, sweltering debut. Regina Black crafts such decadent tension between her characters and their opposing worlds, each word chosen for maximum impact. Achingly raw and beautifully messy—this book is a work of art."

—Rachel Lynn Solomon, *New York Times*
bestselling author of *The Ex Talk*

"As poignant as it is passionate, this marks Black as a writer to watch."
—*Publishers Weekly*

"In this deeply emotional and fast-moving romance, debut author Black writes a sultry story about family, forgiveness, art, and embracing love, even when it's inconvenient." —*Library Journal*, starred review

"The combination of complex characters, gorgeous prose, and a compulsively readable plot made *The Art of Scandal* one of my top romances of all time. It was an ache in my throat, a crackling tension in the air, a haunting melody in my head long after I'd finished reading. I absolutely inhaled every word and am ready for everything and anything Regina Black writes in the future."

—Alicia Thompson, national bestselling
author of *Love in the Time of Serial Killers*

"*The Art of Scandal* is devastatingly beautiful and captivatingly romantic. Every so often, a book strikes the perfect chord of touching, poignant, sexy, and thrilling and this is that book. Black's storytelling draws you in and holds you close and her diverse cast of characters shine with three-dimensional emotion and sizzling chemistry. This one is not to be missed."          —Denise Williams, author of *How to Fail at Flirting*

"In *The Art of Scandal*, Black puts her mastery of character on full display... A riveting debut perfect for readers of *Seven Days in June*."
                                                            —*Shelf Awareness*

"Smart, sexy, and absolutely sizzling with steamy scenes, this book makes the list as one of my all-time favorite romances. Art, scandal, and finding love where one leasts expects it—what's not to adore?"
          —Ashley Herring Blake, author of *Delilah Green Doesn't Care*

"Richly characterized and beautifully depicted, Black brings the political drama and electric chemistry of Shonda Rhimes' *Scandal* to this novel of two starkly different individuals learning to find themselves in each other."                      —Shirlene Obuobi, author of *On Rotation*

"*The Art of Scandal* is a one-of-a-kind story! Sexy and smart with messy yet relatable characters, this is the book you need in your life! Regina Black is a force!"
                      —Catherine Adel West, author of *The Two Lives of Sara*

"Right out the gate, Regina Black charges in to bring drama and sensuality. Black's dazzling use of language creates a compelling novel of heartbreak, passion, and rediscovery. Justice for Rachel Abbott is as delicious as it is scandalous. Readers are going to cheer for her the whole way!"
          —Charish Reid, author of *The Write Escape* and *Hearts on Hold*

"Juicy."                                                    —Sisters from AARP

*For Angel*

# THE
# ART OF
# SCANDAL

# CHAPTER ONE

When your husband of thirteen years sends a close-up of his erect penis, you should not, under any circumstances, ask him why he sent it. Rachel Abbott didn't know much about sexting etiquette, but she was fluent in middle-aged male fragility. It was the theme of the birthday party currently rattling the walls of her home. A massive bowl of pimento cheese sat congealing on her kitchen island, while a dozen lawyers in her living room got wasted on single malt scotch in red Solo cups. Her house was filled with food she didn't eat and people she barely knew, because Matt was turning forty and needed balloons and streamers to blunt the sharp edges of his mortality.

She shouldn't have let Faith talk her into such a big phone. Rachel had trusted her twenty-one-year-old daughter's claim that it was great for watching movies, but it also made the penis inescapable. The detail of the high-resolution image kept her frozen, holding an icing knife in one hand and dick pic in the other, with the muffled beat of "Rump Shaker" as a jeering soundtrack in the background.

Maybe it wasn't him. She tried to remember the last time she'd seen Matt's penis up close but could only picture him drunkenly peeing against their neighbor's crape myrtle after last year's Fourth of July barbecue. Maybe one of his law firm buddies had stolen his phone when he wasn't looking. Abbott and Associates had an aging frat boy vibe that eroded the elegance of every event. When she'd sent out the invitations for Matt's party, one of the senior partners had offered to bring a keg.

Rachel wiped away the buttercream smeared on the screen and tapped the photo to zoom in. No, it was definitely Matt's penis. She had always thought it looked like something out of a textbook—perfectly shaped, and Goldilocks-sized. Not too big. Not too little. The text was probably a dig at their anemic sex life. Or a bumbling request for a birthday blow job. Both possibilities left her annoyed and wilted. She'd been standing for twelve hours straight and had no intention of spending the rest of the night trading pithy sex memes or getting rug burns on her knees.

The kitchen door swung open, and Matt poked his head inside. The phone slipped from her hand and landed facedown with an ominous crack that made her wince. She could almost hear Faith groan, "I told you to get a case, Mom."

"Sorry, I forgot," Matt said. "Where are the cups again?" The overhead light glinted against his glasses, obscuring his eyes. His pale skin was mottled red, and his short dark hair was damp at the temples, like he had just come back from a run.

Or just had sex. That was also his post-orgasm hair, complete with splotchy complexion. He used to tease her about how different they looked after they came—him a strawberry-colored mess, her natural curls a frizzy halo while her dark skin glowed with a dusky pink hue. Now he gave her a puzzled look before stepping into the kitchen. She studied his face as he approached, grappling with the image of him masturbating in the middle of his own birthday party.

"Where are what?" She picked up the knife and searched his cake for a flaw, but it was perfect. Matt's name was written in iced calligraphy she had practiced a dozen times to get right.

"The plastic cups." He shoved both hands into his trouser pockets. They were the same as in the picture—charcoal gray, light Italian wool. Despite a political platform that included the tax policy version of "eat the rich," Matt refused to wear anything that wasn't custom. She'd once gently suggested rethinking his wardrobe when he ran for mayor four years ago. He had brushed her off. "You really think the people in this town would vote for a guy in J.Crew khakis?"

"Hey, isss-everything-okay?" Matt asked, with each word stumbling into the next. Focusing on her face took effort. He was drunk. That had to be why he sent it. Peer pressure plus too many beers had led to a tipsy lapse in judgment.

But wasn't he supposed to reveal the joke, laugh, and tell her to stop being so uptight? She would laugh too, and they would keep pretending it hadn't been a year since they had sex. He wasn't supposed to stand there, blinking through his glasses, waiting for an explanation for the weird air between them.

"I'm fine," she said, though it was directed more at the anxious knot in her stomach than him. She needed him to leave. The kitchen was usually her haven—the room he treated like the backstage area of a play he was invited to attend. "Go enjoy your party. I'll find the cups." *And serve the food. And send the thank-you notes. And deal with the fallout from whatever you've been doing while the senior partners were in the next room.*

He sighed and gave her that look she hated—exasperated but patient—resigned to another teachable moment. "It's your party too. Why are you hiding in the kitchen? People are starting to notice."

"I need to finish the cake." She slid her knife along one side for emphasis.

"No one cares about the cake. They probably won't even eat it."

Her face heated. He was so good at that—making something benign, like baking a cake for a birthday party, feel like a childish mistake. "I don't care if they eat it." She put the knife down and untied her apron. "It exists. That's all that matters."

"Whatever you say." He shrugged. "Are you coming out or not?"

"Do you like it at least?"

He sighed again, flicked his eyes toward the door, and pressed his lips into a smile that looked more like a gassy grimace. "It's perfect. Like always. Now come on." He waved a lazy hand at the cake on his way out. "Bring it with you."

The silence he left behind was smothering. Their snippy argument was nothing new. Yesterday it was about paint colors, the shade of blue she'd chosen for his office. "It's too dark. How am I supposed to work in a room that feels like a cave?" That was who they were. Snippy arguments.

Cold pimento cheese. Not sexy text messages at inappropriate moments. He'd never proposition her this way.

Rachel flipped her phone back over. The screen was covered in webbed cracks, but the picture was still visible. She sent a reply.

I don't think you meant to send this to me.

She put her phone down and dipped her finger into a bowl of leftover icing, careful to avoid the red velvet crumbs in the center. She hated red velvet. The kitchen door swung open and banged against the opposite wall. Matt rushed inside, his panicked eyes darting from her face to her abandoned phone. "Jesus." He shoved both hands in his hair. "God, I'm so sorry."

Rachel held his gaze and slowly pushed the cake over the counter's edge. It fell, facedown, into a bloodred pile at his feet.

---

Two weeks earlier, Rachel had been perched on the edge of her living room sofa while she stared deeply into Matt's eyes and promised to be less of a selfish bitch. Or, more accurately, decided that keeping her mouth shut was the best way to avoid another surprise marriage counseling session. According to Shania Fariss—their wispy marriage-maintenance specialist—their relationship's primary area for improvement was Rachel's lack of gratitude.

"Focus on what your partner gives you," Shania advised. "Not what you think is lacking." Whatever annoying habit of Matt's that Rachel had planned to mention immediately deflated into something so small and petty, it didn't deserve to be spoken out loud. Instead, they focused on the very important fact that Rachel was not, and had never been, very good at being his wife.

A good wife would not have slipped away during her husband's Rising Star Award speech at the Virginia bar luncheon to send their driver to Popeye's Chicken, causing political commentators to speculate whether a white man with a Black wife was a fan of dark meat.

According to Matt, her lack of judgment said something deeper about their marriage aside from Rachel's aversion to underseasoned poultry. The small scandal had called for another counseling session—their third in two months.

"I'm grateful for my family. My daughter." Rachel paused, and then quickly added, "The Abbotts of course," because everyone thought she should be grateful for them. Matt had made her one of *the* Abbotts, a family so royal adjacent that the press had dubbed Rachel "the DC Meghan Markle." And like Meghan, any hint of dissatisfaction with her royal status would be met with skepticism and, occasionally, open hostility. Who wouldn't be grateful to wake up each day swaddled in downy white privilege?

In truth, Rachel was grateful for not worrying about whether her bills were paid or there was food in the refrigerator. She was thankful for the car that always started and insurance that swallowed medical bills like magic. But Matt and Shania wouldn't understand any of that. They couldn't relate. He was born with money, and Shania, with her Wellesley pedigree, would probably launch into a lecture about the pitfalls of focusing on material things as if they were discussing a designer shoe collection instead of basic human needs.

When Rachel and Matt were dating, it didn't matter that she was always broke. Their differences seemed small and romantic. Like how he would order too much food at restaurants because he knew that outside of their shared dinners, Rachel existed on ramen noodles and cheap gas station hot dogs.

"I'm grateful for this community," Rachel continued. "How Oasis Springs has embraced me." Fifteen years ago, she didn't know the place existed. Their suburb was so exclusive that most Fairfax County Realtors didn't bother to include it in their guides. As an outsider, being accepted meant being useful in some way. Rachel was their First Lady. Aside from the chicken incident, a symbol of elegance. Basically, a mascot.

"Jesus, Rache. You're starting to sound like me." Matt exchanged another look with Shania. "I'm grateful for my wife," he said, unprompted, because he was a lawyer and a politician and always said the right thing. "She keeps me solid. I don't know what I'd do without her."

But they both knew exactly what he'd do. He'd hire someone to cook his meals and keep his social calendar. If his office needed an update, a dozen interior designers were a Google search away. Need a pretty girl on his arm? Toss a rock and he'd hit one of the blue-blooded socialites eager to be photographed with the next Pete Buttigieg. Everything he was grateful for could be purchased for the right price.

But she didn't say any of that. She didn't admit how lonely it was to be appreciated for what you did for someone rather than who you were. *Remember when you thought I was funny? Remember when I took a pen from your father's desk and you told me it cost more than a thousand dollars? And I panicked while you laughed and drew crooked hearts along my shin?*

Shania gave her an expectant look. Matt pushed his glasses up his nose with one finger and gazed back at her with soft, encouraging eyes.

"I'm grateful for you too," Rachel said, and repeated how sorry she was for the chicken thing. She mentioned his birthday and suggested a nice dinner, but Matt wanted a party. "Something with shitty food and loud music." She'd agreed and promised to make the cake herself. "It's your fortieth, which is a big deal. I want everything to be perfect."

His eyes had clouded over, and he'd asked if she was happy. "Really happy. Not just... you know."

She'd laughed and said, "Of course!" as if there were no other way to feel.

---

Now, Matt refused to leave the kitchen. His rambling turned him further into a cheater cliché while Rachel seriously considered picking up the knife again. Someone walked into the room and they both froze. It was Kenneth, a new associate and Matt's mentee. His cherubic face took in the messy pile of cake on the floor, his boss's fight-or-flight posture, and what was probably a maniacal gleam in Rachel's eyes. "Cheryl and

I were just leaving," he said with a thumb jab over his shoulder. "But we had a great time. I wanted—"

Rachel left the kitchen before he could finish. Matt hissed her name, following close behind. She needed to get to the stairs. Her heels made clacking sounds against the tile as she moved past the foyer. Matt struggled to keep up without running. She glanced over her shoulder, and he said her name again, this time sharp and determined. Rachel shucked off her shoes and sprinted.

A few party guests watched them, wide eyed. What would people say tomorrow? That Matt Abbott chased his hysterical wife up the stairs at their over-the-hill birthday kegger? Rachel slowed at the landing and Matt gained ground. He darted ahead, blocking her path. His eyes were bloodshot and brimming with excuses. She made a fist, and he stepped back like she'd put her finger on a trigger. "Rachel, talk to me. *Please.*"

Once inside their bedroom, she started pacing, her bare feet sinking silently into the carpet. Maybe it was a mistake. Or an accident. Or some onetime thing he would confess during their next session. Shania would look at Rachel instead of Matt and sigh at his pathetic lapse in judgment.

Matt told her that the affair had started during a monthlong swing of small towns last August. The trip was supposed to make him more appealing to blue-collar workers, and Rachel had been ordered to stay home because she was "too elegant" to fit the narrative.

"You've been fucking this woman since last year?"

Matt lifted his hand to touch her. She probably looked like a wounded animal. Rachel flinched and scooted away. Roadkill didn't look to the driver for sympathy.

"*Seeing.* It's not just…" His voice lowered to a squeamish hiss. "Sex. I didn't plan this. It just happened."

Rachel yanked her dress down over her knees as his affair shifted in her mind from a selfish mistake to a deliberate betrayal. "Is she white?"

Matt blinked, and she could almost see his brain fumbling for the right response. "Yes. Why would you ask that?"

"Because I'm not."

"Are you implying—"

"I'm not implying anything. I'm saying it." That was better. Her anger had wrapped her voice in steel. Instead of being shattered, she'd become a blade. "If you think a congressional campaign would be easier with—"

"Would you stop?" Matt reached for her hands. "It's not an election strategy, Rachel. This is about me falling in love with someone else."

Falling in love? That couldn't be right. Their life was a blur of photo ops and campaign fundraising events. Their nights were surfing cable news shows or mining social media mentions for useful sound bites. Matt's political career had the velocity of a comet that incinerated every free minute in its path—including her minutes, her life, and all that time she spent flourishing cakes with royal icing. When did he find time to fall in love?

Rachel let her eyes roam around the bedroom she had designed—the fluffy white down comforter, the espresso-colored furniture, the bright turquoise accents—everything was coordinated, down to the small fringe hanging from the curtains in the master bathroom. That's what she did in her spare time. Generate new palettes on her color wheel app while Matt kept secrets and nodded absently at variations of ecru.

"Why are you telling me this?" Her voice trembled, close to cracking. "You were obviously fucking her behind my back for months. Suddenly you can't think of a decent lie?"

Matt flinched. He wasn't used to being called a liar to his face. That's what happened when you were the firstborn Abbott golden boy—no one bothered to hold you accountable. He released her hands and put more distance between them. "I was going to tell you once the election was over. I didn't want you to find out like this. It's embarrassing."

He really meant inconvenient. Matt's mayoral reelection was a formality—a small step in his ascension to an empty US congressional seat. The position had been vacated by a ten-term octogenarian who'd been accused of quid pro quo sexual harassment. Matt was being vetted as his replacement because, besides his progressive agenda, he was bankably bland. A young blue blood with a picture-perfect marriage to a Black woman he'd lifted from poverty like some liberal fairy-tale prince. Dumping Rachel for his white mistress would ruin the narrative.

Matt looked down at his hands. They were thinner than when she met him, which didn't seem fair. Her old rings didn't fit anymore.

"*You're* embarrassed?" She waited until he made eye contact again. "I just threw you a frat boy Pinterest party. How do you think I feel?"

Matt didn't answer, which was probably for the best. What could he say besides some cliché like he never meant to hurt her? He might as well admit that ripping her life apart wasn't a big deal because she was the last thing on his mind. "What's her name?"

He tensed. "Does it matter?"

"I should know who stole my life." The woman Rachel pictured was the opposite of herself—blond, willowy, and born swaddled in Chanel. But then she remembered how Matt used to look at her before they got married, like she was priceless. "You've ruined me for other women," he'd said. "How could anyone compare to you?"

Rachel bit back a laugh. Or a sob. She couldn't tell the difference. "We have to separate."

"No." Matt waved away the idea. "I might as well write a signed confession and mail it to every news station in the country."

Her jaw tightened. Even now, it was all about him. "I am done scheduling my life around your career. And I don't want you in my house."

"It's *my* house, Rachel."

She knew it was just his flailing attempt to win the argument. Matt winced, fidgeting inside this new, dickish skin. When his pacing brought him to a wall mirror, he stepped away from his own reflection. Rachel held her breath, waiting for him to take it back.

Two months after their honeymoon, Matt handed her a brochure of real estate listings and dismissed his million-dollar town house with an eye roll. "This place is too small. Faith needs a backyard. Pick something."

Rachel hadn't argued, even though the home they already shared was large enough to have an echo. The Realtor showed them sprawling colonials in subdivisions with names that sounded like resorts. It was overwhelming. When she walked into what would eventually become their three-story Georgian on Millwood Avenue, she had burst into exhausted tears.

One call and the house was theirs. Another call and a blond decorator with a faint Eastern European accent appeared with a binder containing measurements of every room in the house. That was how he managed their life. Matt dialed a number and another hard thing got easier. A decade later, it was Rachel who made the phone calls, because all of it was *theirs*, not just his. That was supposed to be the deal. Matt contributed money. She gave time, attention, and every hour of her day in return.

"Let's think rationally here." His voice was slow and deliberate, like he was taking cues from Shania. "We're not normal people. I can't be seen checking into some hotel with a suitcase. Hell, I can't be seen in public alone without some asshole with a camera asking where you are. Neither of us wants that kind of attention." He gazed at the ground, the window, everything in the room but her. This had turned into a strategy meeting. She might as well have been a member of his campaign.

Rachel's stomach heaved, threatening to empty its contents on the rug. She pushed off the bed with a hand over her mouth, and Matt stopped midsentence, eyeing her warily. The nausea faded, but the sight of him poised to sprint away made her eyes prickle with tears. He really didn't care about any of it. Not about her or their marriage.

She stalked past him, yanked open the door, and was in the hallway before he sputtered her name. "Rachel! What are you doing?"

"You want to stay, stay." She didn't hesitate on the stairs this time. The house was empty. Everyone had likely smelled the rancid air and fled to avoid an awkward goodbye. Her fury intensified as she stared at used cups and paper plates strewn over various surfaces, waiting for the cleaning service she'd scheduled to come in the morning. She should cancel it. She should leave the house so wrecked he wouldn't want it anymore.

"It's almost midnight," Matt shouted. "Where are you going? We're not finished talking. Rachel!"

There was a liquor bottle in a red velvet sack on the gift table. She grabbed it on the way out the door. A hard gust of wind slammed into her face, smothering her briefly before it eased and she could breathe again. She could hear Matt's footfalls against the foyer tile. He matched her pace but didn't go much faster. He didn't want to catch her.

# CHAPTER TWO

Hiding in a public bathroom stall wasn't how Nathan Vasquez usually dealt with awkward social scenes. Although, to be fair, the bathrooms at the Oasis Springs Drive-In weren't the worst place to spend your time. There was something cool and a little creepy about how the sterile walls glowed under the buzzing fluorescents. The apple-shaped air freshener plugged into the wall made the room smell like industrial soap and cinnamon. If it weren't for the toilet paper under lock and key, he could have been in someone's Williams Sonoma'd, rarely used guest bathroom.

Nathan knew that the night's downward trajectory was partially his fault. A boring night out usually called for one of two options: make things interesting or leave. Only assholes suffered in silence, which was exactly what he was doing, sitting on a decorative pouf that he'd stolen from the sitting area, with his legs propped up against the door, ignoring his best friend's text messages to draw on a hot dog wrapper against his thigh.

**Dillon:** Are you hiding in the shitter?

It would be nice to think he was evolving—that turning twenty-six had triggered some adult gene lying dormant all these years. But he'd always hated conflict, and hiding was his newest avoidance tactic. That could count as evolution if you squint.

**Dillon:** Come on Nate. Where are you?

Nathan had sketched a large cheeseburger with razor-sharp teeth gnawing on the leg of a rough self-portrait. The movie playing a few hundred feet away had ramped into high gear with raised voices battling blipping laser guns. He drew lips on the burger before he responded to Dillon's text.

**Nathan:** Third stall on the left.

It took a few minutes for Dillon to find him, which gave Nathan time to add a pair of walking french fries to the scene. The sketch took a darker turn, with the fries reaching for Nathan's likeness, slobbery drool streaming behind them.

"You're not jacking off in there, are you?"

Nathan unlatched the stall door. "I just needed some air."

Dillon frowned and glanced at the wall of urinals to his right. "Cool. Cool. It's just uh... the girls keep asking about you."

The girls were two college students Dillon had picked up at the gas station earlier that evening. He'd arrived at Nathan's apartment with his arms draped over their shoulders, grinning as though he'd won the lottery instead of saddling their night with the awkwardness of two strangers who were old enough to drink but young enough to make the whole thing embarrassing.

"I think Laura really likes you," Dillon said. "She's cute, right? All that red hair."

"What do you think?" Nathan showed off his sketch. "New tattoo?"

The excitement on Dillon's face faded as he focused on the actual image. He glanced at the tattoos covering Nathan's right arm as if trying to picture greasy french fries next to corrido lyrics.

"It's interesting." He squinted at the killer burger. "Very... Adult Swim. But who cares what I think? You're the artist."

There was a whiff of pity in the compliment. They both knew that posting fan art online and doodling cartoon characters on fast-food wrappers wasn't an actual art career. Dillon was starting to make a habit out of lying to protect Nathan's feelings. Last week it was an apology that went on too long when Dillon bailed on plans. Two weeks before that, he claimed a food truck Nathan recommended "*was fire!*" with the same disgusted eye twitch that appeared when someone mentioned sushi. It made Nathan feel like a guy who needed handling, when in the past, he'd always been the handler.

Nathan stuffed the wrapper inside his jeans. "The movie's almost over. We should probably head back to the car." He left the restroom with Dillon trailing close behind, struggling to match Nathan's longer, faster strides.

As always, Dillon never complained. Not even in elementary school when Nathan was a head taller than everyone else, and Dillon had to cheat on the height test to ride a Ferris wheel alone. Back then Nathan was a constant barrier between his friend and whatever bully he unintentionally antagonized that week. Despite getting his ass kicked on a monthly basis, Dillon had never met a bully in his life. He had two labels for people: best friend and God-tier ride-or-die brother. The day they met, Dillon had the brilliant idea to point out that his favorite cafeteria worker wore the same cherry-red Vans as Trunk, an ogre-sized twelve-year-old named after the place he claimed to store his alleged victims. To Dillon, pointing out that his "favorite lunch man" and his grunting buddy Trunk were "shoe twins" was just a way to bring two like-minded people together.

Dillon had smiled and turned his back, thrilled with his good deed for the day. That smile is what Nathan would remember an hour later, sitting in the nurse's office with a busted lip and a fresh suspension. He'd instinctively known that Dillon was a guy who needed protecting. After that day, Nathan ascended to Dillon's God-tier list, while Nathan did his best to make sure no one ruined his new friend's optimism with another sucker punch from behind.

But ever since Dillon traded his Henley collection for dress shirts and a pharmaceutical sales job, their dynamic had shifted. Now Dillon was the one planning ego-stroking boys' nights where he tiptoed through serious conversations like they were riddled with land mines. And Nathan couldn't help thinking that he'd failed at some point. That as Dillon moved forward, it was obvious that Nathan was standing still.

They walked in silence, weaving through the maze of cars at a strolling pace. The new drive-in was still a novelty, which meant almost every available parking space was occupied. Like the bathroom, everything was a little too perfect. There were no potholes in the pavement. The vintage neon sign announcing showtimes sparkled in the moonlight, free of graffiti and bird shit.

Dillon glanced at Nathan's profile. "So, you're not feeling Laura?"

Nathan shoved both hands inside his pockets. "She's nice. But I don't need help getting a date."

"Hell, I know that. It's just been a while since you met anyone. Not since Inez." Dillon's voice tensed, as though mentioning Nathan's ex-girlfriend violated some unspoken code. "I thought you might be depressed or something."

Inez was a server at Nathan's favorite coffee shop. He'd asked her out last year when she slipped him her number with his usual order. She was beautiful and charming, with an influencer side hustle that helped her pay the bills. They had been good together—sexy and fun, with low expectations. But the more Nathan fumbled through conversations about video likes and ad revenue, the more her eyes would dim with disappointment.

She'd dumped him six months ago. Which, yes, was depressing, but it wasn't a heartbreak situation the way Dillon was implying. It was more like an awkward "I wish I could say it wasn't you, but it actually *is* you and your refusal to do anything with your life other than take up space in the world" situation.

He had always been attracted to women with ambition because it required a level of confidence that he didn't have. The laundromat he owned didn't require much effort to keep the doors open, so he had that covered. He owned and lived in the building, so paying a few utility bills on time wasn't difficult either. To someone like him, Inez's color-coded spreadsheets and annotated social media calendars seemed like sorcery. Maybe he thought it would rub off. Or at least point his life in some direction that felt more like progress and less like floating into space.

Nathan spotted his car in the distance. The interior light illuminated the women lounging inside. Laura's bare foot was bobbing outside the passenger window, and Chrissie's blond hair was splayed across the back seat. His Camaro had been taken hostage by two drunk 7-Eleven cashiers.

Fuck. It may not have been his heart, but Inez had definitely broken something.

"I'm good." He turned to Dillon and added a quick smile to make it more convincing. "Just picky."

"Yeah, well, get unpicky before it stops working." Dillon grinned, visibly relieved to switch to one of his favorite topics. "I read that on Reddit a while back. It has to do with chronology or something."

"Chronology?"

"Yeah, like your muscles and shit. What Stan Payton studied before he started coaching that baseball team."

"That's not—" Nathan paused and considered the effort involved in explaining kinesiology versus chronology to his friend. "You know. You're probably right."

A guy in a white Tesla honked his horn when they walked in front of his car, and they flipped him off in unison. "You talk to Bobbi lately?" Dillon asked, ducking his head to focus on an empty Coke can he kicked ahead like a soccer ball.

"Yeah," Nathan said, eager for a new topic. He blocked Dillon with the side of his foot, sending the can skidding to the right.

"Like, a lot?" The parking lot was suddenly flooded in light. Music swelled over closing credits and a chorus of engines turning over. "People around town are saying you guys have some sort of *thing* going on."

People? What people? Nathan could count on one hand the number of people in Oasis Springs he'd spoken to over the past year. Even that customer with the hairless cat who used to nod on her way out the door refused to make eye contact lately. Probably because he didn't smile as much as he used to. Being a big brown guy with ink up to his neck didn't give him the luxury of being antisocial.

"There's no *thing*." Nathan paused at the sight of a black Mercedes parked in the distance, away from the other cars. A woman was sitting on the hood. "Why does that car look familiar?"

Dillon followed his gaze. "Everyone in this town drives a Mercedes. It's like rednecks and their four-wheelers." He glanced at Nathan. "Nice rims, though."

Dillon was right, there was nothing special about a late-model S-Class in Oasis Springs. But the woman sitting on the hood gave him a vague sense of déjà vu. Her clothes matched the car—dark, sleek, and expensive—but she sat hunched over, knees to chest, periodically swiping her eyes. The whole thing looked off, like she'd gotten lost on her way to a cocktail party.

"Wait." Dillon snapped his fingers, eyes widening with recognition. "Is that the mayor's wife? I saw her on some top ten list the other day. Hottest DC Honeys. What's her name? Rebecca or Sarah…"

"Rachel," Nathan corrected hesitantly, because the idea seemed ridiculous, even though he knew Dillon was right. "Rachel Abbott."

If Dillon read anything besides subreddit posts on a regular basis, he would have known exactly who Rachel was. Her husband's rant about Virginia's failed universal pre-K bill had gone viral. Nathan couldn't remember the last time he'd seen a white man in a thousand-dollar suit shout the word "fuck" that many times into a microphone. The guy was genuinely pissed off, even though the Abbotts could have opened their own chain of day cares with a fraction of that British slave trade money they pretended came from "working in textiles." No one had judged Matt for being a trust fund kid shouting about poor people. They thought it made him a good person. Just like being married to a Black woman made him "open minded."

Rachel had also been in that clip. The person filming had zoomed in on her face when Matt mentioned the impact of systemic racism in public schools. As Matt Abbott told the world that his wife used to be a teenage mother who couldn't afford childcare, she'd stood silently behind him like a blank-faced beauty queen, as though someone had put a life-sized cutout onstage instead of the actual woman. Nathan remembered thinking that she was beautiful in that unrealistic way that reminded you some people were God's favorites: flawless skin, full lips, big dark eyes.

Nathan watched her sitting on the car as she covered her face and caved inward, like a turtle retreating into its shell. She became a tiny speck on the midsize sedan, which might have been the saddest thing he'd ever seen. "Is she crying?"

"Dunno." Dillon slapped his arm. "I'm starving. You want to get burgers at The Stand?"

Nathan reached into his pocket and handed Dillon a hundred-dollar bill along with his keys. "It's on me. Bring back some fries if they're open." He gestured toward the movie screen. "I'm going to stay for the late show."

Dillon stuffed the cash in his jeans. "You're really going to stay here to watch an old space movie?"

"*Starship Troopers* is an anti-fascist satire."

"Alone?"

"Just me and my thoughts." Nathan shivered. The temperature had plummeted since they'd arrived. He pointed to the car. "And my hoodie. Pop the trunk."

---

Rachel had come to the drive-in because it was the last place anyone would look for her. Her Saturday nights were usually spent drinking white wine at fundraisers, not watching action movies with greasy pop-corn. It was also past midnight. She and Matt would normally be ready for bed by now, guzzling big glasses of water to chase down the drinks they'd had at the party. She would have popped an Advil before they traded notes on how the evening went with a chasm of space between them in their king-sized bed.

After thirteen years of marriage, she'd settled into the predictable rhythms of their life. But now she knew that they were all lies. Now she was sitting on the hood of the car he'd given her for Christmas, chugging whiskey mixed with a fountain drink the size of her thigh, wondering if he'd fucked his mistress in the back seat before putting that big red bow on top. He probably looked at her now the same way he did that old Honda Accord. "The car is fine, Rache, but we were long overdue for an upgrade."

She used to be wilder. Braver. The girl who dove headfirst into whatever caused the most damage. Making scary, life-altering choices was proof that she was living instead of merely existing. It was the reason she pursued an art career with an obsessive focus that eschewed any other marketable skills. It was how she ended up in Oasis Springs fifteen years ago with no money, a busted car, and a six-year-old who hadn't eaten more than a bag of Funyuns for three days. It was the reason she'd initially placed Matt in the fuck-and-dump category. He was too nice and eager. Like her pussy was a math quiz he wanted to ace with extra credit.

But there was also a cockiness to the way he pursued her. If she said she wasn't interested in anything serious, he would counter with reasons she was the woman he'd eventually marry. She'd never been loved like that before: like a wish that had finally come true. Rachel eventually trusted that feeling, and even though she'd never really believed in happy endings, she'd believed in Matt. He was supposed to be her safe place.

Rachel stared at the few cars left in the parking lot. The drivers were all so young. Her eyes were drawn to a red Camaro with two girls in the back seat. She used to love cars like that, with their loud, growling engines. Now she wouldn't consider one that wasn't at least a fuel-efficient hybrid. Matt was the first person in their neighborhood to go electric.

Two guys stood near the Camaro, a short blond with a pair of keys dangling from his fingers and a tall, dark-haired one rifling through the trunk. She could hear the girls' high-pitched squeals of "Nate, come with us!" that went unanswered.

The tall one, Nate apparently, had a sweatshirt balled under his arm like a football. He didn't look like a Nate. His black hair was cut into an intricate low fade they didn't offer at the high-end salons that shaped

Matt's preppy crew cuts. He had golden-brown skin and colorful tattoos covering one arm. A snow-white T-shirt, stretched over large biceps and broad shoulders, completed his best-kind-of-trouble look. The name Nate was too short and simple, gone just as quickly as you said it. He looked like someone who would linger.

Matt fit his name. He was handsome in a generic way that forced him to rely on charm and earnestness when asking someone on a date. This Nate probably hoarded his compliments like war rations. A guy like him could ignore his girlfriend's calls, party all night on do not disturb, and wake up the next day sure that her devotion would be exactly where he left it. Rachel used to think that way too. She used to look in the mirror and see herself as someone with options.

Her cup was still almost full. She'd chosen Dr Pepper, but after a few gulps, remembered she didn't like the taste. Maybe she didn't know herself anymore. If someone said, "You can have any drink you want," she'd probably stutter and ask for a menu.

Rachel slid off the car and winced when her bare feet hit the pavement. That was the problem with dramatically storming out of a room. There was no dignified way to double back to grab your shoes. She balanced on the balls of her feet as she made her way to a group of empty picnic tables. Tall pergolas covered in string lights were spread around the area. Each table had a ceramic popcorn bucket centerpiece filled with fresh-cut daisies. She dumped the rest of the Dr Pepper into an enormous pot of burnt-orange mums.

A blond woman in a fleece pullover that looked like a poodle devouring her neck paused to stare. "You're going to murder that poor plant," she said.

"My husband donated these in my name." Rachel shook the last few droplets into the soil. "I really don't think he'll mind."

---

The teenage girl working concessions gave Nathan a sour look when he asked for a fountain drink three minutes before closing. She wore the drive-in's teal T-shirt uniform over low-rise acid-wash jeans that probably cost a fortune. He put a five-dollar bill in her tip jar, and the sneer disappeared. She shot him a cheerful "Thanks!" as she retrieved the cash and stuffed it into her pocket.

He turned to grab a straw but shuffled back when Rachel Abbott suddenly blocked his path to the condiment table. She set a bottle of Pappy Van Winkle next to the ketchup packets and leaned into the counter with a tipsy wobble that confirmed she'd been upgrading her soda with five-thousand-dollar whiskey.

"I need a refill."

The girl flicked off the open sign. "We're closed."

"But the movie isn't over yet."

Rachel seemed oblivious to his hooded presence, even though he stood eavesdropping a few feet away. Grumpy Teen yanked the shade down halfway. "We close at eleven," she said, with a dismissive attitude that made Rachel bristle.

"It's two minutes till."

"Is it?" The girl tilted her head and gave the tip jar a pointed look.

Rachel's eyes narrowed. "Are you extorting me for a Coke?"

Grumpy Teen sighed. "It's soda, not revenge porn."

Nathan waited for the inevitable "Do you have any idea who I am?" that would end the face-off. Anyone who worked retail in Oasis Springs probably heard that song at least once a week. The suburb was filled with professional athletes, Washington power players, and retired tech moguls "consulting" from the golf course. There were also people like Rachel, who managed to be a national celebrity while also being so ingrained into the insular fabric of the town that her last name was etched into bricks on four different buildings.

He was surprised when Rachel placed her hand over her heart, fifth-grade Pledge of Allegiance–style. "I get it. It's sweet of you to try to protect me from myself. But I promise I'm not drink." She paused. "*Drunk.* I have been drinking, but I am not drunk."

The girl's blank stare said it all. Nathan smothered a laugh, and Rachel's eyes briefly shifted in his direction. "I'm not," she said to both parties. "I just spilled whiskey on my dress. That's what you smell." Rachel refocused on the girl. "You know, I used to wait tables when I was your age—"

"In the eighties?"

Nathan laughed out loud this time, but Rachel didn't seem embarrassed. Her lips trembled as she looked at him, like she was seconds from laughing too.

The concession shade slammed closed. "Try '03!" Rachel yelled at the ghost of her tormentor. "And those jeans won't age well!"

Nathan pulled out his wallet. "That wasn't very nice."

"Neither was she," Rachel said, watching him add five more apology dollars to the tip jar. "What about you?"

"Me?"

"Are you nice?"

Something in her voice made him pause. Like she had already decided the answer. Her gaze was a challenge, and he met it for a moment, staring long enough for some of her skepticism to fade. But then her eyes dropped briefly to his mouth, and the moment warmed into something else entirely.

Nathan blinked and said, "I'm just here to get a straw."

"Oh. I'm sorry." Rachel shuffled backward and rubbed her arms as if she'd just noticed the temperature. It made him feel like a jerk. The woman was clearly distressed. He only knew her from pictures, but in those she was flawless. Sleek hair. Perfect makeup. Now there were dark smudges under her eyes. Smears of something white dotted the bottom of her dress. Seeing her this way, puffy-eyed and vulnerable, was like discovering a knight without his armor.

He looked at her bare feet. All she had on was a thin little party dress. "Are you cold?"

She looked down at her clothes and frowned like she hadn't considered the possibility. He took off his sweatshirt and wrapped it around her shoulders like a cape. Her fingers grazed his knuckles as she took it from him. They were freezing.

Her eyes widened with recognition. "I saw you earlier."

"Yeah, I saw you too." Nathan took her cup and poured half of his soda into it. Then he grabbed the whiskey and studied her while he unscrewed the top. "You're the mayor's wife."

Her eyes cooled. She probably thought he was one of those hard-up guys sliding into her DMs or retweeting close-ups of her ass. "And you are?" she asked, shrugging into the sweatshirt.

"Me?" He fell silent and focused on the whiskey, carefully eyeballing shots into each cup. "I'm no one. Nathan."

"Right. Nate."

"Nathan." He pointed to her drink. "You're good to go."

Rachel took a sip, gazing at his face. Her eyes were so big and dark, they pulled him in. He stared a beat too long after her soft "Thank you."

She sat at a nearby table, and he noted her bright red toenails, the matching manicure, and the dewy sheen of her skin. Pampered princess. Not his thing. Which was fine because he was just being nice. Now he could find another place to sit while she got wasted to cope with whatever had brought her out there.

But that was his favorite sweatshirt. And the same nagging voice that wouldn't let him watch Dillon get his ass kicked in middle school was whispering in his ear. It was wrong to leave her upset and alone.

Nathan approached the table slowly to give her plenty of time to brush him off. Instead, she scooted over to make room. "I probably shouldn't drink this."

He sat beside her and leaned forward, elbow to knee. "Probably not."

She shoved her hand through her hair, and he reached over to pluck some fluff from the strands. She watched it float to the ground. "Do you have a cigarette?"

He raised an eyebrow. "You know those are bad for you, right?"

She wiggled her drink. "You know this isn't a smoothie, right?"

"I don't smoke tobacco."

"That is very specific. Whatever you do smoke, I'll take it."

He laughed. She had a good voice. Deeper than he'd imagined. A little hoarse, like maybe that cigarette she wanted wouldn't be the first. "Whatever's going on can't be that bad."

"Because I'm famous?"

"Well, DC famous. You're famous adjacent. That's a good enough reason not to ask strangers if they're holding."

"Most of the people I know would refer me to a cannabis consultant who'll make me fill out a fifty-page questionnaire about my lifestyle and weed goals." She pasted on a fake smile and spoke with robotic enthusiasm. "Please use this Likert scale to rate how turnt you'd like to be at the end of your experience."

Nathan laughed, and Rachel watched him with a triumphant grin, like the sound was her prize. It made his face warm. He cleared his throat and looked at the movie screen, pretending to watch the commercials.

"Where's your date?" she asked.

"I'm not on a date. My friend, Dillon, he—" Nathan stopped, and swallowed the explanation she didn't ask for. "I don't know those girls." He glanced at her bare feet. "Where's your husband?"

She thumbed her wedding ring, turning it slowly around her finger, and didn't answer. Marriage trouble—he shouldn't be surprised. But he couldn't imagine being married to a woman like Rachel Abbott and not tracking her like a bloodhound if she were this upset. What was it his father used to say? Behind every beautiful woman, there's a guy dumb enough to think no one else wants to fuck her.

She tucked her hand inside the sweatshirt. "Do you live around here?"

"Yes," he said, and ran a hand over his hair. He'd cut it shorter than usual and was starting to regret it. It made him feel exposed.

"You're not much of a talker, are you?"

"I'm a better listener."

"That's a dangerous combination." She focused on the movie screen. A private school commercial started competing with the drive-in's jazzy elevator music. "Beautiful men aren't known for their compassion. I dated a lot of them at your age. It's all I wanted back then, a beautiful boy who gave me butterflies and paid for popcorn at the movies."

He realized she didn't mean it as a compliment. *You're too handsome to be worth anything* was the implication. But no one had ever called him beautiful before. "So, what do you want now?" he asked, to keep her talking. He liked not being able to predict what she'd say next. The conversation was flowing like a simple painting that went sideways into something beautifully twisted while dragging his brush along for the ride.

"I don't know." Her voice was smaller, as if the question had drained her energy. "I haven't thought about it in a while."

Nathan forced a smile and pointed to the movie screen. "Well…I'd like movie options that were made in the last decade. This one's cool and all, but—"

"You don't have to do that," she said, in a gentle tone still sharp enough to cut him off. "You don't have to pretend it's okay that I can't answer such a simple question."

Nathan nodded, not trusting himself to speak. She was chipping at a crack in a dam. He wasn't sure what he wanted out of life either, which used to feel like freedom, but lately felt more like an excuse for being alone.

Rachel's stomach growled loudly. She shot up with an embarrassed grimace. "Sorry."

"Are you hungry?"

"I'm always hungry." She frowned at her own words. "God, that sounds terrible. I do eat, but it's all vegetables and protein. Fish. Chicken." She groaned. "I haven't had a burger in years."

"Please tell me you're lying."

"I am not." She said each word slowly, with overlong vowels. The drink was kicking in. Her face was softer, and the sweatshirt had fallen off one shoulder. It drew his gaze to a small freckle on her collarbone. He slid the sleeve back up into place, careful not to touch her skin.

"I miss sugar," she said. "And bread."

"There's a gas station down the street. I could grab a Tastykake."

"You don't have a car."

"It's not that far. I can walk."

"You would do that?"

"Of course."

"Why?"

He didn't know how to answer. Because she looked as lonely as he felt? He also wanted to impress her. She'd put him in some exceptional category of "beautiful men" who were worth her time, and he felt a sudden need to live up to the designation. "You seem like you're having a rough night."

She looked away and started chugging her drink. "Have you ever been in love?"

The question surprised him, and he answered "No" too quickly, before he could think. "I mean, I don't think so."

"Do you *want* to fall in love?" Rachel asked.

"Maybe," he said cautiously, because a simple yes felt too small for the conversation. She was so intense and focused on his answer that it was stifling. "Eventually. When it feels right."

"It always feels right," Rachel said. Her dreamy smile burrowed into his chest and slid inside a dozen places it probably shouldn't. "It feels perfect. And you can't imagine loving anyone else. Or even arguing. Or being cruel."

"But there's no such thing as perfect."

"Yes, there is. There are some truly perfect things in this world." She tried to prop her elbow on her knee, and nearly toppled over. He moved to steady her, but she righted herself like nothing happened. "A martini at the Savoy. The *Velvet Rope* album. That fraction of a second before a first kiss, when you realize it's finally going to happen." She tugged his sweatshirt over her knees. "Those things are perfect. It's people who are flawed."

It made him think about Inez. It was scary to think he could have lost the love of his life already because he wasn't paying attention. "Was it perfect for you? With your husband?"

She ducked her head and started maneuvering the sweatshirt until her hands disappeared inside the sleeves. "At first. Then it became unpaid labor."

He thought about that pre-K press conference he'd watched. How her expression never changed, even when her own husband referred to her as an example of the "traumatic toll of marginalization in America." It must have taken a lot of willpower to remain stoic while being used as institutional racism exhibit A.

"People say marriage is hard."

She smirked, like he'd told a joke. "But they never tell you *how* it's hard. It's always a rug being pulled from under you." They locked eyes briefly before hers slid away. That's when it clicked. This wasn't just marriage problems. Matt Abbott had done something bad enough to have her crying her eyes out and drinking herself numb.

"Take it back," he said.

She blinked. "Take what back?"

He realized how gruff he sounded and tried to lighten his tone. "The rug. Someone takes something from you, don't let them get away with it. He shouldn't call all the shots. Seems like he messed up, not you."

"That's nice of you to say, but you don't know what happened. What if it was me?"

"What if you both fucked up, but he fucked up the most?"

That earned him a smile. "I think you're just trying to make me feel better."

She had it half-right. He also liked the way talking to her made him feel. Interesting. Capable. Like he was worthy of influencing her mood. "Is it working?"

"Yes." Her eyes roamed his face. "Thank you."

"You're welcome."

Rachel's eyes shifted down to his neck tattoo, and she rubbed the same spot on her throat. "Did it hurt?"

"Yeah," he said, watching her fingers. There was truth in the way a woman touched herself. Rachel barely grazed her skin, like anything more would leave a bruise.

He must have been staring. She stood quickly and tugged at her dress. "It's getting late. I should go."

Nathan stood. "Are you okay to drive?"

"It's a block away. I'll be fine." She walked backward with the hoodie zipped to her chin and the boozy soda cup peeking up from its depths. "That was your car, wasn't it? The '69 Camaro?"

"You know your cars?"

She kept walking. "A perk of aging. I know lots of things. Good luck getting your car back."

He gestured toward her feet. "Good luck finding shoes."

She rolled her eyes. "I have shoes."

Nathan grinned. "See there? Things are looking up already."

# CHAPTER THREE

It had been a mild summer, so her roses were still blooming. Rachel sat on the ground in front of her house, staring up at large bushes of bright pink flowers the size of her fist. The scent reminded her of her wedding day. Or maybe it was the night of her senior prom, when Thomas Dunn had pinned a white rose to her breast with sweaty palms, the shoulders she'd always considered broad surprisingly small in his father's tuxedo. They had gotten high in the limo and stopped at McDonald's, ordering chicken nuggets and fries. He'd gone down on her in the parking lot before they finally dragged themselves into the gym.

Thomas had cried the day she left for college. At eighteen, she didn't know how rare it was for a guy his age to show so much emotion. She had avoided his calls for the next two months, smugly certain that real men never made snot bubbles or borrowed their daddy's tuxedo for a date. That was one of the last things she'd said to him. "It's time to grow up and be realistic. We were always going to end this way."

Now she knew reality was overrated. Reality was being rewarded for more than a decade of loyalty with a traitorous dick on your phone. Reality was protesting your prenup with a front yard sit-in surrounded by bushes, thorns, and God knows what else. It was sipping a half-empty cup of whiskey and wearing a stranger's sweatshirt that you kept sniffing for reasons you should probably ignore.

"Rachel?" Matt's voice was a sharp whisper. "Are you out here? Rachel?"

She tucked a rose behind her ear, took the lid off her soda cup, and swished it around. Matt stopped a few feet away, hands outstretched, as if he'd found her on the ledge of a building. He had changed into the monogrammed robe and pajamas she'd bought him for his birthday. "Where have you been? You look terrible."

"Good thing you've found a replacement."

Matt's concern evaporated. "I was worried," he chided, as if a broken curfew was their *real* problem. She would have laughed if it wasn't so depressing. Rachel lowered her head and willed it to stop spinning. She could hear mulch crunching under Matt's shoes as he took hesitant steps in her direction. "Are you okay?"

A flash of headlights made her look up. A red Corolla slowed and parked in front of their house. Matt tensed and pivoted like a thief weighing the odds of escape. Everyone in town knew that car. It had appeared at almost every troubled household in the area. Mia Williams worked for the police department as a victim's advocate. On paper, her job was to assist uniformed officers with domestic violence calls to help de-escalate situations and make sure the victim's rights were protected. In reality, she primarily dealt with retirees calling in complaints about their teenage neighbors trampling expensive landscaping.

For more than a decade, Mia had been a mediator for angry spouses, a babysitter to sulky preteens, and the moral authority to single playboys who thought it was a good idea to change clothes near open windows. She knew everyone's secrets, which was why no one ever wanted her around. In a town determined to perform perfection, it was hard to fake it with someone who knew that your wife wasn't at a family reunion because she was on vacation with the nanny you'd both been fucking. Despite Mia's innocent appearance—short and curvy, with dimples so deep, they were still visible even when she wasn't smiling—she had the instincts of a hard-boiled noir detective. Her sudden appearance sent Matt spiraling into a sweaty panic.

"Mia!" Matt's voice cracked with forced enthusiasm. "It's been a long time. What brings you out here?"

Mia moved closer, ignoring Matt. Her gaze was fixed on Rachel. "One of your neighbors called in a suspected break-in. They said a Black man was hiding in your bushes. But the alarm didn't trip, so the uniforms called me. I'm guessing they were trying to keep things in the family."

Rachel and Mia were family in the way two passing ships might occasionally dock at the same port. Despite being first cousins, they'd never met until Rachel moved to Oasis Springs with Faith. As an only child, Rachel had been excited to connect with family members so close to her age. But Mia was intimidating from day one. The oldest of two children, she lived up to the birth order stereotype. The day they met, Mia had introduced herself in one breath and then outlined an Oasis Springs for Beginners itinerary in the next. Mia's brother Niles, four years younger, with a personality composed entirely of charm and optimism, had offered to hire Rachel as a server at a seafood restaurant that never opened. By the time everyone learned he'd lost the financing, Niles had left the country to work as a sous-chef in Belize.

Mia's path had briefly intersected with Rachel's during those initial months when Rachel couldn't afford her own place and had to live with her aunt. Mia had recently quit law school and was staying with her mother for the same reason. During the day, Rachel waited tables at a café, and Mia hunted for jobs with the drive of someone who wanted out of her mother's house. At night, on the rare occasions they were still awake, they inched closer to friendship, trading war stories about Rachel's rude customers and Mia's awkward interviews like they'd known each other for years.

But then Rachel met Matt, and a few weeks later, Mia was offered a temp job at Abbott and Associates, his father's law firm. Neither of them could take the awkwardness of Rachel dating a man who signed Mia's paychecks. Rachel moved in with Matt and limited her interactions with her overly perceptive cousin to occasional waves across the grocery store parking lot.

Now Mia appraised Rachel's current situation—noting Matt's pajamas, the booze cup, and Rachel's bare toes peeking up through the mulch—with grim resignation. She was the domestic drama trash collector, and here they were, dumping another pile at her feet.

"A Black man?" Matt's eyes flashed with familiar outrage. He was gearing up for some rant about racial profiling in the neighborhood. Rachel hated when he did that. His stump speeches were usually smooth and measured, but he couldn't talk about racism to Black people without a hint of desperation. Like if he spoke loud enough with more flailing gestures, they'd finally believe he cared.

Rachel cut him off. "I'm sure they were just worried about us."

"There's a lot of that kind of worry in this neighborhood," Mia said. "I don't think there's been an actual break-in around here in five years. And that was some drunk kid, trying to sneak back into the wrong house."

It was jarring to hear someone say what she and Matt knew but ignored most days: their subdivision was diverse like a corporate recruiting ad—impressive until you realized it was filled with stock photos of the same Black model. Mia lived in a neighborhood filled with Black middle-class families and recent immigrants that reminded Rachel of where she'd grown up. Maybe that was the real reason they'd been so distant all these years. Mia considered her a sellout. In moments like these, a small part of Rachel agreed.

Matt laughed and positioned his body between them. "Lots of retirees with nothing better to do than spy on the neighbors." He tutted like a disappointed schoolteacher and folded his arms. "So, how's your mom? I'm reading the *Post* series Alesha's doing on public school fundraising. Really good stuff."

"You're reading that, huh?" Mia copied Matt's breezy tone, but it was obvious that she wasn't falling for his diversion. "I'll tell Mom. She's convinced people only read the paper for political gossip these days." Her eyes darted back and forth between Rachel's dirty dress and Matt's sweaty face. "Rachel, is there some reason you're..." She waved at the ground. "In the bushes?"

Matt looked nauseated and defeated. Good. Now he knew how it felt. Rachel took another slow sip of her drink and let him stew. He told Mia they were debating landscaping and had come outside to see it up close. "I'm not sure we want these roses anymore."

They were her roses, not his. Just like the house. She'd chosen every tile and light fixture. She had agonized over window treatments and light switch plates while he brushed her off if she asked for an opinion. He'd paid for land and walls, but she was the one who made it a home. That meant something. And she couldn't let him steal it away.

Rachel stumbled upward. "Matt and I need to finish our conversation about chrysanthemums."

"Roses," Mia corrected.

"Whatever."

Mia surveyed the street. "You should probably go inside. It's late and you have some nosy neighbors." She started to say more, but then pursed her lips and nodded. "Have a good night."

Once she was gone, Matt extended a hand but Rachel stepped back. "No. I'm not going in there with you. Not unless—" She looked up at the house, *her* house, and Nathan's question ran through her mind: *What do you want now?*

She wanted certainty. Security. The safe place that Matt had promised her. A dollar amount flashed in her mind, and she blurted it before she lost her nerve. "One million."

Matt tensed. They rarely spoke about money in specific amounts. Big expenses were estimated in "figures" and paid through invoices forwarded to their accountant. He floundered and sputtered, "Wh-what?" before dismissing his own question with a hand wave. "It's late. Let's talk tomorrow."

"I want one million dollars," Rachel repeated. "And the house. I won't say anything about your affair or file for divorce until the election's over. But I won't let you leave me with nothing." She would plant more roses. Once he was gone, she'd cover the yard in enough pink flowers that he'd avoid driving past because they'd remind him of this moment.

Matt looked stunned, his body frozen while his satin robe flapped furiously in the breeze. "Are you blackmailing me?"

"You're a lawyer, Matt. Consider it a negotiation."

"And I thought this was a marriage."

Her first instinct was violence, a kick to the groin or a solid hair pull like girls used to do on the playground. He'd probably call Mia to mediate. Or worse, Shania. She could hear him whining to their therapist: "*That's* why she took off her earrings."

"I know you don't love me anymore," Rachel said, voicing the truth they'd both been avoiding. Matt bristled like a guilty porcupine, ready to argue semantics. But she wasn't strong enough for some debate. Her legs felt wobbly and bloodless, as if her heart were feeding them nothing but adrenaline. "But could you respect me enough to give me what I'm owed?"

His contrite expression quickly cooled into resentment. There wasn't a trace of confusion when he spoke again. Just the bored, rushed tone of someone about to play a winning hand. "*Owed* is a strong word."

"What would you call it?"

"Consideration." He folded his arms. "It's a contract term. A benefit in a bargained-for exchange."

"Okay. I'll say nothing in exchange for—"

"Bargained for," he interrupted. "Not demanded."

This was the most honest conversation they'd had in months. Maybe years. She was drunk and he was eyeing her like a rabid dog he'd backed into a corner. But she wasn't invisible anymore. She had materialized, fully formed, right in front of him. "What could you possibly want from me?"

"You're a part of my campaign, Rachel. I need you at my side, like before. I need you to . . ." He faltered, searching for words. "Do what you normally do. In public. The parties and such."

Rachel had always suspected that Matt didn't know what she did all day. He would ask her to do something at the last minute and get irritated if she said she was busy. She usually agreed to change her schedule, because deep down, she didn't respect it either. Committee meetings, book clubs, and facials. Her calendar might as well be printed on glittery vellum.

The election was in eleven weeks. Eleven weeks of black-tie fundraisers, cutesy interviews, and playing food poisoning roulette to judge chili competitions at local festivals. Eleven weeks of pretending she wasn't just a rage cloud wrapped in Prada couture. Then they'd be done. She could walk away with enough of herself intact to hide any parts that would never heal.

She knew Matt wouldn't budge on delaying the divorce. Protecting his career would always come first, no matter how guilty he felt about cheating. But admitting he needed her had been a mistake. He'd handed her a card to play, and she was determined to take advantage.

Rachel brushed leaves and dirt from her dress. "Rule number one. You don't get to tell me what to do. I will go wherever I want, when I want, and you don't say one word."

"Rules?" Matt tugged at his collar. "If there are rules, then we must have an agreement."

"Rule number two. Never, under any circumstances, are you to say that you're sorry you hurt me, or you never meant for this to happen, or that part of you will always love me. All of the above are grounds for immediate termination."

"Termination?"

"I will kill you."

"Right." Matt paused, his expression softening. "Thank you for... being reasonable."

"Don't say that either." She stepped forward. "And don't pretend that this is a choice. This is *my* home."

Matt glanced at the house. "It's mine, too, Rachel, just like you're still my wife. I know you won't believe this, but that still means something to me."

Rachel leaned in, close enough to smell the mint from his mouth-wash. "I may have to stand by your side and keep my mouth shut in public, but don't ever call me your wife again. That's rule number three."

Matt sniffed and wrinkled his nose. "Are you drunk?"

Rachel gulped the last of the soda. "Yes." She shoved the cup against his stomach. He grabbed it instinctively, eyes wide as she walked past him toward the house. "I'd get used to it if I were you."

# CHAPTER FOUR

Nathan couldn't identify the smells coming from his kitchen, which usually happened whenever Bobbi Kim came over to cook. She liked to pretend it was altruistic, that she was saving him from a sad single-man diet of frozen pizza and takeout, but she actually wanted to use the space. Bobbi's condo barely had enough room for furniture. She also had a roommate who worked from home and complained whenever an appliance ran during her Zoom calls. Nathan lived alone in his studio with a Viking gas range that Bobbi didn't think he deserved. Last week, she bit his head off when he used it to boil ramen noodles for lunch.

"What are you making?" Nathan sat on a bar stool at his kitchen island. Bobbi's hands were a rapid blur, her chef's knife making quick work of a pile of vegetables. A large bowl of beaten eggs sat at her elbow, speckled with black pepper and other spices he couldn't identify. Experimentation had always been her thing. When they were kids, it was a chemistry set. In college, it was switching majors and sneaking around with married women. Three years into being a line chef at a small DC restaurant, it was the aromatic contents of unlabeled jars ground to dust with a mortar and pestle.

"Breakfast," she said. "A real breakfast, not that powdered milk shit your brother got you hooked on."

"It's a protein smoothie." He sipped his coffee and eyed with suspicion the deep casserole dish she had buttered. Nathan didn't remember buying it. His apartment was furnished during a big spending spree when he bought the building. There were probably towels and bedsheets somewhere in shrink wrap with the price tags still attached. "Joe says it's vegan."

"That doesn't make it good for you. Why don't you eat actual food in the morning?"

"I'm not big on breakfast. Too many eggs."

Bobbi paused midchop to glare at him. She was tall, nearly his height, and usually wore her long hair piled on top of her head in a gravity-defying bun. He'd never seen Bobbi fight anyone, but he had once seen her stare down a cop so hard that he ripped up a parking ticket. Nathan took another drink of his coffee and vowed to keep all egg-related opinions to himself.

"I drew that thing you asked for," he said.

She dropped the knife and clasped her hands. "Ooh! Can I see?" Bobbi vibrated with the same energy that she brought to discovering a new restaurant or adding a dish she'd created to the menu at work. Unlike his erratic relationship with art, Bobbi's passion was focused and uncluttered—a laser aimed at whatever brought her joy. Sometimes he avoided putting his work in her crosshairs because he didn't want to disappoint her. But other times, like now, her excitement was contagious. It made him feel like the hours he burned away struggling to capture his daydreams on paper weren't a complete waste of time.

Nathan sent her the image. He didn't draw things for other people very often, but when Bobbi asked for one of her favorite characters from the Phoenix Prophecies series, he couldn't say no. Those books were the reason they'd been friends since junior high. If she hadn't caught him reading *Lost Among the Ashes* during detention, she would probably still be calling him Nate the Late behind his back. He'd racked up more tardies in a single semester than any other kid in his grade that year.

Bobbi was the only person who understood why he posted Phoenix fan art online. It wasn't just loving the books. It was the satisfaction of channeling his compulsive need to draw into creating something that people wanted. This one was for her first tattoo. He had drawn Neptune for her, a water mage cradling the moon as she hovered above the ocean. Nathan had surrounded the character with waves, the whitecaps indistinguishable from the flowing fabric of her dress. Neptune's coloring was similar to Bobbi's golden skin tone. Her hair was inky curls that floated up and merged with the night sky.

Bobbi gazed at the picture with such adoration that he snuck another look at his work, trying to see it through her eyes. But he could only see the flaws, so he quickly dimmed the screen again.

"This is amazing," Bobbi said. "You really outdid yourself, Nettles."

Nathan thanked her with a *no big deal* shrug. His throat was tight, and any attempt at words would probably become some raw and messy confession about how down he'd been feeling lately. Bobbi would freak. Then she'd tell Dillon and both of his friends would converge, wringing their hands because *Nate's not himself,* which would force him to admit that he actually *was* being himself. He'd been this needy his whole life, but had never let them see it.

Nathan popped a chili pepper into his mouth. The burn cleared his head, but quickly escalated into a coughing fit that made his eyes water. Bobbi nudged over a bowl of shredded cheese and resumed ogling the picture.

"You keep getting better," she said. "Did you try a new technique this time? No, don't tell me. I like trying to figure it out on my own."

The cheese helped, but his mouth was still on fire. "Don't put those peppers in whatever you're cooking."

"Did you get the link I sent you about selling your designs online? People would pay a fortune for something like this."

"For a tattoo of some book character?" His laugh was strangled by another cough. "I don't like encouraging questionable choices."

"Okay, hypocrite." Bobbi pointed to the evidence of his Phoenix devotion tattooed on his forearm.

"A phoenix is objectively badass." He ran his hand over the image. "I can make up ten stories about where this came from."

THE ART OF SCANDAL

She put her phone away and ate one of the demonic peppers without wincing. "You shouldn't be ashamed of what inspires you."

Nathan wasn't interested in starting another debate about whether he should post his work under his real name. While Bobbi's hobbies were indistinguishable from her career, Nathan preferred to keep his life in separate, tidy compartments, to ensure the different parts never touched. She saw his obstinate expression and huffed in defeat. "Dillon's been blowing up my phone since you ditched him last night."

"I didn't ditch him. I wasn't feeling those two girls he met at the gas station."

"Sounds like you were being an asshole." She dumped a handful of vegetables into the eggs, picked up a whisk, and stirred with super-human speed.

"I bought them all dinner!" Nathan looked away from the bowl, his stomach rolling at the slimy consistency. He wasn't totally recovered from his whiskey binge the night before. After mindlessly finishing the bottle, he'd called a Lyft and spent the rest of the night on his couch, scrolling through articles and social media posts about Rachel Abbott.

People used #BlackElsa to post about how cold and boring she was. But the photos hit differently now that Nathan had the husky Demi Moore voice and dark sense of humor to pair with the flawless face. She put on plastic smiles for the camera, but last night she'd been viscerally real, electric and changeable like a summer storm.

He read through a few posts debating whether she wore a wig to a cancer research fundraiser before he switched to reading news articles that were probably planted by her husband's staff. Apparently, the buzzed woman who'd asked him, a stranger, for weed was passionate about drugs and alcohol education in schools. She also taught kinder-gartners how to garden. He'd drifted off scrolling through photos of her squatting next to starry-eyed kids.

Bobbi closed the oven and tossed her potholders on the counter. "What is going on with you?"

If he didn't answer, she would keep prodding. Bobbi's stubbornness about helping the people she loved could occasionally be obsessive. The last time he tried to freeze her out of one of his dark moods, she'd planted herself on his couch for a week.

But each time he tried to pinpoint a specific thing that was bothering him, the opposite thing felt just as true: He was lonely, but he was also tired of being around people. He was bored, but the things he enjoyed weren't appealing. Sometimes it felt like he was existing underwater, looking up at everyone thriving above the surface, breathing the stale air he couldn't stomach. But he couldn't say that to Bobbi. She'd lecture him about wasting time running the laundromat and tell him to research art schools again. He loved drawing, but he hated school. Or school hated him. Every teacher unlucky enough to have him walk through their door had been relieved to see him walk back out again.

When he was young, Nathan would get in trouble for daydreaming while he was supposed to be paying attention. It came to a head when his fifth-grade teacher, Donald Green, said that he would be better off repeating the same grade next year. Nathan was sent to a guidance counselor who suggested he keep a journal to help him focus. But he was a shitty writer. Now he knew it was the dyslexia, but back then, the idea of trying to put what was in his head down on paper made him want to give up on education completely.

So he'd started drawing. Doodling at first, and then illustrations of his teacher's lessons. His grades had improved, which led to accusations of cheating. The notebook was used as evidence of his laziness during parent-teacher conferences.

In high school, Nathan tried becoming someone else. He stopped drawing, joined the wrestling team, and learned to flirt. It worked for a while, but then the rumors started. He was an asshole only looking to get laid. He only liked white girls. He had a monster dick that made some girl cry when he tried to fuck her. It was like being back in Green's class, with his patronizing warnings not to bother trying—he would never be more than this.

Nathan needed somewhere to put all that rage and frustration. At first, it was heavy layers of graphite pressed so hard into the paper that it would rip before he finished. Then it was oils and acrylics, plus numbing himself with such a myopic pursuit of perfection that he'd lose time, like he was working while blackout drunk. Eventually, he learned to let other things fuel his work. Friends. A fandom community. Things that made him feel good about himself, instead of trapping him in a dark place he'd done his best to leave behind.

Sometimes he envied people who could put their messed-up feelings into words. Like Rachel. Sitting next to her while she worked through her tangled emotions had lit him up inside. Now he was restless and resentful of that younger version of himself who'd committed to staying strong and silent as a way of coping with life.

He met Bobbi's eyes. "You've been in love before, right?"

Her brow furrowed. "Yeah. Why?"

"How did you know?"

She turned on the oven light and knelt to look at the dish inside. "I just knew." She stood and fixed him with a direct stare. "Did you meet someone?"

He thought about Rachel with her perfect bow lips. He could swear there were moments when they'd swayed closer, like magnets surrendering to their natural pull.

"No," he answered. Because he didn't. Not the way Bobbi meant it. "No, it was just a conversation. The subject came up and it's been on my mind ever since."

Bobbi wiped her hands against her apron. "I'm not surprised you haven't. I've seen the girls you date. Your taste is garbage."

"I dated you."

"Oh, fuck off." Bobbi propped her elbows on the counter. "We were in eighth grade and you kissed me once, on a dare."

"I was nervous."

"You were ambivalent. You always are. You asked me to be your girlfriend because we were already friends, and I was literally the girl in closest proximity." She paused and he thought back to the half-hearted note he'd slipped her in English class. Bobbi had read it, snorted a laugh, and written, *This is a sentence fragment*, instead of saying yes.

"You always choose the path of least resistance," Bobbi said. "That's not how you fall in love."

Nathan thought about the last time he saw his ex-girlfriend Nina. He'd run into her at the grocery store and learned she was engaged to an accountant in the Treasury Department with three small kids she referred to as "our littles." She'd asked if Nathan wanted to get lunch sometime, which was good, right? That was how relationships should end; polite and easy, not as some bitter stain that would never wear off.

Nathan reached for a dish towel and started wiping the counter. "You seem to know a lot about it. Have *you* met someone? What happened to that one girl with the glasses who used to flirt with you at the library?"

"She moved." Bobbi pointed a finger at his face. "Don't change the subject."

"I'm pretty sure it's the same subject."

She took a deep, patience-fortifying breath. "No, it's not. I love you, Nathan. You're like the brother I never wanted. But things get handed to you, which makes it harder for you to appreciate them."

"Keeping things light reduces conflict. I don't like drama," Nathan said, even though his fixation on Rachel's freckle screamed he was a liar.

"Intimacy isn't drama. It's a basic human need."

Bobbi proceeded to lecture him about emotional vulnerability until the oven timer buzzed. She pulled her creation from the oven and set it down with a smug flourish. "You should ask this person who has you all introspective to hang out sometime. It sounds like they could be good for you." She pointed to her finished dish. "Veggie frittata."

Nathan nodded. "Right. So basically..."

She rolled her eyes and tossed him a fork. "Yes, eggs, asshole. Eat up."

---

Rachel didn't know how long she stayed in bed. Checking would require opening her eyes, which she refused to do. The shades were still open from the day before because Matt had ignored her request to close them before the party. "The sun is my alarm clock," he said. He had to know she would be hungover with the sunlight tolerance of a vampire. They used to laugh at how two drinks could have her stumbling around, begging for electrolytes and Advil. Then he'd call her his "little teetotaler" while stashing bottles of Vitaminwater near her bed.

Rachel rolled onto her side and opened one eye into a narrow slit. According to the clock, it was almost noon. She never slept this late, especially on a Sunday. It was her planning day. She usually spent the early morning hours adding reminders to Matt's phone so he wouldn't overlook any events.

Her phone vibrated. She ignored it. The noise stopped for a moment and started again, somehow seeming more insistent than before. She glared at the caller ID: Ben Abbott, Matt's younger brother. He wouldn't call just to chat.

"I got your text from last night." Ben's voice was low and measured, similar to Matt's, but more cautious. Rachel always imagined him running words through his mind like a script before he said them. "I'm sorry, but I'm not sure I understand what sort of help you're asking for."

When had she texted him? Before or after she'd been mistaken for a criminal breaking into her own home? "Um, okay. Could you hold on a minute?" She squinted at the cracked screen and navigated to her sent messages.

**Rachel:** Matt fucking chrysanthemums. Need your help.

She sighed. "I'm sorry. I had too much to drink last night."

"You know I'm happy to help with home improvements, but gardening isn't really my area."

Being the overlooked, second-born Abbott son had given Ben the breathing room to develop practical skills while attending Harvard Law School like his brother and father. On the day he met Rachel, Ben was covered in grime and sawdust from building cabinets in a house he'd purchased to flip. She later learned he had briefly flirted with starting a contracting company that specialized in restoring Victorian homes. Matt told her the story as a joke because Abbott men didn't work with their hands. Their calluses were from gripping mountain bike handles or holding pens with an awkward grip. Even though Ben had ultimately caved to his family's expectations, his ability to see the value in creating something beautiful had always made him different in her eyes. He was her Abbott ally—the person who sent her Gordon Parks postcards each year for her birthday because he spoke a discerning creative language the rest of his family didn't understand.

"That message wasn't about flowers." She hesitated. "Ben, if I speak to you as an attorney, this conversation is privileged, isn't it?"

A long stretch of silence followed her question. "Yes, it is. Are you in trouble?"

"Your brother is leaving me for another woman."

Another pause. "*Shit.*"

It was only the second time she'd heard Ben swear. The first was during a Christmas dinner, one of the obligatory Abbott family gatherings. Matt announced he was writing a memoir and Ben had declared it "a fucking joke."

"I'm so sorry, Rachel. My brother's a jerk."

"Don't be. I just need to talk through some next steps."

"The prenuptial agreement."

He was too polite to say it, but she heard the *I told you so.* Thirteen years ago, Ben had told her not to sign the prenup without speaking to an attorney, but Rachel couldn't imagine taking money she hadn't earned. She'd thought signing it made her a better person. At least now she could tell him she hadn't rolled over and played dead last night when Matt threw the prenup in her face. "He agreed to give me money and the house."

"Agreed? He just offered that to you?"

She was afraid of this. An agreement made during a drunken argument probably wouldn't hold up in court. "Not exactly. I blackmailed him. A little."

"Jesus, Rachel. Why would you do that?"

"Because I don't have a choice." She kicked the comforter away from her overheated skin. The conversation had her covered in sweat. "It's my house. I need money to keep the lights on long enough to figure out my next move." Saying it out loud made her chest hurt. She shouldn't have to explain herself to a man like Ben who would never understand what it was like to be financially vulnerable. He'd tell her to apply for a job like she didn't have a decade-long gap in her anemic work history.

The first time she'd explained to Ben how she ended up in Oasis Springs, she could tell he had a hard time believing her story. He couldn't reconcile the Rachel he knew—an art history major and devoted mother who had finally convinced Matt to take the Metro into the city—with a woman who had experienced homelessness. Despite his relative sophistication in the Abbott household, he wasn't immune to the privilege that kept him isolated from the rest of the world. Ben liked to believe that bad things only happened to bad people because it gave him a sense of control. But Rachel had learned years ago that control was an illusion. Tragedy was indiscriminate and ruthlessly patient, waiting until you let your guard down to strike. Before she met Matt, it had stolen her life. She refused to let it happen again.

Ben shifted back into attorney mode. "Okay. Well, you'll want to get the clock moving on the separation waiting period."

"Is there any way to file that without people knowing?"

"You mean a legal separation? Those don't exist in Virginia. You need to live separately for a certain amount of time. With a no fault, that's one year."

"A year?" She ran a hand over her face. "Is there any way to speed up the clock?"

"You could file for cause." Ben paused. "Cheating is cause."

It would feel good to reveal Matt's affair. No, it would feel *great*. Better than sex. But she would also lose her leverage. After last night, Matt would happily kick her out of the house if he thought she was no longer useful. And she'd be back to where she started, struggling to pay rent and bills while people gossiped behind her back.

Ben gave her a number for an attorney and extracted a promise to keep him updated before they disconnected. Her phone was dying, so she rifled through her dresser drawers, searching for a charger. Her gaze caught on a Bic lighter and a half-empty pack of cigarettes shoved to the back. The contractors they hired to update the master bathroom last spring had left them on the new vanity, enraging Matt. She'd taken the cigarettes and hidden them in her nightstand.

Rachel lit up and inhaled, remembering Nathan's slow grin as he warned her, "Those are bad for you." She imagined him plucking it from her fingers, only to replace it with something worse but better. Something potent and destructively sweet.

She wandered over to Matt's closet. The dark blue Hugo Boss was his lucky suit. He had worn it the night he was elected mayor. She aimed for that one first, exhaling smoke on the sleeve and lapels as she worked her way along his closet.

Rachel straightened and admired her handiwork. Then she yelped, spun around, and pointed the lighter like a weapon against a dark-clad figure in her doorway. But the intruder was just their housekeeper, Lenora, eyeing Rachel with a laundry basket balanced against her hip.

Rachel never realized how devoted domestic employees could be until she was exposed to the people who kept the Abbott household running. Matt's mother, Matilda, always claimed that they were part of the family. As if the monogrammed rubber gloves handed out at Christmas were a sign of love, and not because she refused to let them use anything but industrial-strength cleaner on her toilets.

Lenora had been picking up after Matt since he was in diapers. He insisted on keeping her around, even though watching Rachel cook his meals and pick up his dry cleaning seemed to cause the woman physical pain. At the moment, she looked ready to tackle Rachel to the ground and smuggle Matt's suits away for safekeeping.

"What are you doing?" Lenora gaped like she'd stumbled into a crime scene.

Rachel knelt to attack his favorite shoes. The suede loafers were custom, handcrafted by little old European ladies, according to her mother-in-law. Rachel pressed the cigarette tip against one toe and burned a small hole all the way through.

"You know Matt's allergic to cigarette smoke," Lenora huffed. She rarely addressed Rachel by name. It was always *you* or *pardon me*, or when she thought Rachel wasn't listening, *that woman he married*. It was a constant reminder that Rachel would always be a guest in this family.

"That's probably a lie." Rachel stood and took another drag. "He's very good at those."

Lenora swallowed hard, her hands twisting on the edge of the basket. Rachel held her gaze as she puffed out small rings of smoke. She used to tie herself into knots wondering why this woman hated her so much. Whenever Rachel completed a chore, it was deemed inadequate and had to be redone. Dinner was always supplemented by one of Matt's "favorites since he was little."

Maybe she hated Black people. Or women. Or Black women who fucked her precious Abbott prince.

"I need to get the laundry," Lenora sniffed. "I tried to wait until you woke up, but well…" She glanced at Rachel's nightgown. "It's noon," she said, with a tone that added, *you lazy drunk*.

"Why don't you take the day off?" Rachel moved closer and reached for the basket. "I can do the laundry."

Lenora's grip tightened. They engaged in a brief standoff that Rachel considered ending by blowing smoke into the woman's face.

"The washer's broken," Lenora said. "I called the repairman, but he won't be able to come out until Monday. I was going to the laundromat."

"I can go." Rachel tugged at the basket, harder this time. Lenora finally relented but eyed the dirty clothes as if Rachel had stolen her purse.

"With all due respect, Mrs. Abbott, when was the last time you used a washer and dryer?"

Rachel hitched the basket up on one hip and leaned close enough to make the older woman flinch. "With all due respect, Lenora? That's none of your goddamn business."

———

Rachel hoped her exit was actually as dramatic as she'd intended. She wanted Lenora to be stunned silent and maybe a little intimidated, for her words to echo as she got dressed and threw her hair into a disgraceful ponytail, then carted the dirty socks and undershirts downstairs like a trophy. She was flying on wings made of spite as the door slammed behind her.

Once outside, three things immediately became apparent. One, she didn't know where the laundromat was. Two, her car was parked in the garage, which meant she'd have to retrace her steps to reach it. And finally, Sofia Cárdenas's bright green Corvette was headed directly for her house.

Rachel's biggest humiliations during her early attempts to navigate the social cliques that ruled Oasis Springs could all be traced back to Sofia, a former telenovela star and the wife of a billionaire coffee mogul. Rachel received her first lesson about Sofia's influence when she was forced to reschedule a dinner party that was supposed to be the soft launch of Matt's political career. Every caterer Rachel contacted was unavailable. One chef who declined advised her to have a signed contract in hand before she sent out invitations. "Thursday night is Ms. Cárdenas's book club. You should get the schedule and avoid those altogether."

Then there was the green dress fiasco. Matt had recently announced his candidacy, and they were invited to the charity gala Sofia's nonprofit held at the National Portrait Gallery each year. Rachel had agonized over her dress and eventually chosen a custom chartreuse satin. No one had bothered to tell her that the important women in town all had a signature color. Her mother-in-law wore purple. Joanne Wilson, whose family owned the oldest Black investment firm in the state, always wore marigold. And Sofia, the first person Rachel saw when she arrived, was a vision in chartreuse satin. Sofia's expression remained placid as she joked about how similar their outfits were, but Rachel was never invited to the gala again.

Despite those early missteps, Rachel had become a woman other people admired. She had her own signature color now, crimson, which screamed sex and power. If she wore a scarf from a local Etsy shop, it sold out within twenty-four hours. The rosé she brought to a dinner party would soon be prominently displayed in local liquor stores. Since Matt had elevated their profile beyond Oasis Springs, there wasn't as much pressure to keep up with her neighbors. Most felt pressured to keep up with her.

But Sofia existed on a different plane of influence. Most of the money that flowed through their community could be traced directly back to her family. If Oasis Springs was its own overpriced suburban kingdom, then Sofia was the de facto queen. Queens didn't follow trends. They didn't acknowledge trends existed. That was what Rachel envied, the freedom that came with removing yourself from the conversation.

A cloud of Jasmin des Anges wafted toward Rachel as Sofia glided up her walkway carrying an elaborately wrapped gift. The woman's insistence on bathing in expensive perfume was considered her single social misstep. But Rachel knew better. Sofia managed her image like a chess master. That familiar whiff of bergamot and jasmine inspired fear in every socialite in DC.

Rachel ran a hand over her ponytail and pushed her shoulders back as if she were wearing an Armani pantsuit instead of a vintage Santana T-shirt from college. Sofia's pleasant smile wavered when she got a closer look at the black-and-white raglan. "Hello, Rachel," she said. "I'm so sorry for stopping by like this. I should have called."

"No, it's fine. I was just—" Rachel's eyes fell to the laundry. Sofia followed her gaze with raised eyebrows.

"Well, I don't want to interrupt your chores," Sofia said. "Beto and I were so disappointed we couldn't make it to Matthew's birthday party." She offered the present. "Could you give this to him, along with our regrets?"

Rachel had sent the invitation with no expectation they would accept. She'd never seen this woman at any event that didn't have valet parking.

"Thank you." Rachel accepted the gift and tried to resist the urge to drop it on his dirty undershirts.

"Great." Sofia flashed another blinding smile. "I also have an ulterior motive for stopping by. Again, I could have called, but I hate asking for favors over the phone."

"A favor?" Rachel tried to keep her voice neutral. The lingering throb at the base of her skull intensified. Was this a trap? Sofia was one of Matt's biggest financial donors and was actively lobbying behind the scenes for his congressional bid. Had he called to complain about what happened? Were they colluding to fix a situation that needed *handling*?

"I'm sure you know our foundation chooses a couple to host the art gala every year," Sofia said.

Rachel tensed when she mentioned the origin of chartreuse-gate. She tried to keep her voice steady. "Herman and Matilda were chosen one year, I believe." She remembered how bored her mother-in-law had been by it, announcing the honor during the salad course at dinner. "There are no plus-ones, unfortunately," she'd sighed. "That family is very cheap."

Sofia nodded. "The Abbotts ran one of our most successful campaigns. This year we chose Judith and Karl, but with everything that happened..."

Everything being Karl Harris running off with his wife's twenty-seven-year-old hairdresser and moving his medical practice to Tampa. Judith's settlement wasn't enough to cover the mortgage, and she was currently living in exile, otherwise known as a two-bedroom condo on the southeast edge of town. The women she used to consider friends would only whisper her name behind their hands with down-turned eyes as though she were dead instead of working at a Pottery Barn.

"Anyway." Sofia shook off the thought with a delicate shudder. "We need new hosts. I know it's last minute, but would you be interested?"

"You want me to help find new hosts?"

Sofia's plush lips tightened briefly and then curved into a fresh smile. "No, darling. I want you and Matt to host this year. He told me years ago about your art background, and I thought—well, that makes you the perfect choice, doesn't it?"

Whenever someone brought up Rachel's art, it felt like they were talking about a different person. That woman had been raised by a musician who believed that creativity unbound by expectations was the best way to live your life. Her father, Peter, used to say that Rachel's photography was a gift she was obligated to share with the world. She'd convinced herself that leaving Faith, then two years old, to have a *real* college experience was necessary to live up to all that potential. She'd planned to settle down with her daughter after she graduated, and build another life of swirling creativity, unbound by rules or expectations.

But none of that was true. She wasn't destined for greatness. And sometimes Faith still held her hand so tight it hurt. Like her mother might disappear.

"Matt told you about that?" Rachel struggled to keep her voice steady. "About my photos, I mean?"

"Photos? No. He mentioned that you studied art history. My cousin had the same major at UCLA, but she owns a smoothie shop now. Benita's Batidos." She shrugged. "They taste like dirt. But the Instagram is impressive."

Rachel tried to think of a tactful way to ask what the woman's angle was and failed. Maybe she could cultivate the offer into a strategic friendship. Once her divorce hit the news cycle, Sofia could be a powerful ally.

"What would hosting involve?"

Sofia pinched the air between her fingers. "Very little. A few planning committee meetings. And the hosts typically commission a collection from a local artist."

A familiar warmth spread through Rachel's body at the mention of an exhibit. Before she met Matt, she had envisioned a life filled with creators and patrons brought together by her curatorial eye. Now she had to settle for rearranging the landscapes in her dining room. "I would work with a local artist?"

"Work with? No, no." Sofia waved again and added a soft chuckle. "Lyric Patterson is consulting for us. Have you heard of her? She's worked for the Met. I convinced her to help us find an artist and curate the event."

Rachel knew *of* Lyric Patterson. They'd both attended Howard and applied to the same graduate programs a year apart. Rachel had read about Lyric's success through the regular alumni newsletters. She'd interned in Europe, been mentored in New York, and made a name for herself curating pop-up exhibits featuring artists of color around the country. It was as if Rachel had drawn up blueprints for the professional life she'd abandoned, and Lyric had found them, dusted off years of neglect, and then built her career.

"Lyric's amazing," Rachel said, while her insides steeped in envy. "I'm sure she'll put together a wonderful collection."

"No, what's amazing is that you're willing to help us out with this. I promise it won't be a burden. All we need is your gorgeous face and the Abbott name."

And that was it. Sofia's real reason for putting her vendetta aside and inviting Rachel to host: She needed a flashy distraction from the scandal, and Matt and Rachel were at the peak of their moment. Sofia wanted to sell two-thousand-dollar tickets to see the Washington "It Couple" up close and in person.

"So we show up and greet people?"

"Exactly," Sofia said, beaming as if she had given Rachel another gift. *No need to worry your little head about actual work, just keep posing for the cameras.* "You'll do it then? Oh, that's wonderful. It's a relief to know the gala will be in your hands."

Rachel tried to match her enthusiasm. "Tell me where and when to smile."

Sofia touched her arm with a soft laugh. "You're funnier than I thought. Let's talk more about the gala next Saturday."

"Next Saturday?"

Sofia frowned. "My anniversary party? It's our fortieth. You're both coming, right? People would notice if the mayor wasn't there."

"Right, yes. We wouldn't miss it." Rachel forced the smile that Sofia wanted, one that suggested fawning gratitude that she was married to someone who mattered.

# CHAPTER FIVE

The only laundromat in Oasis Springs had forty washers and dryers, a Pepsi machine, and a television mounted onto the wall that played CNN twenty-four hours a day. Nathan had considered changing the name to something like Fluff n Dry, or the Rinse Cycle, but in the end, he stuck with Oasis Springs Laundry Center, because he believed in truth in advertising. This was not some quirky, upmarket laundromat. It was just a place to wash clothes.

Owning a small business was never the plan. He was supposed to go to college like his brother and major in something that would make him useful. His abuelita pushed him to pursue a degree because getting an education had changed her life. "It made me into a woman," she used to say proudly, pointing to the diploma on her wall. Nathan heard the part she didn't say out loud: that he needed to become a man. "Boys like you will always be underestimated. If you attempt nothing, no one will expect more."

She died two weeks before his first application deadline, and if Nathan weren't grieving, he might have remembered her advice. Instead, he deleted his admissions forms as soon as the money she left him hit his bank account.

The real estate listing was for a self-service laundromat with a studio apartment attached. Later, he would wonder if he was seduced by the business model: the automated service, the small and sporadic customer base, the ease of living and working in the same building. He'd made a cash offer for a business that wasn't profitable, instead of doing the smart thing and calling his brother before he signed any paperwork. Joe would have swooped in with his big MBA brain and a PowerPoint presentation to lecture Nathan about how the local market didn't justify the overhead. But Nathan had always been better at gut feelings than thinking things through. Yes, the decision was impulsive, but he had learned a lot over the last eight years. Front loaders were more efficient than top loaders, even though they cost more up front. Providing coin-operated machines meant people without a bank account wouldn't have to buy prepaid cards to wash their clothes. Owning it also made him feel useful to people who were often overlooked in Oasis Springs, like frazzled single mothers waiting for a landlord to fix their dryer, or overworked domestic workers venting about their employers' finicky appliances.

The day-to-day didn't take much effort. Nathan usually worked out with Joe before opening the doors at six a.m. Then he'd take a cup of coffee to the back office and work on unfinished sketches while listening to Spotify at a volume that would eventually destroy his hearing. Sometimes it took a while to get started. He'd been drawing for years now, but whenever he touched the tip of his pencil to paper, a voice whispered, *Still drawing wolves and wizards? Aren't you embarrassed?* It sounded a lot like his father.

Nathan heard a grunt followed by a string of hard clangs that usually signaled his washers were under attack. He eyed the customers scattered throughout the room. One was a middle-aged housekeeper he'd seen three times this week. A young white woman stood in the corner folding towels with AirPods wedged into her ears. And then there was the short Black woman on his left. It took him a minute to recognize Rachel Abbott as his washer's attacker. Judging from the hard furrow of her brow, it wasn't about to escape her wrath anytime soon.

She had ditched the cocktail dress for a T-shirt and tight jeans. Her hair was pulled back into a loose ponytail that made it look like she rolled out of bed with no fucks to give. Wild, wispy curls framed her neck.

"Damn it!" She slammed the door closed so hard the sound echoed, startling the other customers into nervous frowns. Nathan moved forward as she grabbed a bottle of detergent. "Fuck you, you . . . machine."

"Whatever happened, I'm sure it's not the washer's fault."

She spun around and her eyes widened when she saw him. "You! What are you doing here?" Her voice was rushed and a little breathless, like she was excited. Or maybe that was just him. His pulse was racing.

"I was about to ask you the same thing."

Her gaze shifted to the other customers. The blond woman still looked oblivious, but the housekeeper kept glancing in their direction. Rachel tensed. "I'm doing my laundry." She jabbed a thumb at the washer. "This thing keeps eating my change."

Nathan moved to a different washer. "Try this one. It's credit cards only." He tapped the sign. "You also need to put your clothes in first. They have sensors that adjust the settings based on what you put inside." He pointed to her clothes on the floor. "May I?"

"Sure." She stepped aside and avoided his eyes. "Do you work here?"

Anyone else would have gotten a curt yes in response, but Nathan replied, "I own the place," with a cockiness he didn't actually feel. Twenty-four hours after the drive-in and he was still trying to impress her.

"You *own* it? Seriously?" She grimaced and quickly added, "Sorry! You're just so young."

He was relieved she hadn't said something ignorant about him not looking like a business owner. She didn't seem like the type, but she was still an Abbott.

"I'm not that young." He leaned back against the washer and folded his arms. She stared at his bicep, and he flexed a little for her benefit. "Plus, I've got a birthday coming up, so I think they'll let me keep it." The last bit of tension vanished from her face, and her eyes softened to umber velvet.

"Don't let last night's drunken tragedy fool you. I'm not that young either."

"You weren't tragic."

"That's nice of you to say."

"I'm not that nice."

Her eyes raked over him, lingering in places—his chest, his shoulders—before returning to his face again. "I don't buy you as a tough guy."

"It's the dimple, right?" He rubbed his left cheek.

She laughed. "You're right. It's mesmerizing. I'll try to focus on the right cheek instead."

"Good. And you're gonna pay me for that wash." He nodded to the machine working behind her. "It's on your tab."

"My *tab*?" She scanned the room. "What kind of laundromat is this?"

"The friendly neighborhood kind." He grinned. "No cash, no problem. It's also a good excuse to come back and visit the next time your housekeeper goes on vacation."

Her smile dimmed. "How do you know I don't do my own laundry?"

Because he'd lived here long enough to know that women like her rarely separated their own colors and whites. But they also didn't look at him the way she did, like some decadent dessert they were tempted to try. They never looked at him at all. "You're right. I shouldn't assume."

"It's been a while since I used a laundromat. But I'm not from here." She said it like it meant something. Or like she needed it to.

"Where are you from?"

"Southeast DC. My neighborhood was mostly rental houses and apartments. Not like this place. At all."

"Yeah, I bet." She kept glancing out the window at his car parked near the entrance. "Are you a gearhead?" he asked.

She jerked her eyes back like she'd been caught. "Me? No. I don't know what's under the hood or anything."

"But you like cars."

"I like *those* cars. Loud and temperamental tanks that might kill you in a crash." She paused. "Or save you, depending on where it lands. And the body . . . a hard frame with soft curves. I love a contradiction."

Nathan thought about her public persona. How rigid and rehearsed she seemed, adopting the same pose in every photo. But last night she'd been tearstained and vulnerable. A hard frame with soft curves. His eyes drifted lower to the swell of her hip. She caught him looking. They stared at each other with lust flooding the air like dopamine. Her face reddened and she turned away.

"How long do these usually take?" She gestured toward the washer. "I could probably come back."

If she left, he might never see her again. Not alone like this. Not after that look. "Do you want to go for a ride?"

She froze. "With you? Don't you..." She scanned the empty room. "Don't you have to work?"

"I own this place. So no, I don't."

She looked at the car and then back at him. "I shouldn't."

"But do you want to?" He was surprised at how even his voice was. His heart was pounding in his throat.

Rachel sat with his question for the longest five seconds of his life before a reckless grin lit her face like wildfire. She held out her hand. "Can I drive?"

---

Nathan tried very hard not to look at her ass on the way to his car, and Rachel appreciated the effort. She might have ignored it if he hadn't defaulted to sidelong glances at her face. His brown eyes became amber in the sunlight streaming through the windshield, transforming his handsome features into something ethereal. It was hard to keep her eyes on the road.

Men were better listeners when they were attracted to someone. Rachel had been told from an early age that she was a pretty girl and should be grateful for her looks. That people would kill for good hair like hers and she wasn't *that* dark, so the guys who only dated light-skinned girls would probably make an exception. Which was another way of saying that she wasn't worth much. *Don't waste what little you have. Take advantage of every door that opens wider when you smile.*

Rachel had met Faith's father at a house party in Georgetown when she was fifteen and still believed the number of eyes that followed her across the room was the measure of her value. Her flirting was giggly and indiscriminate, fueled by foul punch that consisted of different fruity vodkas mixed together. One cup had her buzzed enough to trip over someone's purse. Adrian caught her. He was dark and lean, with an easy smile that made her stomach flip when he offered to buy her coffee. They left the house and he walked her toward a 1970 cherry-red Chevy Chevelle with thick white lines across the hood.

She'd spent the next three days being chauffeured around the city in white leather seats. People with vintage cars never shut up about them, and Adrian was no exception. She learned more about horsepower than she ever cared to remember. But she also loved to sink low against the leather and let the loud rumble of the engine drown out everything but the road.

Adrian had just turned eighteen and drove in from the West Coast to celebrate his birthday because he loved fishing and Maryland crab cakes. He was almost too gentle when they had sex, like he didn't believe she was as experienced as she claimed. Rachel didn't know much about what she wanted from men back then, but she knew it wasn't a pedestal. When he gave her his number and said he'd like to see her again, she'd waited until his taillights were gone before throwing it in the trash.

Not keeping that scrap of paper was her biggest regret. Whenever Faith asked about him, that careless mistake gnawed at her insides. If she could travel back in time and tell that version of herself that she'd conceived her only child in the back seat of that car, things might have been different. The hardest parts of her life might have been more bearable with someone who considered Faith a piece of their own soul too.

Now she understood why Adrian had never let her drive the Chevelle. Nathan's car was like steering a wild horse on a two-lane road. The first turn was terrifying. The next was amazing. When she gave it gas, it rattled her body like an earthquake.

Nathan was almost eerily calm when she gunned the engine or underestimated a turn. He kept both hands resting against his thighs, still stealing glances when he thought she wasn't looking. His attention made her skin feel tight and sensitive. Every look was like a touch. Combined with the adrenaline of the drive, she was turned on in a way that felt as sacred and vital as the blood coursing through her veins.

Matt used to call her insatiable. He meant it as a compliment, but it was also judgment, something to distinguish her from the other women he used to date. Once they were married, insatiable became a switch that she had to turn off to be more palatable. She was a Black woman, with a teenage mother bio that everyone loved to applaud in public but mentioned skeptically behind her back. If a woman flirted, Rachel never played along. If a man held her gaze too long, she'd avoid him the rest of the night. She even hid her sex toys in a plain black bag, deep inside her closet so her own husband wouldn't be reminded that he'd married a woman who owned a dildo.

But that was before she'd extorted Matt for money. She'd felt the change in herself the moment she'd asked for Nathan's car keys. The insatiable switch was back on and dialed up to its thirstiest setting. Nathan took up so much space in the car that his body was impossible to ignore. He had to be five or six inches taller than she was. His biceps were nearly the size of her thigh. What would it feel like to be held by someone like that? Someone big enough to block out the sun.

He pointed to a street on their right. "Don't miss the turn."

Rachel jerked the steering wheel left and then tried to quickly spin it in the opposite direction. The car fishtailed. This time, Nathan covered her hand with his. Her pulse skyrocketed from a rush of fear and adrenaline. And his touch. Their intertwined fingers guided the car onto the side of the road.

Her hands trembled as she turned off the ignition. Nathan touched her headrest and leaned closer, watching her with worried eyes. "Are you okay?"

"Yes." It came out as a gasp. Her body was still humming. "Nathan, that was amazing. It made me feel so...*alive*." She groaned. "That's corny, I know."

"No, it's not." He smiled. One side of his mouth lifted a little higher than the other. A perfect face with an adorable, perfect flaw. "I could tell as I was watching you. Made me remember driving it for the first time."

"I always wanted one of these. I forgot until I saw yours." She ran her hands over the steering wheel. "I think I've forgotten a lot of things about myself."

They fell silent. His eyes were on her again, but this time it felt more like analysis. She was a riddle he wanted to solve. Maybe he'd see something she couldn't. She could barely track her own emotions from one minute to the next. An hour ago, she'd been standing in front of Sofia Cárdenas, desperate to be seen as something more than Matt's appendage. Now she wanted to turn the gas back on and keep driving until she disappeared completely.

Rachel looked away and focused on their surroundings for the first time. She didn't recognize the neighborhood. "Where are we?"

That crooked grin sprang to life again. "A block from the best burger of your life."

———

The restaurant was a walk-up with picnic tables out front. *The Stand* was printed on a large sign in bright red letters and repeated in Spanish on the bottom. If they had been on the west side of town, there probably would have been more kitschy nostalgia like shiny chrome napkin holders that doubled as credit card readers. But this place was authentic and lived-in. The walls had been repainted numerous times. The tables showed signs of repeated weather exposure. The poles that held up a wide awning were covered with rust and overgrown weeds at the bottom.

It was late afternoon, and the tables were empty. Rachel stopped to study a menu posted on a bulletin board, but Nathan kept walking to the counter. He tapped an old-fashioned call bell and leaned through the cashier's window. "Can we get some service out here?"

His rudeness surprised her. But maybe that was his thing—nice to pretty girls, mean to the waiter. "Hey," she said, catching his eye. "Can you give them a minute?"

A stocky, gray-haired man appeared in the window and snatched the bell away. "¡Tócalo de nuevo y escupiré en tu comida!"

Nathan rolled his eyes and smiled at Rachel. "He said he's going to spit in my food." He gestured toward the man. "This is my friend Miguel. He owns this place."

She relaxed. "It's nice to meet you."

Miguel glanced at Nathan. "¿Tu novia?"

"I'm not his girlfriend," Rachel interjected, with a quick scan of the parking lot.

Nathan leaned against the counter. "Don't sound so offended."

"I'm not offended. I just—" He stood there grinning while she fumbled. Her face warmed. "Forget it."

"She's my aunt," Nathan said, with a different, less crooked smile. This one was broader, all teeth and flirty dimple. "Can't you see the resemblance?"

She rolled her eyes. "Okay, ha ha, fuck you."

"What's your name, beautiful?" Miguel asked.

She hesitated. Nathan must have noticed because he moved to block her from Miguel's view. "Princesa."

Miguel shook his head. "*Reina*. Get it right." He winked at her over Nathan's shoulder. "I'm single, by the way. In case you really are his aunt."

Nathan groaned. "The food, man, come on."

"It's coming. Two with everything?"

Nathan looked at her to confirm. She shook her head. "No onions."

"No onions on either."

Miguel nodded. "Give me ten minutes."

They sat down at an iron-lattice table with unlabeled bottles of chili sauce in the center. Nathan grabbed two and set them to one side. "How hot?"

"Nuclear."

He grabbed another dark red bottle. "Figured."

"Did he really not recognize me?"

"Who, Miguel?" His eyes slid over her face. "You don't really look like yourself right now."

She caught her reflection in the silver napkin holder. Her hair had nearly escaped from her ponytail. Without eye makeup and lipstick, her features looked smaller—plainer. She should have put on eyeliner, at least. "I wasn't planning on seeing anyone today."

"That's not how I meant it. You look good." His eyes fell briefly to her shirt. "Just different."

She wanted to press him for more details. Did she look single? Like a jilted wife? Between him and Miguel, this was the most open interest she'd received from men in years. She still wore her ring, but she didn't hate the idea of being perceived as someone who had evolved beyond believing in wedding vows.

"At least I remembered to wear shoes this time."

Nathan folded his arms on the table, displaying a phoenix drawn in swirls of red and gold from his elbow to his wrist. "I like that you went out that way. It told me a lot about you."

"Such as?"

He paused and considered the question. "You're not who everyone thinks you are. But it's intentional. You prefer it."

It was a little too close to being called fake than she was comfortable with, but that didn't make it any less true. Hiding was safer. And was it really hiding when the world was watching? Wasn't that more like self-preservation?

The worst part of being the woman standing beside a man that everyone adored was the constant pressure to prove that you deserved it.

"It makes things easier," she said. It was also lonely, something she'd only realized last night when Nathan had given her his sweatshirt.

"Easier for who? You?"

"Yes," she said, her voice sharpening. She hated when someone who would never have her problems thought they could fix them in five minutes. "You don't have to understand."

"I know," he said sheepishly. "Sorry, but it seems miserable. You should be able to blow off steam and make mistakes like the rest of us." He leaned closer. "Tell me about one. Something messed up, that deep down you really don't give a shit about. Something juicy and formative."

Rachel laughed. His thumb trailed lazily over his forearm as he waited for her to speak. Watching him made her skin tighten again. She averted her eyes. "I have an incomplete tattoo."

He smiled. "I'm listening."

The story was embarrassing in a way that most college freshman stories were. At that point in her life, she was still naive and insecure. The most dramatic thing she'd experienced was childbirth, and people like her friend Shauna were so dismissive of the concept of motherhood that Rachel had stopped mentioning her daughter in their presence. One night, Shauna had gotten drunk and called Rachel a white-girl prom queen pretending to be down. "It pissed me off," Rachel said. "While yes, I pretended to be interested in her shitty performance art, I was never a fucking prom queen. And her family owned a house on Martha's Vineyard!"

Nathan pitched forward with laughter. There was something melancholic in him that disappeared when he found something funny. It made her possessive. Like each time she made him laugh, more of that delicious, eye crinkling sound belonged to her.

"So this was a spite tattoo?" Nathan asked. "This girl called you basic and you got a fleur de lis on your ass?"

"That is not what it is. And it's not on my ass. But it really hurt, and I chickened out halfway through. Now I'm stuck with it."

Miguel rounded the corner with two plastic baskets filled with food. He set them down and eyed the last bottle of chili sauce that Nathan had placed between them. "That shit'll burn your lips off."

Rachel grabbed it and unscrewed the top. "Challenge accepted."

He laughed and gave Nathan a pointed look. "Ella me gusta."

Nathan's eyes never left her face. "Me too."

Miguel waved and returned to the stand. The burgers were huge, and the fries were seasoned with so much salt that it formed a crust on the surface. Rachel used a paper napkin as a placemat and then used three more to cover her lap. She shook out a generous amount of chili sauce into a small paper cup filled with ketchup.

Nathan opened his burger and started covering it with fresh pickles. "That's a very specific situation you got going over there."

"Specific?"

"With the napkins." He pointed to her ketchup. "And your chemistry experiment."

"I don't want grease all over my jeans." She dipped a fry in the spicy ketchup. "And please tell me you've tried this."

"I don't eat ketchup."

"Not even with fries?"

"Nope." He picked up his burger, took a bite, and grunted his appreciation.

She looked down at her burger. "I should cut this in half."

"Just bite it."

"It's messy."

"Messy's good. Get a little grease on your chin. It's sexy."

She groaned. "You're making it weird."

"Why is that weird?" He laughed. "I'm just messing with you. I can go get a knife."

"No, no." She picked up the burger and took a big bite. Tomato slid out of the bottom and hot grease coated her fingers, but it was delicious—salty and spiced with cumin and chili—probably one of the best burgers she'd ever had. A contented sigh burst from her throat. "Oh god. It's been so long."

Nathan cocked an eyebrow and grinned. She quickly changed the subject. "So, how long have you owned the laundromat?"

Something slid over his expression too fast for her to identify. He ducked his head and took another bite of his burger before answering. "Eight years."

"Eight?" She lifted her brow. "How old were you?"

"Eighteen," he said. "I live in the apartment upstairs."

So he was twenty-six. Who buys their first business at eighteen years old? And why would he choose Oasis Springs? "Before I moved here, I didn't know what these people were like."

"These people?"

"Wealthy people. Like the Abbott and Vasquez families, with their piles of money earning interest in a vault on some island."

He took another bite and swallowed before responding. "I don't really think about it."

That was hard to believe. Living in Oasis Springs meant that your kids ran around playgrounds named after Tomás Vasquez. He was the founder of the original Vasquez Coffee plant that was built when the town was still a small immigrant community in the 1950s. Today, that small plant was a billion-dollar conglomerate run by his son, Beto. And the community Tomás nurtured through real estate investment and philanthropy had become one of the most affluent suburbs in Fairfax County.

While the Vasquez family had been the economic lifeblood of the town for decades, compared to the Abbotts, they were still new money. The presence of Matt's family in this historically Black and brown town was like a beacon for a richer and whiter group of business owners looking for commercial property at bargain prices. Eventually, small generational businesses were pushed to the fringes of the city that had once been a haven. Miguel was a prime example of the type of business owner forced to settle for what was leftover once people with more money and influence took more than their share. Rachel had researched all of this when Matt told her he was running for mayor.

"No one has ever been rude to you?" Rachel asked. "Handed you their dirty laundry and asked for a ticket like they were at a dry cleaner?"

Nathan smiled. "Of course. But I grew up here, so I kind of expect it. Most people are harmless. If they realized how they came off, they'd probably be embarrassed."

Rachel shook her head. "Tell me again how you're not a nice guy?"

He shrugged. "You never know what someone's going through."

"Especially if they never talk about themselves. I'm a good listener too." Their conversation kept pivoting back to her, but she didn't want to keep taking the bait.

They faced off for a moment, and it slowly tipped into something dangerous. Like she was a sharp curve, and he was debating whether to accelerate or pump the brakes. Eventually he shook his head, pushed his chair back, and said, "We should probably get going. Make sure no one stole your clothes while we were gone."

"You're right," she said, trying to ignore the sudden dip in her mood. She had no right to be disappointed. "It's getting late. Someone will be looking for me."

The feeling eased when Nathan asked for her phone number and then sent her a text so she'd have his. She started to save it and hesitated. "I don't know your last name."

He shoved his phone back into his pocket. "It's Vasquez."

Her hand froze. "Wait. Are you—" She stopped midsentence, embarrassed by the assumption. It was a common name in the area. She'd run into two distant Vasquez cousins last week.

"Am I related?" Nathan chuckled and shook his head dismissively. "I mean, in this town, isn't everybody?"

# CHAPTER SIX

Nathan hadn't seen the inside of his parents' home in six months. Its imposing exterior, however, was inescapable. The Vasquez estate loomed over Oasis Springs—a Spanish tiled fortress that defied every restrictive covenant the neighborhood association had passed over the years. While his father would stop short of claiming his family was above the law, Beto Vasquez had no problem saying that they predated it. Vasquez Industries was one of the largest privately held corporations in the country and had been the economic center of the town for half a century. The sprawling fruit orchard and forty-five-foot saltwater pool that technically extended over his property line were things Beto felt entitled to.

Inside, Nathan sat opposite his brother, Joe, in an almost identical position—shoulders hunched and heads bowed over their phones. The matching wing chairs were uncomfortable for both of them, but that never seemed to bother his brother as much as it did Nathan. Joe had been the chief operating officer at their family's company for seven years, but still used the wobbly office chair left by his predecessor. That was his brother in a nutshell—impatient with comfort, ambivalent about ironing, and constantly annoyed that he was mentally three steps ahead on every project while everyone else was just showing up to the meeting.

Nathan took his time typing a response to the photo Rachel had sent, trying to avoid as many spelling errors as he could. It was one of those annoying things about living with dyslexia. When he was alone, he could use the speech-to-text function and clean it up. But he wasn't about to dictate a reply to Rachel's post-workout selfie with his very nosy and opinionated brother sitting across from him.

In the photo, Rachel wore a baggy Up in Smoke tour tank top that was soaked with sweat. Her cheeks were flushed, and clumps of wet curls clung to her neck. Her smile was an endorphin-fueled sunbeam.

**Rachel:** No one ever sees me like this.

**Nathan:** It feels good to be no one.

He paused and then sent another message.

**Nathan:** You look beautiful.

Rachel had been messaging him for three days now. Her timing was random and the subject matter unpredictable. But every text seemed confessional, like things she'd never admit to anyone else. That tattoo story had opened the floodgates, and now he had the paparazzi's favorite "ice queen" whispering secrets in his ear.

Nathan leaned his head back and stared at the decorative red plates lining the wall above his brother's head. He should be confessing too. He should tell her that no one ever saw him like *this*, waiting to be summoned to dinner like one of his father's employees. He should tell her that while every other Vasquez was content to live on the estate that had been in their family for generations, being in his parents' house for more than five minutes made him into a person he despised. The baby of the family. The troublemaker. The afterthought his parents tried to ignore.

Nathan dimmed his screen, but Joe kept typing, probably some multi-paragraph text with bullet points and footnotes. Abuelita had nicknamed his brother Apollo, because Joe was basically perfect. Grades. Sports. Table manners of the gods. He was twelve when Nathan was born, and instantly became the ideal older brother, helping with feedings, changing diapers, taking trips to the park. But at some point, Joe missed a step and brought home a B+ instead of all As. Their parents staged an intervention and took him off babysitting duty. While Joe became entrenched in high school and everything that came with it, Nathan's favorite hobby was pushing Carla, his nanny, to the point of cursing him out in Spanish. She quit the day he hid in a toy chest for six hours and popped out like a giddy, deranged jack-in-the-box when the police started searching for ransom notes.

Joe finally stopped texting and dialed someone's number. "It's me," he barked into the receiver. "Did you get my text?"

Nathan leaned forward and whispered, "Hey, Joe. That's not how texting works."

Joe ignored him and snapped, "It's all in there!" at the poor bastard on the other end of the line. "Go read it."

"The guy can't read the text if you won't let him off the phone."

Joe angled away from Nathan and lowered his voice. "Hey, so uh... I'm gonna hang up now so you can read it."

Nathan gave him a thumbs-up and mouthed, "Good job!" Joe responded with a middle finger and disconnected. The change in his brother's demeanor was immediate. He relaxed his shoulders and unclenched his jaw, studying Nathan's clothes with a bemused smirk.

"Do you even own a shirt with buttons?"

Nathan grinned. "Yes. Do *you* own anything that isn't from some tragic Arthur Miller play?"

Before Joe could respond, they were smothered by a cloud of perfume. Sofia was dressed casually for dinner, which meant a multicolored caftan with jewelry and no makeup. Her dark hair was piled on top of her head in a complicated swirl of thick braids that probably took half an hour to create. Her sense of fashion would only give so much in the name of casual comfort.

"Joseph! It's been so long since we've seen you at dinner." She pulled him down into a hug. "I'm going to have meals sent to your office. You're too skinny."

"You only say that because I'm vegan."

She patted his face. "Please don't talk about it like it's an identity."

Meat was their mother's love language. Most of her family lived in Monterrey, and all Nathan remembered about their rare visits was eating his weight in machaca and carne asada. When Sofia learned Joe had switched to a vegan diet, they didn't speak for days.

"How is my grandson?"

Joe beamed and quickly brought up photos on his phone. "Angel's doing great. He got these new Nikes and only takes them off for bath time." He tilted the phone so Nathan could see a photo of his six-year-old nephew wearing white Air Force 1s with a puffy-cheeked smile that flashed all five of his remaining baby teeth. It was a full-on cuteness assault that made Nathan feel guilty for not reaching out more. He made a mental note to hype Angel up over FaceTime later. "He keeps talking about showing them to Uncle Nate." Joe paused, and added, "Zara's fine too."

Sofia's smile slipped. "It's been a while since we've seen Xiomara."

Joe pretended he didn't notice his mother's obvious contempt for his wife. Over the years, he'd become adept at hearing only what he needed to when it came to their parents. But Zara wasn't. She'd once admitted to Nathan that she could never eat in Sofia's presence. "She watches me like a movie villain waiting for me to keel over because she's secretly poisoned my food."

"She's been busy," Joe said. "Her last film just wrapped in New York."

"Yes, yes, how wonderful." Sofia spun around and beckoned Nathan closer with a wary look that reminded him why he hadn't been home in months. They embraced, his arms stiff and cautious, hers a little too tight for comfort. When it came to Nathan, Sofia would always waffle between ambivalence and outsize concern, and he could never tell which was genuine. She'd never wanted two kids and would often joke about the number of pregnancy tests she had taken with Nathan, hoping to see a negative result. Then she'd quickly follow up with sugary soliloquies. "Of course, I *adore* him. My little Rivera, always gifting us with beauty and light." But to Nathan, it felt like being loved in fits and starts, as if the feeling vanished when he wasn't standing right in front of her.

"How have you been?" Sofia asked. "I hate thinking about you alone in that laundry place. What if someone broke in while you were sleeping?"

"For what? A midnight merlot stain emergency? There's a basket of Tide sticks by the door, so I'll be safe."

She nudged his arm. "You're not funny."

"You're right. No one uses Tide sticks in Oasis Springs. They'd buy another outfit."

Sofia tried to hide her smile. "Be serious," she said. "I know you're attached to that business, but there's an open position in marketing at the company—"

"Mom," Joe interrupted. "Leave him alone. Nate's not interested."

"Let him tell me that."

"Nate's not interested." Nathan parroted his brother's clipped baritone.

"Listen to him, Sofia." Nathan's father appeared by the doors of the dining room. "He clearly wants nothing to do with the company."

Beto cast a shadow over their mood in his black suit and bloodred pocket square. He was tall and broad, like his sons, but with dark eyes, unlike the golden-brown color they'd inherited from Sofia. When Nathan learned about black holes in school, how nothing escapes them, not even light, he pictured Beto's eyes, placid as midnight, absorbing his excuses for a bad grade with the apathy of a gravitational pull.

Zara had it wrong. If Nathan's family were cast in a movie, his mother would be the critical mentor who was impressed only if you saved the world. Joe was the hero who walked into a zombie apocalypse, inspiring hope in everyone that they would make it out alive. But Beto was the real villain, and not the easily defeated kind who monologued while you reloaded a gun. He was sinister like a shadow, the devil that struck as soon as you forgot he was there.

Nathan liked to think of himself as the comic relief, but in reality, he was an expendable bit player who was too sensitive and emotional to survive till the end. As a kid, Nathan was quick to shed tears or have emotional outbursts. After Joe read him *Where the Wild Things Are*, it gave him nightmares for weeks. Even now, he could recall the terror that seized his five-year-old chest when Beto yanked the night-light from his wall, grumbling, "There are better things to be afraid of."

Joe tried coping with the pressure of being Beto's favorite by having modes he switched on and off like a computer. Big brother mode was the annoying, overprotective know-it-all who was obsessed with collared shirts. The Apollo mode made him the charming boyfriend who convinced Zara he'd make a good husband, even though he showed up late for his own wedding. Finally, there was the workaholic: the version of his brother who only left the office to yell at someone else for leaving work early. That mode put everything else on the back burner. Eating. Sleeping. Family. If it stayed on too long, it was almost impossible to turn off. Beto liked that mode the most.

Twelve years ago, Joe pushed himself so hard, for so long, that his body finally gave out. Nathan was fourteen when he had found his brother slumped on the floor of his office, sweaty and pale, staring at a coffee cup he swore had been put there by their dead grandfather.

When Beto arrived at the hospital, his favorite son was sleeping off sedation, strapped to beeping machines, while his youngest son sobbed incoherently in the corner. Before the doctors explained that Joe had experienced anxiety-induced psychosis and sleep deprivation, Nathan could tell Beto blamed him for Joe's condition. That was the type of father he was, a man who viewed his children through a lens of bitter cynicism instead of empathy.

Nathan was sent to boarding school on the same day his brother was checked into an inpatient program. Joe had reassured Nathan they'd both be fine. "I know this feels big, but it's not. We're going to do what we have to and shrink all of this down to nothing. Things will get better. You'll see."

Nathan thought Joe meant he was done working for their father. What he had really meant was that he would take medication and stop eating meat because it was better for his heart. Joe could work twenty-four hours a day, whittling *himself* down to nothing, and never be convinced it was enough. Not for the favorite. Not for Beto's Apollo.

Eventually, Nathan learned how to face Beto without falling apart, particularly during lectures about the family business. His father was predictable. Years had passed but the insults never changed.

"You can't force a grown man to respect his legacy," Beto grumbled, his eyes stubbornly fixed on Sofia. Criticizing Nathan directly would imply that his youngest son was present and visible, not a vague source of annoyance. "Particularly when it's taken for granted."

Joe moved closer to Nathan, ready to act as a human shield if necessary. "Come on, Dad, that's not fair. Not everyone wants to pick apart coffee markets twenty-four hours a day."

"Since when is *work* about *want?*" Beto punctuated his words by slapping his knuckles against his palm.

Nathan focused on a brass wall sconce and drained his voice of emotion. "It's not the work I'm avoiding."

"Same old excuses," Beto sneered. "Repeating something doesn't make it true."

Beto had never liked that Nathan owned the laundromat, but on some level, he understood it. Nathan's grandfather, Tomás, had started a billion-dollar corporation by purchasing a small Oaxacan coffee farm from his wife's family. Tomás's father was a banker who opened a chain of grocery stores that eventually became a subsidiary of Vasquez Industries. Being a true Vasquez meant taking ownership of your life and never answering to anyone but your family. Even Joe, burning through the days to keep their father happy, would never truly be respected until Beto decided he was ready to be CEO.

When Nathan told Beto he bought the laundromat, his father's face had shown a rare glimmer of respect. But in his excitement, Nathan let it slip that he planned to use the basement as an art studio, and Beto had immediately dismissed the business as the whim of a spoiled son "too lazy to commit to something real."

Beto moved to the head of the table and said, "Come sit down. All of you. I didn't call you all here to chat in the hallway while my food gets cold." Nathan chose the chair farthest from Beto. Sofia sat at the opposite end of the table, while Joe claimed a seat in the space between them.

Joe went straight for the vegetables. Nathan stacked his plate with as much food as it could contain and vowed to spend the rest of the evening silently chewing and swallowing. It wouldn't be hard. The food was delicious. His mother hired only the best chefs to feed her family.

"Still got that appetite, I see." Beto speared a piece of chicken. "Both of you look good—healthy. Are you still working out together?"

Joe glanced at Nathan, who bit into a bread roll instead of responding. "Yeah, we are," Joe said. "Every other morning, I drag this one out of bed for a run. We lift at Abel's Gym."

"Nathan, you're getting so big," Sofia said. "Nice broad shoulders." She glared at Joe's plate. "It must be all that meat."

Joe started grumbling about a late conference call and glanced at his watch. Nathan shoveled down more food, mentally drafting excuses about why he had to leave early. Beto recaptured their attention with a raised palm. "So, I asked your mother to extend this invitation because I wasn't sure you would accept one from me."

"You were right," Nathan muttered and stabbed a potato. Joe gave him a look that would have been a kick under the table if they weren't separated by an ocean of mahogany wood. Nathan took a breath and tried to soften his voice. "So, what's going on?

Beto picked up his wine and took a long drink. He eyed his wife and children over the rim and took a deep breath. "I'm dying," he said. "It's a brain tumor. Inoperable. I've got…I don't know…a few months. Maybe more, maybe less."

Nathan's fork slipped, crashing to his plate. He stared at the splattered mess and thought, *This is just like Beto. Ruining dinner before anyone can enjoy it.* But then he looked up and saw the truth in Joe's horrified expression. Beto had a tumor. His father was dying.

"Wait," Nathan said, and tried to push more air through his lungs. "That can't be true."

"How long have you known?" Joe looked like he was suffocating. "I mean, are you sure?"

"Wait." Nathan's brain was stuck in a loop. He focused on his mother, an old habit since childhood. His father would say something that rocked him, and he'd look to her to be his anchor. But her eyes were fixed on Beto.

"I'm dying, so it's the kind that kills you." Beto fixed Nathan with a hard stare. "And I don't plan on spending my last days trading insults with my youngest." He looked at Joe. "Or letting my firstborn play hero when I know he can't save me."

Nathan reached for his water glass, but his fingers were numb and stiff. It fell over, and he watched the water drip onto the rug.

"You do this now, Beto?" Sofia hissed. "I finally get them here and you won't let us have one more dinner? One evening without—"

"What do you expect me to do, Sofia? Wait until dessert to tell my boys they're about to lose their father? Things need to be done." His eyes shifted to Nathan. "I'm out of time."

Beto's gaze pinned Nathan to the chair. He couldn't speak. There was a lump in his throat so big that he would choke if he tried to swallow. He'd spent most of his life wishing that his father were anyone but the man sitting across from him, but he'd never thought about something like this. He watched his parents exchange a look he couldn't decipher, and something cold ran up his spine.

Deep down, Nathan still believed Joe's promise that things would change. That at some point, his family wouldn't cringe at the mention of his name. Eventually, he would do something or become someone that would make all the grief he'd caused worth it. It was a thin hope, like wisps of smoke he'd stupidly tried to grasp.

"What do you need from us, Dad?" Joe's hands rested awkwardly alongside his plate. His brother wasn't used to being helpless.

"There are decisions to make, things I've been putting off—and I . . ." Beto faltered as he gathered his thoughts. "I need to know that you'll be okay when I'm gone. That you'll support each other as a family."

Joe started firing off more questions, and the next few months unfolded in Nathan's head like a movie. With Zara out of town, Joe would move from the guesthouse to his old bedroom to be closer to

Beto, working even longer hours to make up for their father's absence. Sofia would hover over Beto's care, second-guessing his doctors to micromanage her grief. And Nathan would . . . wait until someone needed him.

As if on cue, Sofia moved to Beto's side and muttered something about eating to keep up his strength. Beto gazed at her with a raw adoration that made Nathan's eyes burn.

Maybe he shouldn't wait to be useful. Maybe he could be a respite to his family, the person who listened when they needed to talk without judgment. He didn't have an office job like Joe or a dozen charities depending on him like Sofia. He just had unencumbered time. Time he could use to be a shoulder they could lean on.

The wisps of hope that he could help them grew thick and weighty; all he had to do was hold on to them. Nathan stood and said, "I'm here. Like Joe said, tell me what you need."

Beto's expression curdled. "What I need is for your existence to have a point."

Nathan jerked back. He folded his arms tight, as if he could stem the humiliation flooding his system. It was his own fault for thinking he could offer anything his father would want. Beto kept going, twisting the knife to ensure a hemorrhage. "Stop screwing around with your finger paints and be a goddamn Vasquez. I need you to be my son."

---

After the first week of their deal, Rachel admitted to herself that she might have been overconfident about her ability to play nice with Matt for the cameras. On Monday, as they stood beside each other at a ribbon cutting for a newly accessible public playground, she could barely focus on the instructions his people whispered in her ear. "Wave at that donor. Now stand closer to Matt and hold his hand." Rachel's skin crawled the minute their fingers touched, and she jerked them away in full view of a dozen photographers. She'd thought she'd blown it until she saw that everyone was too busy laughing at Matt's *I was that lonely kid on the seesaw* story to notice.

Once the press was gone, Matt pointedly asked everyone but her whether he should do tomorrow's event alone. He was scheduled to sit piously in the front pew of a Black megachurch while the pastor spoke about the importance of voter registration. Hailey Dearwood, his communications director, told him it was a bad idea. "Think of the optics," she said, and smiled at Rachel like it was their private joke.

Matt and Rachel never talked much about race when they started dating. They would sidestep hard conversations while bantering about the differences in their upbringing. But one night, a month into their relationship, Matt had been uncharacteristically quiet on the way home from one of their favorite restaurants.

"I've noticed something," he said, and reached for her hand. "When we eat out together, they always ask whether we want one or two checks."

Rachel nodded. She'd noticed, but hadn't pointed it out because she assumed he'd call her paranoid. They were still in that murky place of caring for each other without knowing what that meant. The conversation he was hinting at was used to test the foundations of something permanent. Twentysomething Rachel would always default to the easier option, so instead of confirming his suspicions, she said, "I think that server was new."

Matt gave her a side-eye. "It's not just her. You haven't noticed? It's every time. 'Is this one check? Are you two together?'"

"Yes, I've noticed," she snapped. "What's your point?"

"Why didn't you say something? I'm over here thinking I'm paranoid, and you—" He sighed, like she'd put the world on his shoulders, and pulled the car over to the curb. By the time he killed the ignition, Rachel was furious. What gave him the right to give *her* attitude? He wasn't owed her outrage. She wasn't his racial conscience.

Matt stared at the windshield while Rachel braced herself for their first argument. But then his breath caught, and he rubbed his face until his skin was red. "You don't want to talk to me about it, do you. About race." His voice was low and halting, like the words were painful. And Rachel realized that, for Matt, this wasn't some social justice debate.

This was a part of herself that she'd been withholding, a closed door he'd observed but never tried to open, and instead had waited patiently to be invited in.

Years later, she would wonder if she'd made a mistake that night. Maybe she should have said, "No. I don't want to talk about it," because love wasn't entitlement, and she had the right to decide when and if she had those conversations. But she'd convinced herself it was selfish not to try, so she'd grabbed his hand and spent the rest of the night reassuring him it was okay to ask questions if he had them—saying that she'd rarely dated outside her race before, so she was still learning too.

In hindsight, that night set a precedent for their marriage. Matt felt safe discussing race with the woman he loved, and Rachel didn't want to discourage it because he was trying and learning. But she never told him it was exhausting, and that his staff would pepper her with questions like she was the only safe Black person to ask why it wasn't okay to say *dreadlocks* anymore. And Hailey Dearwood was the worst of them. She scheduled Rachel for every event in Black neighborhoods whether she was needed or not, as if her presence would obscure Matt's obvious whiteness.

Now, with the additional burden of selling their fake marriage, Rachel thought she'd earned the right to skip the church service. But Matt switched course and agreed that she should be there. He couldn't look her in the eye when he said it. Neither of them had thought about the way this dynamic of mutually assured destruction would feel: the uncomfortable grossness of forcing each other to do things against their will. He mumbled something about "important depositions" and practically burned rubber leaving the parking lot.

Rachel had her car keys in hand when Hailey informed her they'd scored a last-minute profile that afternoon with the *Washington Post*. "We need to capitalize on the gala, and Alesha is game, but she wants to focus on the education angle. It's at OS Elementary West. I need to make a stop, so can you meet us there?"

"Did you say Alesha? As in Alesha Williams? My aunt?"

Hailey's eye twitched, but her smile didn't falter. "Yes! And we didn't even have to beg this time. She called the campaign and insisted on interviewing you herself."

---

Rachel had grown up knowing that her father had a sister named Alesha and that they were estranged for reasons he never told her. But she'd never asked for an explanation. Peter Thomas didn't keep secrets; he revealed information when it was needed. Rachel had always trusted his judgment and she knew their world was held together by the fragile strings he'd woven to ensure she would never have to sacrifice anything. She loved him for it. But when her father died swiftly, without warning, she resented him for it. Because in addition to withholding her family history, he'd never told her about his cancer diagnosis, or his lapsed medical coverage, or the predatory loans he'd been using to pay the bills. She was alone, with a young daughter, and no one to turn to for help. By the time she found Alesha's phone number in one of Peter's old books, Rachel and Faith had been sleeping in a car for weeks.

Alesha had sent her an Oasis Springs address, wired gas money for the trip, and told Rachel to arrive as soon as possible because as a journalist who specialized in exposing local political corruption, she didn't have time to "wait around for visitors" during an election season. Rachel had been so grateful for the possibility of finally sleeping in a bed again, she'd ignored the rudeness of Alesha's charity. Once they arrived, Alesha made Faith a sandwich and asked what color she'd like to paint her new bedroom. Later, when she showed Rachel the room that she'd be sharing with her cousin Mia—a home office with two austere twin beds shoved against the wall—the reality of her situation set in. While Alesha had fallen in love with Faith at first sight, Rachel was a burden she had no intention of carrying for long.

Their relationship was combative and vicious, a yearlong stream of shouting matches that Rachel struggled to hide from Faith. Once she got married, Rachel had tried to put the woman behind her. But Matt was obsessed with winning Alesha's approval. Sometimes Rachel wondered if he'd conflated earning acceptance in the Black community with being accepted by a woman who'd made a career out of dismantling privilege. Like he needed her permission to stop flinching at his own reflection.

That afternoon, the parking lot at Oasis Springs West was virtually empty. A large bulletin board displayed little smiling faces with *Our Kids Have Character* in bright red letters across the top. She read the captions: *Amy brings the crossing guard bottled water every morning. Max picks up the litter on the playground. Chase used a 3D printer to make an accessible staff directory for blind students.* It read like a shrine to the Ivy League hopes of their parents. Meanwhile, on the other side of town was OS South, smaller with lower test scores, fewer PTA funds, and perilously close to a "failing" designation. It was also majority Black and brown kids. When Rachel first moved to Oasis Springs, Faith had attended OS South, but once she got married, their zoning changed, and Matt was aggressively anti–school choice. Faith told her years later that on her first day at West, an older boy called her ghetto and threw her backpack in the trash.

Rachel heard footsteps heading her way and looked up, expecting to see Hailey's exasperated face, but Mia turned the corner instead.

"There you are." Mia sat down beside her, stretched out her legs, and sighed. "My mother is looking for you."

Rachel eyed the casual comfort of Mia's sweatpants with envy. "She wants to interview me."

"I know."

"I'm hiding."

"That's obvious. I'm surprised you agreed."

Rachel wanted to confess that she was in marital purgatory and didn't have a choice. "The gala funds the art programs here," she said instead. "Surely she'll play nice for the kids."

"Mom never played nice for Niles and me." Mia looked up at the colorful display filled with tiny, gap-toothed faces. "I hate this school."

Rachel followed her gaze. "They do look a little brainwashed, don't they?"

Mia laughed. "No, it's not the kids, it's the parents. They called an emergency PTA meeting. Like those exist. Mom hitched a ride."

"I joined the PTA," Rachel said. "But I wasn't..." Interested? Welcome? Half the women resented her for snagging Matt. The other half were obsessed with vaginal steaming and charcuterie in a way that felt cultish. "I wasn't very active. What was the emergency?"

Mia rolled her eyes. "Fall bake sales are evil now. Filled with sugar and gluten and problematic messages about the gender binary. There was so much shouting." Mia shuddered. "Mainly from me. I think I blacked out yelling about brownies. It's embarrassing." She shrugged. "But I won, so who cares?"

"Well, congratulations. Enjoy making all those cookies."

"Girl, I can't bake. I'm booking a vacation that week."

Rachel snorted. "You yelled at the OS West PTA, which is basically an organized crime syndicate. I would leave and never come back."

They burst into laughter. Rachel wiped her eyes and said, "Let me know if you need help."

Mia nodded. "I'd like that. Why don't you come to my house, and we can—" She stopped and listened to the sound of high heels clicking against the floor. Alesha rounded the corner with Hailey trailing close behind.

"Ms. Williams," Hailey sputtered. "If we could talk—"

Alesha held up her hand and cut off Hailey's protests. "I don't need your permission to speak to my niece."

Mia stood. "It's my fault Rachel's late. She was too nice to tell me to shut up."

Alesha looked at Rachel. "I need to speak with you alone."

Hailey dove forward with splayed hands. "Wait, no. That isn't what we agreed to."

"This isn't about the interview. It's a family matter."

Hailey bit her lip. "I'll call Matt."

Alesha snatched the phone from her hand. "No, you won't. He's not her overseer."

Rachel was sweating. If Alesha knew about Matt's affair, it would be in the paper by morning. "It's fine, Hailey. Leave us alone."

Hailey hitched up her chin. "I'm not comfortable with that. This is completely unprofessional."

It was like waving a red flag in front of a bull. Alesha looked giddy. "You'll be even more uncomfortable if you stay."

"I'm just doing my job," Hailey said.

Alesha shrugged. "Okay, fine. On the record. Why is your staff conducting focus groups on Rachel?"

Hailey seemed startled. She looked at Rachel and Mia as if she'd just realized she was outnumbered. "We always monitor public opinion about the candidate."

"This wasn't about the candidate. A member of your focus group goes to my church. You asked whether Rachel was an *appropriate fit* for a US congressman."

Hailey's eyes were on Rachel now, pleading. Alesha spun around and positioned herself between them, blocking Hailey's view. "You didn't know about any of this, did you?"

"You're mischaracterizing it," Hailey sputtered. She sidestepped Alesha with an outstretched hand. "This was nothing. A last-minute addition to our regular polling. The feedback was disappointing, but we can pivot a little. Find a new direction."

Rachel realized that Hailey expected some sort of life raft from her. Did she really think they were friends? "So, I'm the wrong direction?"

Hailey's neck snapped back and her eyes widened. "Absolutely not. You are incredibly impressive. *Stunning* is a word that was used, more than once."

*She's pretty like a picture.* That's how these people thought of her. Vapid. Boring. Useless. "So, they like my face, but not me."

"You know how this works." Hailey was all-business now, her clipboard angled toward Rachel like a weapon. "People need to know what box to check. It's human nature. You can be difficult to categorize."

Rachel had heard this complaint before. She was a homemaker who wasn't domestic enough. A socialite that was too introverted. A Black woman whose struggle-bus backstory included studying art history at one of the best HBCUs in the country. But at least she was pretty. She could stand in front of the cameras and give them something nice to look at while they searched for the least offensive box to stick her in.

Mia raised her hand. "Okay, I think everyone needs to take a deep breath right now. This sounds like something that should be between Rachel and her husband." She looked at Alesha. "And off the record." Her voice was different, like that night when she found Rachel sitting in the rosebushes. It was probably the same tone she used to keep abusive husbands from becoming unhinged.

"The public has a right to know that Matt Abbott is doing sketchy shit behind his wife's back," Alesha said. "Rachel deserves better. That man is going to humiliate her and then—"

"Stop! All of you, just..." Rachel's breathing was shallow and erratic. She closed her eyes and tried to regain control so it wouldn't become a full-on panic attack. But she could still sense them hovering. Watching. She was tired of being around people who borrowed pain for a living. Mia's contrived handholding. Alesha's greedy outrage. They thought they knew her, but really, they only knew which vulnerable spots they could exploit to get their way.

Rachel walked away, ignoring Alesha's protests. She had just reached her car when her phone vibrated.

**Nathan:** Saw this. Thought you might like it for your next burger.

It was an ad for an adult bib—a big napkin that snapped at the neck. Rachel smiled. And then she was laughing, so loud and hard that a woman passing by stopped to stare. He always seemed to show up just in time to undermine her misery until it vanished.

**Rachel:** Does this mean I'm on your mind?

**Nathan:** All the time.

# CHAPTER SEVEN

It had been a while since Nathan accepted Dillon's offer to get high, and it had been even longer since Bobbi joined them. Earlier that day, Joe had dropped off an invitation to their parents' anniversary party. The envelope sat on Nathan's coffee table, currently being used as a coaster. Bobbi grabbed the card and pinned it to his refrigerator with a magnet. "Forty years is a big deal," she said. "Try to be happy for them."

Bobbi viewed his parents the way everyone else did—as the Mexican Obamas, an untouchable power couple who still engaged in socially acceptable public displays of affection. But Nathan had seen the ugly side of his parents' marriage more often than anyone realized. At sixteen, he'd overheard them arguing about a pregnant woman who had shown up at Beto's office. Nathan didn't stick around long enough to know whether his father had denied the baby was his. Secrets that big were parasitic. Life was easier when you kept it small: girls, parties, rinse, repeat. His parents taught him that he wasn't built for marriage, or mortgages, or any other notarized lifelong commitment; not when he'd spent his whole life feeling like an obligation. He'd rather spend the rest of it being chosen.

Dillon slipped a vape between his lips and inhaled. He held his breath, speaking in tight bursts. "What about *Forged in Flames*?"

They'd been debating movies for over an hour. Nathan had thought he was being clever by limiting their options to the *Phoenix Prophecies* series, but he'd underestimated how deep their divisions on the subject ran. Bobbi shook her head and motioned for Dillon to pass the vape. "Not an option."

Nathan sighed. "Dude, you know she hates that movie."

"There's nothing wrong with *Forged*," Dillon said. "You're both biased because *she's* not in it." He pointed to the new tattoo of Neptune on Bobbi's shoulder.

Bobbi twisted her arm to admire the fresh ink. It looked good. Better than Nathan had expected. She propped her feet on the coffee table. "You're just jealous because no one wants to draw you anything."

"Nathan would draw me something," Dillon said, nudging her sneakers away from his beer. "Right, Nate?"

Nathan smiled. "Sure, man. I'll draw whatever you want. Name it."

"No way." Bobbi sat up quickly. "Don't you dare waste your talent on mermaids with giant tits."

"Oh my god," Dillon groaned. "That was *one* anime, Bobbi. *Nine* years ago. I thought the main character was cute."

Bobbi smirked. "And you've been dating her ever since."

Nathan took the pen from Bobbi's outstretched hand while Dillon defended his tendency to swipe right on photos of girls with beach waves on paddleboards. He inhaled just as his phone vibrated. Rachel's message made him choke.

**Rachel:** I'm checking my swimsuit bottoms for ticks.

Since his bib joke, they'd been texting nonstop for three days. But after an early morning confession about how she regretted throwing away her old journals (*I was terrified some reporter would find them*), she'd gone quiet for several hours. Nathan had nearly called her. Then he remembered that he'd only known this woman for two weeks. You couldn't let your insecurities drip over relationships like a leaky faucet. You had to keep boundaries with people, otherwise they'd try to fix you.

**Nathan:** I hope that's some kinky metaphor.

**Rachel:** No. They're actual ticks. I signed up for a charity float trip that I thought would be in canoes. It was inner tubes on the river. You can picture the rest.

**Nathan:** I'm trying. Bikini or one piece?

**Rachel:** Trikini. A handkerchief and saucers. It was freezing but I needed the ego boost.

**Nathan:** Come find me if you ever need another one.

**Rachel:** Next time I go on vacation, you're coming with me. Do you like the beach?

He thought about the last-minute trip he took to Miami two years ago with Dillon for spring break. All he remembered was puking up sugary mojitos and realizing he was too old for spring break.

**Nathan:** Sometimes. I liked visiting my grandmother's family in Oaxaca. We'd visit Bahía Tangolunda and swim for hours.

He hadn't thought about those trips in a long time. His family would go every year before Abuelita passed. His cousins would call him flaco and make fun of his terrible Spanish. Then they'd take him to clubs and tell everyone he was an American reality TV star so people would buy them drinks. Before the trip was over, they'd have him acting like a local. It gave him a glimpse of what it might be like to have a normal family, with brothers and sisters his own age.

**Rachel:** I just looked it up, and it's beautiful. Your family lives there?

**Nathan:** Great-uncles and cousins. I haven't seen them in a while.

As soon as he typed it, he knew she'd ask him why. So he quickly typed another message.

**Nathan:** You want to go? I'll book some tickets.

**Rachel:** Ha ha.

"Nettles!" Bobbi snapped her fingers in his face. "Who are you talking to?"

"No one." Nathan shoved his phone in his pocket. "Are you done fighting?"

"He's hopeless." Bobbi pointed at Nathan's hidden phone. "Is it a woman?"

"A woman?" Dillon stood beside Bobbi. "Are you seeing someone?"

Nathan leaned back on the couch. "You guys are kind of close right now. Could you back up, please?"

Dillon rolled his eyes. "Booty call. He's embarrassed."

"No." Nathan paused until they both retreated. "I'd like to have a private conversation without being interrogated."

"Is Dillon right?" Bobbi cornered him like a sniffing bloodhound. "Or is it serious?"

"There is no *it*," Nathan snapped. "Could you guys talk to each other for a minute while I text her back?"

"*Her!*" Dillon pointed to Bobbi. "Told you. Our boy is back!"

Bobbi shuddered. "Uh, no. Fuck boy Nathan is your boy. Not mine."

Nathan waited until they'd settled into another debate before picking up his phone.

**Nathan:** Anytime you feel like running away just say the word.

Those marching dots taunted him as she typed her response. He suddenly, intensely hated text messages.

**Rachel:** I feel that way every day.

He reread it, lifted his thumbs to type, and then lowered them again. He wanted to say, *So do I. I'm not sure why I never could.* But you didn't put big things like that in a text.

Nathan stood and loudly announced, "I'm making a beer run. You guys need anything?"

Dillon looked confused. "Uh...more chips?"

Nathan took the steps down into the laundromat two at a time, barely reaching the stoop before dialing Rachel's number. She answered on the first ring.

"I know that last message was pathetic, but you didn't have to call."

Her voice washed over him, soft with a hint of huskiness and smoke. He might never text her again.

"It wasn't pathetic." He leaned forward and propped his elbows on his knees. "I like hearing your voice."

She was quiet long enough to give him palpitations. "I actually hate texting," she admitted. "I'm too slow."

"That's because you care about punctuation."

"Commas increase readability, and I will die on that hill." She laughed. It was like audible honey. Nathan rocked forward, leaning into the sound.

"You've got a good laugh."

"Really?" She laughed again, but this time it was muffled, like she was covering her mouth with her hand.

He groaned. "Did I make you self-conscious? Don't be. Yours is sexy."

She didn't respond. Fuck. The filter between his brain and his mouth had been smoked down to nothing. "Rachel? Are you still there? Hey, I didn't mean it like that."

She cleared her throat. "It's okay if you did."

Nathan leaned back on the stairs and stared at the empty parking lot. His body felt heavy and light at the same time, like any minute, all the darkness weighing him down would fall away.

"God, this house is so empty," she said. "There's an echo."

"You're not alone. I'm here." He could also be there if she wanted, even though he probably shouldn't. But what was the point of playing by the rules while everyone else broke them? What would he get from standing still? "You know that, right? You can talk to me whenever you need to."

"I do," she said quietly. "And you can do the same."

He wanted to. But their situations were different. Rachel's big secret was that beneath that shiny, Instagram-ready exterior, she was chaotically sexy, smart but reckless, and viewed the world like a cynical poet. Meanwhile, scratching beneath his surface would be a disappointment.

Whatever mysterious persona she'd conjured in her mind was better than the reality of how little was there. Bobbi was right. Having everything handed to you on a silver platter made it hard to know what to value. Which made it all worthless. Except his art. Money couldn't make it easier to put his vision on paper. The starving artist was a cliché for a reason. The only time his life had meaning was when there was a risk of failing.

"You're so quiet," she said. "I didn't mean to ruin your mood. Ignore me."

"That is impossible." He pictured her legs, smooth and bare beneath that cocktail dress. "Believe me, I've tried."

She didn't respond, but she didn't hang up. She also didn't say what she should have said, that he was out of line, and whatever this was, wasn't happening. Her silence sparked the air like a dangling live wire.

"Nate! I thought you were getting beer!"

He whirled around as Dillon clattered down the stairs. Nathan made a *shut the fuck up* motion across his throat.

"You should go," Rachel said.

He gripped the phone tighter. "Hey, no—"

"Go spend time with your friends. I think my housekeeper just drove up."

He heard a sound on her side, the soft slam of a door closing. Rachel said goodbye and rushed off the phone.

"Sorry I ran off your supersecret mystery woman." Dillon lifted both hands in a helpless shrug. "But you *did* say you were getting beer."

---

Matt sent Rachel a message the morning of the Vasquez anniversary party, asking to meet downstairs at eight. They hadn't spoken since he'd left town after the ambush interview for a series of solo appearances. It was clear avoidance, but Rachel liked the idea that he was afraid of her. She had learned about the focus group while he still needed her around and Matt didn't know how she would react or what she was capable of. She wasn't sure if she knew herself.

She was certain of one thing. Nathan wasn't some fun distraction. Checking her phone for his messages had become a compulsion. Now there were meandering late-night calls when they should both be asleep. In every conversation, they said the same thing beneath their words.

"You alone again?" *I want to see you.*

"Lenora's here." *It's a bad idea.*

"Does that woman have a hobby?" *I don't care.*

"Upholding the patriarchy. And ironing sheets." *I have to care. And I don't trust myself with you.*

Rachel knew that if she were in the same room as Nathan again, she would kiss him. He wouldn't even have to do that half smile or say something sweet, insightful, or infuriatingly wise for a guy his age. She'd just kiss him. She replayed the fantasy of his lips on hers so many times it was almost a memory. No, this wasn't a fun distraction. There was nothing fun about being swept into an undertow when you weren't even swimming.

Rachel stared at the navy-blue cocktail dress hanging on her closet door. It had been there since the ghostly pale woman Matilda Abbott paid to dress every member of her family had stopped by with the pre-approved attire. Rachel had never actually agreed to let her mother-in-law pick out her clothes. It was more like a slow erosion of agency that she stopped resisting when the Abbotts made it clear they didn't trust her judgment.

She used to love fashion. It tapped into that same part of her that could spend hours rearranging canvases on a gallery wall. She used to love taking risks with outfits and watching the reaction when she walked into a room. But it only took one *Hot or Thot?* caption in a local gossip column for her mother-in-law to suggest developing a quieter brand.

"People are cruel," Matilda Abbott had said in her typical terse, bored tone. There was no judgment. Only disappointment that Rachel hadn't figured it out sooner. Matt could marry a Black woman. He could have a Black daughter. He could even marry a Black woman with a Black daughter she conceived as a teenager. He could *not* have a Black wife who dressed in a way that reminded everyone that she might actually enjoy sex and wasn't ashamed of having a child out of wedlock before she was old enough to vote.

"Who is blowing up your phone?" Keely White approached her with a bottle of leave-in conditioner and a blow-dryer. She was the only member of the Abbott-approved glamour team that Rachel had hired herself. Clothes were one thing, but she drew the line at a European waif smearing ashy makeup over her face. "Is it Faith? Tell her I got that tea tree shampoo she likes."

Rachel hid her phone against her thigh. "I'll let her know. So, what are we doing with my hair this time?"

Keely plugged in the blow-dryer. "Same as always? Silk press, bump the ends." She paused. "Maybe we could add some barrel curls since it's a party." Her eyes brightened and she held up a finger. "Oh, I got something for you. Hold on." She moved away and started digging through her bags again.

Watching her, Rachel realized that Keely was the only person in her life who wasn't connected to Matt in some way. Rachel had stopped reaching out to her college friends when her father died, because watching them succeed at what she'd abandoned was too painful. She'd barely gotten to know her coworkers at the café before Matt swept her off her feet and into his exclusive social circle, people who acted as her judge and jury.

Rachel picked up her phone and put her panicked thoughts into a text.

**Rachel:** I don't have real friends anymore.

Nathan responded almost instantly.

**Nathan:** That's not true. You have me.

His words were reckless, chipping away at all the reasons she should keep her distance. But he couldn't know how vulnerable she was right now—exposed and raw in places that hadn't seen daylight in years. "Be careful with me," she whispered.

"Did you say something?" Keely appeared behind her holding a hair clip. It was a flower made of pavé diamonds and black crystals that glittered when she tilted her hand. "I know it's a little flashy, but there's not much going on with that dress over there."

"A black dahlia." Rachel took it from Keely's hand. "You know what they mean, don't you?"

"Murdered white lady in the forties, right?"

"Betrayal." Rachel set the hair clip on her vanity next to her phone. "They're supposed to be a warning."

When Rachel walked downstairs, Matt's face turned the crimson color of her lipstick. The black dahlia was pinned above her ear, and the Abbott-approved dress was still upstairs on the hanger. Instead, she wore a black leather dress that fit her like a pair of driving gloves. The right side flashed a mile of leg whenever she took a step, and the low neckline plunged a few inches above her navel. "Welcome home."

Matt didn't respond. He stormed out and, five minutes later, pulled up to the front of the house in a new Maserati. That car had the same infuriating effect on her that the cocktail dress had on him. A seamless exchange of passive-aggressive *fuck you*s.

He didn't speak until they were on the road. "I don't know what you're trying to prove."

Rachel stared out the window as their neighborhood floated by. "That my tits still look amazing without a bra?"

"Jesus." He glanced at her chest. "Is this how you're going to be now?"

"You're the one who wanted me to stick around. I'm just maximizing what is apparently my lone asset." She gestured from her face to her body.

Matt tightened his grip on the wheel. "Hailey shouldn't have told you about the focus group."

"How could *you* not tell me?" She shook her head. "Oh, right. You're a fucking liar. Of course you wouldn't."

"Okay, that's a bit—" His jaw clenched. "You're being overdramatic."

"Well, this *is* a hostage situation. I'm probably not being dramatic enough."

"No one's forcing you to take my money."

"You just want me to pretend I don't need it."

She crossed her legs, and the dress parted over her thighs. Matt's gaze followed her movements before he jerked his eyes back to the road. "Are you trying to sabotage me? There are important people at this party." He was getting louder, while she had a death grip on her tone that kept it at an even level. "This should be easy," he snapped. "What I'm asking you to do is *exactly* what you were already doing before. Show up, smile, and drink some goddamn champagne." He slammed his hand against the steering wheel. "Why do you have to make everything so hard?"

Matt made a sharp turn, the tires screeching on the asphalt in the Vasquez driveway. The valets stopped talking to stare as he braked to a sudden stop.

"Don't kid yourself. *This?*" Rachel gestured between them. "Was never easy." She glanced at the gawking guests, already raising their phones to take pictures. "Now pull yourself together. Your fans are watching."

# CHAPTER EIGHT

Nathan bypassed the valets and parked his car between the west entrance and the lemon groves. No one entered that way unless they were working in the kitchen. Tonight, the lot was filled with small cars and catering vans. A group of guys standing in a cloud of cigarette smoke passed a bottle of Smirnoff back and forth while they spoke loudly about going to Adams Morgan after their shift. Nathan imagined joining them, blowing off the party, and throwing back shots at some college bar until his brain was numb. But he'd promised his family to make an effort.

He reached the foyer and instantly recognized a few people from his father's company, gray-haired executives wearing dark suits and big gold watches. None of them recognized him. He wasn't eight years old anymore, stealing pens and paper from their offices. They were clumped together, shout-talking over glasses of brown liquor. One of them called Matt Abbott a "pandering prick" and laughed so hard it made him cough.

The other guests were from his mother's world—people who planned, attended, and critiqued parties like this for a living. Their outfits were brighter and more complicated, with leather straps in strange places and suits in fabrics that had no business being made into clothes. One guy was suddenly camouflaged against the damask cushions when he perched on a love seat.

Servers in white dress shirts weaved through the bodies with trays of drinks, and Nathan swiped a glass of wine. A white guy with a handlebar mustache pointed to his glass and asked, "Hey, fella. Can I get another one of those?" Nathan handed the guy his unwanted drink and walked away, searching for a dark corner to brood in.

Joe found him lurking in the shadows a few minutes later. "Look who finally showed up, only…" He glanced at his watch. "Forty-five minutes late."

Nathan pointed to his own shirt. "And with buttons."

Joe's lips twitched as he cocked an eyebrow. "Congrats on the bare minimum."

"Apparently that's all I'm capable of."

"Dad didn't mean it like that," Joe countered. Nathan knew his brother was trying to stay neutral, but just once, he wanted Joe to pick a side and stay there. Or at least call their father out on his objectively fucked-up bullshit. Beto was imprinted on his brother in ways that ran so deep it was scary.

"That's exactly how he meant it," Nathan said.

Joe propped both hands on his hips, revealing a creased shirt and wrinkled pants. He'd probably come straight from the office. "All right, so what? He's a seventy-year-old asshole that doesn't care about anything but a stock option. Toss a coin in this room and you'll hit five more just like him."

"That makes it okay?"

"No, but your attitude is pointless. Who gives a fuck what he thinks? Let it go."

Nathan bit back a laugh because Joe never let go of anything. He balled things up and choked them down with a chaser of sleep deprivation and antacids. Then he dragged himself to events like this to avoid dealing with their parents' disappointment.

Sometimes, when Joe would visit Nathan's apartment, his brother would slouch on the couch with his tie loose and his shirtsleeves rolled high. They'd drink beer, make guacamole, and watch some romantic Korean drama that Joe refused to admit was his favorite. He'd tell jokes, and laugh, and sound like the teenage boy who used to squeeze Nathan's fingers to distract him when he was frightened. That was the real Joe, a goofy romantic who didn't think twice about holding his little brother's hand, not this brittle Brooks Brothers drone constantly beating his life into submission. Talking to this guy made him miss his brother.

Nathan surveyed the crowd of party guests. The men checked their watches while the women greeted each other with slack-armed hugs to preserve their hair and makeup. It was like watching an *SNL* sketch about what rich people do in their spare time. "How do you deal with this every day?"

"It's just a party."

"You know what I mean."

Joe sighed and claimed a bare spot of wall to lean against. "I haven't left the office before eight in months. Most nights I skip dinner. In the morning, I hit the gym before five. I never see Mom. Don't see Dad outside the office. Makes things easier."

Nathan laughed. "And I'm the one getting shit about ghosting this family?"

"It's not the same thing and you know it. You left *us*, Nate."

Nathan could hear the rest of his brother's accusation. Joe had learned that Nathan moved out the same way everyone else did—in a group text of his new address. They'd argued about the way it went down a few times, but Joe had never said out loud what his eyes were saying now. *Why didn't you talk to me? You didn't even try.*

"I left *him*," Nathan said, and nearly added *not you*, but stopped himself because they weren't having that conversation.

"He built this life for us," Joe lectured. "Like Tomás did for him. Call it pride, machismo, whatever, but what you did broke his heart." He sighed. "Look, I know he talks shit about your art—"

"Finger paints. Get it right."

"Come on, Nate." Joe looked up at the ceiling, probably praying for patience. "I know what it means to you. I know you better than anyone, don't I?" He paused, waiting until Nathan nodded in agreement. "I'd never let them take it from you. But you can do more. We've got a dozen subsidiaries with creative teams at Vasquez. Take your pick."

Nathan's head was starting to hurt. He rubbed his neck and fumbled for a polite way to say that becoming his brother's clone was one of his worst nightmares. "I can't kern fonts on coffee bean labels every day."

"You can't—hold on, what the fuck is kerning?"

"Adjusting the space between letter—"

Joe lifted his hand. "Stop. Forget I asked." He sighed. "Dad is dying. If you want to do something about your relationship with him, you need to do it now, before it's too late."

Nathan's patience snapped. "Our *relationship*? You mean the one where he sent me away because he drove *you* to a fucking breakdown? That relationship?"

Joe tensed. He looked like he wanted to grab Nathan and shake until something rattled. "Don't make this about me. I'm not the one about to bury his father holding grudges like a spoiled kid."

Nathan's vision tunneled, blotted by rage. "I buried that fucker eight years ago. I'm not digging him back up again."

Joe looked stunned and then defeated, like Nathan had destroyed the last of his hope. The sight was sobering. Nathan didn't want to hurt his brother. He wanted to save him.

"Joe, please," Nathan pleaded. "Stop burning through your life trying to make him happy. Or he won't be the only one digging his own grave."

———————

Rachel made the entrance she wanted. The outfit turned a sea of heads in her direction and prompted a rush of whispers as she made her way through the room. One of the board members from the public library stopped to compliment her new look. A close friend of Sofia's looked Rachel in the eye for the first time and said, "That damn dress is killer." Dennis Marks, a partner at Matt's law firm, who always flirted with her when Matt wasn't around, practically leered at her over his drink.

Rachel reached for a glass of wine, but the server moved away too quickly. Someone touched her arm, and another glass appeared in front of her. "This look is definitely a statement, though I'm not sure it's the one you were going for."

Alesha's presence deflated Rachel's confidence. She accepted the glass and sipped instead of responding.

"I'm sure your husband had something to say about it." Alesha was dressed in her signature white, with a wall of pearls wrapped around her neck. A reporter had once asked if she chose the color to symbolize solidarity with women like Hillary Clinton or Kamala Harris. Alesha said no. "My husband left me to either go find God or fuck his way through South America. Neither would be surprising. White represents rebirth, and I did that. I started over."

Alesha scanned the room. "Where is that son of a bitch? Did you ask him about it?"

Rachel gulped more wine. "Ask about what?"

"Don't play dumb."

"It's nice that you think I'm pretending."

Alesha took Rachel's glass and thrust it at a server. "Oh, you're smart. A little too smart for your own good. It makes you reckless."

Rachel thought of the dick pic saved in her photos. The one she could easily forward to a tabloid with a time and date stamp. These last few weeks, she'd been the pinnacle of restraint. "It's just a dress."

Alesha grabbed her arm and squeezed. "I'm not talking about your damn dress. I'm talking about you keeping your head in the clouds, while your husband is plotting against you. I told you years ago not to trust that man, but you wanted what you wanted. Now you're walking in here dressed in dead animals with murder flowers in your hair, telling me everything is fine." The grip on Rachel's arm slackened. "I can help you."

Alesha's eyes were wide and pleading. But the lesson Rachel had learned about accepting her aunt's "help" couldn't be undone with a few supportive words and lukewarm wine. While Rachel had grown up knowing nothing about Alesha Williams, the woman knew everything about her. She knew that Rachel's mother had abandoned her. She knew that Peter was taking care of Faith while he was sick and Rachel was in college. She knew that after he died, Rachel didn't have a job and couldn't afford childcare. Alesha offered to help only out of obligation. Or maybe guilt.

Now Rachel could finally say the words that she couldn't back then. "I don't need your help." She shook off Alesha's hand. "I'm not that desperate anymore."

"No," Alesha said, exhaling a frayed sigh, like she'd been holding it in for years. "I don't think you're desperate. Just lost."

"There you are!" Sofia's voice startled them out of the moment. Rachel turned away, relieved to have something else to focus on. She forced a smile as Sofia grabbed her hands. "You look stunning." She swept appreciative eyes over Rachel's dress. "Can we wear leather now? Who's the designer? There must be a story."

"It's actually vegan." Rachel angled herself to show off the intricate stitching at her sides. Alesha was still hovering, so Rachel injected a sugary lightness in her voice that she knew would grate on her aunt's nerves. "But I told Giovanni to make it impossible to tell."

Sofia threw back her head and laughed, causing a dozen eyes to turn their way. She wore a green cocktail dress with a matching bolero shrug. A diamond choker sparkled at her throat.

"Alesha, did your niece tell you she's hosting the gala this year?" Alesha didn't respond and Sofia kept talking, uninterested in her answer. "People still get so excited about the Abbott name. Ticket sales have almost doubled since we made the announcement."

"Rachel is also a Thomas," Alesha corrected. "Our family was here before the Abbotts, remember? The first Black family to settle in the region? Her great-grandfather's bank financed the first Vasquez Coffee plant. Did you put that on your little flyer?"

Sofia's gaze sharpened. "You know we don't print *flyers*."

Alesha had left out the fact that while Vasquez Coffee had flourished, the savings and loan had the same fate as other Black-owned small businesses in the 1960s. They closed when their customers moved on to bigger and whiter financial institutions. Alesha enjoyed reminding anyone who would listen that the Vasquez family had abandoned their lone Black investors as soon as the Abbotts had opened their wallets. The bank closure had bankrupted the Thomas family, and according to Sofia, Alesha had been "trying to claw her way back to relevance ever since."

Theirs was an old beef that predated Rachel, and despite her last name, she didn't want to be put in the middle of it. "Excuse me. I'm going to get another drink."

"Stay." Alesha grabbed her arm. Rachel tried to pull away, but her aunt's grip was fueled by intergenerational spite. "Did you know Rachel curated exhibits for the Museum of Modern Art?"

Sofia turned surprised eyes to Rachel. "Is that true?"

No, not completely. Rachel's time at MoMA was a summer internship drafting exhibition outlines for shows she wasn't around to see. It was also sixteen years ago. She hadn't worked for another gallery since. But Sofia's tone was starting to grate. Her brows were too high, signaling disbelief.

"It is true," Rachel said, and name-dropped six of her mentors who were only famous in New York art circles. Sofia's eyes got bigger and her mouth rounder with each one. Rachel prayed Sofia didn't have them on speed dial. By "mentors" she meant listening to them speak on panels in crowded lecture halls.

"You attended Howard, right? So did Lyric." Sofia spun around and waved at a tall, tawny-skinned Black woman with waist-length locs. Rachel's former classmate looked the same as she did sixteen years ago. Ethereally beautiful and effortless—like she had gotten dressed by wandering through three different closets, pulled out the worst pieces, and reconfigured them into mixed-media art. This was Rachel's punishment for being a liar. Not only the humiliation of being outed as one, but being outed by an accomplished, gorgeous woman who had also been cryogenically frozen in time.

Sofia touched Lyric's arm. "I want you to meet our local First Lady, Rachel Abbott. Rachel and her husband are hosting the art gala."

Lyric offered her hand with a blank smile. "It's nice to meet you."

Rachel's spirits soared at the possibility she'd been forgotten, but crashed again when Sofia said, "She also attended your alma mater and studied...art history, wasn't it?"

Rachel braced herself for Lyric inevitably asking which year she graduated, and Rachel would be forced to admit she hadn't. Her father died during her senior year, and she'd left school three credits short of her degree. Then the conversation would spiral with Lyric realizing she was *that* Rachel, the one who left in a cloud of scandal surrounding her final project, and Sofia's nose would be sky-high again, while Alesha added public embarrassment to her long list of Rachel's failings.

"Oh?" Lyric's expression didn't change. "DC is such a small world sometimes," she said. "But you must be excited about hosting this year. Sofia has a wonderful theme planned. *Spectacle.* It should make for some interesting interpretations."

Rachel exhaled the breath she'd been holding. "Agreed. I bet the featured artist is excited to work with you."

Sofia and Lyric exchanged glances. "Actually," Lyric said, "I received a job offer in London, so I won't be here to work on that collection."

"We're devastated," Sofia said, with a hand pressed to her chest. "Thankfully, she's offered to help us find a replacement." She looked at Lyric. "I just found out Rachel curated for MoMA. She might know someone who could help at the last minute."

Maybe it was the dress. Or the murder flower whispering in her ear. They drowned out the rational parts of her brain that reminded her that it had been more than a decade since she'd held an actual job. Inflating her résumé at a party was one thing. But working with a respected artist would immediately expose her as a fraud. Even Alesha looked wary. Sofia was still eyeing her like a show dog performing tricks. Lyric looked idly amused, like she'd turned on a reality TV show. Rachel couldn't tell whether she was rooting for her success or failure.

"I can do it," Rachel said. "I'm hosting anyway, so I'm happy to work with the artist. It's for a good cause."

Sofia looked at Lyric, who continued to be only mildly interested in the conversation. "That's incredibly generous, but I'm sure your husband wouldn't be happy about me monopolizing your time in the middle of his campaign."

"Matt isn't here," Alesha said tersely. "And I think it's an excellent idea. Another Black woman curating, and this one with actual ties to the community." She glanced at Lyric. "An upgrade, if you ask me."

Lyric's smile finally faded, and Sofia's eye twitched. Rachel pressed her lips together to suppress a laugh.

"It'll be a tight deadline," Sofia said, focusing on Rachel. "The pieces are still in the planning stages, and the artist is Circe Gavin. Have you heard of her? She's incredibly in demand and can be a bit...eccentric. But with your experience, I'm sure you can handle it."

"Of course I've heard of Circe," Rachel said, with a smug chuckle that made her hate herself a little. She made a mental note to google the name later. "The timeline won't be a problem. I'll make it my top priority."

Sofia squeezed Rachel's hands again, tighter this time. A warning. "I'm sure you will. Now if you'll excuse me. I think my husband has a speech planned."

Lyric drifted away once Sofia left. Alesha tried to grab Rachel's arm again but pulled back when she flinched. Her aunt looked worried. As if she had the right.

"Watch yourself," Alesha said. "Sofia Cárdenas is a venomous snake. Be careful she doesn't bite you."

———

Nathan's mother once told him that she could always tell when it was time to leave a party by how much the temperature had risen in the room. The longer people talked and the more they drank, the more stifling it would get. Make an exit as soon as you started to feel uncomfortable, because, according to Sofia, "that's when it doesn't feel like a party anymore." Using her logic, Nathan should have left five minutes after he'd arrived. Then the fight with Joe never would have happened.

He was typing out an apology as he walked through the foyer and nearly ran into someone's back. His father turned around and looked surprised to see him. Beto wore his usual black tux with a green tie that matched Sofia's dress. He glanced down at Nathan's clothes, checking for anything offensive. "We're about to do the toast. You boys should stand with us."

The crowd had migrated to where his mother stood on the stairs. She stared down at their upturned faces, like royalty greeting her adoring subjects.

"I can't stay," Nathan said. "But tell her I said happy anniversary."

Beto fell silent, and Nathan knew what would come next. An insult. Cold ambivalence. Whatever it was, he'd take it. He was too raw from arguing with Joe to do anything else.

"Nathaniel," Beto said. He stepped closer and lowered his voice. "What I said at dinner. I shouldn't have—" He grimaced and frowned, frustrated. "I want more for you. I always thought it would happen sooner, I guess. Before I . . ." Beto looked away, toward Sofia. "She looks good, doesn't she? Stuff like this makes her shine." His eyes softened. "Like the sun."

Nathan studied his father's face. He tried to see past Beto's wistful smile to the motive behind his confession. Was it guilt? Regret? Nathan would take anything that wasn't disappointment.

Beto clapped a hand on Nathan's shoulder and gently squeezed. Then he left to join his wife. Nathan spun blindly in the opposite direction, into a nearby hallway. He caught a glimpse of a woman slipping into his mother's office, then stopped short and locked eyes with Matt Abbott.

Matt seemed scrawnier in person than in his photos, with ruddy skin and wire-rim glasses that made him look like someone who spent most of his time bathed in the blue light of a computer monitor. This was the guy who had Rachel falling apart at the drive-in and beating up washers at the laundromat? *This* guy, with a cowlick in his hair?

"Hey there uh..." Matt's eyes drifted to Nathan's chest, briefly searching, and then flicked back up again. "Young man. Will you leave an empty tray out here for dirty glasses?" Matt pointed to a spot on the floor next to Sofia's library. "My friend and I would rather not be disturbed."

Nathan was tempted to ask how he'd done it. How did this pompous hobbit persuade a woman like Rachel to be his wife? But Matt's eyes were bloodshot and boozy, like he'd already started whatever private party he intended to have behind closed doors. Nathan nodded and said, "No problem," so he could leave. Matt raised his glasses and strolled toward the office with the awkward swagger of an incel who was finally about to get laid.

Nathan stepped aside when an actual catering employee approached him from behind. The hallway was the quickest route from the party to the kitchen, and he may not have been the only person who'd seen Matt sneaking off with a "friend." A few more servers slipped past him, but they seemed more interested in balancing crowded trays than spying on party guests. Only one person stood motionless, staring at the door that Matt had closed behind him.

Rachel. With her curly hair and leather dress, he almost didn't recognize her. This wasn't the woman with the blank eyes of a mannequin in Matt's viral video. This was the Rachel who drove his Camaro like a race car driver and slid into his texts, seducing him with proper comma usage and tiny secrets dropped like bread crumbs.

Everything made sense now. The drive-in cocktails, her chaotic emotions, and the bitter rants about marriage. She already knew her husband was cheating. That's why she stood motionless instead of chasing after him and demanding answers. She was intensely focused on the door, like if she glared hard enough, she could see the face of the woman who'd slipped in before she'd arrived. Nathan might as well have been invisible.

She spun around and stalked toward the kitchen. Nathan followed her. Rachel's rapid pace and his obvious pursuit startled the servers into wide-eyed stares as he followed her out the side door. It was nearly pitch black. Unlike the front of the house, there were no streetlamps or decorative lanterns to light their way.

He was about to call her name when she stopped and crouched to pick up something from the ground. She straightened, standing in front of a gray Maserati. He saw the rock when it was too late, after she'd already wound up like a baseball player. The window shattered, spraying glass at her feet and setting off the piercing wail of the car alarm.

Nathan spun her around. He gave her a moment to realize who he was, grabbed her hand, and ran. He heard shouting and dodged a flood of light from a door opening. Valets spilled into the parking lot, frantically searching between the cars.

They rounded a corner, and Nathan pulled her into a grove of fruit trees. They weaved through oranges and lemons until they reached the garden shed near the back. He pulled her inside. Moonlight briefly illuminated her face before the door shut and they were both covered in darkness.

There were no footsteps or sirens. Nathan heard yelling, but it sounded far away. Rachel's eyes caught the light, and they were all pupil, black and glittering. He touched her cheek. "Are you okay?"

She pressed against him and exhaled a soft "Nathan" on his lips. He'd never liked his name. Nathan, Nathaniel, the shortened Nate everyone insisted on using. But he'd never heard it that way: whispered like a prayer. Lust flooded his body like the tide dragging him beneath the ocean. Maybe they were both drowning. But instead of doing the right thing, and pulling back, he dove deeper, drinking her in until there was no saving either one of them.

Their kiss was rough and greedy, as if at any moment she'd be snatched away. Everything else receded until there was nothing but the wet glide of her tongue, the press of her fingers against his neck, and her warm breath against his lips. Rachel made the sweetest sounds, little gasping moans, that made him hard enough for her to feel it. Blood rushed through him, plummeting so hard and fast that he felt high, or drunk, or both. She broke the kiss to catch her breath, and the loss of her mouth made him dizzy.

The voices outside were louder and the faint wail of a siren too close for comfort. "Come with me," he whispered, and kissed her palm. "Let me take care of you."

# CHAPTER NINE

Rachel had a habit of picking at loose threads. It was something she'd done since childhood. She would pick holes in furniture, pry apart dress seams, ruin the stitches on crocheted hats—all because she couldn't stand the sight of a dangling string. She could never shake the hope that she could fix something broken without it unraveling.

But she had gotten arrogant. The dress, the taunts, lying her way into a position she wasn't qualified for—pick, pick, pick. But Matt had won anyway. He was always two steps ahead in the twisted game they were playing. And she was the one who unraveled. When Nathan found her standing next to Matt's car, she might as well have been those glass shards scattered beneath their feet.

Rachel didn't get a good look at Nathan until they were in the car. He was dressed in a white shirt, unbuttoned enough for her to see the tattoo on his throat. His clothes looked expensive and tailored. Dry-clean only. When she was his age, she washed everything with cold water and prayed the colors didn't bleed.

He was quieter than usual. Both hands were glued to the steering wheel. Had he decided she was more trouble than she was worth? Or maybe it was the kiss.

No. That wasn't a kiss. Kisses were questions. Kisses started tentatively and gradually intensified, with plenty of time to draw conclusions in between. What happened in that shed was a demand. When Nathan pulled away, she thought it was because of the sirens. But now, in the safety of the car, he still wouldn't meet her eyes.

"What were you doing at that party?" she asked. Sofia's big events were very exclusive. Distant maybe-cousins weren't usually on the guest list.

He kept his eyes forward as he pulled into the parking lot. "Someone invited me."

His studio apartment was bigger than she'd imagined. A large kitchen with stainless steel appliances took up one corner. The living area was filled with dark wood tables and brown leather furniture. A king-sized platform bed took up the rest of the room, covered in white linens he'd tucked into hospital corners. She remembered how in the garden shed he'd pitched forward, both hands gripping her waist as if he was seconds from lowering her to the ground. Nathan caught her staring at the bed, and their eyes connected for a blistering moment before he looked away.

The whole place was neat—bookshelves arranged by color and size, open kitchen shelves with identical plates. The only clutter was a pile of sketchbooks scattered over the kitchen counter. A large wooden drafting table sat empty against the wall.

"You're an artist." It came out like an accusation and she tried to soften her tone. "Why didn't you tell me?"

Nathan tossed his keys into a small bowl near the door. "Because I'm not an artist."

He moved to the counter and gathered the sketchbooks into a neater stack. Watching his slow, methodical movements made her want to throw something to reclaim his attention. "That is a five-thousand-dollar drafting table."

He shoved the sketchbooks out of sight. "How do you know how much it costs? Are *you* an artist?"

"Why do you do that?"

"Do what?"

She raised an eyebrow. "*That.* Answer a question with a question."

"Is that what I'm doing?"

"*Yes*. Or are you only this way with me?"

He stared at the table. "It was a birthday gift from my brother. I've never used it."

"But you kept it."

"It was a gift."

The table obviously had history, which was none of her business. Despite shoving her tongue down his throat thirty minutes ago, she needed to remember that she barely knew this man. Nathan had an entire life she knew nothing about. He was entitled to keep some things private.

"I studied art history in college," she said. "Black American portraiture. One of my professors owned the same table."

"So you're a photographer."

"Yes. No. I used to be. Now, it's barely a hobby." She bit her lip and scanned the room, searching for a different topic. "Did you decorate this place yourself?"

He frowned. "It's not decorated."

Rachel pointed to a throw pillow on his couch. "That's not functional."

"Are pillows ever?"

She smiled. He was starting to sound like himself again. "Ask me in ten years when you need five different sizes to avoid getting a crick in your neck." She leaned against the sofa. "Do you want to ask about the car?"

Nathan tensed. "Not really."

She understood his reluctance. She'd been a chaos demon since the day they met. Drunken confessions. Needy late-night phone calls. Now she'd committed vandalism right in front of him. "It was Matt's."

"I assumed."

"You saw him at the party?"

He unfolded his arms. "With the woman? Yeah, I did."

"A warning would have been nice, a note—he loves notes—letting me know his girlfriend would be there." Her eyes were drawn to a loose thread on one of his pillows. She clasped her hands and looked away.

"Do you still love him?"

His voice was gruff and rushed in a way that implied there was a right answer. Maybe that's what was on his mind. "No," she said, handing over another secret buried so deep, she'd only just realized it was true. "And he's not why I kissed you."

"No one would blame you for wanting revenge."

"You're not revenge." She paused. "The car, *that* was revenge. And not because I still love him. I'm jealous of him. I always have been."

Nathan's shoulders slacked as the tension faded from his body. His shirt was still wrinkled from where her hands had gripped his shoulders in the shed. He pushed off the counter and moved closer, preserving enough distance to stay out of reach.

"I'm jealous of his friends, his career. The way he walks into a room and assumes everyone will like him. How it never occurs to him they won't."

She ran a hand through her hair, dislodging the dahlia. Nathan watched her yank at the hair clip for a moment, and whispered, "Stop. Let me." He started untangling her hair, a few strands at a time, like he was doing to her insides—unfurling truths from places she didn't know existed. She closed her eyes when his fingers brushed the shell of her ear.

"I'm jealous of how easy it is for him to let other people do things for him. He delegates every second of his life. Every burden. How do you do that and not float away?"

Nathan stroked her back and she leaned into it. "I'm angry," she whispered. "I'm fucking furious at myself." Her eyes burned and she closed them until the pressure passed. "This wasn't supposed to be my life. And now I don't know who I am without it."

He set the hair clip on a table. "What life were you supposed to have?"

Rachel thought of Lyric. "There was a woman at the party tonight. A former classmate. We were a year apart." She wrapped her arms tight around her waist. "She didn't recognize me. She looked right at me and saw the First Lady of Oasis Springs and not Rachel Thomas, because I buried her. I gave her up and I grieved for her because it was the right thing to do. I became a wife. And a mother. And that should be enough." She met his eyes, desperately searching. "Why isn't that enough?"

---

Bobbi had once told Nathan he had a hero complex, but he didn't believe her. He'd never wanted to be someone's savior. And Rachel didn't need saving. She was strong and brave. Brave enough to be vulnerable with someone who was practically a stranger without expecting the same in return. She leaned into him after her confession, dazed but content, as if he'd done enough for her by existing. But it wasn't close to enough. He wanted to make things better. Solve her problems. Be her hero.

He also wanted to kiss her again. It was all he could think about. In the car. At the door. As he pried that pin from her hair, he'd wanted to press his face into all that softness. But that wasn't what she needed. If he was being honest with himself, he didn't know how to help her. He had no idea what it was like to stare down the end of a marriage. But he did know how it felt to lose something that was a part of you, and how lonely it was when no one knew or cared.

"Let me show you something." Nathan grabbed the tablet hidden underneath his sketches. His stomach coiled in protest as he pulled up his Instagram account. He hated this moment—that sliver of space between someone's eyes hitting his drawings and the reaction they thought he wanted. When he'd shown them to his ex Nina, she'd said all the right things, compliments that a good girlfriend would give early in a relationship. But he'd seen her true feelings the second she'd looked at the screen: confusion and amusement. *This is what he does in his spare time?*

That was the last time he'd shown it to anyone he was dating. But this was different. Rachel wasn't his girlfriend. *Friend* also seemed inadequate. Rachel was a *feeling*. She was the reason he woke up every morning and checked his phone with his heart in his throat. She was the flutter in his chest when he drove by The Stand. She was a spark that made him want to draw again. He wanted to fill the empty sketchbooks he'd been ignoring for months with renderings of her face.

Rachel saw the first drawing and whispered so softly that he could barely make out the words. "What did you say?" he asked.

She pointed to his username. "FireBird84. That's you?"

He nodded, and she started scrolling—stopping to study each picture. He tracked every beat of her reaction: faint gasps, wide eyes, and soft smiles. "It's just fan art," he said, filling the painful silence. "They're characters from the Phoenix Prophecies, a fantasy series I read in junior high."

"I know those books. Faith loved them."

His face warmed. "It was a long time ago. The main characters are based on Greek mythology, but they're ethnically ambiguous. So I started drawing my version as Black and brown people, and it kind of took off. I do other stuff now, but this is mostly what I post online."

She studied the screen. "These three posts have more than a hundred thousand likes." She scrolled through more posts. "How many times have you gone viral?"

He shrugged. "I'm not sure." When something took off, he would usually mute the notifications.

Rachel's eyes widened. "Tim Sale follows you!"

Nathan nodded, even though he had no idea who that was. "Lots of people read those books."

"It's not the books..." She scrolled down and pointed to a portrait he'd made of the main character, Inara, once she'd come into her full power as a Phoenix mage. He'd drawn her with ebony skin and glowing glyphs etched into her arms. "I don't even know how you did this one. What did you use to make the fire?"

Inara was framed with flames that he'd created by scanning red and yellow leaves and manipulating the digital image in Procreate. Once he'd fully explained the process, Rachel shook her head and laughed. "How can you say you're not an artist?"

"Because I'm not," he said. "I'm not trained. I never went to college or took a class. I've never even sold anything. I—" He rubbed the back of his neck. "I do it because I can't *not* do it, if that makes sense."

She looked down, still chewing her bottom lip. He desperately wanted to kiss her. Lust knifed through him, sharp and visceral, and he had to look away.

"Can I see those?" She was staring at the sketches on his counter.

"No."

"Why not?"

*Because they're of you.* He'd been drawing her for days now. "They're not finished."

"Well, you definitely sound like an artist."

The way she said *artist*, like she was daring him to disagree with her, was almost enough to make him believe it was true. "They're pretty rough. I just made you smile with my old stuff. Let me thump my chest for a little while before I show you anything newer."

She laughed and moved to the couch, the tablet on her lap. A languid smile settled on her lips. "Come sit with me."

Nathan quickly complied because resisting Rachel felt like rejecting ambrosia. She smelled sweet and expensive, like something you'd want to roll around in.

"Do you want to draw professionally?" she asked.

"I don't really think about it," he said, which wasn't a complete lie. Thinking about an art career was pointless because it would never happen. His ideas were too small, his inspiration unpredictable and fleeting. He didn't understand why some things worked and others didn't, or how to produce good art on demand. Beto used to say that luck wasn't enough to build a life with, and that's what his best work felt like: a lucky accident. Nathan wasn't some prodigy. He was a guy with enough money and free time to ruin a dozen canvases until he drew a straight line.

"The laundromat is fine. I mean, it's something to do." He wiped the sweat from his palms and tried to focus so he wouldn't ramble. "I've never been good with deadlines. Right now, I can paint whenever I feel like it. It's..." He looked down at his fingers, at the flecks of blue acrylic lining his nails. Rachel followed his gaze. He folded his arms. "It's fine."

"How often do you paint?"

The past week, he'd been in the basement every night until two a.m. Ideas kept coming, like a flood. "Sometimes daily. Sometimes I don't paint for months."

He rubbed his neck again. Rachel watched him, staring at his tattoo. She pointed to his wrist. "May I?"

He nodded, and she inched over, her body heat sparking his skin like static as she leaned in to unbutton the cuff. Her fingers grazed his arm, rolling his sleeve up to his elbow, slowly revealing his phoenix.

"Those books meant a lot to you, didn't they?" She touched the inside of his wrist, almost like she was taking his pulse. "Why is that?"

His heart was knocking against his rib cage, and he wondered if she could tell. Stringing words into sentences suddenly took all his brainpower. "Stories like that make you want to believe that what makes you different also makes you special. That it's your superpower." He twisted his forearm to show her the flaming tips of its wings on the other side. "In Phoenix, Inara was brown like me. She was always in trouble, like me. But ultimately it was because she'd been kidnapped and hidden from her real home and family. Her powers only manifested once she went back to where she belonged." He briefly met her eyes. "You know, kind of your basic adoption fantasy."

Rachel's fingers grew bolder, leisurely tracing one image and then the next on his arm. "Did you draw all of these?"

It should have felt strange to be examined like a sculpture, but instead it was gentle and sweet, and kind of hot. "How can you tell?"

She leaned in closer, her dress revealing more of her chest and thighs. "You use these soft dark lines that look like smoke." Her gaze moved up. She parted his collar to reveal the words that extended to his neck from his shoulder. "What's this one?"

"A song," he said, pinning his hands under his legs. It was the only way he wouldn't reach for her. "'Y Llegaste Tú.' Abuelita, my grand-mother, she used to play it all the time." He unbuttoned more of his shirt and pulled it back so she could see all the lyrics. "It says, 'And you arrived. Entering my soul. As a sweet note, from a tender song.' She said it reminded her of her wedding."

Since Rachel started her exploration of his body, he'd hoped her curiosity would override her better judgment, that she might stroke him with the gentle reverence of a lover. He wasn't prepared for how she traced the line of his neck like it was precious. Like *he* was sacred. No one had ever touched him that way. Her fingers were hesitant at first, a flutter of movement. Then she whispered, "Your beautiful secret," with astonishment that ground his willpower into dust. "This song. Your art. Nathan, why are you hiding?"

"I'm not." He ran his thumb along her cheek and nudged her chin higher until she met his eyes. "You're the only one who sees me."

———————

Rachel grabbed his shirt as he clasped her waist and they both pulled at each other, colliding. The taste of him, already familiar, made her head swim. She gave him her tongue, and he sucked and swirled until she was gasping. They broke apart so she could wrap her legs around him and the dress bunched at her hips. He slid his hands underneath and squeezed her thighs.

"We probably shouldn't," Nathan said, his voice thick and rough while he stared at her mouth. "I'm really trying not to be an asshole here."

She braced against his shoulders and rocked into his erection. He made a guttural sound low in his throat. "You're not an asshole, Nathan."

Nathan sank both hands into her hair and gently pulled her head back. He pressed his mouth to her neck, and mumbled, "You don't know me, Rachel," into her skin. She felt his breath, his teeth, the flick of his tongue against her pulse. "But I really want you to."

He cupped her breast. She arched into his hand while he teased her nipple, whispering, "Harder," against his ear. He slipped his fingers beneath her dress to give her what she wanted—blurring the line between pleasure and pain, making a thrilling mess of her senses.

He kissed her again, tracing the strip of lace at her hip. "Can I taste you?" His hand stilled as he waited for permission. She said, "Yes," and his expression shifted, darkening to something so greedy and determined, it might have been the sexiest thing she'd ever seen.

He lowered her to the couch and paused to stare at the crooked half circle drawn on her hip. "Is this the mystery tattoo?"

She propped herself on her elbows. "Oh. It was supposed to be a moon, like in *Starry Night*." Nathan tried and failed to hide his amusement. She rolled her eyes. "I know."

He circled it with his fingertips. "I could draw something for you." His hand slipped beneath her panties light and teasing, which she loved but also hated. Her legs trembled as he tugged them down her thighs. "You're not a moon girl."

"What am I?" she rasped. He held her gaze as he finally massaged her clit. She ignited.

"You're the fucking sun."

He pressed his lips against her like a kiss. One side, then the other. It had been so long since anyone had seen her like this—wet, exposed, and swollen. It made her want to hide from the hungry way he looked at her. She also wanted more.

She felt his tongue, slick and cool, and the intensity made her startle. Nathan leaned back. "Do you want me to stop?"

"No!" She extended a hand. "It's not you, it's—it's been a while. I don't know if... It might take a while," she said, and hated that it sounded like an apology.

"I plan on being down here awhile, so I think we're good." He grinned, but his gaze was steady and measured, closely tracking her reaction. "Do you trust me?"

She was sprawled over his couch, her panties crumpled on his floor. "Of course I do."

Nathan sat back on his heels. "I want to learn you." He guided her hand between her legs. "Show me, Rachel."

It felt like too much. Too intimate. But as he watched her, his thumb sweeping a reassuring trail over her knuckles, she realized that this was what he'd meant. *Do you trust me enough to be seen too?*

She closed her eyes and leaned her head back. He hovered close, the heat from his body warming her sweat-glazed skin. She pressed her fingers inside, deep, the way she liked. Nathan voiced his approval in taut, chanting whispers.

She pictured him watching with those beautiful eyes—amber, like whiskey, and threaded with gold. The image nearly pushed her over the edge. His breath caressed the back of her hand, tempting her to look. She'd just caught her rhythm when he licked her, in the perfect spot, with the perfect pressure, and then settled into a slow, efficient devastation. Rachel broke apart. She came, hard and trembling, slurring his name. A filthy unraveling.

He straightened, flushed and short of breath. "Are you okay?"

She nodded, afraid that if she spoke, it would be a stream of babbling *thank you*s. Or worse. She might burst into tears.

By the time they moved to the bed, she had started to recover. She slid naked between the sheets and watched him undress. Nathan could have been a Greek sculpture with his contoured chest and defined six-pack that tapered in a V into his pants. She was in good shape, but she was also older—softer in places that used to be firm. Nathan's body looked healthy and new in a way that made her feel every one of her thirty-seven years. She sat back on the bed and pulled the sheet up over her breasts.

"Hey." He sat beside her. "What's wrong?"

"Nothing." Her gaze roamed over his chest. His tattoos were a living painting on a bronze canvas. "You're a little too beautiful. It broke my brain for a minute."

His face reddened, and he ducked his head—smiling big enough to make his eyes wrinkle at the corners. "I'm not thinking clearly either." His eyes slid over her, lingering where the sheet covered her breasts. "I pictured this, you in my bed, but the real thing is just..." He shook his head. "I shouldn't say what I'm thinking."

She sat up, and the sheet slid lower. His eyes tracked its progression. "What are you thinking?"

"It's inappropriate."

A laugh burst from her throat, and that crooked grin slid across his face. "I think we're past that," she said.

"We are? Good." He unfastened his belt and dropped it on the floor.

He spent the rest of the night proving with his body—hands on her wrists, hips between her legs, his mouth hot and greedy against her skin—that this was what she was made for. That she was just blood and muscle, skin stretched over atoms colliding. They came, shuddering and gasping, bodies hot and slick as they collapsed into an exhausted heap.

She loved the heavy weight of him pressing her down into the mattress. Nathan pushed her hair back and smiled. "Like I said. My thoughts were inappropriate." She laughed. When he spoke again, his voice was quiet and serious. "How are you feeling? Was that—"

"I am fine," Rachel said, cupping his cheek. "And that was incredible."

"You're incredible." He kissed her and climbed out of bed. "I'll get you some water." He paused to look at her. "Promise you'll be right there when I get back."

She settled against the pillows, the pull of sleep already thickening her words. "I promise."

# CHAPTER TEN

Nathan had never been ghosted. It was something he'd never even thought about until he woke up alone, grasping at empty sheets. Rachel was gone. He checked his phone, assuming she'd sent a message. Nothing. Not even a missed call.

Once the realization hit, he spent the next forty-eight hours drafting whiny texts he would never send. What could he even say? *On a scale of maybe someday to blocking this number, what are my chances of ever seeing you again?*

On the third day of silence, he decided to let it go. When his alarm went off, he got up long enough to open the laundromat, before crawling back under his covers to lick his wounds. He dozed off again but was startled awake by someone knocking on his door. He didn't move. But then it turned into pounding.

"Open up!" Joe yelled. "I know you're in there. I saw your car."

Nathan squinted at his alarm clock. It was five thirty a.m., the usual time for their workouts. They started this ritual when Nathan moved out, and now, three times a week, Joe would bring breakfast, harass Nathan into getting dressed faster, and then drive him to the gym.

Nathan opened the door. "I heard you the first fifty times."

"Then you should have answered. And what is this?" Joe took in Nathan's undressed state with disgust. His brother wore black gym shorts with a sleeveless mesh top and had two bright green smoothies in his hands. "We're gonna be late."

"The gym's not going anywhere."

"I've got a meeting at seven and a lunch thing with—"

"You're important. Got it."

Nathan walked to his dresser to search for his workout clothes. Joe set the extra smoothie down in front of him. "Breakfast."

Nathan's irritation faded. Joe guarded the homemade mixture the way their mother hoarded her cabrito recipe. He pulled on a pair of workout shorts. "Hey look, that stuff I said at the party—"

Joe grunted and shooed the rest of the sentence away. "You ever use this thing?" he asked, pointing to the drafting table.

Nathan immediately thought about Rachel asking the same thing. She'd walked into the room and zeroed in on all his vulnerable spots. He never should have brought her here. He should have taken her home and reminded himself of his no-drama policy, which included women who made you forget to hide how desperate for affection you really were.

Teasing Joe was easy. It was also a good distraction. Nathan shrugged, picked up his cup, and gave Joe wide eyes over the rim. "It's a good clothing rack. No wrinkles."

"A good *clothing rack*?" Joe whipped around to stare at the table. "I spent weeks searching for this thing. It's the top brand, specifically designed for left-handed people and—" Joe dabbed at the air like he was holding an invisible paintbrush. "Art...stuff." He paused and said, "Do you have any idea how much this cost?"

Nathan took a drink of his smoothie and tried not to shudder at the taste of vinegary kale swimming in frozen bananas. "Five grand." He pointed to a loaf of sourdough. "Do you have any idea how much *that* cost?"

Joe's face slacked at the sight of the bread. George W. Bush was in office the last time he'd gone to a grocery store. "Whatever. I accept your non-apology. Make it up to me."

Nathan grinned and slammed back the rest of his smoothie. It was like guzzling a juiced fern. "How?"

"Mom asked me to go to this luncheon for Matt Abbott. You're coming too."

"I don't think—"

"Didn't ask you to think. Find another shirt with buttons and show up to the club Thursday at noon."

"The *club*? Joe, I can't—"

"You can. And don't pretend you hate the *club*. You and that Dilbert kid wore out Dad's membership at the pool every summer break."

"It's Dillon, not Dilbert."

"Is that supposed to sound different to me? Look, Dad's been pushing me to show up to stuff like this a lot lately. He's about to step down." Joe turned on the faucet and filled the empty cups with water. "They have to replace him."

His brother's voice was calm, but the compulsive cleaning gave him away. He was a wreck. Being Beto's heir was Joe's entire identity. At some point, his brother must have had dreams of his own, like being an astronaut or a firefighter or even an executive at someone else's company. But those dreams couldn't compete with all those expectations. It had to be lonely. Which was probably why he'd never let Nathan skip their workouts.

Nathan promised himself that from now on, Joe wouldn't have to browbeat him out of bed so they could spend time together.

"CEO," Nathan said. "It's what you've wanted."

Joe gripped the edge of the sink. "Not like this. How can I care about some promotion when Dad is dying?"

"Beto cares," Nathan said. "And you'll make him proud the way you always do."

Joe smiled weakly, and Nathan wished he knew how to lift his brother's spirits, even temporarily. He would never admit it, but growing up, he'd wished that Joe were his father. Joe kept up with his doctor's appointments, taught him how to shave, and forced him to see a financial advisor so he wouldn't blow through his money before he turned thirty. Having Joe as a father might have even made a difference in how Nathan turned out. Maybe he'd have made better choices if he'd been raised by a better person.

"So, is Zara flying in with Angel?" Nathan asked. Sometimes Joe's wife could get through to him when his anxiety got out of hand. But Joe shook his head and scrubbed the cups for a second time.

"She's directing that documentary on the LA public school system." Joe's voice was flat, like he was delivering an earnings report to the board. "It's not a good time to visit."

"Visit?"

Joe froze. "You know what I mean."

"Yeah, but—" Nathan couldn't bring himself to say the obvious. Beto was dying; this wasn't like scheduling a vacation. "Do they know what's going on?"

Joe started to speak, then shook his head with a grimace.

"Hey..." Nathan's voice trembled. He tried to push away the memory of his brother babbling to himself on the floor. "Are you uh...you doing okay?"

Joe squared his shoulders. He knew exactly what Nathan was asking. *Is it happening again?* "I'm fine," he said, with a firmness that meant it wasn't up for debate. He picked up the cups and put them on a drying rack. His voice was softer when he finally spoke again. "But it'd be nice if you had my back through all this. Like I've had yours."

Nathan paused so he wouldn't dissolve into an incoherent mass of guilt and gratitude. "You know I do. Always."

Joe held his gaze like there was something more he wanted to say. Instead, he looked at the calendar on his watch. "The luncheon starts at twelve thirty. Club sandwich or chef's salad?"

His brother was right—Nathan needed to make more of an effort. "I'll take the sandwich."

Joe smiled. "Great. Now tell me about this girl you've been seeing."

Nathan froze. "What girl?"

Joe pointed to his right. "Well, I assume those aren't yours."

Nathan turned around and spotted Rachel's underwear near his bed. He snatched them up and stuffed them into his pocket, shrugging. "I had company the other night."

Joe slapped his shoulder. "Good for you! Glad you could blow off some steam."

"It wasn't like that." Nathan winced at how defensive he sounded. Joe finding out about Rachel was the last thing he needed. His brother had firm ideas about right and wrong, which probably included not sleeping with a married woman.

"Oookaaay," Joe said. "So, what was it like?"

It was amazing. And it was awful. He wanted to relive that night on a loop while also wiping it from his memory. "It's complicated." The truth was dangerously close to spilling out. Joe knew what it was like to want someone who was off-limits. He'd dated Mia Williams, even though their mothers hated each other. But Mia had broken his brother's heart. Joe would probably warn him not to waste his time pining for someone he couldn't have.

Nathan yanked at his shoelaces. "I won't be bringing her around. She's got a lot going on."

Joe searched his face as though he could identify the source of Nathan's frustration if he stared hard enough. "Sounds like you care about this woman."

"Yeah," Nathan said too quickly. "I mean, I care about what happens to her," he added, even though she clearly didn't want him in her life. The faster he could work up the courage to delete Rachel's number the better.

Joe tried to probe, but Nathan stonewalled with a shrug. "Be careful, Nate," Joe said. "Complicated things usually stay complicated."

---

When Faith was little, a therapist told Rachel that her daughter was highly sensitive and "extremely connected to the world around her." Faith was more likely to notice things that others didn't: temperature shifts, textures, and sounds were all experienced with a greater intensity than the average person. If someone was nervous, Faith would be the first to notice. Or if they were hiding something, she could always spot that too. Now, at twenty-one years old, Faith's powers of perception had extended to spotting the stress behind Rachel's eyes through her small iPhone screen.

"Are you okay, Mom?"

Sitting up straighter on her bed, Rachel tried to remember to smile with her eyes instead of only her mouth. When Faith had moved to New York, she'd promptly negotiated their weekly phone calls down to biweekly check-ins, with text message status updates in between. So far, Faith was thriving. She had her own apartment, a graduation gift from the Abbotts, which she shared with a friend enrolled in the same applied food studies program.

Rachel held the phone up a bit higher, hoping to obscure whatever anxiety Faith could spot. "I'm fine," she said. "How's the thesis coming?"

Faith launched into a rambling story about reaching out to her favorite food historian in hopes of finding a new mentor, and how her research into Black American foodways had her exploring the idea of a PhD in agriculture after graduation. "Professor Fine is fine," she said. "And I'm not being mean, so don't start. It's a joke. He's nice, but I'd really like a Black woman to help guide me since I'm exploring motherhood and the generational inheritance of Black food traditions. And maybe homemade conditioner? I know that's random, but you'd be surprised at the overlap."

"I get it. Homemade conditioners are basically recipes, when you think about it."

"Exactly!" Faith beamed. "I knew you'd understand."

"Well, I pay attention," Rachel said. She almost added how proud she was of the work her daughter was doing, but thinking about it always made her too emotional. It was hard to put into words how good it felt to watch her little girl doggedly pursue her dreams.

"I think if you explain your reasoning to Professor Fine, he'll be—" They locked eyes, and burst into identical giggles. "It'll be okay," Rachel said finally. "You'll make the right choice. You always do."

Faith cradled her chin in one hand. "Thank you."

Rachel would give anything to hear someone say the same thing back to her. That person was usually Faith, putting a positive spin on difficult situations. On Rachel's wedding day, Faith had taken her hand and said, "We're happy, Mommy," with the gravitas of a Baptist preacher. *This is joy*, her eight-year-old daughter was saying. *It's okay to feel this.*

"Anyway," Faith, said, sitting up straighter. "Enough about me. What's happening back home?"

"Here? Nothing. Same old boring stuff. Dinner. Paint swatches. Nothing exciting."

"Paint swatches? Really?" Faith was teasing, but Rachel knew that the boring minutiae of her life was soothing and comforting for her daughter. Faith ate the same breakfast every day. She'd painted her child-hood bedroom once, when she was nine, and kept the same pearlescent lilac until she left for school. To her, paint swatches and boring dinners was code for *Mom and Matt are where I left them.* The truth would be devastating. Thinking about it had caused Rachel to panic when she'd woken up in Nathan's bed. She'd looked at his gorgeous face and thought, *What if I stayed? What if this were my life instead?* But then her thoughts immediately turned to Faith, and she'd left as quickly as she could gather her things.

Rachel forced her mind back to the present. The camera image tilted as Faith relocated to her bed. "You're all dressed up," Faith said. "Where are you guys going?"

"There's a donor lunch at the club today. Like I said, same old stuff."

"Oh, no wonder you look stressed. You hate those things."

Rachel forced another smile. "They're more fun when you're here."

"Yes, they are!" Matt appeared behind Rachel and waved at Faith. "Hey, sweetheart. How's school?"

Rachel tried not to visibly tense. They hadn't stood this close in almost a month, not since his birthday party.

"I already bored Mom with my thesis, so I won't make her suffer again. School is good. Nice tie."

He touched the green and navy plaid at his neck. "Can't remember where I got it, but someone has good taste." Faith gave him a new tie every Christmas. It was their in-joke, a wink to the fact that it was impossible to buy gifts for someone who had everything.

They weren't always so close. It took Rachel a year to introduce Matt to Faith. He was nervous and overcompensated with adorably awkward jokes that made Rachel fall for him even more. Two years later, the night before their wedding, she overheard him tell Faith how excited he was to be her father. "How lucky am I? Finding two loves of my life at once?"

The memory gathered sharply in Rachel's throat like broken glass. "We should probably go," she said, with more edge than she'd intended. It was too much, seeing their lying faces next to Faith's on her screen. "Honey, let me know if you need anything."

"And me," Matt said. "Did you get the last transfer? I hope that's enough for books this year."

"Yes, Matt. I'm learning to cook, not do brain surgery, so I think your overly generous deposit will be fine." Her smile made Rachel's chest hurt. She wanted to shove Matt away and warn Faith not to love him anymore. That they both had made a mistake that day. *That wasn't happiness, baby. We were just finally breathing.*

"Try to have fun," Faith said to Rachel. "Love you both. See you in a few weeks."

Rachel frowned. "A few weeks?"

"For Niles's sip and see. Did you forget?"

Of course she had. Mainly because she had planned to avoid it. But her cousin was the head chef at his future father-in-law's new restaurant, and this would be a good networking opportunity for Faith.

Rachel assured Faith that she'd be attending, disconnected, and immediately moved away from Matt. If he noticed the slight, he didn't comment on it. Instead, he glared at her dress.

"I know you do the signature color thing for parties, but you can't wear red to my fundraiser." He propped his hands against his hips, forcing his suit jacket to flap behind him like wings. "It sets a tone.

I'm running as a progressive Democrat. I can't have my wife parading around in Reagan red."

"That's not an actual color."

"Come on, Rachel, you can't phone it in. That is not what we agreed to."

"I agreed not to file for divorce."

"*And* maintain the status quo. Which includes not humiliating me in public. You look like you're headed to a singles bar." The laziness of his insult stole her breath. So this was who they were now. Petty. Bitter. He used to preen in public whenever she wore something revealing on a date. Now he glared at her low neckline like it was a thong peeking out of her jeans.

"Why does it bother you so much?" She pressed a hand to her chest, over her pounding heart. "I *like* my body. I look good in red." Since Matt's confession, wearing the body-conscious clothes at the back of her closet had become an affirmation instead of a constant source of anxiety. They hugged every curve the Abbott publicity machine had tried to hide. "Is there something wrong with people finding me attractive? Does that mess with your poll numbers in some way?"

"Everyone knows you're a beautiful woman." He sighed, and his voice softened as if he were explaining things to a child. "You don't need all this." His gaze dripped with pity. "I know you're hurting, but trust me, this isn't the attention you want."

She opened her mouth to speak but closed it quickly so she wouldn't tell him it was too late. That Nathan had already proved him wrong. A laugh bubbled inside her throat and escaped her pressed lips.

He glowered in silence until she finished. "So everything is a joke to you now? Is that why you're playing these games? I know you're the one who broke my car window, by the way."

Rachel shrugged. "You should be more careful about where you park it. You *are* up for reelection. Maybe it was a dissenting voice."

"This is my career, Rachel. Forget this mayoral bullshit. I'm a year and a half away from Washington. Don't ruin this for me." He inhaled and his voice softened. "Please."

She grabbed her purse and walked to the door. "Your tie is crooked."

He looked down at the awkward knot. "Damn Windsor. I can never get it right. How do you—"

"Fuck off," she snapped, stunning him silent as she left the room.

———————

Whenever Nathan walked inside the Oasis Springs Country Club, he felt like he'd traveled back in time. It was opened in 1964, the same year Tomás Vasquez opened his first coffee plant a few miles away. The floor was still covered in the same ugly shag carpeting, so thick it was a tripping hazard. When he brought Dillon, they used to sneak into the supper club between the lunch and dinner crowds to steal leftover desserts and half-empty wineglasses from neglected tables. They would bake beneath the sun with a buzz they struggled to hide from their parents. Sofia and Beto never noticed, but Joe would catch him almost every time.

Today, the dining room was filled with potential donors for Matt's congressional run pretending they were there to support his mayoral campaign, though most didn't live inside the city limits. A popular cable news host held a plate filled with shrimp and stood next to a woman who was recently named CEO of one of the biggest social media platforms in the world. Nathan wove through the sea of designer suits and heavy jewelry, catching snippets of conversation along the way. "What we really need is universal pre-K, like Matt is saying. It's all about food insecurity. Did you read that piece in *The Atlantic*? Black Lives Matter unless they're four-year-olds who need a carton of milk."

Growing up, Nathan would be forced to sit through dinner parties with conversations like these—virtue signaling from people who had never used a social program in their lives. Even when he was young, he understood that it took more than caring about an issue to form an opinion on it. They'd whine about access to mental health care in one breath and complain about a panhandler obstructing traffic with his wheelchair in another: "If you give him anything, he'll just keep doing it."

Nathan had finally made it to the bar when he saw Matt Abbott smiling broadly, with his hair flattened into a *Leave It to Beaver* part. Matt's voice projected over the low buzz of the crowd, who listened to him babble about billionaire tax brackets with the smug smiles of people who paid their bills with capital gains. It was the first time Nathan could glimpse what might have made him appealing to Rachel. He was telling animated stories with the same intensity that struck a nerve in that viral video. Nathan could imagine her being seduced by his passion.

Last night, Nathan had googled her in a moment of weakness. The first result was a tabloid headline speculating about the identity of Faith's biological father. Another, shorter article mentioned an art project Rachel did in college that was banned for being obscene and damaged the department due to the scandal.

Reading it had made him want to call her. Instead, he had closed his computer and lied to Bobbi about being hungry so she'd come over to hang out and make dinner.

Nathan had just placed his drink order when Sofia appeared, and leaned in for air-kisses, steeping his lungs in bergamot and jasmine.

"You look so nice." She ran approving eyes over his outfit. "I know you hate dressing up, but it's such a good look on you."

She was in full-on mothering mode, and he appreciated the attempt to make him feel better about standing out in the crowd. They were surrounded by clean-shaven men in dark blazers and light-colored pants, with solid ties. Nathan wore dark pants, no blazer, and a five-o'clock shadow because he'd been too preoccupied with Rachel to shave.

"I don't hate nice clothes." He accepted his drink and tossed a twenty into the bartender's tip jar. "But I only own two of these shirts. Got to space them out so no one notices."

Sofia gave him a familiar *you're adorable, but please behave* look and guided him away from the bar. "You should make more of an effort with your father. I know he's difficult. But you do things to make him angry."

"My breathing makes him angry."

She stopped walking and rounded on him. "You're not a teenager anymore, Nathaniel. Your father is flawed, but he's also human. And like you, he makes impulsive choices without thinking about how they affect the people who love him."

"I'm not like Beto."

"Oh, please," she sighed. "You are *exactly* like him. I warned him not to pressure you. He was so obsessed with being right that he pushed you away from us. Away from me." The hand on his arm tightened. "I never wanted you to leave home. But getting away from him—and being *right*—was more important to you."

Nathan untangled himself from his mother's grip. "We're not the only stubborn people in this family. Nothing matters to you more than Beto. No one. Not even—" Nathan stopped and clenched his jaw. "Forget it."

Sofia's voice hardened. "You think I would choose him over my children?"

"No," Nathan said, because it would have implied that she'd made a choice at all. Instead, she'd hovered, waiting for Beto to finish browbeating Joe or making Nathan feel worthless, to then swoop in with hugs and kisses, saying, "It's okay, he doesn't mean it. I'll talk to him, I promise." But she never did. In their home, Beto was king. And Nathan grew up watching his mother defer to a man who didn't respect her enough to keep his dick in his pants. "I think you chose him over yourself."

Her face iced over. "I know you're angry, but you don't have to be disrespectful."

He wanted to tell her that honesty wasn't disrespect—it was kindness. But she'd gone stiff, her eyes darting to the people around them. He hadn't bothered to lower his voice, and they were starting to attract attention.

"I'm sorry." He touched her arm. "We shouldn't even be talking about this here."

"Well, you barely return my calls, so when are we supposed to talk?"

He smiled, attempting to lighten the mood. "I return all your calls. You're too busy being the town badass to answer."

She rolled her eyes, but grinned. "You should leave a message."

"You could text."

Sofia grimaced. "You sound like your brother. He tried to add me to a group chat with your aunts and cousins. It's an endless live feed of arguments about tax policies and whether you should wash raw chicken. I won't take part in it." Her eyes softened and focused somewhere over his shoulder. "Speaking of Joseph..."

Nathan's stomach dropped. Joe was deep in conversation with Matt and Rachel. Sofia took a step forward, but Nathan stayed rooted to the floor. Why the hell was she here? Standing next to *him* like everything was fine?

"I need to make a phone call," Nathan grumbled, avoiding Sofia's eyes. "I'll find you after."

"It'll only take a minute. Matt is the guest of honor." She grabbed his arm and started walking in their direction. "It would be rude not to say hello."

# CHAPTER ELEVEN

Unlike Matt, who constantly sold his charm with the zeal of a used car salesman, Joe Vasquez didn't have to say anything for people to know he was the most important person in the room. It wasn't just the imposing figure he struck with his gray-streaked beard and dark suit, or that he was taller than everyone at the luncheon except a retired NBA player running for state senate. It was his indifference to the social posturing surrounding him, as if he were immune to any need for approval. When Joe did look away from his phone long enough to speak, it was often in clipped shorthand, like his time was too valuable to waste on fully formed sentences.

Rachel knew that Joe was one of the few people in Oasis Springs that Matt envied. He would practically strain a muscle attempting to bond during conversations.

"You should join us out on the green one weekend," Matt said. "The guys at the firm would love to see you." He took a sip of red wine. Rachel would normally have told him to stick with white. Red stains your lips, and you never knew who would take a photo and post it online. Now she was perfectly happy to let him look like a toddler who had too many suckers while chatting up potential donors.

"Yeah, I don't golf," Joe said. "Something about riding around in those little carts. Not a fan of tight spaces."

Rachel raised an eyebrow. "They don't have doors."

Joe shifted his eyes over, a half smile lifting his lips. "Well then, maybe it's the company I keep."

Rachel laughed. She didn't know Joe that well, but he was always polite in an impatient way. Kind enough to give you the opportunity to impress, but not nice enough to stick around if you failed. She'd approached him thinking it would draw Matt's attention away from her. He'd been shadowing her movements since they got there. When she emptied her wineglass, he offered to bring her water instead. It was a warning. He didn't want a repeat of what happened at Sofia's party.

Matt touched the small of her back while he questioned Joe about Vasquez Industries' federal grant eligibility. For the last hour he'd been leaning close to speak, cupping her elbow to walk through the room. It sent a clear message to everyone watching. They were together. They were partners. After all these years, they were still in love. To Rachel, it felt like revenge. Intimate touches from the man who betrayed you inspired a special kind of revulsion.

"Who's that woman over there?" Matt stared at someone over Joe's shoulder. Rachel followed his gaze to see Lyric walking in their direction. "She's been staring at you since we got here."

"Lyric Patterson. She's an old classmate," Rachel said, and averted her eyes. She wasn't in the mood to deal with Lyric's ambivalence. But Matt waved her over with a large, welcoming smile.

"Well, hello there." Matt shook her hand. "I don't think we've met. Lyric, right?"

"Yes," she said. "It's nice to finally meet the man behind the trending video. I feel like I should get your autograph or something."

Matt flushed and dipped his head modestly. "How embarrassing. I was angry and lost my head for a minute. No idea it would take off like that."

It sounded so sincere. But Rachel was there when Hailey had fed him lines for this exact situation, when someone implied that he was a celebrity. "Remind them it was spontaneous. That feels more authentic." When Rachel asked how repeating a canned answer a dozen times would "feel authentic," Matt had laughed. "No one gets their news from multiple sources anymore."

"I actually have a bone to pick with your wife," Lyric said, and looked at Rachel. "When you introduced yourself, I didn't realize. You're Rachel *Thomas*. The collage artist who did the piece on sexuality and shame. Dr. Smith changed his thesis policies because of you."

Joe looked up from his phone with raised eyebrows. "I'm sorry. You did a collage about what?"

"Dr. Smith didn't actually change the policy," Rachel said quickly. Joe was eyeing her with more interest than he'd shown during his entire conversation with Matt. "Parts of the syllabus were vague, so he made them more specific."

"More regressive, you mean," Lyric said. "I don't know how someone that uptight ended up teaching art. But I thought your work was real and important. No one talks about the way we police Black women's bodies nearly enough." She glanced at Matt, who opened his mouth as if to agree, but then shut it quickly. "I wish Sofia had asked you to step in earlier. Maybe we could have explored spectacle through a womanist lens."

"You're curating?" Matt asked.

Lyric looked back and forth between them. "Rachel's taking over next week. I'm sorry, was I not supposed to—"

"It's fine," Rachel said. "We've been so busy I didn't have time to tell him the good news. Sofia and Lyric have asked me to work with the featured artist on pieces for the gala."

"Really?" Matt's voice lifted with a saccharine enthusiasm that meant he was secretly seething. "How exciting! I didn't realize Sofia was interested in feminist art."

"Womanist," Rachel corrected.

Lyric snapped her fingers, and said, "Womanist is to feminist..." She trailed off, smiling at someone behind them.

A familiar deep voice finished the quote. "As purple is to lavender."

Rachel spun around and locked eyes with Nathan. He stared for a charged and volatile beat before he turned to Matt and said, "Alice Walker. You should look her up."

The glass Rachel was holding slipped and shattered. Matt watched in stunned silence as she crouched quickly and reached for a broken piece.

"Don't!" Nathan grabbed her hand and moved it away from the glass shards. "You could hurt yourself."

His touch made her light-headed, and she tightened her grip without thinking. His thumb grazed her palm, and she yanked her hand away.

Sofia cleared her throat. "I think she's been sufficiently rescued, Nathaniel."

Matt stared at Nathan. "I'm sorry, are you the manager or something?"

"No, he's just obnoxious," Joe said with a laugh. "This is my little brother, Nathan."

"Well of course," Lyric said with an airy chuckle. "Look at the three of you. It's so obvious you're related."

Rachel's body went numb, like she'd been doused in ice, as all her foolish assumptions rushed back at once. She could still hear his dismissive laugh. *Isn't everybody?*

---

She looked happy to see him at first. Later he would rewind that part over and over in his mind, how she'd squeezed his hand and pulled him into those dark eyes. A second longer and he would have ignored everyone in the room, maybe said something stupid like, "I miss you."

But Matt's voice brought them back to reality: him wearing his good little Vasquez uniform, and her with that big diamond ring that hid most of her finger. He wanted to pull her aside and explain that this wasn't what it looked like. He was never hiding who he was. He was hiding from it. That he'd been doing it for so long, that it never felt like a lie until today.

"I forgot you had two sons." Matt smiled brightly at Sofia. "I met Joe before, but—" He studied Nathan. "Where have you been hiding yourself?"

Nathan couldn't look at him. Instead, he focused on Rachel, trying to coax her into meeting his eyes so she could see that he was...what? Sorry? Hurt? That morning, he'd given up on ever speaking to her again. Now he was ready to walk out that door with her if she wanted.

"Nathan owns his own business," Sofia said when it became clear to everyone that Nathan had no intention of responding. "It keeps him busy. We barely see him anymore."

Matt whistled, and said "Impressive!" with raised eyebrows, like Sofia had revealed that Nathan had started SpaceX. "You're pretty young for an entrepreneur. I would have guessed you were still in school. What are you, twenty-one, twenty-two?"

"I never went to college." Nathan finally met Matt's eyes. "I own a laundromat."

"A laundromat?" Matt's smile faltered. "You mean like a chain?"

"Nope. Just the one."

"Oh. Well, good for you."

"We were talking to Lyric about the gala," Rachel said. "I'm looking forward to working with Circe as our artist. She has an impressive body of work."

Sofia tensed. "Actually, Circe won't be featured this year. It seems our efforts to fund art programs for at-risk children aren't authentic enough for her public relations team." Sofia's tone was somber, like a eulogy, because she'd probably already ordered a hit on the woman's career. "Unfortunately, that leaves us without a big name to bring in donations."

Rachel looked stunned. "What does that mean for the gala?"

Lyric pushed her hair back over her shoulder. She had angled away from Sofia, which was probably a mistake. His mother was known for stabbing people in the back. "Don't worry. I'll find a replacement before I leave. We might be able to use one of the other artists we've already recruited," she said. "They're not flashy names, but there isn't much time to commission anything else. And we need an artist of color to showcase."

Joe looked up from his phone. "Wait, you need an artist? Nate can do it."

"I can do what?" Nathan tried to catch his brother's gaze, but Joe was staring at his phone again.

"His username is FireBird84." Joe showed his screen to the group. "He's got a ton of fans."

Lyric eyed Nathan with an odd expression. "You're FireBird?"

"Uh, yeah. I'm sorry, who are you?"

"Lyric Patterson," she said, extending a hand. "I'm an independent curator. And also one of your biggest fans."

"Cool. Thanks." She didn't look like the type who was into fandom, but he'd learned not to make assumptions about those things. One of Nathan's oldest followers was a seventy-year-old retired teacher who had her art printed and framed in her living room.

"My friends will never believe this," Lyric said. She was holding his hand in a firm grip. "I work with a group of niche gallery owners and art collectors across the country. We discuss your work all the time. We all read the books growing up, but your take is so fresh and subversive. You're like our fan art Banksy."

"Wait," Matt said. "I thought he owned a laundromat." That mocking smile from earlier was gone. Now Matt was staring at Nathan like a threat instead of a child who'd done a cute trick. Nathan suddenly realized Matt was *that* guy. The insecure D-lister who sulked without a captive audience to feed their ego.

"He does both," Rachel said. "His work is inspired by the Phoenix Prophecies, a young adult book series, but he draws the main characters as people of color in modern-day settings that..." She paused and looked at Nathan. His insides had levitated as she spoke. It probably showed on his face because she blinked and looked away. "Faith showed them to me. They're very good."

"Do you have other pieces?" Lyric was staring at him the way Joe leered at a steak when he thought no one was looking. "Not that your Phoenix Prophecies art isn't impressive, but I've always wondered."

Nathan's first instinct was denial. But he could feel Rachel's eyes on him, and he didn't want to lie to her again. "A few," he admitted. "Not ready for public eyes, though."

Lyric smiled at Rachel and said, "You're thinking what I'm thinking, aren't you?" She turned to Nathan without waiting for confirmation. "I know I'm being pushy, but you have to be the featured artist for the gala." She splayed her hands to mimic a headline. "*FireBird Revealed: The Long-Lost Vasquez Son Returns*. Think of the publicity we could generate with a few family profiles. This event will go viral."

It sounded ridiculous. He couldn't imagine anyone paying thousands of dollars for a night of kid lit art and nepotism. Nathan watched his mother mulling over a tactful way to tell the woman that this was a terrible idea. "Lyric," Sofia said calmly. "We didn't *lose* Nathaniel. He moved into a studio on Park Street. And while my son is talented—" She looked at Nathan. "*So* talented. I'm not sure he's ready for an event like this. We're six weeks away from the foundation's biggest fundraiser. That's a lot of pressure for someone who's inexperienced."

Joe cleared his throat. Sofia ignored him and continued speaking, but he grunted again, louder and deeper. She turned to face him. "Do you have something else to say, Joseph?"

"I'm no art expert, but Nate's been drawing his whole life." He lifted his phone. "Better stuff than this. He's got experience. All he needs is an opportunity."

"There will be other opportunities," Sofia said. "Something more appropriate. With mentorship."

Joe's support had infused him with confidence that his mother's rebuke swiftly deflated. Sofia was right. While Lyric may like his art, she was also treating it like a gimmick. But it was still hard to hear his own mother put his insecurities into words. She didn't trip over a goddamn one.

"I'll be his mentor," Rachel said. She kept her eyes on Sofia, like it was safer than looking at Nathan. "You asked for my help with the commission. I can guide him through the process. I've done it with other artists before."

He thought about what she'd said that night, about how she'd walked away from the life she'd wanted. Was that why she was pushing this so hard? Maybe she thought working with him would make up for some of what she'd lost.

"Really, Rachel?" Matt gave her a patronizing look that made Nathan want to stuff that crooked tie in his mouth. "It's been a while since your last internship. Maybe you should listen to what Sofia's saying."

Joe's face turned to stone. He couldn't stand bullies either.

Rachel kept her attention on Sofia. "If Lyric's enthusiasm is a reflection of Nathan's reputation in the art community, we'd be foolish not to take advantage." She paused, and added, "The theme is spectacle. I would say revealing that your youngest son is a reclusive fan artist with a mainstream following would qualify, wouldn't you?" Rachel aimed doe eyes at his mother, daring her to disagree. Sofia blinked rapidly, searching for a counterargument, but failed.

Nathan wasn't even sure he wanted to be some marketing hook to sell more tickets. But it was hard to process anything beyond *Rachel needs this*. When he looked at his brother, Joe seemed hopeful again.

"I'll do it." Nathan saw Joe's grin widen as he turned to look at Rachel. "If you're willing to work with me."

She finally met his gaze, and he saw the clash of hurt, anger, and stubbornness flicker into something warmer. Though maybe that was wishful thinking. "Of course," she said with a breezy tone so strained, he could swear he heard a vein pop. "I'm looking forward to it."

"Great," Matt said, smiling at Lyric. "Problem solved." His eyes flicked briefly to Rachel. "This'll be good for you. Give you a chance to use that expensive art degree on something other than decorating the bathroom."

A tense silence followed as everyone struggled with how to ignore the comment. But Nathan caught Matt's gaze. He was done with this asshole. "Don't talk to her that way."

Matt took a step back. "What?"

"I hate to be rude," Rachel interrupted, with a tone that implied she didn't hate it all that much, "but like everyone said, we don't have much time to work on this." Rachel nodded toward the exit. "Do you mind stepping out, so we can talk specifics?"

Nathan glared at Matt, who stared back with a newfound wariness. Lyric excused herself and mumbled something about being late for another event. Sofia offered to walk Lyric out. Joe studied everyone too long and too closely before his phone vibrated and pulled his attention away.

Nathan touched the small of Rachel's back. "After you."

---

The hallway was empty except for a woman in pale pink Chanel who gave Rachel a startled look before disappearing inside the restroom. Not good. Rachel probably looked like a wild animal caught in a net. She found an empty conference room and motioned for Nathan to follow her inside.

He had Sofia's eyes. All that time she didn't notice, but now she couldn't unsee it. He and Joe had the same mouth and nose. "Would you say something, please?"

Nathan shrugged, like he was bored by the question. "I told you that my last name was Vasquez."

"Oh, that is bullshit, and you know it."

"Fine," he snapped. "I didn't want to tell you about my family. I still wish you didn't know. I knew it would change how you see me. It always does."

"Of course it does!" She groaned. "I am such an idiot. Of course you aren't *no one*. I mean, who buys a laundromat before they can legally buy a drink?"

"What does that have to do with my family?"

She barked out a bitter laugh. "How did you pay for it? A trust? Something that hit your bank account when you turned eighteen?"

He didn't answer. But his jaw twitched, and that was enough confirmation.

"And I doubt a fluff and fold was your childhood dream," she continued. "So, who were you rebelling against? Who was the target of the *fuck you* that is your nonexistent college education and your designer T-shirt wardrobe? Sofia? Your father?" His eyes flashed. "Ah," she said, and folded her arms. "Daddy issues makes total sense."

Her scorn was laced with old resentments of college classmates like Nathan, spoiled into wearing their ambivalence as threadbare jeans from Goodwill. They'd been pretending. *He'd* been pretending to be an outsider, like her. Or at least, the way she used to be.

"Are you done?" Nathan's voice was ice. "Because I don't think you should throw stones about giving *fuck you*s to shitty families."

And this was precisely why she didn't trust people. They kept your secrets locked and loaded, ready to use against you. She'd ignored her instincts because she'd needed to feel something, anything besides rage. She should have known better than to think that salvation came in gorgeous Nathan Vasquez–shaped packages.

Being married to Matt had always been lonely. Even when he'd tried to be thoughtful and empathetic, there were parts of her that he could never understand. But Nathan had. Not everything, but more than anyone else. He knew what it was like to walk into a room of white faces wearing dark skin made of stone so no one could hurt you. He knew what it was like to love your art like it was a thing that made you, instead of the reverse. She didn't have to explain it. He *knew*, and that had meant so much that she'd ignored everything else.

Now he was just like Matt. Rich and privileged. That easy confidence so rare for a guy his age was just a perk of having money.

Rachel moved in closer until they were inches apart. Even in heels she had to tilt her head back to glare at him. "Are you seriously comparing your situation to mine? If anyone finds out about us, I am done. I will be run out of town with pitchforks, and your mother will chair the witch hunt's planning committee. I could lose everything—" She stopped when he cut his eyes in disbelief. Like he knew the first thing about her life.

"You knew who I was," she said. "That Sofia and I are...friends. Is that why you slept with me?" She hated the quivering strand of hurt inside the question. "To get back at her for something?"

"I wouldn't do that."

She tried to wave him away.

"Rachel." He grabbed her wrist. "I would *never* do that to you."

He was close. Her focus narrowed to his chest, his shoulders, the musk of his aftershave. She searched for a safer place to rest her eyes, but her gaze landed on his mouth. She wanted to believe him. She wanted to be back there, sitting on his couch tracing his tattoos while he handed her pieces of himself. She didn't want to be here. But this was the cost of letting someone in. The minute she let her guard down, they drew a map to the quickest way to hurt her. "I don't even know who you are."

Nathan's eyes flashed and he put more distance between them. "Well, I don't know you either. All that stuff you said about your husband? How you don't love him anymore? If that's true, then what are you doing here? With *him*?"

"It's none of your business. You don't get to ask about my marriage."

"What marriage? He doesn't want you. And you spent Saturday night riding my dick for hours, so you sure as hell don't want him. How can you act like nothing happened?"

"Because *nothing* happened!" He blinked, his hard expression cracking. She knew it hurt, but she kept going. She had to. What they'd been doing was dangerous. "We fucked. It was a mistake. So let's get through this, keep it professional, and move on with our lives. Can you do that?"

Nathan's eyes glinted against the light, damp and hazy with some emotion she wasn't brave enough to identify. Then he blinked and it was gone. "I don't think that'll be a problem," he said, and the gulf between them became an ocean.

# CHAPTER TWELVE

Nathan had underestimated the size of Lyric's network. News about FireBird84's work being featured at the gala leaked before the Vasquez Foundation could issue a press release. Sofia sent someone over to help him with public relations, and the woman hijacked his schedule so completely, a week went by before Nathan realized that he'd been neglecting his brother.

They didn't work out on Thursdays, so Nathan stopped by The Stand, picked up Joe's favorite lunch, and drove to his office. He was halfway through his trek across the parking lot when he spotted a tiny figure running toward him.

"Mom! It's Uncle Nathan!"

Joe's son had become a gangly six-year-old. Nathan crouched so Angel could launch himself into his arms.

"We saw Dad! And Grandpa! I mean, Abuelo. ¡Me compró un *Millennium Falcon*!" Angel started speaking rapidly, and Nathan struggled to follow the confusing story about the *Star Wars* LEGO set Beto had bought for him.

"¡Habla despacio!" Nathan finally said, and lifted palms of surrender. "I can't keep up."

Nathan greeted Zara, who was smiling a few feet away. "Joe hired another new tutor," she said. "This one's big on immersive education and wants Angel to only speak Spanish, even to family. Your dad was annoyed."

"Are you surprised?" Beto wasn't raised in a bilingual household like Sofia. He was like Nathan, speaking Spanish only to explain that he wasn't fluent. Joe spoke more than all of them after taking classes as part of his business degree. Once he had Angel, he became determined to raise a son that knew his heritage.

"Maybe you can tutor me, huh?" Nathan said. Angel flushed and pretended to punch Nathan in the stomach. Nathan groaned and doubled over. "You taking boxing too?"

Angel laughed. "No! I'm too little!"

Zara asked Angel to wait in the car with his nanny. Nathan hugged him goodbye, long and tight, reveling in his nephew's scrawny arms around his neck. He needed to steal hugs more often, even if it meant hopping on a cross-country flight.

Zara didn't speak until Angel was in the car. "I'm so sorry about Beto. I couldn't believe it when Joe told me."

"Yeah, I know." She looked like she was expecting tears at any moment. But when Nathan thought about the tumor killing his father, it felt like a story someone had told him about a weaker man he'd never met. He couldn't believe something that small could defeat a giant. "Joe finally asked you to come home?"

She hesitated. "He asked me to send Angel with Nadia. I decided to come too."

"Oh. Okay." Nathan knew to tread carefully. Living with his parents had taught him that there were some things about a marriage you'd rather not know.

"We're separated," she said, and folded her arms around her waist. "It's been eight months now, but he won't talk about filing papers."

"Divorce papers?" Saying it out loud made his chest hurt. Family meant everything to Joe. A divorce would devastate him. "Is it that bad?"

Zara sighed. "I met someone. It happened during filming. Joe and I spent so much time apart—"

"I don't think I need to hear this," he interrupted. Nathan loved her, but if he had to pick a side, Joe would win every time. "It's between you and my brother."

"He won't *talk* to me." Her eyes watered and she pressed a hand to her mouth. "I still love him. I just..." She shook her head. "I don't know how to help him. He seemed fine with Angel earlier, but he always seems fine."

Joe was usually so open about his therapy and medication that he sounded like a self-care influencer on social media. Now he avoided eye contact whenever Nathan asked how he was feeling. Joe had been looking out for him for years. It was time he returned the favor.

"I'll take care of him," Nathan said, "I promise."

Later, Joe's assistant did a double take when Nathan walked out of the elevator. He lifted the greasy food bag and pointed to Joe's door. Once inside, he found Joe sitting behind his desk, staring out the window. The sound of the door made him start, swivel around, and reach for a file without looking up. "I said I'm busy, Carrie."

"Doing what?" Nathan closed the door behind him. "Admiring the landscaping?"

Joe frowned. "What are you doing here?"

"Brought you lunch."

"I don't have time." He stared at the bag. "Are those—"

"Fries from The Stand?" Nathan pulled out a tiny condiment container. "Yeah. Miguel sent extra sauce."

Joe's eyes sparkled like a kid on Christmas morning. He really needed to eat something besides juiced grass and tofu.

"Give it to me," Joe said.

Nathan sat down but kept the food in his lap. "I have a question for you first."

"Fuck you, I'm hungry."

"Thought you were busy."

"Don't make me call security." He reached for the phone for dramatic effect.

Nathan laughed. "So they can what? Shake me down for fries?"

Joe grunted and rocked back in his chair. "What's the question."

"What's going on with you and Zara?"

Joe's face fell. "Can I at least eat while I tell you?"

Nathan tossed Joe the bag and watched him pull out a tray of greasy fries. "You know they probably cook those in anim—"

"Shut up." Joe dipped a fry into the sauce and closed his eyes as he took his first bite. "Do not ruin this for me."

After a few more fries, Joe started talking. Zara was the one who had suggested separating, and Joe was half listening at the time, as always. To him, it wasn't much different from their regular living arrangement. "With me at the office and her running around making movies, we barely saw each other. I thought she just wanted another condo, but she started seeing this other guy a few months later." Joe sounded irritated, like his wife falling in love with someone else had screwed up his work calendar.

"I'm sorry, Joe," Nathan said.

Finally, a streak of pain broke through Joe's stoicism. "Yeah, it's fucked. But I can't change it."

"Does Mom know you're splitting up?"

"Do you see her twerking in the streets? No, she doesn't know. And now she's wrapped up in your art thing. It's a good distraction."

Nathan snatched a paperclip from his desk. He pried it apart while Joe finished his meal. "So, about that," he said. "What makes you think I can do something this big without screwing it up?"

"I don't know." Joe rocked back in his chair. "I don't have faith in much anymore. Maybe I need something to believe in. Even if it's you and your blurry dragons." He rolled his shoulder, as if he were trying to shake off the admission. Being raised by Beto made sentiment feel like a hazard.

"They're not dragons."

"Whatever. Get out of your head. Mom and Dad are proud. That art lady loves you. And Rachel Abbott does too, for some reason." Joe narrowed his eyes. "Is that why you punked her husband?"

He should have known. Joe liked people to think he was constantly distracted, but he never missed anything that didn't bore him. "He was being a jerk."

"Right. But she's also hot, so I understand the impulse to rescue." Joe dug out another fry from the bag. "How did Abbott pull her anyway? He's fucking stupid and his face looks like a potato."

Nathan tried to sound bored with the conversation. "Are you interested in her or something?"

Joe snorted. "You mean am I a piece of shit? No. I don't date married women. But I thought after she fought so hard for you, that you might have a crush."

Nathan slumped lower and flattened his voice. "I just met her."

Joe pointed at Nathan's chest. "Sit up straight, man. Jesus. Your posture's a power suit."

Nathan didn't respond with his usual "Okay, Dad." That joke only worked when your real father wasn't dying. Or when it didn't feel vaguely true.

"Speaking of unlikely marriages, I could never figure out what Mom saw in Beto," Nathan said. "He's not exactly a good time."

"Money." Joe popped a tiny fry in his mouth and shook the bag, seeking more. "He was better looking back then too. More Diego Luna and less Gomez Addams."

Nathan laughed and shook his head. "I don't think it was only money. Mom's not like that."

"Not like what? Human?" Joe sighed. "They're just people, Nate. You get that now, right?"

He thought he did. Or at least, he was starting to. It was getting more difficult to see Beto as an all-powerful malevolent force if he was being defeated by a few mutated cells. Joe had been saying for years that Nathan gave their father too much power over his life. Nathan used to think it was hypocritical, but now he realized that it was a warning. Joe had really been saying, *Don't be like me. I took these hits so you don't have to.*

Nathan sat up straighter in the chair. "Thank you. For believing in me."

Joe cleared his throat and started shuffling papers on his desk. "It's nothing," he mumbled. "Now get out of here so I can get some work done."

Nathan saw a picture on the wall on his way to the door. Joe was at the family lake house, beaming, holding up a tiny fish Angel had caught, while Zara leaned away with exaggerated disgust.

"Is it really over?" Nathan asked. "With Zara?"

Joe stared at the picture. "Yeah, it is." He paused. "I always thought I'd be good at this family stuff. Because I wanted it so bad. But I don't know. First Mia. Now this. Maybe it's not my thing."

His brother had nearly fooled him. Nathan had almost walked out of this office thinking that while Joe was stressed, he wasn't on the verge of another breakdown. But Joe never mentioned Mia Williams. Not since she dumped him by leaving her engagement ring with his assistant, wrapped in a Post-it with a note written on the back: *Tell Beto he wins.*

Nathan still saw Mia regularly at the laundromat because she couldn't afford to replace her washer and dryer. She would always bring something with her, like muffins from a new bakery or a book she'd been reading, and use it as an excuse to stay and talk. But he never told Joe about those conversations. Knowing that she'd stayed in Nathan's life would break his brother's heart all over again. After she ended things, Joe had barely spoken to anyone but his assistant for months. Beto had finally snapped him out of it by threatening to fire him. Nathan always wondered if things would have turned out differently if Joe had fought for Mia the way he had his job.

"Why don't you ever fight for anything, Joe?" It slipped out before Nathan could stop it.

Joe was still staring at that photo. "I don't know," he said, and then looked at Nathan. "Why don't you?"

---

The Law Offices of Julia Beaumont was practically hidden between identical storefronts in a strip mall on the southwest edge of town. The reception area consisted of a pair of cheap chairs and a scarred wooden desk. A sign was propped beside a dated call button that instructed Rachel to ring for service. She knew that ringing for service wasn't how most reputable lawyers greeted new clients. But Ben Abbott had been adamant about his referral.

Rachel rang the bell and waited. A door opened behind the reception desk, and a stunning Black woman with huge dark eyes appeared in the doorway. Her natural curls were cut into an angled bob that framed razor-sharp cheekbones and a 1950s pinup mouth. She wore a suit with dark suspenders, tailored so perfectly to her body, it could have been a sexy-lawyer Halloween costume.

"Rachel Abbott." The way she said it made Rachel sound infamous and inevitable, as though Julia Beaumont had always known she would show up at her door eventually. "You're a long way from home."

"Ms. Beaumont? A friend of mine referred me here. He said you were one of the best attorneys in town."

"It's Julia. And your friend is wrong." Julia nodded toward her office. "I'm *the* best lawyer in town. Come on in."

A few minutes later, Rachel sat on the opposite side of an L-shaped desk, while Julia drummed her fingers. Rachel spotted a framed photo of Julia smiling at the camera, standing next to another woman. It took her a moment to recognize Mia, with loose hair and Mardi Gras beads draped around her neck. "You know my cousin?"

Julia didn't look at the picture. "We've been best friends since high school."

There really was nowhere to escape in this town. "Oh. Well, maybe this isn't a good idea."

Julia's fingers stilled. "I'm a professional, Rachel. Whatever you tell me won't go beyond this office. Not unless you want it to."

Maybe it was Julia's bullish tone that made Rachel believe her. Or maybe she needed to confide in someone whose only vested interest in her life was a contingency fee. Rachel told her everything. From dick pic to rosebushes to the million-dollar hush money. Julia's expression didn't change, except for a slight nostril flare when Rachel mentioned Matt's election.

Julia wrote something on her legal pad. "Why one million? Why not two. Or ten?"

"Because I was drunk, and math isn't my strong suit."

Julia had no reaction. Just more notes. "What's your current net worth?"

"I have less than a thousand in a joint account."

"Have you started looking for work?"

The line of questioning was starting to make sense. Julia thought she was spoiled. A woman with a law degree, working long hours in a modest office, would probably consider her situation a joke.

"I haven't worked in over a decade," Rachel said. She listed her résumé—unpaid internships, a few cashier positions, and waiting tables. "The utilities for the house are more than three grand a month. I can't pay for that on tips. I need to keep the lights on while I figure out what to do with my life."

Julia slipped off her glasses and placed her pen on her notepad. "Okay," she said. "You made this deal because you need money. I get that. You've been married awhile and it's more than fair." She folded her arms. "But I don't really do fair. Or nice. Or neat. Whoever referred you to me is aware of that. So why don't you tell me what you really want, Rachel. Deep down. With attorney-client privilege attached."

That word: *want*. Rachel had initially brushed off her lack of "wants" as a side effect of domestic life. Her wants, her needs, even her name had been overtaken by her personae of "Faith's mom" and "Matt's wife." But abandoning her own wants had started well before her marriage. A few days after Matt had proposed, Herman Abbott had pulled her aside, handed her a glass of wine, and calmly explained that while he understood that she loved his son, people don't get things simply because they want them. "Relationships like yours only work in the movies," he'd said. "I'm not talking about race. This is about pedigree. My son could end up in the White House and you're a scandal waiting to happen."

When she'd told Matt about Herman's warning, he assured her they'd be fine. "Dad has a messed-up way of saying 'grow up and be respon-sible.' We'll figure this marriage thing out together, Rache. As a team." And that's what they'd become. A unit. Strategic partners, instead of the naive fools who fell in love. Rachel had remade herself into the wife Matt needed instead of paying closer attention to everything he didn't say. He'd never told her that she was already enough.

Now, she looked at Julia, with the memory of that day still raw and burning. "I want thirteen years of my life back," she said. "I want the long nights working on his campaign, the boring vacations with his toxic family. I want to get back every time he told me to wait. To just *wait*, for a better time to go back to school. Or to open a business. Or do anything that was for me. I want every second of every day that I trusted that man refunded. And I want it with *fucking* interest."

Julia opened a drawer and pulled out a client agreement form. She slid it over to Rachel. "I can work with that."

———————

Nathan was nervous about seeing Rachel again, so he picked a casual but suitably public setting for their first meeting. Sunlight streamed through the windows of his favorite coffee shop. The long tables at Press were filled with people studying, reading, or scrolling through their phones. He'd usually take a seat at the bar so he could people watch while he drank his coffee. Today, he stopped a few feet inside and looked around until he spotted Rachel.

Unlike the rest of the Saturday crowd, she was dressed for business—high-heeled pumps, navy dress, a strand of rich-lady pearls around her neck. Her hair was long and straight, and she held a dainty teacup with a death grip. The whole look had a definite *don't fuck with me* vibe.

Rachel didn't see him until he was almost to her table. She didn't smile or speak, so he took a cue from her and sat without a greeting. "How long have you been waiting?"

"I don't know. I had two espressos already, so I switched to tea." She tapped the cup again. "I've never been here. It's busier than I expected."

No one was looking their way, but Rachel's posture was beauty queen proper and her face was deliberately flat, like she was about to take a polygraph.

"Are you afraid someone will think we're on a date?" he asked.

Her fingers clawed against the teacup, which wobbled and threatened to spill its contents. "Could you keep your voice down?"

"No one's listening to us."

"Everyone's listening. Don't be naive."

It was tempting to remind her that he was born into this kind of scrutiny and knew how to handle nosy people. She was the one bashing in car windows and crying barefoot at the drive-in.

"Naive?" He laughed. "You really think you're fooling anybody? You can't stand Abbott. I saw the look on your face when he touched you. Like you wanted to file off your own skin."

Rachel pitched forward and lowered her voice to a rough whisper. "Stop pretending that fucking me opened a window to my goddamn soul. You don't know me as well as you think you do."

She was closer to him than she realized. Her hair brushed against his forearm, and the memory of that night ran through him like a current. Rachel was right, they barely knew each other. And this was the second time she reminded him that they had "just fucked" and nothing more. His one-night stands were usually skin deep, but that night with Rachel had burrowed and rooted somewhere deeper. It ate at him that a guy like Matt Abbott had years of memories with this woman, while he was stuck mentally rewinding a few stolen moments. But that was his problem, not hers.

"Rachel—" he started, but stopped when she averted her eyes. He leaned back and pulled his hands down to rest against his thighs. "I'm sorry. You're right. I know you're dealing with a lot right now. It was wrong of me to throw it in your face like that."

He could see her winding up, like she wasn't ready to let go of the fight yet. But then her shoulders caved. "I didn't come here to argue. I'm sorry. It was unprofessional and won't happen again."

A server approached and put a drink down in front of Nathan. Once they ordered food, Rachel laced her fingers on the table, with a straight spine. All-business. "Are you nervous about the gala?"

"Aren't you? This is a big deal for you. It's okay if you'd rather work with someone else."

Her neck snapped back. "Why would I do that?"

"Come on." Nathan touched his chest. "Me? Featured artist at some thirty-thousand-dollar-a-table dinner? It's a punch line to a shitty joke." He'd made the mistake of looking up the gala last night. He'd always thought of it as another one of his mother's numerous parties. But it was held in a large courtyard at the National Portrait Gallery and typically attracted over eight hundred people. Last year, the featured artist had sold a single painting for six figures. And here he was with his blurry non-dragons.

"What if no one shows up?"

She smiled and said, "They'll show," with conviction that threatened to melt away his anxiety.

"What if no one bids?" he asked quickly, clinging to the cold comfort of his doubt. Borrowing her confidence seemed hazardous. Like the path to leaked-sex-tape-level disaster.

"I know this is a lot," she said. "But I was serious about helping you. Everyone gets stage fright their first time out. It's normal." She leaned closer. "We are partners. You're the talent and I'm like..." She paused, searching for words. "I'm like the director, guiding you through a performance."

"So I run everything past you?"

"Yes. But not for approval, just for a fresh perspective. Like an editor for a novel."

"I think I get it. You'll pull me back if I go down some weird rabbit hole—like Catholic saints as Marvel characters. Or naked popes."

She pressed her lips together, but he could see the hint of a smile, which was a relief. Working together would be hell if she was too mad to laugh at him. "Are these your actual ideas?"

He shrugged. "There might be a few sketches in my drawer."

"Let's keep them there."

As the afternoon passed, they both seemed to settle in. She was all about the work, and he was all about convincing her not to glare daggers at his face. When the food came, he made sure she had plenty of napkins and offered to wave down the server when he forgot her hot sauce. He also finally made her laugh again with an embarrassing story about his brief detour into community theater. "In my defense, I was really bored," he said. "I'd been living alone for a year, and it felt like adulthood was just constantly running the dishwasher. But then I realized it was filing taxes too, and that seemed like *a lot*, so I quit the play."

She ducked her head and gave in to that wind chime giggle he loved. It fed a hunger that had been gnawing at him since she snuck out of his apartment that night. If he couldn't have her, maybe he could still have this.

Rachel steered the conversation back to art. She explained she was going to work with him the way she used to work with high school students during undergrad, mentoring them through a development period that ended with an artist showcase. "I remember all of their names," she said, her voice filled with pride when she listed how many of them had gone on to successful careers. He imagined it had to hurt, watching kids she mentored do what she couldn't, live out the dreams she'd abandoned for something that was slowly eating her alive.

The difference between her now, radiant while she discussed the work she loved, and the aloof woman at the luncheon was stark. This was who she was. If the work they did together was the huge hit that everyone kept predicting, maybe she wouldn't have to hide that anymore.

They ate in silence for a while before she looked at him with expectant eyes. "Did you bring your portfolio?"

Nathan shifted in his chair. "I don't have one. Just the stuff online."

"Well, let's look at that and brainstorm."

This was the point of no return. He was starting to form this half-baked dream of putting his name on something meaningful. From here on out, she would know that he really wanted it.

"What if I did something else? Portraits. Maybe."

She steepled her hands under her chin. "Interesting. Go on."

The pose was an adorable assault on his willpower. Was he really supposed to ignore that for five weeks? "Some of my favorite artists do things using photo references."

"Like Kehinde Wiley."

"The guy who did Obama's portrait, yeah. A little. But I like using charcoal. And stuff from nature—grass, leaves, and fire?" His face was warm. "Sorry. It's hard to explain."

"Don't apologize." She moved to touch him but let her hand fall to the table instead. "You mean mixed media. And it sounds interesting."

He studied her fingers. She wasn't wearing a ring. "I'd like to use photo references. But I'm not much of a photographer."

"I can help with that. You don't need anything fancy. Your phone is fine." She smoothed a wisp of hair back into place. He missed her curls. He liked how they would wind around his fingers like tendrils of silken rope.

"I have a camera," he said. "An old Nikon that I don't know how to use."

"We can try it out," Rachel said. "I'll show you some basics to get you started. How about Monday?"

"Monday's fine. So's Tuesday. And Wednesday. I'm free every day."

She laughed. "So am I. I keep myself busy, but sometimes I wonder if anyone in this town would notice if I was gone."

That night at the drive-in, when they'd met as strangers, he'd had a similar thought. That he'd made his life so small, her smile might be the biggest thing in it.

# CHAPTER THIRTEEN

Rachel listened to Vivaldi to calm her nerves while Faith drove through rush-hour traffic. *The Four Seasons* was long enough to make it to Potomac, where Niles and his fiancée lived. Faith had been so eager to get behind the wheel since coming home, she pulled her blue Mini out of the garage with a flourish that nearly took out their mailbox.

In addition to her daughter's rusty driving skills, Rachel was also anxious about the party. Alesha would be there, and so would Mia, with her bloodhound ability to sniff out messy secrets. Thinking about it made her stressed and lonely, so Rachel distracted herself the same way she had all week, by texting Nathan about his photographs. In between messages, she snuck wistful glances at Faith.

Sunlight lit the angles of her daughter's face and sharpened her features in a way that made her briefly unrecognizable. That always happened when Faith returned after long periods away; her daughter would seem like a different person. She'd suddenly care deeply about things she'd never mentioned before or notice nuances in situations she used to overlook. That morning, Rachel had gotten up early to beat Lenora in their ongoing war to control the laundry, and Faith had asked, "Why are you fighting for something you hate doing?"

Her daughter wasn't growing up anymore. She was growing into herself, uncovering morals and values that she'd formed on her own. As a mother, Rachel found it gratifying, but also scary. Her little girl had been raised, past tense, and was now a full-blown adult, reckless driving habits and all.

Faith motioned for Rachel to turn her music down. "Who were you texting earlier?"

Rachel considered lying. But those were starting to pile up, and it was hard to hide things from Faith anyway. "The artist whose work we commissioned for the gala."

"Nathan Vasquez?"

Rachel paused. "Yes. Do you know him?"

"Do you remember Celia? We went to junior prom together. She wore that baby-blue suit, and—"

"It got covered in makeup when you two hugged. I remember that. I felt so bad for her."

"Yeah, well her current girlfriend's cousin dated Nathan's best friend, Dillon, who, according to Celia, is a drug dealer." Faith's eyes briefly flicked her way. "She also claimed that Nathan is his connection to a cartel, which is why he got sent away for high school and no one talks about him."

Faith recited the story with the flat inflection of a newscaster. "That isn't true," Rachel said. "About Nathan. I don't know any Dillon, but that cartel stuff is really racist."

"Right? Who would believe it anyway? He's a bubble kid. Probably paints landscapes of the hood with thousand-dollar paintbrushes."

Rachel thought about Nathan's expensive drafting table. "What's a bubble kid?"

Faith turned in to a long driveway. "It's what we used to call people who were born and raised in Oasis Springs. Rich, diverse utopia. None of it's real."

"You grew up there."

Faith shook her head. "We *live* there. It's not the same."

Faith pulled into a half-circle driveway with a derisive nod at the large house owned by Niles's fiancée. It was a sprawling estate that reminded Rachel of the Vasquez property. The builder had added structural flourishes like Corinthian pillars and elaborate lawn sculptures that would have made the conservative property owners association in Rachel's neighborhood march with torches. It wasn't Rachel's taste, but she respected the sentiment: a middle-finger-up, *less isn't more, it's just less* attitude.

Faith unlatched her seat belt with the keys still in the ignition, but Rachel didn't move. This wasn't one of Matt's campaign events. This was family—her family, even though they felt like strangers. But she wasn't really an Abbott either. Which meant today she was simply Rachel, unmoored, with no prep or sound bites. It made her feel exposed.

"Let's get this over with," Rachel said, and hoped Faith didn't notice the way her hand trembled as she reached for the door. They both walked slowly, trying to take it all in. There was so much *house.* Everywhere you looked, there was a sprawl of space lit by the early evening sunlight streaming through floor-to-ceiling windows. The tile was a custom ombré mosaic that gradually changed from burnt orange to gold as they moved closer to the ballroom. Who besides royalty and those *Sound of Music* kids had an actual ballroom?

"Holy shit," Faith mumbled beneath her breath.

Rachel looked around and realized that she'd made a huge mistake. Everyone was dressed in costumes—1920s-style outfits that made them look like they'd stepped into East Egg. There were drop waists and fringe, double-breasted suits and long cigarette holders perched on people's fingers. The centerpieces were plumes of pale pink ostrich feathers mixed with red carnations. An all-Black jazz quartet played in the corner, while a group of women attempted the Charleston in four-inch heels.

"Uh, Mom?" Faith and Rachel exchanged confused glances. "Did Niles say anything to you about costumes?"

"No," Rachel said, though she wasn't sure if that was totally accurate. She remembered a brief period of phone tag, followed by an email that she'd skimmed with the RSVP request. "I don't feel like Tyler Perry's *Chicago* is a dress code I would have missed."

Faith snickered, and the proximity of her daughter, unimpressed with the artifice of opulence as always, eased some of Rachel's embarrassment. This was supposed to be some sort of post-birth baby shower. She'd brought a Boba wrap and leather diaper bag for Kat.

"You came!"

Their eyes widened as Kat Jones, in a black bob with a white ostrich plume that curved against her cheek, grabbed Rachel's arms and pulled her into a tight hug. "Niles said you wouldn't make it, but I told him you're family! How would you not see the baby?" She stepped back and looked at the present. "Oh, how sweet! What is it?"

"A Boba wrap."

Kat's excitement dimmed. "Drop it off on the table by the kitchen," she said. Her eyes swept over their clothes. "I guess Niles didn't tell you guys about the theme?" She forced a smile through her obvious annoyance. Kat was a part-time event planner and full-time trust fund diva. In Rachel's experience, people who planned parties for a living attached an unnatural importance to the uniformity of their vision. She wouldn't be surprised if Kat had them escorted off the premises at some point.

"He probably did," Faith said, swiftly going into damage control mode. "School has my brain fried. And Mom's been really busy lately."

"With the gala!" Kat squealed. "I can't believe you're hosting! When's the last time a Black person was asked to run that thing? You would think as another woman of color, Sofia would try harder, but she's all about that old, white money. If you don't own an island, do not apply." Kat laughed, even though Rachel was pretty sure Kat's father owned enough land on an islet off the coast of Virginia to also qualify.

Rachel scanned the room. "So, where's Serena?"

Kat made a whirling gesture toward the ceiling. "Upstairs with Alesha. I think Niles is hiding from his mother. She brought baby formula and threw away my waist trainer." Kat rolled her eyes and started venting about milk production and baby weight. When she mentioned eating raw placenta, Faith gulped back a gag. Thankfully Rachel's phone vibrated.

**Nathan:** Busy?

**Rachel:** Trying to escape a sip and see.

**Nathan:** A what?

She looked up to see that Kat had disappeared, while Faith had found a group friends from her Jack and Jill chapter. Rachel strolled away from the ballroom, typing a long message explaining why Kat considered a pre-birth baby shower for her "spotlight-loving Leo" an insult.

**Nathan:** Is it a good party at least?

**Rachel:** I think the theme is the Harlem Renaissance? There are napkins with Langston Hughes quotes everywhere.

**Nathan:** Baby is a Hughes-head already? Good for her.

Rachel laughed as she walked outside. The sun had almost set, and the party had spilled into the rose garden. The smell of sweet smoke drew her attention down a winding walkway to a set of lawn chairs. Mia and Niles reclined in the matching loungers, smoking cigars. Niles stood quickly and squinted in the dim light. "Shit," he said, relaxing. "I thought you were Kat." He sat back down, stretching out his long legs, and then smiled, a blinding flash of white teeth that lit up his handsome face. "Pull up a chair, cousin."

Niles was always like this—warm and familiar, lovingly teasing in a way that made her ashamed for not reaching out to him more.

Mia blew circles of smoke. "He's not hiding from his fiancée at a party for his own baby. In case you were wondering." She looked at her brother. "Did I say that right?"

Rachel sat in a chair next to Mia, who offered her the lit cigar. Rachel didn't hesitate. She took it and filled her mouth with smoke. Niles watched her with wide eyes. "Okay. Unexpected."

"I used to smoke a long time ago." She rounded her lips and puffed out her own circles.

"I bet," Niles said. "Living that *artist* life at Howard."

"Okay, *Chef,*" Mia said. "You should talk."

"I sowed some middling wild oats back in the day." Niles stretched long and pushed back the black fedora perched on his head. Mia wore a navy romper with gold earrings. Rachel was starting to see a trend in who didn't get the memo about the theme. "Those were good times. I did some shit. Saw a *lot* of shit." He shook his head. "I was broke and tired and working my ass off for nothing. Wouldn't have changed a minute of it." He looked up at the house looming above them. "I'm grateful for all of this, but sometimes having nothing to lose sounds easier."

"You miss it," Rachel said. "Because you're grieving."

Niles frowned. Or stopped smiling, which was as close to negativity as he could get. "Grieving what?"

"The old you," Mia interjected. "The one without a fiancée, or a kid, or things to lose. And you're thirty-four, so it's even worse. You've got decades of a former life to mourn."

"I miss staying up all night," Rachel said. "Because there was a TV show I wanted to watch or a book I wanted to finish. And then I would sleep in the next day because it didn't matter. No one was waiting for me or expecting anything."

"I used to sing in the shower," Mia said. "At the top of my lungs. Now the walls are so thin, I'm afraid my daughter will hear me and have one more thing to hate about her mother."

Niles tsked. "Livie don't hate you."

"Not today, no." Mia sank into her chair. "But there's always tomorrow."

"Wait," Niles said. "If I'm over here grieving, why is Kat fine? She's too cheerful for me, and I'm a pretty happy motherfucker."

"She's twenty-three," Mia said. "Sleep deprivation is for the young."

"She's also not doing as fine as you think," Rachel said. "I spoke to her earlier."

Niles winced. "Did she talk about the placenta?"

Rachel nodded and they all shuddered.

"This is probably none of my business," she said. "But what's it like being engaged to someone so much younger?"

Niles shrugged. "Kind of like being married to a white man, I guess. Some parts fit. Others don't. Try to have more that fits."

He stood and offered to bring them food. Mia gave him a long list of appetizers she'd seen on the way in. Rachel requested cake. "Two slices. I'd like to take one home."

Mia and Rachel smoked in silence once Niles was gone. This far from the city, she felt like someone else. The Thomas girl who could smoke and drink and eat whatever she wanted, with whomever she chose. She'd worked so hard to be a good Abbott, but never thought to do the same with her own people. Years of neglecting them had robbed her of this kind of peace.

Mia looked up at the sky. "I hate my job," she whispered, and her hesitant tone made Rachel realize why her cousin had been trying to connect lately. She'd seen Rachel's restlessness and it had resonated with her own.

"You should quit," Rachel said softly. Tonight, her fragile tie to this family had grown stronger, and she wanted to settle into the feeling. She wanted to be a shield between this woman and anything that tried to hurt her.

Mia didn't speak for a long time. "I need the money," she said finally, with a weight that Rachel felt in her bones.

---

When Rachel said she wanted to keep things professional, Nathan thought he knew what that meant. It was no more late-night text messages. It was scheduled meetings instead of stopping by. They'd been working together a week and for the most part, he'd been doing okay. Daytime-only texts. Plus, that one video call to show her a messed-up Dixieland mural so they could debate whether all censorship was technically bad. But that was all work related. He really was, actually, doing fine.

But then Rachel brought him cake.

She stopped by late, after the sip and see, and the laundromat was empty. It took him a minute to spot her hovering near the door, backlit by a streetlight, and holding a small Tupperware container. The dress she wore was something out of a dream—like spun sugar, tied at the neck, and swirling around her thighs.

"Sorry to just stop by."

"It's okay," he'd said quickly. "I'm, uh…" He trailed off, gesturing toward the office like that would explain that he'd been fucking around on YouTube. "It's fine."

"I brought you cake," she said, and looked embarrassed. There was no way to fit this into the just-business framework she'd created.

"What kind is it?"

She smiled one of her rarest smiles. Pure joy that brightened the room. "I don't know," she said and laughed. "I left the party before I could try any."

He got forks from upstairs. They ate the lemon raspberry cake slowly, leaning on their elbows at a folding table. She told him about the party, and he told her about playing LEGO with his nephew, the whole time thinking, *Yes this. This is the way we should be.* She smelled like expensive perfume and cigars. It made him want to press her against the table and breathe her in.

They were stretching out the time, taking smaller mouthfuls and longer pauses between bites. Once the cake was gone, he tried to think of something that would stop her from leaving. But all he said was "Thanks for stopping by," like some clueless jackass with better things to do. For the rest of the night, Nathan picked at the scab of that moment, imagining all the ways he could have persuaded her to stay.

He was used to being alone. It was how he'd spent most of his life. But Rachel had slipped into his daily routine when he wasn't paying attention. Now, he couldn't go an hour without sending her a message. He was lucky that the increasing demands of the gala gave him an excuse to be in constant communication with her. The event had been sold out for weeks. Publicity requests seemed to take up more of his time than working on the art they were trying to sell. Which didn't matter much, since so far, the only "work" he'd done was cursing himself while staring at a blank canvas and blowing off the freewriting exercises Rachel recommended to draw cheesy doodles of her name.

He was actually relieved when his mother called the next morning and asked if he'd do a last-minute photoshoot for some DC society magazine he'd never heard of. Nathan wore a white T-shirt and jeans, while Sofia posed in a fuchsia blazer with one hand on his shoulder, staring down the camera as her hair billowed in artificial wind. The photographer told Nathan to fold his arms and show his tattoos. "We like the contrast," the jittery British man said. "Elegance meets street, or something. Maybe glare a bit more, and lift your chin so—"

"Excuse me," Sofia said. "Could you shut up and take the picture."

The guy clammed up after that and took a break.

"Thank you for doing this," she said to Nathan.

"I was surprised you asked. I know you didn't want to pick me for the gala."

Her eyes shot to his. "Excuse me?"

"This is a big deal. You had a right to be anxious about them choosing me."

"Because I thought they were pressuring you. Joe put you on the spot in front of all those people and I didn't want you to feel obligated." She paused. "Being associated with me and my work can be difficult. I'm an easy target and I didn't want my critics aiming at you too."

Nathan had seen the snide comments online about corruption and nepotism. His family was accused of using their money to buy corporate-friendly congressional seats. He'd ignored it because, honestly, some of it was true. And the worst stuff wasn't even aimed at him.

"Rachel's helping me tune out the noise and focus on the work. I'll be fine."

Her mouth twisted. "Rachel? Not Mrs. Abbott?"

"That's not her name."

Sofia pulled out a small gold compact from her purse and rubbed away a smear of lipstick. "That woman can be so difficult to read. Has been since she moved here. It's unnerving."

"You can be intimidating."

Sofia snorted. "I doubt she's intimidated by much. Did you see the dress she wore to our anniversary party? Looked like she'd skinned a calf. And then she needled her way into curating for the gala. So manipulative." She shrugged. "I almost admire it."

He had to change the subject before his desire to defend Rachel overrode his common sense. Beto could be ruthless, but that was all-business. When it came to her sons, Sofia had a vicious streak that was extremely personal.

Nathan never brought anyone home, so his dates were spared Sofia's venom. Joe always looked like a soldier recounting war stories whenever the subject of Mia meeting Sofia came up. "Mom hates the Williams family. And me loving Mia made her hate them even more."

Zara hadn't fared any better, though she definitely tried harder to win Sofia over. She always arrived with a gift, something expensive and handcrafted that she'd picked up while she was filming. Nathan remembered the year she'd invited them all to Brooklyn for New Year's and served six courses on an elaborately decorated table that was supposed to represent tranquility and rebirth. As soon as she left the room, Sofia righted a crooked candle and told Joe that his wife was trying too hard. "It's supposed to look effortless, but we can all see the seams."

Nathan wasn't interested in hearing his mother go in on Rachel, so he quickly changed the subject. "How's Beto doing?"

She pulled out her makeup compact again. He was starting to understand its function better now: a fancy fidget spinner. "Your father is your father. He works. I never see him."

"Have you talked to him about it? Asked him to spend more time with you? Or to—"

"To what? Become the sort of dying man who counts his blessings? I'm not a magician, Nathaniel. Just the wife." She ran a hand up and down his arm. "I'd rather focus on my boys."

Abuelita used to tell Nathan not to believe his own eyes when it came to his mother. "I told your father not to trust a novela actress. Only a fool marries a woman who pretends to fall in love for a living." She would grab her crucifix and rub it, like she was warding off the memory. "He didn't listen. And he chose her, over me, every time."

Sometimes, Nathan thought that was what his mother feared most: that stealing someone's son created a debt you eventually repaid by losing your own.

# CHAPTER FOURTEEN

Before Matt was launched into the public eye, the average person had probably never heard of the Abbotts, despite being on a *Forbes* list of America's Richest Families. If it was up to Matt's parents, things probably would have stayed that way. People with generational wealth understood the power of anonymity. They knew that shady offshore accounts and tax loopholes only mattered to anyone if *you* mattered to anyone. There were levels of invisibility: ignored and undetected. The Abbotts preferred being the latter.

Matt, as the spoiled first son, tended to flail when he wasn't the center of attention. Rachel had seen that side of him when they were dating, when he'd grow irritable around her café friends, who were never as impressed with him as he needed them to be. But back then, she didn't consider it a red flag. She thought he wasn't loved enough. But as the years wore on, she realized that it was entitlement. It was living in a world that was constantly rearranged to accommodate your seat at the table.

If Rachel was given anything resembling a seat by the Abbotts, it was an uncomfortable stool, wedged in a dark corner with a wobbly leg that constantly threatened to throw her off-balance. But Faith was different. She had come into the Abbotts' lives still young and impressionable. Maybe they liked the idea of molding her into the perfect Black Abbott since Rachel had too much baggage to be comfortably claimed. Or maybe they wanted a parenting do-over—to feel like they could love a child without ruining them. They doted on her in ways that, according to Matt, they never extended to their own children. They showed up at boring dance recitals and bought cookies they wouldn't eat to support her fundraisers. They threw elaborate birthday parties with Disney characters in the middle of their formal dining room. For Faith, they didn't just offer a chair at the Abbott table, they threw the whole dining set out and built a new one.

During Faith's weekend visit, Rachel and Matt had executed a carefully choreographed avoidance routine in which they were never together in the same room with her for long. By Sunday they'd run out of excuses, and Faith wouldn't accept the campaign or the gala as a reason for skipping an Abbott family dinner. The fifteen-minute drive was torture. Matt announced that he was in the mood for car karaoke, something they hadn't done since Faith was twelve. He cranked up Billy Joel to earsplitting levels and warbled "Piano Man" while Faith lip-synched along out of pity.

All of the Abbotts had dressed in their usual uniforms to attend the dinner in Faith's honor. Matilda was the unimpressed academic matriarch, dressed in beige layers from head to toe, as though her massive brain couldn't be bothered to deal with color coordination. She never wore jewelry or accessories because, like everything else, they made her bored and impatient. She greeted Matt and Rachel with a half-hearted gesture that could have been either a wave or dismissal. Faith, however, was given eye contact and asked whether she was old enough for a cocktail.

Ben was the emo poet who was too busy pondering the mortal coil to greet anyone. He stood in a dark corner, wearing a dark suit, and watched them all through dark eyes and an even darker expression. His glass was filled with whiskey that he sipped slowly while glowering at his older brother. He tried to catch Rachel's eye, but she avoided his gaze, and was relieved when Faith finally coaxed him into playing a game of chess.

Almost an hour later, Herman appeared, wearing the Russian doll of Abbott costumes—the starched shirt and tailored pants of a powerful patriarch, beneath a gray cashmere cardigan with a rolled collar that shouted, "Dad!" at the top of its lungs. With his steel-colored eyes, and gash of a smile that bared all his teeth, he looked like a shark trying to convince everyone he was a guppy. The room quieted and leaned in at his arrival.

"I'm so glad you all could be here," he said. "We need to get together more often. Thank you, Faith, for giving us an excuse to do that." He bared his teeth again. "I think the food is ready. Matilda?"

She sipped a vodka tonic while gazing at the faceless figures in a large Tomoo Gokita hanging above the fireplace. Long, awkward seconds ticked by before she realized everyone was staring. "I'm sorry, what?"

"The food," Herman said.

"What about it?"

"Do you think it's done?"

She stared at her husband for a long beat. "I think you should ask the person who's cooking it, don't you?"

Herman's eyes narrowed. Matilda's face remained placid and serene. Rachel stood with a raised hand. "I'll go check." It was the best way to handle these dinners. Keep your hands full and try to look busy. Herman protested, but Matilda cut him off with a bored drawl.

"Oh god, let her do it."

Rachel moved down the hallway, putting the escalating argument between Matilda and Herman about whether he was merely sexist or a raging misogynist behind her. She spotted an abandoned cart covered with silver serving dishes and raised a lid to reveal a brothy soup. She took a picture and sent it as a reply to Nathan's earlier text asking what she was eating for dinner.

**Nathan:** Could be the lighting, but I'm pretty sure that needs salt.

**Rachel:** Ha ha. Well, what are you eating?

"Are you texting Julia?" She jumped at the sound of Ben's voice. He stared at her phone. "Is that why you're sneaking back here?"

She dimmed her screen. "I'm not sneaking. And no. Though I did hire her. I told her everything and she's working on it."

He relaxed. "Everything? Including the deal you struck with my brother?"

"What the hell are you two doing?" Ben flinched and turned to face Matt. Rachel closed her eyes and willed the ceiling to cave in. When she opened them, Matt was frothing at the mouth. "What did you tell him?"

Rachel started to speak, but Ben cut her off. "She needed help. You were railroading her."

Matt laughed. "Is that what she said? Rachel, tell him whose idea this was."

She opened her mouth, but Ben spoke over her again. "I'm sure she didn't force you to fuck someone else."

"That's not—you know, I don't have to explain myself to you. This is between me and my wife."

"Don't call me that," Rachel hissed, and then looked at Ben. "And while I appreciate your help, I don't need you to fight my battles for me." She heard footsteps and looked over their shoulders. Faith turned the corner and stopped short at the sight of them gathered around the cart.

"Um, the Russian woman with the apron said dinner is ready. Also, who is she? And why am I a little afraid of her?"

Rachel spent the next three courses dodging Matt's eyes while he did his best to avoid his brother's glares. Matilda and Herman were too busy offering unsolicited advice about which Ivy League graduate program Faith should attend to notice the tension.

Matt wanted Faith to take a break. "You've been in school a long time, sweetheart. It's okay to live a little." He patted her hand, and Faith leaned over to rest her head on his shoulder. Watching him continue to excel at being a loving stepfather was torture. Rachel looked down at her barely touched plate, searching for something to stab with her fork.

Matilda filled her wineglass to the rim. "Is that what you called postponing the bar exam, Matt? Breathing?" She leaned back in her chair. "It looked more like hyperventilation."

Herman touched her arm. "Tilda—"

"No, Dad, let her vent," Matt said. He gestured toward her glass. "Finish your wine and keep recycling the same boring stories. I'm waiting for the part when you admit to preferring those grad students over your own children."

"That's not true," Matilda said. "All of you are tedious. They're just better read." She stood up, grabbed the wine bottle, and walked out of the room.

Matt looked at Ben. "You should go after her."

Ben blinked, like he'd been asleep the whole time. "Me? Why?"

"You're her favorite."

"That's a low bar. And you're the one who called her a drunk."

Faith kept her head bowed to hide her grimace. She used to compare their dinners to Real Housewives reunions. Rachel's theory was that the Abbotts needed to argue because without it they wouldn't know what to say to each other. Rehashing petty conflicts was the closest thing to a love language this family had. One of the many gifts of shedding the Abbott name would be avoiding a front-row seat to the way they tore each other to pieces.

She pulled out her phone to check the time and saw Nathan's reply. His name on her screen was like a beacon guiding her to an Abbott-free shore.

**Nathan:** You should swing by and see for yourself. I'm here until ten.

It was almost nine. She looked around the room, and no one was paying her any attention. She looked at the text again, the address he'd sent. Her heart was pounding. She shouldn't leave. But she couldn't stay.

Faith pushed away from the table. "I have to go."

Everyone stopped speaking. Herman cleared his throat. "So soon?"

"I promised a friend I would stop by before my train leaves tomorrow." She looked at Rachel. "You said you would drop me off, remember?"

Rachel stood quickly. "Yes. Sorry, I forgot about that. We'll be late if we don't head out. Matt, you can get a ride, right?"

When they got into the car, Rachel froze with her finger on the ignition. "I have a thing to take care of. For the gala. Did you want me to take you home?"

"You can drop me off at Alesha's. I'm still hungry and she made gumbo." Faith paused. "Is something going on with you and Matt?"

Deep down, Rachel knew this was coming. All the clever scheduling in the world couldn't hide the rancid air in their house. "Why do you ask?"

"It's kind of obvious," Faith said. "He's always attentive, but this weekend he was hovering. And buying me stuff I didn't need. Why do I have a sleeping bag now? I can't take that on the train."

"I'll take care of it." Rachel took a deep breath. "And you're right, there is something going on that I'm not ready to talk about yet. But you and Matt are fine. You always will be."

"How bad is it?"

Rachel tried to smile, but her mouth trembled with the effort. "Nothing I can't handle."

Faith fell silent, studying Rachel's face. "I know you're strong, Mom. But if you can't talk to me, promise you'll find someone else to confide in. Someone who cares enough to really listen."

As Rachel promised, she realized that the person who immediately came to mind was someone her daughter would never approve of. Faith had called her strong, but watching her walk up the stairs to Alesha's house, Rachel felt weaker than she had in years.

The address Nathan sent was on a street in Southeast DC she'd never been to before. It was a redbrick building, with *Annabelle's* written on the window in gold letters. The sign read CLOSED, but there were lights on inside. She saw Nathan's car next to a small Toyota with a Bi Pride flag on the bumper.

Rachel started to check her hair, but then stopped herself. It was easier to pretend this was nothing if she didn't care how she looked while doing it. But when Nathan opened the door, the wattage of his smile made her wish she would have at least reapplied her lipstick.

"Didn't think you'd come," he said.

"Curiosity got the best of me. I've never heard of this place."

"My friend Bobbi works here. Come on in."

The kitchen lights were on, but the dining room was still dark enough that Rachel stumbled over a chair. Nathan steadied her, telling her to be careful. She wanted to laugh. Like he wasn't the real hazard.

Rap music blared from a phone, and the sound of pots and pans warred with shouts across the kitchen. Nathan introduced her to a tall East Asian woman with keenly observant eyes. She took in Rachel's wool pants and silk blouse, then lingered on the pearls around her neck in a way that made Rachel feel uptight and ancient. "There's grease flying all over this place," Bobbi said. "I'll get you an apron."

Rachel pointed to Bobbi's *Annabelle's* T-shirt. "I'll take one of those if there are any extras lying around." Bobbi's expression warmed, and she led Rachel to a small office with piles of branded swag. By the time they rejoined Nathan, Rachel was swimming in her new T-shirt. She had also peppered Bobbi with enough questions to learn how long they'd been friends, and how successful Bobbi thought Nathan could be if he believed in himself. The affection woven through her voice was obvious. Knowing he had someone like Bobbi looking out for him eased a worry Rachel hadn't realized was there.

"I saw him whining about your food earlier," Bobbi said. "Nathan's my guinea pig for new recipes, so I probably created this picky-eating monster."

"It's called standards." He nodded at Rachel. "She's picky too. Just less vocal."

"My daughter is at the Institute of Culinary Education," Rachel explained. "I'm sure it's the same with your family. They know just enough to be a chef's worst nightmare."

Bobbi glanced at Nathan. "Oh, I never went to culinary school."

Rachel's face heated. "I'm sorry. I didn't—"

"It's fine. Lots of people make that mistake, but it usually comes after

they've eaten my food. Because I'm fucking brilliant." She smiled imp-
ishly and winked at Nathan. "Like this one and his art."

Nathan rolled his eyes. "Okay..."

"You're right. He is brilliant," Rachel said softly. Their gazes caught
in a brief tangle and slid away. She leaned forward to peek at Bobbi's
cutting board. "Are you making catfish?"

"Yeah. This place is southern fine dining. Fancy grits and shit." She
picked up a jar of cayenne pepper. "Nathan says you like things spicy."

"Nuclear," Nathan corrected. Bobbi added it to the fish batter, and
Nathan signaled that she should add more. Soon they were dividing
up the labor—Bobbi handled seasoning while Rachel cooked the fish.
Nathan made a roux for macaroni and cheese and laughed when Rachel
told him to sprinkle cayenne in the sauce.

"Your tongue is Teflon."

She propped a hand on her hip. "Well, you have toddler taste buds."

Nathan smiled and brushed a bit of cornmeal from her shoulder. "No,
just a little sensitive. But that's a good thing, right?"

Rachel stared at him, suspended in a heady moment that she knew
was fragile and fleeting. For the span of a breath, she felt pure longing.
To be someone else. To fully belong here, in this moment. To be able to
reach up and straighten his collar without caring if anyone saw. Because
he was hers.

It was torture, daydreaming of a different life, one with close friend-
ships and trust. And love. Everything she wanted but couldn't have.

Bobbi had stopped cooking to stare at them. She'd seen everything.
She'd probably figured it all out the minute Rachel stepped into the
kitchen.

"I should probably go," Rachel said, overwhelmed. "It's getting late."

Nathan frowned. "But the food's not done."

"I'm sorry." She gave Bobbi an apologetic smile. "I promise to stop
by some other time."

She started to leave, but Nathan blocked her path. "It's dark. Can I
at least walk you to your car?"

They left together in silence. Nathan opened the driver's side door, but held it ajar. "I get it now," he blurted, like he was afraid she'd leave before he could finish. "Why you love taking pictures."

He was close enough to warm the air between them. Rachel kept her eyes fixed somewhere between his neck and shoulder. "You do?"

"Yeah." He didn't speak until she met his eyes again. "Looking at the world through that lens makes you notice things. Shapes. Colors. Change a setting, and you see something else. Something you might have missed if you weren't paying attention." He hesitated, like he was still debating his next words. "I don't think I ever did that before. Paid attention. Appreciated things." He paused, studying her face. "I wanted to say thank you."

A surge of tenderness tightened her throat. She couldn't speak. Instead she nodded and attempted a small smile that trembled and dissolved as she climbed into the car. Nathan closed her door and stepped back with folded arms, as if he was holding himself in place.

---

"Try not to fuck the mayor's wife."

Nathan nearly choked on a piece of fish. Bobbi didn't look up at his sputtering and continued stirring a pot of mustard greens with her usual, mildly irritated resting face. He'd suspected that inviting Rachel over wasn't a good idea. Now he knew it was aggressively stupid. Bobbi could read him like a book, and this one was filthy.

"Excuse me?" He did his best to sound offended.

"You heard me." She took a bite of greens and grimaced. "Too salty."

He tapped the table for attention. "Bobbi, come on."

She sighed and added lemon juice. "It's obvious. The fact that she came all the way out here to stir mac and cheese says a lot. And your face does this thing when you talk to her. All dreamy and tense at the same time. It's totally you when you're into someone."

Excellent. He was doing a piss-poor job of hiding his feelings and that was probably why Rachel left so fast. Though to be fair, she wasn't doing a great job at hiding anything either. Talking taste buds and sensitive tongues, swaying into him like a flower seeking light. "There's nothing going on," Nathan lied. Fumbling. Flailing.

"Okay, fine," Bobbi said. "Pretend if you want, but like I said, I know you. Every other word out of your mouth is Rachel. Rachel said. Rachel thinks. Rachel, Rachel, Rachel. The only other time I've seen you like this was when you were sixteen and your dad said you couldn't have that old Mustang. It made you obsessed."

"I don't know how you get from me wanting a car to me fucking Rachel Abbott."

"*Not* fucking her, remember? You've never coped well with being told you can't have something. And I'm sure you understand that you cannot have someone else's wife."

Nathan protested, listing reasons why it made complete sense for Rachel to be on his mind: They were working together. They were friends. Real friends, and he didn't make those anymore. Rachel understood him. Talking to her was like finally finding someone who spoke the same language.

"Don't you feel that way too? When you meet someone who loves food as much as you do. Something just falls into place."

Bobbi's eyes grew wider while he talked. She covered her mouth with both hands and peered at him over her fingers. "Holy shit, Nettles. This is so much worse than I thought. Are you in love with her?"

"What? No! *No.* I barely know her." He was speaking too fast and too loud, but he needed his gut to listen to his brain for once. Rachel had secrets. Things she kept hidden from him on purpose. Love didn't work that way. You didn't fall for pieces of someone and gamble on the rest. Love should be sure. Some enlightened knowing. This was a roller coaster he'd never asked to be on in the first place.

Bobbi, convinced she'd solved the mystery of his secret girlfriend, was insufferable the rest of the night. She kept asking questions about his art for the gala, and with every mention of the event, Nathan's mood got progressively darker. He'd taken hundreds of photographs and still painted nothing. There wasn't much time left. Which also meant there wasn't much time left with Rachel. That particular thought stole his appetite completely. He had to leave.

The next day, he woke up and decided to stay away from Rachel for a while. No more camera lessons. No more flirting. He pulled out his sketchbooks and some of the photos he'd taken and opened his laptop to play videos on rendering realistic motion in a scene. With everything spread over his table, he looked productive even if he didn't feel that way. He was trying to figure out how to use a French press he didn't know he owned, when he got a text.

**Rachel:** We need to talk. Can you come over?

---

Rachel's house belonged in an old movie. The white siding, black shutters, and wraparound porch reminded Nathan of some small-town drama with tense conversations in rocking chairs over lemonade. Large pink roses lined the foundation. When he stepped up to the front door, the tinkling sound of wind chimes floated toward him. It was the type of place you would expect a mayor to live, quietly opulent but also generic and inoffensive—a politician's dream.

The door swung open. Rachel leaned against the frame with a cocktail in one hand, looking like she'd just rolled out of bed. Her light pink dress was a slightly longer version of his T-shirt. The thin fabric skimmed her body close enough to make out everything underneath. Curvy hips. Thick thighs. She wasn't wearing makeup or shoes. Or a bra. He snatched his eyes back up to her face and cleared his throat.

She stepped back and waved him inside. "Do you want a drink? The kitchen is this way."

"No, I'm good."

She started walking like she didn't hear him. He followed and let his eyes roam on the way. The house was bigger than it looked from outside. It was also aggressively clean. He hated that about his parents' house. It always had to be photo ready. Growing up, there were never any toys left on the floor, or even a speck of dust left on a windowsill. He thought homes should have clutter and dust. Lived in, not maintained like a museum.

"This isn't working," Rachel announced as they reached the kitchen. His stomach plummeted. How often did he reach out to her now—five, six times a day? She probably thought he was obsessed.

Rachel poured a finger of bourbon into her glass. "You still haven't finished anything, have you?"

Nathan's heart settled back into his chest. "No, I haven't." He pictured the pile of false starts in his apartment. None of it felt honest. That was the only thing he knew he wanted. His name next to something true.

She slid the glass in his direction. "How do you usually get inspired?"

He swirled the bourbon around and watched the light filter through the liquid. "Read the Phoenix books again."

"Right. But you were drawing before you read those. What inspired you then?"

Nathan hesitated. "Not much. I bought into that toxic, macho bullshit in boarding school. Paints were for girls. Real men didn't know indigo from violet. I joined the wrestling team in high school, and I don't even like sports. My coach hated me. And I was angry all the time. It came from that."

One night, after losing a match, he'd picked up a chair and slammed it against the wall until it splintered. It felt good enough to scare him. "I quit the team, bought a sketch pad, and drew a bunch of raging, fucked-up shit that I burned as soon as it was finished."

He took a drink and tried to clear it from his head. He hated going back there. He wasn't that guy anymore, but he had been once, which meant that he could be again.

"I don't want to have to be angry to make something real," he said. These days, she was his only inspiration. Her laugh. Her smile. The dark glisten of her sweaty skin against his sheets. He could trace it all from memory onto his canvas.

Nathan drained his drink. She topped off her own glass, eyes moist with pity, like she'd discovered a limping puppy.

"Hey. It's fine," he said. "Ancient history."

"Right. When's the last time you saw an exhibit?" She snatched up the glass he just put down and returned it to the kitchen island.

Jesus, she was wound tight; the glass didn't even have a chance to sweat. "Never."

She stopped to stare at him. "Not even a museum?"

"No." He paused, thinking back. "Maybe on a field trip once. But I'm pretty sure it was dinosaur fossils, that kind of thing."

She set the glass on the island. "Are you seriously telling me you've never been to MoMA? The Met? The Portrait Gallery? Nothing?"

"It's not really my thing, Rachel."

"How would you know? The walls of those places speak to you. It's impossible not to be inspired."

He disagreed. There wasn't anything inspiring about random paint splotches dribbled on a canvas. But just talking about those places had her glowing. Visiting one would probably make her radiant. Two hundred miles from Oasis Springs, he'd be free to enjoy it, uninterrupted. "So, let's go!" He threw out the suggestion, watering the faint hope of being alone with her until it sprouted and bloomed. "We can drive up to New York and you can show me around MoMA."

The glow dimmed. "I can't—" She paused, and chewed her lip for two agonizing seconds, before nodding to herself. "You know what? Yes. Let's do it. How's this weekend?"

"Good!" Nathan said, trying to rein in his enthusiasm, even though his greedy heart was still spinning. "It's great. It'll be fun."

She nodded and touched an empty glass. "Would you like another drink?"

He glanced at a clock. "It's five thirty. I should probably slow down."

She blinked and shook her head. "You're right. It is early, I'm sorry. I wasn't thinking." She poured the rest of her drink down the sink, flipped on the faucet, and chased everything with an aggressive wipe-down using a dishcloth that she threw in a small basket next to the refrigerator.

"What's wrong?"

"What?" She blinked like he was shining a flashlight in her face. "I'm okay."

"You don't look okay."

She touched her ponytail. "Excuse me for relaxing in my own home."

"I'm not talking about your hair. I like your hair. I like—" *Every inch of you.* "Did Matt—" The name was acid in his throat. "Did he do something to you?"

"No. I'm fine." She inhaled sharply. "Could you move that back, please?"

Nathan frowned, realizing that he'd been absently fiddling with a porcelain bird figurine. It was part of a collection that lined the table beside him.

"Sorry." He put it down.

She shook her head. "Not there."

He looked at it again and realized how ugly it was. It was a robin redbreast, covered with a glossy sheen that gave off *Flowers in the Attic* vibes. "Are these yours?"

"They belonged to Matt's dead aunt," she said. "His mother looks in on them whenever she stops by."

Nathan nodded. "Got it, right." He took the bird, walked across the kitchen, and set it on the counter. "You should throw that thing in the trash."

A startled laugh burst from her throat. "Why?"

"Because it's ugly. It also stresses you out. Who gives a shit if it's a millimeter to the left?"

"I like things a certain way."

"I think *need* is more accurate." He pointed to the figurine. "I dare you to leave it right here. Or at least two millimeters away from where it should be. All night—don't move it, don't even look at it."

She walked around the counter to face him. The top of her ponytail barely reached his chin. He looked down and got an eyeful of bright red toenails. What would people think if they saw her like this? Barefoot and tipsy. Vulnerable.

"You're making fun of me," she said.

"Never." He grinned. "A little."

"I don't do dares."

"You mean you don't win them." He tapped the bird's head with one finger. "That's surprising. I thought you were a low-key suburban badass."

Her lips twitched as she fought a smile. "Now you're trying to provoke me."

Her fingers darted toward the bird. He snatched it away, laughing, and grabbed her wrist. "Cheater."

Her eyes fell to his lips. He wondered if she realized how often she did that—stared at his mouth like she was desperate for him to kiss her.

"I'm not playing a game," she whispered.

Nathan tugged her closer and brought her hand to his chest. Her fingers splayed against his heart. She had to know what being this close to her did to him.

"Neither am I."

# CHAPTER FIFTEEN

That second drink was a mistake. It was working inside her, alchemizing with the lust rushing through her veins. She was warm, but Nathan was burning. He cradled her neck, thumb to her pulse, then gave her a look that was yearning and haunted, like an ache.

Rachel knew what falling in love felt like. The beats were as instinctual as holding a camera. She could go months without taking a photo, but her hands would know what her mind had forgotten. Just like her heart. Last night, she'd tossed and turned, rehashing all her choices. Love wasn't a free fall; it was surrender.

"Why did you bring me here?" Nathan whispered.

She pulled his hand away and stepped back. "I'm sorry. I shouldn't have done that."

Nathan swayed, unsteady. "Rachel—"

"You're too young. And I'm still—" She couldn't bring herself to complete the thought. She didn't feel married. She felt like a prisoner promised early release for good behavior. "My life is a mess. It isn't fair for you to be a part of it."

A harsh laugh erupted from his throat. "Like I'm not already?" He moved forward, closing the distance she created. "I think about you all the fucking time. And not just—" He swallowed hard. "I'm no good at this. Every time I think I'm okay with how we left it, that I've gotten it together, you take me apart. Who was I before I met you?"

Her eyes filled. "Don't say that. Please—"

"Look at me." He cupped her face in both hands. "I'm not too young. I'm *not* a mistake. I just want you to see me."

She heard a soft click and the creak of a door swinging open.

Rachel pushed him away and stepped back a moment before Matt appeared in the doorway. She caught a glimpse of herself in a mirror on the far wall. Her eyes were still glassy from too much bourbon.

"There you are," Matt grumbled. It sounded like an accusation—as if she'd failed the moment he realized she wasn't where he'd left her. "Have you seen the *Post* today?"

"No, I haven't," Rachel said. The intensity of the interrupted moment still lingered, cutting through her voice. Nathan had backed away, and Matt hadn't moved far enough into the kitchen to realize they weren't alone. Matt unlocked his phone and glared at the oversized screen. "*The 'Inevitability' of Mayor Abbott.*" His eyes flicked up. "*Inevitability* is in quotation marks. Your aunt wrote this. This isn't that puff piece of yours on the school."

"It wasn't my puff piece," Rachel said, praying that Nathan wouldn't move closer. She could feel his gaze prickle along her skin. Even the room smelled incriminating—like liquor and guilt.

Matt squinted at the screen. "*A blue blood prince raised on the spoils of a capitalist oligarch dynasty that he hides in the footnotes of his press releases like a dirty secret.*" He looked up, seeking support for his outrage. "This last part. Now this takes the cake. *Don't be fooled by his sleight of hand. He's not a progressive. He's a Democrat. There is a difference.*" He sighed. "She hates me."

Matt moved farther into the kitchen and blinked when he spotted Nathan. "Sorry. There was a car outside, but I thought it was another decorator Rachel hired for the house. Nathaniel, right?"

"Nathan," he corrected.

"Right," Matt said, nodding. "How is, uh…how's your family?"

Nathan leaned back against the counter and gripped the edge with both hands. "They're fine."

"Great." Matt was still nodding, the strained conversation thinning his voice. They eyed each other until the tension was stifling. Rachel cleared her throat.

"We were discussing Nathan's gala pieces."

"Of course," Matt said. "Makes sense." His eyes skimmed her shirt-dress. "I'll leave you to it. The team's stopping by in an hour to trouble-shoot the article in the dining room." He glanced at Nathan, flashing a tight smile. "Say hello to your mother for me. Her last donation was incredibly generous."

Nathan didn't respond, and Matt didn't wait to be acknowledged. He lifted the phone to his ear and walked out of the kitchen. Rachel's body slacked with relief as she watched him leave. She glanced at Nathan. "Lenora will be back any minute. She'll come straight here, and—"

"We need to talk." He made it sound inescapable, a ticking bomb about to go off.

———————

If Nathan were more like Joe, he probably would have outlined all the reasons they could work as a couple. They would plan everything together. Her divorce. Their new life. Thieves plotting an escape route. But instead, Nathan's thoughts were scattered, incomplete sentences piling on top of each other in a mental junkyard. He just wanted to tell her how he felt, that she didn't have to go through any of it alone.

Rachel led him to a small guesthouse near the back of the property. Dust floated into the air, and the only furniture was a writing desk and two unused chairs. He spotted a large box marked *Rachel's Photographs* next to a camera bag and tripod.

"This was supposed to be my studio," Rachel said. "But after Matt got elected, we decided it would be my First Lady's office, which was a joke. Now it's storage."

He pointed to the box. "Can I see?"

She pulled out a photo book and flipped the pages. "I put them in chronological order so I could see improvement. It made me want to push myself. Keep getting better."

He paged through slowly, studying every photo. When he was done, he pointed to another large portfolio case. "What's in that one?"

"My senior thesis." She grew solemn as she opened it. It was a photo collage with a small white label that read *Fast Girls*. The photos formed an X on the canvas. At first, he saw only bare arms and legs in various shades of brown. Then he looked closer and noticed hands resting on bare hips and breasts. Ambient light licked their skin and made their bodies glisten. His chest tightened, like he was seeing something he shouldn't, but he didn't want to turn away. "Jesus. Rachel, this is amazing."

"My professor had a rule that prohibited real or simulated sex in our final projects. And I knew that. But I'd had this idea stuck in my head, and I had to do it. It felt wrong not to, like I'd be betraying myself if I didn't. So I turned it in." She looked at the collage like someone might look at their child: a prideful *I made that*. But then she swiped a hard hand over her eyes and looked away. "I got an incomplete," she said. "And an email about professionalism that I forwarded to the student paper. It sparked this huge debate on college campuses about censorship versus academic freedom. And then my dad got sick, so I had to leave. The incomplete became an F and I never graduated."

"You never got your degree?"

She shook her head, a small, stiff motion that looked more like flinching. "That's who I was back then. Someone who would wreck her own career prospects to get what she wanted."

Nathan knew what she was trying to say. He could list a dozen reasons why their situation was different, but he couldn't compete with that soft waver in her voice. You can't rationalize your way out of fear.

She touched his hand. "You said earlier that you wanted me to see you."

Nathan shook his head. "We don't have to talk about that right now."

She leaned closer, scanning his face, and whispered, "I *see* you," directly into his heart. That's when Nathan stopped fighting. He stopped pretending that he wasn't hopelessly in love with this woman. He lifted her hand and trailed kisses over her fingers, knuckle by knuckle, bracing himself for what he knew was coming.

"And I want you. But wanting something doesn't mean you should have it." She pulled her hand away. "I won't let you make the same mistake I did. You could lose everything," she said. He knew that by *everything*, she meant the show, the press, and the possibility that this could lead to an actual career. But she was also saying they weren't worth it. That he should ignore how sitting this close made his body feel like it would crack and burn. How could she look at him as if he were oxygen one minute and hold her breath the next?

"Do you want me to stay away?" he asked. "Is that what you need?" She looked so panicked at the suggestion that he added quickly, "Or we can be friends." It was a lie, but she knew that, right? He could hear the desperation in his voice. "I'm a good listener, remember?"

The way she looked at him and nodded—she knew. This was a Band-Aid over a gaping wound.

———————

Rachel's photos were original prints. Nathan offered to scan them into digital files, because it seemed like something a "friend" would do. He also wanted a chance to look through them at his own pace. Three days of sifting through the photos in his apartment introduced him to a younger Rachel, with devious grins and long languid limbs draped in clothes that typically left something bare. He thought about that collage, and the way her professor had shamed her for submitting it. The woman in those pictures wasn't ashamed of anything. She was the center of the universe. Combustive. She leaned into the camera with a cigarette in one hand, laughing so hard it made her eyes squint. This was the woman at the drive-in. Buried and resurrected through pain. The woman he loved.

Nathan was interrupted by a knock on his door. He opened it and stood motionless, staring at Beto on his stair landing, waiting to be let inside. Beto's gruff voice snapped him out of his trance. "Are you going to invite me in?"

His father strolled around and studied each component of Nathan's apartment like a landlord conducting an inspection. He stopped occasionally to glare at something that irritated him. The leather couch was too flashy and the PlayStation was too childish. The drawing table, however, was ignored.

"It's a nice place," Beto said. "I wasn't sure what to expect with the, uh…" He snapped his fingers and pointed to the floor.

"The laundromat?"

"Yeah, downstairs. One of my cousins had a place over his bodega. Looked like a storeroom with a mattress on the floor. But that's never been your style." He glanced at the closet. "Nice car, fancy shoes. Didn't run away from everything, did you?"

Nathan ignored the criticism. He wasn't a teenager with an allowance anymore. He had brokerage accounts and a financial advisor, which meant he didn't have to justify his spending habits to his father. "Why are you here?"

"I was driving by and saw your car outside. Figured I'd say hello."

"I've lived here for eight years. You've never stopped by before."

He shrugged. "Yeah, well, I never had cancer before either."

Nathan couldn't argue with that. They sank into an awkward silence, both at a loss for what to say next. "Do you want to sit down?" Nathan asked. "Have a drink?"

"A drink would be nice." Beto paused and added, "Thank you," like he'd been invited to a tea party.

Nathan walked into the kitchen and hesitated. "Uh…water?"

"Booze, Nathaniel."

"Right." Nathan grabbed a bottle of bourbon and poured generously.

"What's all this? You taking pictures now?" Beto was staring at the photos. Nathan wasn't sure if his father knew Rachel well enough to recognize her twenty-year-old self.

"Just doing a favor for a friend," Nathan said, handing over the drink.

His father took a sip and sat on the couch. "Lady friend?"

Nathan sat and did his best not to look at the photos. "It's a woman, yeah."

"Amazing how helpful we are when there's a pretty girl involved."

Beto settled into the couch and crossed his legs. It was jarring for Nathan to see his father relax in his living room. Beto always seemed guarded, like he could never trust a good thing to stay good. This version, with his easy smile, was a stranger. "Did I ever tell you how I met your mother?"

Nathan sipped his drink before answering. "I think Mom told us about it once."

Beto waved his hand. "That's her story. I never told you mine."

"Is there a difference?"

"When two people fall in love?" Beto smiled that crooked smile everyone said was identical to Nathan's. "Always."

According to Sofia, Beto was the opposite of the man she thought she'd marry. He was cocky and arrogant, two unattractive traits to his mother, who was admittedly vain and wanted all the attention. When Beto finally proposed, too soon and with an enormous princess-cut ring that she hated, it took a while for her to say yes. "Not because I didn't want to. But because I knew I would say yes to everything after. It's frightening to love someone that much."

"She was dating someone else when we met," Beto said. "Nelson something. White guy with big teeth. I think they were veneers, but she swears to this day they were his. She had this guy ready to propose. But one look at them together and I knew she wasn't in love with him." Beto drained the last of his bourbon and tapped the glass. "You have any mezcal?"

"No, just this and beer."

"I should have taught you how to keep a bar."

Beto continued his story, recalling how they had met in Miami, on the set of Sofia's telenovela. The CEO Beto was courting for a merger was a fan of the show, and Sofia played his favorite character, Lourdes Santana, the red-lipped femme fatale. Beto got backstage access to win him over. "She comes out—you know your mother—she's wearing this sheer robe." He chuckled, and nodded his thanks when Nathan handed him another drink. "Beautiful body. An hourglass, with huge—"

"Dad, *no*."

"Sorry. You get it. She was gorgeous. And I wanted her." He took a deep breath. "It was her eyes. You could fall into those eyes, right? Never stop, just keep going." He glanced at Nathan and cleared his throat. "We walk into her dressing room, and there's this guy in the corner holding her purse. Now, I'm all for gender equality, but seriously. He's holding her purse. A woman like that, it's not where your hands should be."

Nathan shuddered. "Please move on."

Beto paused to drink before continuing. "This next part I'm not proud of. Your mother had every right to knock me on my ass. But as everyone's saying goodbye, I pull her away from him. I'd never do that shit now. It's classless. But she was getting away from me and I couldn't let that happen. She looked up and—" His voice caught, and he looked at his fingers. "Those goddamn eyes."

Beto went back to the set the next day, waited until she was done shooting, and asked her out to dinner. "The day after that, I did the same thing. Every day, for three weeks. It was supposed to be a weekend trip, but I couldn't leave her."

"What about Nelson?"

"Who?"

"The boyfriend."

"Oh. What about him?" He shrugged. "I'm sure she let him down easy. I asked her to marry me a few months later."

Beto's version differed from Sofia's. Listening to his dad, it was more like some soul mate, love-at-first sight connection that anyone would have been happy to tell over and over. But Sofia downplayed everything that came before they were engaged.

"So when did things…"

Beto frowned. "When did things what?"

"You know, change between you two?"

"What change? I love your mother."

Nathan laughed. "Yeah, but you two fought a lot when I was in the house, about everything. Especially—"

"Especially what?"

Nathan was too stunned to speak. Years of earsplitting shouting matches about Beto's affairs came tumbling back. As a kid, he used to hide in his closet with his fists in his ears and a ball of fury lodged in his throat. Now that same lump kept him mute as Beto reddened with rising anger.

"Spit it out." Beto set his drink on one of Rachel's pictures. Nathan moved it to the side. "I see how you look at me. Is that why you hate me? Because you think I don't deserve your mother?"

"I never said that."

"You've always been a shitty liar. When you even bother to try. It can be a kindness, you know. Not throwing a man's mistakes in his face whenever you get the chance."

Nathan stood, grabbed both empty glasses, and headed to the kitchen. "Only you could turn lying into a virtue."

Beto stood. "You always do this. Pick a fight and play innocent."

"I didn't pick this fight. You're the one who came here, to what? Make yourself feel better? Check me off some list?" Nathan had almost fallen for it too. No matter how hard he tried not to be that gullible kid who wanted his father's approval, Beto would pull it out of him every time. And it hurt. He was so sick of this feeling.

Beto flung his hands at Nathan's chest. "So now I can't reach out to my son?"

"For what? Your last play to get into heaven?"

Beto grimaced like he'd been punched. Until now, Nathan had never thought of his anger as destructive. Not when it got him into trouble at school. Not when he broke that chair and had to pry splinters from his hand. Not when he decided to leave home. To him, it was survival, not some bitter, spiteful choice that left his family in pieces. But in that moment, seeing his father practically stumble back, Nathan finally realized the damage he could cause. That he could cut deep enough to leave a scar.

"That wasn't..." Nathan trailed off, floundering. "I—"

"You goddamn brat! You're still holding grudges about shit that happened years ago? Grow up!"

Grow up. Do better. *Don't you fucking cry because some little shit hurt your feelings.* A hundred old humiliations came back to Nathan all at once: that he was weak, that he was worthless. Nathan slammed his glass into the sink so hard it cracked. "Get out."

Beto waved a hand. "There you go, quitting when things get hard. That's not a solution."

"I'm not a fucking problem. So stop trying to fix me."

"Fix you?" Beto gestured frantically between them. "I'm trying to fix *us*! Everything I've ever done has been so you could become the man I know you could be. Is that wrong? Did wanting the best for you make me a bad father?"

Nathan heard the desperation in Beto's voice and realized what his father really wanted. Absolution. He was a dying man, chasing down his sins, wondering if there was still time to be forgiven. But Beto had taught him how to hate himself. Those lessons were embedded so deep that Nathan was terrified he could never unlearn them. It wasn't the kind of damage you healed with bygones over drinks. Nathan couldn't give him that.

"No," Nathan said. "That's not what made you a bad father."

Beto stopped pacing. The anger fueling him was gone, like someone had yanked out the cord. "You told me once that I talked *at* you, not to you." His lips twitched into a sad smile. "But you've always been a moving target, Nathaniel. I could never seem to..." He shook his head. "I'm gonna go."

Beto walked to the door and paused with one hand on the doorknob. He finally looked at the drawing desk. "Abuelita used to call you her light. A bighearted little joker who could find something beautiful in any shadow." He blinked, eyes shimmering. "But things have been so dark for this family, for so long. I think that when you gave up on us, we lost our light."

# CHAPTER SIXTEEN

Rachel didn't hear from Nathan until Friday morning, the day of their MoMA trip. She told herself that he was probably busy with the latest publicity push for the gala, which was less than a month away. But after three days of silence, she was convinced that her attempt to slow the runaway train of their relationship had derailed it instead. Matt was avoiding her with another round of rural campaign stops that would last until Monday. He'd barely been gone five minutes before Nathan's car pulled up to the curb.

"It's a long drive," she said, adopting an airy tone as she slid into the passenger seat. She was determined to hide how much his silence had upset her. The trip would take four hours if they were lucky. Stewing in tension the entire time would be miserable. "We should take turns."

"I don't mind driving," Nathan said absently.

"Is something wrong?"

He paused as he pulled onto the road. "It's not you," he admitted. "I mean, it's not us." He fell silent, clearly debating whether to tell her the rest. "I think I need to talk to someone. Like a professional." He paused. "Beto is dying."

"What?" It burst out before she could stop it. Nathan gave her a pained look, like he didn't want to repeat it. "I'm so sorry."

"Don't be. I don't give a shit if he dies." His voice cracked and she touched his shoulder.

"Yes, you do."

Nathan didn't argue. He swallowed hard and twisted his hands on the steering wheel. "He's got six months, maybe. They're not sure." Rachel rubbed his arm. His muscles were rigid, coiled into a useless armor. "He came by my place last night. We got into it. He's always been disappointed in me. Like I've failed at being his son."

Nathan told her stories about his childhood, casting Beto as a neglectful tyrant whose rare acts of kindness only left Nathan frustrated and confused. But Rachel was slowly becoming fluent in the man sitting beside her. He rushed through softer memories because they made the thought of losing Beto hurt more, while focusing on the pain kept him numb.

"I've been so angry with him all my life." He met her eyes. "But I don't want to live like that anymore."

"Do you think you can forgive him?"

"Maybe." Nathan swallowed hard. "But I don't know how."

She'd forgotten this part of falling in love with someone, how hard it was to watch them hurt in ways you couldn't heal. There was nothing she could say to make it easier, so she reached for his hand instead.

That small touch shifted the air between them. Nathan moved his arm to the back of her seat for the rest of the drive. Rachel drifted closer to him with every mile, until she was practically nestled against his side. They spent the next five hours trading intimate stories and lazy finger grazes to the low bass of Nathan's slow jams playlist. It was kindling on a fire.

At MoMA, Nathan seemed more intrigued by the wispy curls at Rachel's ear than the art. After her second sidelong glance, he started gazing blankly at installations. They stopped in front of Yves Klein's *Blue Monochrome* and Nathan examined the large canvas with polite apathy.

"What do you think?" she asked.

"Honestly?"

"Yes."

"Nothing," he said. "I mean, I know there's some deeper meaning, but it just looks like blue paint to me."

"It is just blue paint."

He sighed. "Look, this is why I don't come to places like this. I don't get it. I won't have the right reaction."

"There is no right reaction. I can tell you the history. I can tell you what Klein said about his inspiration, but no one can tell you how to feel. And that's the whole point."

"I don't feel anything," Nathan countered. "That's *my* point."

"Close your eyes." Nathan chuckled and shook his head but did as she asked. "What do you see?"

His lips twitched. "Nothing, because my eyes are closed."

She batted his arm. "Really? *Nothing?*"

He paused. "Well, now all I can think about is blue."

"That's it! That's the point."

He opened his eyes, looking doubtful. "Really?"

"Klein was fixated on this exact shade." Her words came faster and slightly winded, which always happened when she talked about art this way—as something to be experienced instead of observed. "He said he wanted the viewer to become 'impregnated in sensibility' by this shade of blue."

His eyebrow shot up to his hairline. "Become *what*?"

"Impregnated. He was also known for using nude women as paintbrushes, so don't be surprised that he reached for that analogy."

Nathan laughed and studied the painting again. "I use bright, saturated colors too. On purpose. I never think my work is good enough, so I use color to hide the flaws."

"Those imperfections make them yours," she said. "You're not a machine making perfect images for mass consumption. You're a man. An *artist*. With emotions and flaws. That's why something like this"—she pointed to the painting—"has immeasurable value. This is a moment. It's a feeling, movement, and time that can never be repeated. That's in every piece you've created."

Nathan studied her with such intensity that her face warmed. "You are *really* good at this," he said softly. "Did you know that?"

Years of practice had taught Rachel how to accept compliments gracefully, even when it felt like being praised for wearing a lovely shell. This was different. She'd revealed the unvarnished depths of her passion, and

Nathan thought it was beautiful. For the first time in years, it *felt* like something beautiful, instead of the source of her biggest regrets.

They strolled through the rest of the museum in companionable silence until Nathan stopped at a photo exhibit about the history of colonialism. "But it's different for us, though, right?"

"What's different?"

"We don't get joy." He gestured toward the new realism exhibit they'd just left. "They get to deconstruct things and slap colors on a canvas because they like the way it looks. But we get what?" He gestured to the photos. "The special collection for heritage month? Places like this only care about our oppression and suffering."

Rachel took a step back. He was right, but she couldn't help but feel defensive. "I get your point, but that erases the effort of people working to change that. I used to be one of them and my work was never about suffering."

"It's not hanging up in here either," Nathan said. His gaze bounced from canvas to canvas before he noticed her discomfort. "Oh, fuck. I'm an asshole. I didn't mean—"

"You're right," she said. "Even if I hadn't quit, I doubt any work like mine would have been displayed somewhere like the MoMA. Most museum acquisitions are still conservative pieces from white male artists, which makes women like me invisible to this part of the art world. But we're also getting louder. Kara Walker. Amy Sherald. It's glacial, incremental change, but their work was shown here and it's impossible to ignore. Just like yours." Nathan still looked skeptical, and she quickly squeezed his hand. "This is one museum. There's another one in Harlem, that—"

"Let's do it," he said quickly. "Harlem, Brooklyn, Paris, whatever. I'm ready to learn. Show me more."

--------

Nathan wasn't superstitious. He didn't believe in luck or karma, and while he liked the thought of a higher power, he could never fully embrace the idea that a deity powerful enough to create the universe would care about whether he went to mass on Sunday. And yet, as he stood on the side of a two-lane highway, staring at his blown tire, it felt like the universe was trying to tell him something: There was no such thing as a perfect day. You couldn't spend hours talking art with the off-limits woman of your dreams without some sort of penance.

He'd had the brilliant idea to take the scenic route so they could stop by the infamous spring that gave the town its name. Rachel had never seen it, and he talked up the landmark by sharing a folktale he was pretty sure Abuelita had made up. That swimming in the spring would lead to your heart's desire.

Maybe it was more like a Robert Johnson's crossroads deal for the price of his soul. Nathan had figured that being alone with Rachel for twelve uninterrupted hours would be worth the risk of someone noticing they were both gone. But the real price for their perfect day was this: Lightning flashes, the "no signal" message on his phone, the unsettling feeling of being alone but not *alone* in the racoon-friendly backroads of Maryland. God or no God, there was a devil laughing somewhere.

Rachel opened her door. "Is it flat?"

"I messed up," Nathan said. "I'm sorry, I don't have a spare in the trunk. I used it a while ago and never replaced it."

She pulled out her phone, and he waited while she figured out what he already knew. The stretch of road was a dead spot. There wasn't a decent signal for miles. A large thunderclap brought more rain.

He got back into the car as Rachel stared at her phone as though she could will it into working. "We need to get somewhere to make a phone call. How far would we need to go?"

"I'm not sure. The next town is a thirty-minute drive. Maybe a few hours on foot." Nathan examined the clouds. "That looks nasty. We probably shouldn't try it until this dies down."

"It's supposed to rain all night."

"I know." He twisted around to the back seat. "I have a blanket. You can have the back and I'll stay up here."

"No."

She glared at him. Had he missed something? "Do you want the front?"

"No, I need a phone signal." She looked at the sky. "It's not that bad. If we left now—"

He waved at the sheets of rain outside her window. "It's pitch black and the road is narrow. Someone could easily sideswipe us. We should wait here until it eases up."

"I said no," Rachel snapped. "I'm not sleeping in your back seat because you can't handle basic car maintenance. If you won't go, I will."

Nathan was baffled by her sudden hostility. Then he noticed the way she held herself rigid, breathing erratically, panting and then labored. Her eyes fluttered, and she covered her mouth like she was close to vomiting.

It was a panic attack. Joe had told him once that they felt like your chest was caving in, while your worst fears played on an endless loop. "Hey," Nathan said, touching her hand. "Breathe."

"I am breathing."

"Do it slower. Count with me—"

"Stop." She looked away. "I'm not hysterical."

"I know," he said, evening his voice. "I know you're not." Her hand was a fist. He ran his thumb over her knuckles. "Help me understand. What is it? Is it being stranded? Is it—" He hesitated, not sure if he wanted the answer to his next question. "Is it being alone with me?"

"No." She closed her eyes. "I can't sleep here."

"Outside?"

"No, in the car. I can't sleep in the car, it's—" She covered her mouth again. "I know it's stupid. I'm sorry for yelling at you."

"Look at me." He waited until she met his eyes again. "It's not stupid. I'm sorry for making you feel this way." A tear slid down her cheek. It was his fault. Him and his careless, fuck-it attitude about something that would have kept her safe.

Rachel's breathing had slowed, but she still looked frazzled and nauseated. He squinted through the windshield at a sign in the distance, desperate for a solution. It was a closed bait and tackle shop. The red siding and white trim seemed familiar. Then it came to him—that one-off fishing trip with Joe where he caught nothing but the hem of his own pants and his brother vowed never to let him near a fishing rod again.

"Hang on, I think I know where we are." He looked out the passenger-side window. "This is at the edge of my parents' property. Their lake house is that way. I could—"

"Alone? Through the woods?" She was breathing too fast again.

"It's not that far," he said softly. "Fifteen minutes on foot maybe? I wouldn't be on the road."

"But it's the *woods*."

"Plenty of people walk in these woods."

"During the day. Not at night during a rainstorm. What if something happens to you? I don't have a phone. I wouldn't know where you were, or how to find you."

Her words were running together. He tried to keep his own voice calm, even though he knew the plan was risky. "It's not that far. I used to play out here when I was a kid."

Rachel's hand crept closer to his leg like she wanted to hold him in place. "I'll go with you," she declared, trying to sound braver than she looked.

He gestured toward her white dress, which was obviously expensive. "In that? In those shoes?" She wore a pair of thin leather flats. "No, you should stay."

"Please. I don't want to be alone out here." She folded her arms and seemed steadier. More confident. "You're the one who said it wasn't far."

He studied her, debating whether to keep arguing or to let her have her way. Her face was determined, but those flimsy shoes were screaming that she had no business walking through brush and mud.

"Fine." He reached into the back seat, grabbed a blanket, and tossed it into her lap. "Put this on."

---

Rachel knew she deserved every miserably muddy step. Her fears were irrational, and she should have stayed behind. But she couldn't handle that silent, closed-in feeling of being parked in the middle of nowhere. Not again. The panic attack had left her drained, weak, and incapable of being alone. And so, despite the open sky dumping sheets of rain over them, and Nathan's assurances that she'd be safer in the car, she'd followed him anyway.

Nathan paced himself so she could keep up. Rachel pulled the blanket tight over her shoulders and tried to move faster, but only managed a few steps before her foot sank in mud up to her ankle. She yanked it out and stumbled backward, minus her shoe. When Nathan spotted her bare foot, his expression was so incredulous she wanted to return to that mud hole and see if it was big enough to hide her entire body.

"You can't walk like this," he said. His face tightened, like he was readying for a fight. "I'm going to carry you. Please don't argue."

The situation was now beyond embarrassing, but she couldn't summon the energy to protest. Nathan turned around and crouched low so she could climb onto his back. At first, she held her body stiff and upright as if she could make herself lighter. But then he squeezed her ankle, said, "Relax," and like some magic spell, it made her sink into his warmth. He smelled like rain, fabric softener, and aftershave. She buried her face against his neck and closed her eyes.

Exhaustion made her lose track of time. One minute they were surrounded by dense forest and the next the lake house was looming a few feet away. She loosened her arms and said, "I think I can walk from here."

Nathan's grip tightened, like he wasn't ready to set her down yet, but he relented. A few minutes later, they were standing at the door of a rustic two-story cottage, almost as tall as the surrounding pine trees. Nathan typed in a security code, and a motion sensor kicked the heat on as soon as they crossed the threshold.

The living room was long and lean, the walls covered with bay windows that framed a cinematic view of the storm still streaking across the sky. Nathan yanked a protective cover away from a chair and told her to sit. Then he disappeared upstairs to look for towels.

Rachel stared at the puddle forming beneath her feet and thought of how furious Sofia would be if she ruined the gleaming hardwood. She stripped a cover from the sofa and crouched to her knees. By the time Nathan found her, she'd mopped up most of the water and cleaned the mud from her bare feet.

"What are you doing?" He dropped a stack of towels on the couch. She ignored him. There was a smaller puddle near the front door, and she scooted toward it, still on her knees. He touched her arm. "Rachel!"

She shook him off. "I'm almost done."

His grip tightened. "You need to get dry."

"I'm almost—"

"Rachel, *stop*." He knelt and met her eyes. "You don't have to do this."

"Neither do you." She tried to blink back tears and failed. "We could have stayed in the car."

"No, we couldn't." He gestured to the room. "We're here. We're safe. I'll call a tow truck and we'll be back on the road in a few hours." He pried a wet strand of hair from her cheek. "The shower is upstairs, first door on the right."

She rose with the towel balled in her hands. "You're mad at me."

His eyes were on the floor. "No, I'm not."

"I know I was horrible to you in the car, I was rude, and I'm so sorry." Her voice was pitched and fractured, the words tumbling in jagged pieces. "It'll never happen again. I don't want to lose our...our friendship over—"

"I'm not your friend," he said gently, with the exhaustion of someone tired of explaining the obvious. Her eyes filled. This was it. This was how she lost him.

"Nathan, please don't—"

He stepped back. "I can't do this. I can't be around you and not..." He looked at her, finally, and took a deep, ragged breath. "I love you. I'm so in love with you, but I don't know *how* to be in love with you." There was no joy in his confession, only anguish. Like it was a sickness without a cure.

"I never meant for this to happen," she whispered. They never should have met that day at the drive-in. She never should have kissed him in that garden shed, sending them both hurtling over a cliff, hurtling to *this*, to something they could never really have. "I'm so sor—"

"*Don't.* I don't want your apology. I want *you*. If you don't want me too, please just stop. Stop touching me. Don't hold my hand. Don't look at me like—" His gaze fell to her mouth, to her soaked dress. "You look at me like—"

"Like what?" Rachel could feel herself changing, shedding an old skin that couldn't contain her. She moved closer until the sliver of space between them was as charged as the thunder rumbling outside. "Tell me how I look at you."

---

He practically lifted her from the ground. A sound burst from his throat, her name anchored to a groan. He kissed her with everything boiling inside him—the frustration, the longing. The love. But his brain couldn't be trusted. It had been taken hostage by that look in her eyes—dark and hungry, beautiful enough to hurt. *"You could fall into those eyes, right? Never stop, just keep going."* He'd dove in headfirst like the fall wouldn't break him.

"Rachel." He scanned her face. It had gone hazy and lust drunk. He could feel it—all that waiting and wanting arcing between them. "Is this you? Or is this the car and the storm—"

She grabbed his shirt with both hands. "I want you, Nathan. *Please.*"

It pierced him like a bullet. That word. Her mouth, swollen from his kisses and begging for more. Begging for *him*. This was what it felt like: to be wanted, and to be enough.

"Are you mine?" He kissed her again, claimed her with his tongue. "Because I'm yours."

Rachel pulled back, but just far enough to whisper, "Yes." Her hands slid beneath his shirt and Nathan yanked it off by the collar, nearly ripping the fabric in the process. That's when he knew this would be different. Rougher. Dirtier. After all that time, they were starved for each other. She put her mouth on his neck, kissing and licking like she'd been thinking about it all along. Drawing a map. Then she urged him back and down, until he was sprawled on the couch and looking up at her, a siren bathed in rainwater. She raked her eyes over his body like she wanted to devour him whole.

Rachel tugged at her dress and pulled it down over one shoulder. Teasing him. Savoring this. "The night we met, you asked me a question about what I wanted," she said, and the rasp of her voice made his stomach clench.

She pulled her arms free. "I couldn't answer you." The dress collapsed around her waist, revealing a white bra, soaked to transparency.

Nathan sat up so he could touch her. He *had* to touch her. His fingers found that indention at the top of her stomach, just beneath the lace of her bra—the soft dip before heaven. "You'd been through a lot."

Rachel's eyes were all shimmering want. "That's not why I couldn't." She unfastened her bra as he slid his hands up and palmed her breasts. She arched her back and made sinfully grateful sounds when he tugged her nipples. "I've never wanted what I should," she said. "My whole life has been selfish cravings. Guilty pleasures. Being desperate for things I can't admit that I want out loud."

This was how they started, with confessions and cravings, exposing all the dark places they were supposed to be ashamed of. Nathan reached beneath her skirt, prying away the strip of lace and satin, and sank two fingers inside her wet heat. She hissed and groaned as he trailed them out again, a leisurely stroke that settled into steady circles over her clit. "You can say them to me."

He watched her eyes flutter as she rocked against his hand. "I don't want you to be gentle," she whispered. "And I don't want to be careful." She stroked his hair and kissed him, hard. "I want to make you come apart."

She straddled his hips, rubbing herself against the rigid fabric of his jeans. It was torture. It was bliss. It was enough to spark the base of his spine but would never ease his suffering. He nearly begged her to give him more, something. Anything. But then he remembered what she said, about wanting him in pieces, and the thought coiled low, into a throbbing ache that made him groan.

Nathan thought he'd seen everything. Every part of her. But this was different. She didn't move like the woman he'd known before. Her body practically glided over his, so sure of its beauty. He kissed her neck. She tasted like heat, salt, and rain.

"I want all of it," he said. "All your secrets. Every filthy last one of them."

She slithered lower, her mouth on his chest, kissing, licking, nipping him with her teeth. Her hair was light and cool on his skin. He sank his hands into the curls.

"This is my fantasy," she mumbled at his waist. "You. Like this." She unbuttoned his belt. "I touch myself, but I want you."

Nathan felt the heat of her breath as she pressed her lips against him. When she took him in her mouth, his body seized. She pressed her hand to his chest, to his heart, like she wanted to measure how thoroughly he was being wrecked. His hand fisted mindlessly, a gentle hair pull that made her hum in pleasure. Soon he was begging for release, pleading for mercy.

Rachel climbed on top of him, and he entered her with a long, rough stroke. They were wild and frantic, fighting to move deeper and harder than their bodies would allow. Eventually, they settled into a rolling, seductive dance, one body instead of two. Rachel came with a series of moans into his mouth, and Nathan held them in his chest like smoke. His release was a punishing, spiraling thing that gripped him so hard that he shouted her name. When it finally receded, he collapsed on the couch, shattered and wasted.

Rachel lay on top of him, and he studied her face as they both came back to themselves. Her eyes were soft and hazy. He touched her chin, tracing the perfect line of her mouth with his thumb.

She was his. But once they left, she wouldn't be. Not completely. "What if we stayed?" he asked.

Rachel hesitated. "What do you mean?"

"Stay with me. Just for a few days." He kissed her temple, her cheek, the corner of her mouth, trailing small *I love you*s over her skin. "Let me take care of you."

# CHAPTER SEVENTEEN

Rachel's dad used to say that instincts were your heart trying to be heard over your head. If you ignored them too often, they would eventually go quiet. Her instincts, her heart, used to fantasize about running away. She thought about it when she wandered through a bookstore until they took down the open sign. Or when she ate her muffin slowly at a coffee shop so they'd keep refilling her mug. It happened the day she dropped Faith off at culinary school. Rachel had roamed around the city for hours because she didn't want to go home.

But those were fantasies. Her head would remind her of how grateful she should be for her life. Over the years, it happened less and less. So when Nathan asked her to stay, it felt like her heart, tired of being ignored, had put those desires into someone else's mouth instead, hoping this time she would finally listen.

"The tow truck just left." Nathan handed her a coffee mug. "The guy sold me a used tire, so we're not stranded anymore." They'd woken up on the couch after a heavy night's sleep and migrated to the sunroom for breakfast, which seemed redundant given the entire house was one big atrium. Someone had designed it with sunrise backdrops in mind.

"I was about to go shopping," he said. "We need actual food and a change of clothes." Nathan had found a collection of T-shirts and sweatpants Joe had left in a drawer upstairs, but the weather had settled into a brisk fall chill. They both needed something warmer. Nathan was bursting out of clothes that were a size too small.

"I should go with you."

She sat up, but Nathan touched her arm to stop her. "I can go.

You look tired." He stroked her cheek. "Do you want to talk about yesterday?"

She wondered if he realized his hands were extended, palm up, as if he might need to catch her. "I had a panic attack."

"I know," Nathan said. "I also know they can have triggers." He hesitated. "Did something happen to you? In a car?"

"No, not like you mean. It's a long story." She was stalling. People who love you think they want to know everything about you. Like the unseen parts are wrapped gifts they're eager to open. But Rachel knew it was more like reading someone's diary or going through their internet search history. Once you know, you can't unknow.

"When Faith was two, I left her with my dad so I could go to college. My freshman year, I came home to visit them over Christmas and again the following summer. After that, I stopped going home at all."

A mother can decode their child's pain by the way they cry. Faith's was a breathless whine when she was hungry and a hiccuping staccato when she wanted attention. The high-pitched scream that burst from her tiny body when Rachel came home for the holidays was pure pain. It was *Where were you?* and *Why did you leave me?* and *Please don't go*, in one long scream. All Rachel could do was hold her arms down in the center of the bed so she wouldn't hurt herself.

Later, her father would say that Faith was never like this. "She's just tired, most likely." But Rachel knew better. She heard the damage she'd caused in Faith's wail. It was an echo of the pain she felt when someone mentioned her mother's name.

Ramona Thomas was a woman who dreamed of singing on Broadway but paid the bills by fixing the soles of rich white women's shoes. She'd named her only daughter Rachel because it was her favorite from the Bible, a fact she'd written in a notebook filled with unfinished song lyrics and her bitter resentment, which coated her life like oil. All of it was bound to catch fire eventually.

Rachel was three when her mother left. Too young to have anything but the memory of her smell: vanilla and Pink Oil Moisturizer singed with a hot comb. The memory of her touch: firm but careful. The memory of a sweater: burnt orange, like sunsets, with little fuzz balls Rachel used to grab. Her voice was a melody that started to fade as soon as she left—like a song Rachel listened to less and less as she got older.

"I hated my mother for a long time." Rachel didn't look directly at Nathan while she spoke. She kept her eyes on the lake and let the water's motion lull her into a calm. "But after Faith, I think I finally understood her a little more. You can't straddle both sides of your life. Living in one means losing something from the other. That's just the way it is."

Despite her father's assurances that Faith was fine, the tantrums were worse when she returned home for the summer. Rachel spent the first two nights rocking Faith to sleep, only for her to jolt awake, look at Rachel's face, and start crying all over again.

"That's when I had my first panic attack," she said. "I didn't know what it was. I'd sit outside her room and listen to her breathing while my heart was burning up inside my chest. I was nineteen years old. I remember thinking that we couldn't live that way. That this couldn't be what we were to each other. Nothing but damage."

Her hands were trembling like she'd never left that narrow hallway. She pressed them hard against her legs. "I stopped going home. Phone calls would trigger another attack. Dad wrote letters, but I could never bear to read them. I got high a lot. It helped. But I couldn't look at old pictures or be around kids." She paused. "I wonder if that's how my mother did it. Erased me from her life so that it was easier to stay away." She glanced at Nathan but wasn't brave enough to read his face. "Two years later, the dean of students told me that my father was in the hospital with pancreatic cancer. They'd put him into a medically induced coma."

Nathan made a wounded sound, a strangled loss of breath. "I'm so sorry."

"Please don't be." She rubbed her eyes. "I don't deserve sympathy. I never will." She took a deep breath. "I read all his letters. There was nothing about him being sick. It was all about Faith and—" The memory bled through and made her choke. She swallowed hard and kept talking, but her words stopped and started, tumbling together. She'd dropped her classes and returned home, but he was already gone. Faith was with a neighbor. She was five and there was no tantrum this time, but she didn't eat for several days. Like she wanted to hurt in ways her mother couldn't see.

The little money Peter had was put toward unpaid medical bills so large they looked like mortgages. The landlord gave her six weeks to get current on the rent. Rachel applied for retail jobs, but the hours never worked with Faith's school schedule. After-school programs were full. Sitters were too expensive. Eventually an eviction notice went up.

"We stayed with a neighbor for a while, and then we went to a motel." Her face warmed. "It was too expensive. To this day, I don't know how I could have been so careless with my money."

He slid a hand up her spine. "You were doing the best you could."

"Well, you can guess what happened next. I ran out of money. I applied for public housing, but..." She paused and he finished the thought for her.

"Waiting list."

"For everything. No one's ever in a hurry to help someone when they're poor. Maybe they figure since you don't have anything, there's no harm in making you wait." Her voice cracked as she spoke, and she covered her mouth.

Nathan's hand stilled. "Hey. If this is too much for you—"

"No." She took a deep breath. "You asked, I want to tell you. We slept in the car because the shelters weren't safe." Bile rose in the back of her throat. "I would drop her off at school and take whatever work I could find. I made enough for gas and food. And then we would park on some quiet street for the night and hope no one saw us and called the police." She could still picture Faith's curly head bobbing beneath the blanket. Her daughter was still afraid of the dark back then. She'd prop a flashlight on her shoulder and read a worn copy of *The Runaway Bunny* that Peter bought for her. Rachel would stay up all night, staring at the expensive houses with their landscaped lawns and home security signs, thinking, *I have to fix this.* And at dawn, for a few hours between dusk and day, sometimes she'd sleep.

"I knew that if someone caught us, they'd take her away from me," she said. It was the only thing that kept the panic attacks away. And that's when she knew having Faith had fundamentally changed her. That it had rewritten her DNA. All that time, she'd been afraid that love would break her, but instead it made her stronger than she'd ever been.

Even during the worst of it—when people walked by peering into her car window, looking for a purse or forgotten keys, that moment when they made eye contact and she never knew if they would see her as a deterrent or an opportunity—Rachel didn't fall apart. She'd covered the windows with newspaper and started carrying a knife. And then one day she'd found Alesha's address in one of her father's old books. A scrap of paper that nearly fell to the floor before she noticed.

"She found me a job waiting tables," Rachel said. "Faith was enrolled in school. A few years later I met Matt and..."

And she got her own big house. A manicured lawn. She got the security of Matt's bank account. She got to wake up every day next to a man she loved. Someone who had vowed in front of hundreds of people not to disappear like her mother or be stolen away like her father. She got the Abbotts, a family more flawed than she was. And she could finally tell Faith that everything would be fine and know it was true.

Rachel had signed that prenup to prove to everyone, including herself, that she married Matt for love, not money. But in reality, she was exactly like her mother, bending herself into awkward shapes to become the perfect wife, when she never really wanted any of it. She had fought for a life she didn't want because losing it scared her more than losing herself.

And here she was, still fighting. Still afraid. Loving Nathan was a ledge, and she had no idea what was on the other side. What would happen if she jumped? Would she just keep falling?

"Does Faith have any idea how much you've sacrificed for her?" Nathan asked.

Rachel bristled at the idea that she'd earned her daughter's sympathy. "She knows I didn't finish school. But it wasn't a sacrifice. It was doing the right thing."

"Is that how she sees it? You never graduating, moving in with strangers, being a full-time wife and mother while your art collects dust in storage?"

She thought about the few times she'd mentioned her art to Faith, and how quickly her daughter would change the subject. Rachel had always assumed her former career aspirations were a reminder to Faith of being abandoned for something her mother thought was more important. "I put her through a lot. She has a right to be cautious when it comes to me."

"No, she doesn't," he said. "I couldn't boil water when I was eighteen. You were learning to be a mom before you even knew how to be a person."

"Being a mother was more important."

"What does that even mean?" Nathan reached for her hands. "My mother never left the way you did. But there were times when she was so bored with her life that she might as well have been gone. I never knew her when she was passionate about something. I never learned how to fight for what I wanted. I didn't have examples of that. But being around you these last few months has made me into a man I never knew existed. And if Faith is as brilliant and brave as you say she is, it's because you raised her."

Rachel could feel herself recoiling from his praise. She was a cautionary tale, not a source of inspiration. And never a good mother. But how would she even know what that meant? The only thing Ramona taught her was that good mothers didn't leave. But now here was Nathan, someone's son, telling her there was more to good parenting than being present. She could be a safe place. She could be a warrior. She could be the roots that her daughter craved.

Rachel felt like he'd rummaged through the truth of her and cut away the heaviest parts. Her quiet "Thank you" felt inadequate. She climbed into his lap, wrapped her arms around his neck, and repeated, "Thank you," with her love woven through the words. Nathan pressed his ear to her chest. To her heart. Then he closed his eyes and listened.

———

Nathan woke up twice that night. The first time was on the tail end of a dream. He was in Mexico, swimming with his cousins. They called him flaco, like when he was smaller, and warned him about swimming out too far. "Come back, or you're going to miss it," they yelled. "You'll be too late."

He tried yelling back, "Too late for what?" but he couldn't speak and swim at the same time. He'd just decided to turn back when the ocean pulled him under.

He opened his eyes expecting a blue haze of salty sea, but instead he saw Rachel's hair splayed against the satin pillowcase he'd bought for her. He slid a hand around her waist and moved closer, until her back was against his chest. She woke like he did, with the grogginess of an interrupted dream, and he wedged against her until every inch of his body touched some part of her skin. He'd never fallen asleep seared to another person before. It was sweaty, hot, and addictively uncomfortable. He didn't want to move away. He didn't want it to end.

The second time he woke was to the sound of a door slamming. He reached for Rachel, but the bed was empty. His stomach did a hard flip. Then he saw her standing next to the window, staring with clear agitation.

"I think your brother is here."

That's when Nathan knew that it was over. Like in his dream, they had swum too far.

He put on jeans and grabbed a T-shirt. Rachel started to follow, but he shook his head and pressed a finger to his lips. Maybe Joe thought he was alone. Maybe he would assume Nathan brought a date to the lake without telling anyone. The maybes ran through his mind as he took the stairs down to the living room two at a time, but Joe's expression killed them instantly. His eyes were flint. He said, "Put your shirt on," with a coldness that Nathan had only heard once in his life before.

Joe had a pen that Abuelita had given him when he graduated from college. It was a monogrammed Montblanc that he carried around like a witch cradling a magic wand. He would use it to forge their mother's signature when Nathan brought home another failing test grade. Nathan had loved that pen. He loved the onyx color and the clean lines of ink it left on paper. He had loved how Joe's penmanship would gleam silver in the light as he wrote out their shared lie. And most of all, he had loved the fact that every now and then Joe would let him use it. He would entrust this beautiful thing that symbolized all his accomplishments to his little brother without a warning to be careful, or to put it back where it belonged. And Nathan had been careful—right up until the day he wasn't. It took him three days to finally admit that he lost it. Joe hadn't yelled. He'd stared at Nathan with stony eyes and said, "It's just a fucking pen," in that same icy tone.

That look was worse than yelling. It was Joe, giving up and calcifying his expectations of his little brother. *I guess this is who you are.* And standing in front of Joe at the lake house, Nathan couldn't argue. Instead, he shrugged into his shirt.

Joe looked past him, at the stairs. "Is she here?"

"Is who—"

"Don't lie to me. Matt Abbott told Mia that Rachel was missing. She asked if I'd seen you." He finally met Nathan's eyes. "I said of course not. What would Nate have to do with Rachel Abbott going missing? She probably thinks I'm an idiot."

"Mia knows?" Nathan winced at how guilty it sounded. "What did Matt say to her?"

Joe's face was red. "You mean does he know that his wife's cheating on him with the local laundry boy? Pretty sure he doesn't."

Nathan's guilt vanished. If Joe wasn't pulling punches, neither would he. "He's the one having an affair. I saw him with his mistress at the anniversary party."

"And that makes it okay?" Joe shook his head. "What the hell has she gotten you into?"

Joe looked up at the sound of footsteps. Nathan turned to see Rachel, dressed in the baggy sweatshirt and leggings he'd bought for her. "You can ask me," she said. "My answers will probably disappoint you, but it's not fair to take it out on him."

Joe shook his head. "The whole way up here, I didn't believe it. Mom said you two were close, and I thought, well, that's great. My brother needs a mentor. But then I got the notification about the alarm out here being disabled. And then I remembered that Nate's seeing some woman, and it's *complicated*. You two are terrible at covering your tracks."

"We weren't trying to," Rachel said. She walked down the stairs and stopped before she reached Nathan. He wanted to build a wall between her and his brother. "Nathan's right, this wasn't an affair."

Nathan could sense Joe winding up to say something cruel and raised his hand. "We didn't come out here on purpose. It was car trouble. I blew a tire on the east highway."

"That was Friday," Joe said. "It doesn't take thirty-six hours to fix a tire."

Nathan shifted to one side, blocking his view of Rachel. "The rest is none of your business."

Joe laughed. "You're kidding, right? What did you two plan to do, run away together?" Joe paused. "You can't do that, Nate," he said, his anger fading into concern. "You can't disappear again. Not now. Dad—" He swallowed hard and looked at Rachel. "We need him here."

Rachel touched Nathan's shoulder. He reached for her hand, but she stepped past him to face Joe. "We're not running away," she said. "And I'm sorry about your father."

"If you're sorry, maybe don't wreck what's left of our family before he's gone." Joe looked at Nathan. "What do you think will happen when word gets out that you've been fucking Matt Abbott's wife? That guy is on every cable news show in the country. So is she." He flung a hand at Rachel. "They'll rip you both apart along with anyone else who gets caught in the crossfire. Me. Mom. Beto." He looked at Rachel. "You have a *daughter*—"

"That's enough," Nathan yelled. Joe looked shocked. Nathan had never yelled at his brother before. "Joe, you need to leave."

"No," Rachel said, facing Nathan. "I should leave. If Matt called Mia, it means he knows something. I have to go."

Nathan could barely process what was happening. He sputtered, "No. No, don't," and moved toward her, but she stepped back and looked at Joe.

"Can I take your car?"

Joe offered her his keys. Nathan thought of what Beto said, how he didn't think before he reached for their mother. That's what had stopped him from losing her. Holding on.

Nathan grabbed Rachel's hand. "Please don't do this." If his brother weren't there, he might have been on his knees. "Stay. We can figure this out. We'll go back, together."

Rachel didn't look at him. She stared at the floor, rubbing her eyes hard enough to mark her skin. "You have to let me go."

# CHAPTER EIGHTEEN

I t was six in the morning when Rachel finally arrived home. The still-
ness she encountered when she walked into the foyer made her uneasy.
She'd been expecting fireworks. Shouting. Instead, Lenora had quietly
taken her bag of dirty clothes and asked if she wanted coffee. Rachel
declined because while she was pretty sure Lenora wasn't trying to poi-
son her, the whole situation was strange enough to make her cautious.

She found Matt in the kitchen, hunched over a cast-iron skillet. He
never wanted her to cook for him when they were dating. He'd pour her
a glass of wine, tell her to put her feet up, and listen to stories about her
café customers while he struggled with a recipe. The food was terrible.
But it was a lot easier to choke down underseasoned vegetables when it
was someone's love for you on the plate.

Rachel sat at the kitchen island, unnerved as he served her charred
bacon with runny scrambled eggs. She took a bite to be kind, but it
turned to ash on her tongue. She decided to abandon kindness and get
to the point instead. "Why did you call Mia?"

"I was worried." Matt poked and glared at the food like it had
betrayed him. "The outdoor stops got canceled because of the storm.
When I came home, no one knew where you were. I thought something
might have happened to you. That you'd been in an accident, or someone
had taken you." He shook his head. "I know it sounds ridiculous, but I
was just frantic about my missing wife."

He said it smoothly, like the last few months had never happened.

"I'm not your wife."

Matt poked his eggs again. "We need to talk about that. I want to make a new deal. To save our marriage."

She thought he'd exhausted ways to hurt her. But now she knew he'd probably always have that power. They made vows to each other, trusted each other enough to build a life. And he'd waited until now, when they could barely make eye contact without wincing, to decide it was something worth saving.

Rachel grabbed the edge of the table so she wouldn't throw eggs in his face. Matt held up his hands and said, "Hold on," like she'd already taken aim at his head. "I know you're angry. And so was I, for a long time. But I think that was the problem. I was angry because I thought you'd abandoned me. You seemed so unhappy, that it was like you'd completely checked out of this marriage. But I think I was the one who abandoned you."

Matt explained how her disappearance had put things in perspective. "This is our family, Rachel. We owe it to each other, to Faith, to at least *try*." He started to reach for her, but she flinched, and he splayed his hand against the table instead. "I don't expect you to forgive me right away. But I'd like to work on earning your trust again."

If he'd said the same thing a few months ago, the night of the birthday party, she might have listened. She might have handed over her heart, again and again, because that's what "for better, for worse" meant. Matt had always been good with words—pitch perfect and so sincere that you felt them in your stomach. But he wasn't safe. He was a fairy tale she'd repeated to herself enough times to forget it wasn't real. She'd never make that mistake again.

Rachel stood, dumped out her food, and walked out of the kitchen. He didn't follow her. She went upstairs and called Julia, who was equally skeptical about Matt's sudden change of heart. "Herman Abbott responded to my request for financial records instead of Matt. They're closing ranks, so watch your back."

She was right. An hour later, Rachel's father-in-law was on her doorstep. Herman's smile faltered when she skipped her usual polite greeting.

"Matt isn't here."

"I'm actually here to see you."

She paused. "I was about to head out."

His eyes went from her face to her bare feet. The last time he saw her without makeup was probably the family beach trip when she was twenty-five. "I don't think that's true."

"I also don't want to talk to you."

"That I believe." He placed a hand against the door. "Please, Rachel. A few minutes of your time."

His voice was even and polite in a way some people found seductive. Rachel wasn't fooled. He was pretending to ask permission while his hand blocked the door. She didn't have the strength to argue.

"Are you going to stand there?" he asked as he sat on the sofa.

"You're wasting minutes."

"Okay." He laced his fingers. "You're angry. It's understandable."

"What are you talking about?"

"My son's stupidity."

"You know he cheated on me?"

"Yes, I do. I also know that you agreed to stay until the election." He studied her face. "How much did you ask for?"

She sighed. He was sitting there, calm as a frog on a lily pad, asking how much hush money his son paid his wife to keep his secrets. This family made her sick. "Not enough."

He smirked. "When it's for your dignity, it never is." He scanned the room, eyes resting on a framed wedding photo. "I'm impressed you kept things together this long. I never would have known it was so bad if he hadn't told me. My son can be very shortsighted about his own best interests. He only thinks about what he wants in the moment. At one point that was you."

"Which you never approved of."

"Not at first, no." He paused. "But I was wrong about you, Rachel. I know I should have said something before now, but sentiment doesn't come naturally to me. You've been a good influence on him. Calming.

Rational, when he lost focus." He leaned forward. "When we poll Matt as an unmarried candidate, he's unelectable. No one trusts him. Not without you there. Beautiful. Respectable. You convince voters he's more than just another trust fund, Ivy League kid."

The revelation turned her stomach. She should have known Matt's change of heart was prompted by the numbers on some spreadsheet. "Why are you here?"

"To fix his mistake." Herman leaned back and crossed his legs. "Neither of you has any idea how to negotiate. He should have made the initial offer. And you should have demanded enough to make following through worth it. You have no incentive to keep your word."

"I won't tell anyone about his affair."

"But you won't stay either." He tilted his head. "Will you?"

It was like being pinned beneath a microscope. She needed to get rid of him before he started plucking away her defenses like the wings on a dead fly. "I can't do this anymore."

"Because you've decided money doesn't matter," he said. "But what about Faith? Matt told me how well she's doing at that expensive culinary school. And that apartment in New York? It'd be a shame to lose all that so suddenly."

His nonchalance was terrifying. She eyed a nearby vase. It was light enough to throw but heavy enough to do damage. "Are you threatening her?"

Herman looked insulted. "Faith is family. I don't threaten my family. I help them." He pulled out a white envelope from his suit jacket. "This is an agreement, already signed."

Rachel stared at the envelope. Deciding whether to accept it felt like haggling over her soul. But her curiosity won. She snatched it from his hand and pried it open. The amount made her gasp. "Oh my god."

She looked up at him, and he stared back, inscrutable. "You'll stay through the congressional primary next year and we'll negotiate an additional agreement after. You and me. Matt will have nothing to do with this."

She wanted to fling it back into his face. She wanted to have never seen the trust agreement, with all the zeros under Faith's name. But her fingers tightened around the envelope, like they had a will of their own. "I need to think about it."

Herman stood and straightened his jacket. "I would expect nothing less. Like I said, Rachel. You were always the smart one."

---

Nathan had expected Joe to leave for the office as soon as they reached the laundromat. Even on a Sunday. Instead, he stood in the middle of Nathan's apartment, scowling at the air. His brother was never this quiet. It went on for so long that Nathan finally lost patience. "Is this silent treatment some kind of punishment?"

"She's a distraction," Joe said. Nathan started to protest, but Joe lifted a hand to stop him. "It's what you do. Escape somewhere..." He glanced at Nathan's sketchbook. "Into something, so you don't have to feel anything."

"You're wrong." Joe had it backward. He felt too much, all the emotions, firing on every cell at once. "I'm in love with her."

Joe looked pained, like it was the worst thing Nathan could have said. "It doesn't matter."

That's when Nathan realized that a part of his brother, the romantic, was slowly being poisoned by his two broken hearts.

"This family needs to heal," Joe continued. "You don't get to flit around infatuated, while the rest of us are putting in the work. Not this time."

Nathan thought about his last fight with Beto. How he'd frozen when confronted with his father's suffering. The next day he was in New York with Rachel, pretending it never happened. "The trip was last minute," Nathan said. "I wasn't trying to run away. I just needed a break to get my head on straight."

Joe laughed, and it was so sad and bitter that Nathan's throat tightened. "A break? I've lost my wife. I might lose my kid. The livelihood of our entire family—no, half this goddamn city—is about to be on me!"

He flung a hand at Nathan's chest. "And now I've got you, trying to make a terrible situation immensely fucking worse, by going down in flames where the whole world can see."

Nathan could feel himself retreating, his body instinctually trying to escape his brother's wrath. Joe was right. He'd been hiding from this. Cowering on the other side of town, behind a wall of fucking dryers. "I'm sorry," he said, even though the words felt thin and inadequate. "You're right, it was selfish. I've just always been—" Nathan stopped, because he'd nearly said *alone*. But it wasn't true. Because Joe had been there. As always. "It won't happen again. I promise."

The next day, Nathan was forced to follow through on that promise when he received a text from Beto asking him to stop by the house. After the argument with Joe, he'd decided to focus on what he could control. If Beto insulted him, Nathan didn't have to argue. He could ignore it and engage with his father as an equal instead of a wounded son. He could keep the peace for both their sakes. And for Joe.

An hour later, he pulled into his parents' driveway behind a car he didn't recognize. A housekeeper let him in, explaining that Sofia was visiting with guests. Nathan started to seek out his mother but froze at the sight of Rachel in the foyer. She'd straightened her hair. The pearls were back, tucked inside the high collar of a stiff white shirt that made it look like she was wearing a uniform. When she finally looked up from her phone and saw him, he couldn't think of anything to say except "Rachel?" It was a question, accusation, and plea all at once.

He started to reach for her. She shook her head and stepped back as Matt walked out of the living room. Rachel stiffened when Matt touched her lower back, and shuffled sideways, out of his reach.

"Nathaniel!" His mother walked out of the sitting room with a freckly redhead holding a camera trailing behind her. "What a surprise!" Sofia gave him air-kisses to preserve her lipstick.

"I came to see Beto," Nathan said.

Sofia dismissed the explanation with a flick of burgundy-tipped fingers. "Since everyone's here, let's all get a picture." She gestured toward

Rachel and Matt. The suggestion broke through Rachel's frozen posture, and she took a step back, swinging horrified eyes between the two men. When Beto appeared at the top of the stairs, Nathan nearly groaned with relief.

"I'm in the office," he said, and beckoned for Nathan to follow.

Sofia grabbed Nathan's arm. "We need to get a quick photo."

"Need?" Beto laughed. "I doubt that. Nathaniel, come on."

For once he was grateful for the smothering effect his father's bullish behavior had on the people around him. Nathan kissed Sofia's cheek and escaped up the stairs without turning back. Music floated into the hallway and grew louder as he walked into his father's office. Nathan listened for a moment and recognized "Habanera" from *Carmen*. "Is that Grace Bumbry?"

Beto sat in his high-back leather chair. " 'L'amour est un oiseau rebelle.' You listen to opera?"

Rachel had played it for him on their trip to New York. He remembered this piece in particular because she'd called it "the sexiest aria ever written."

"I've just heard it before."

Beto turned down the volume. "You're full of surprises, mijo."

Nathan sat in the chair on the opposite side of the desk. Beto grabbed a crystal decanter with golden liquid inside. "Mezcal," he declared pointedly, apparently still traumatized by the poor drink selection at Nathan's apartment.

I have something for you. Here." Beto handed Nathan a leather book. "It's my mother's photo album. You were looking at those old pictures the other day, and I thought you might want to have it."

Nathan's heart pounded as he accepted the album. He didn't know why their last vicious argument had inspired such a thoughtful gesture, but for the first time, he didn't care. He just wanted the same thing as Beto, to fix something between them, even if it was merely being able to take his father's kindness at face value.

Nathan opened the album to the first page. Abuelita's face smiled back at him from beneath a lace wedding veil. He'd heard stories about her wedding, how the whole city was in attendance and the reception lasted so long they had to serve breakfast the next day, but she always said that looking at the photos was painful. After his grandfather's death, she would talk about him as though he were still there. "Tomás always buys the perfect flowers for my birthday," she would say, years after he was gone.

He flipped through the pages of mostly black-and-white photographs until he came to one of Beto as a pimply teenager, standing next to a wood paneled car with a wide grin. A calmness washed over Nathan, like he'd found something he didn't know he was looking for. Confirmation that his father wasn't infallible. He was just a guy who went through the same nerdy growing pains as everyone else.

"First time taking her out," Beto said, tapping the car. "It took six months to convince my mother that I could handle it without crashing."

"You look so happy." Nathan wondered if Beto had ever smiled like that again. Maybe at his mother. Or when Joe was born. "It's a good picture." Nathan closed the album. "Thank you for this."

Beto studied his face. "You look like something's bothering you."

"No, I'm just—"

"Don't lie, Nathaniel, please." For once, it was a request instead of a command. Beto leaned back in his chair and motioned for Nathan to continue.

His hands were clammy. He set his glass down and wiped them against his thighs. "I'm..." He thought it would be hard to say, but the truth spilled out in a rush. "I'm in love with someone. A woman."

Beto nodded. "First time?"

"Yeah."

"Do I know her?"

Nathan hesitated and Beto must have sensed his struggle. "You don't have to say. But good for you."

"It doesn't feel good." Nathan drained his glass and flinched at the trail of fire it made down his throat. "It actually feels like shit."

"She doesn't love you back?"

He thought about how Rachel was downstairs right now, letting Matt Abbott touch her like they were still together. "I don't know what she feels. I don't think she knows either. But I'm not sure I can wait around while she figures it out."

"That's understandable." Beto tapped his chest, over his heart. "It hurts though, right? Thinking about letting go."

Nathan nodded. He tried to remember whether Beto had ever been this insightful before, but kept coming back to one memory, so old and worn that he could barely trust the details anymore. Beto loved cocoa and used to make oversized marshmallows from scratch. It was always strange to discover his father in shirtsleeves, studying a candy thermometer like a chemist. Once, when Nathan was six, Beto had caught him watching and beckoned him closer, inviting him in. Nathan had run away. For years he wasn't sure why, but now he realized it was unnerving to see your parents as more than the caricatures you'd created in your mind.

He was always running. But what if this time he stayed?

Beto drained his glass and set it on the table. "You boys are like me."

Nathan stilled. "Excuse me?"

"I know what you're thinking. Our history. We butt heads, but it's because we're too much alike. I knew that. I've always known, but you make it hard to—" He shook his head and mumbled something under his breath. "What I mean is you're very passionate, mijo. You and your brother. You love like..." He paused. "Like it's who you are. It's not simply a feeling. Losing this love will mean—"

"Losing myself," Nathan finished.

"Give her time," he said, with a bittersweet smile. His voice was filled with decades of regret. "That's what we all need to get it right sometimes. A little more time."

Beto's phone rang, and the extra-large font setting made it easy for Nathan to see Joe's name pop up. "This boy never slows down, does he?" He waved at the door. "Let's finish talking another time."

Nathan left but stood for a moment at the closed door, still reeling at one of the softest conversations he'd ever had with his father. There had been kindness and mutual respect. The exchange was so different from what they'd always been, it felt like a waking dream.

The foyer was empty when he finally walked downstairs. Nathan stopped to look at his mother's favorite piece of art, a framed textile piece by a local artist influenced by Feliciano Centurión. A small print by the same artist hung in his apartment. He should have told Sofia that. He should have thanked her for raising him in a house filled with inspiration. He should have looked up. But every day he'd kept his eyes stubbornly fixed to the ground, as if he had all the time in the world to appreciate what he'd been given.

Nathan left without anyone noticing. By the time he got home, he was so keyed up and itching to work, he almost tripped on his way up the stairs. He opened Abuelita's album and started to sketch. Once he had a rough idea, he pulled out a larger canvas and laid it on the floor.

He used every tool he could think of—pencils, charcoal, his fingers, the different positions of his body—to create light and smoke, heavy lines and whisper-thin shading. And then he'd move to another canvas, and start again, like a machine. He turned his music up so loud the table beneath the speaker started trembling. "Y Llegaste Tú" played on a loop, while the memory of her spilled from his fingers.

Nathan only stopped when someone knocked on the door. He turned off the music, and the sudden silence made his ears ring. There was another knock, softer this time. Like an apology. That's when he knew who was on the other side. But he still didn't move. Not yet. Every second he waited was another second they weren't broken. Loving her felt like holding the pin of a grenade.

He finally let Rachel in. The red lipstick was still there, perfect lines of deep red that made her mouth look like acrylic on canvas. She'd ditched the pearls, but this was a stranger. The mayor's wife. Someone who would pass him without a second glance.

---

Asking for water wasn't technically stalling. Rachel didn't want her voice to crack as she explained how broke she really was, that over the past few months, she'd barely scraped together enough money for her lawyer's retainer. Her voice was steady as she admitted the truth, so at least she had that. Because the way Nathan looked at her—like her confession was the plot of a horror movie he was forced to watch—was worse than Matt's sneering contempt.

"You asked for *money* to stay with him?" His question was drenched in judgment, like she'd traded her silence for Bitcoin.

"One million—plus the house." She found a loose thread in her skirt and wrapped it around her finger. "Herman offered me more. A lot more. But he wants me to stay until the Democratic primary is over. That article Alesha wrote isn't going over well. Add a messy divorce to all that and they might pass him over for the nomination."

"Good. They should." Nathan paused. "What did they say when you turned them down?"

She should have started the conversation differently. She should have pointed to the art supplies littering his floor and asked what he was working on since the gala was only three weeks away. Or she should have kissed him. She should have peeled off her clothes and pretended that she wasn't trying to imprint his memory on her skin.

"I haven't answered him yet," Rachel said, and omitted the rest. He wouldn't care about how she'd filled her schedule with donor lunches and gala committee meetings to anesthetize his absence. He wouldn't care that she'd failed completely.

Nathan's irritation slipped briefly into confusion before darkening into anger. "Why the hell not?"

"It's complicated."

"He's treating you like a—"

"Prostitute?"

His confirmation was a brief tightening around the eyes. "I wasn't going to say that."

She knew he couldn't accept her motivations because he didn't understand them. With his background, she doubted he ever would. "And it was my idea," she continued, pushing harder, because neither of them deserved to get off that easily. "It must be nice to have the luxury of a moral high ground sitting on a pile of your grandmother's money."

Nathan's jaw clenched. "This isn't about me."

"No, it isn't." Fury strained her voice. Rachel gouged her nails into her palm, using the pain to stay focused. "You've never been desperate. You've never had your entire life snatched away by things you couldn't control. We've both made bad choices, but you've always had better options. I'd love to walk away, buy a building, and wipe my slate clean, but I can't. I have to live with my mistakes. But Faith doesn't. And I owe her this."

"She wouldn't want it this way!" Nathan spoke in a rush, one word tripping over the next.

"Yeah, well, she's young," Rachel said. He stiffened, and she knew he heard the implication. *And so are you.*

Nathan seemed lost for a moment, scanning her face, looking for a tether. "Let me help you," he pleaded. "I'll pay your rent, find a lawyer—whatever you need to walk away from Abbott, free and clear." He was so sure. So confident that he'd figured out the obvious solution to her problems. But Rachel knew that look: another man playing a winning hand.

"No."

"So you'll take his money, but mine's not good enough for you?"

"I thought you were a good listener." She'd forgotten how loving someone could slowly convince you they were perfect. But like she told him when they met, people are flawed. "I earned every dime of that money. Thirteen years of propping that man up so far that it buried me. I'm not taking anything. I am *owed* a piece of the life that I built."

"But you shouldn't have to be miserable to get it! Pretending to be his wife, everyone judging you all the time. It's not fair to you." He finally reached for her, clasping her hands tight. "Let me help you. *Please.*"

Rachel closed her eyes. She was so close to saying yes. The desire was a flood strong enough to wash away the little willpower she had left. But she'd been here before. Seduced by the fairy tale. Now she knew the way it ended, with sour resentment, and all that gratitude twisting into contempt. "It's one more campaign," she said. "Once it's over, I'll be free to figure things out for myself."

He dropped her hands. "What do you want from me, Rachel? Why did you come here?"

*Because I love you*, she thought. *Because you said you were mine.* "I came to tell you the truth, so we could figure out how t-to..." She gestured between them. "We can just—"

"Keep fucking behind Matt's back?"

His voice was lifeless. She reached for his hand, but he jerked away. She panicked, her thoughts fracturing into excuses that were too embarrassing to admit out loud. Instead, she said the worst possible thing, at the worst possible time, which she regretted the moment it escaped her mouth. "It wouldn't be behind his back."

Nathan went still. Rachel grabbed his arm, this time ignoring the way he flinched, and blurted, "No, that's not what I meant—"

"You should leave." He gently pried her fingers from his wrist.

She started to cry, hard blinding tears. "Nathan, *wait*—"

"For *what*!" His face was ravaged. But asking her to pick him was also asking her to walk away with nothing. After all those promises she'd made to Faith, he was asking her to go back there, to a world that was constantly shifting beneath their feet.

"I can't," Rachel whispered. "I can't choose you. Not right now."

Nathan reared back. "You're better than this," he said, though his anger was crumbling. His eyes were glazed and red. "Better than all of them. And you deserve more than just what they're willing to give you." He looked away. "And so do I."

Nathan opened the door and gestured for her to leave. She was tempted to stay and argue, to try and convince him he was wrong, that even a flawed piece of what they had was worth saving.

But no one got to keep stolen moments. They were always going to end this way.

# CHAPTER NINETEEN

**Dillon:** Just ate a cheese ball and watched three seasons of The Golden Girls. Am I Rose?

**Dillon:** Bobbi is definitely Sofia.

**Dillon:** Wanna draw me a tattoo?

**Bobbi:** NATHAN. Where the fuck are you?

Bobbi and Nathan had a rule about never letting Dillon choose a bar without vetting it first. But when Dillon resorted to calling instead of texting, Nathan agreed to meet him and Bobbi for drinks at a dive bar they hadn't gone to in years. Nathan had also taken an edible Dillon left at his apartment, and after getting impatient when he didn't feel anything after thirty minutes, he also took some Molly. They'd both kicked in while he packed the final pieces for the showcase. The gala was tomorrow, and Nathan handed everything to the delivery guy with his heart thundering and his thoughts blunted into uselessness. It took him three tries to request a Lyft, because he kept tapping Postmates instead.

He sobered up when he walked into Mirrors, assaulted by the smell of stale cigarettes and urine. It was Thursday night, and the place was nearly empty. An ancient TV mounted to the wall was playing HGTV with the captions on. The faint strains of a Richard Marx ballad trickled through the speakers of an old jukebox.

Dillon spread his arms like a game show host. "Blast from the past, right?"

Bobbi immediately declared the place a "filthy shithole," with enough volume and conviction to earn dirty looks from a group of men clustered around a table. She gave them a "Sorry" that implied it was their fault for lacking standards.

"There's our booth." Dillon rushed to claim a red plastic booth in a shadowy corner. Bobbi grabbed Nathan's arm to stop him from following.

"Say something," she demanded.

Nathan's tongue felt thick and unqualified to comply. "Huh?"

"Okay, so you're not mute." She glanced at Dillon, who had started taking selfies beside an old Britney Spears poster. "You know, I'm used to you avoiding me, but ignoring Dillon is like ghosting a kitten. He'll never say it, but you hurt his feelings."

Nathan had been ignoring them for two weeks. He could tell by the tremble in her voice that Bobbi was hurt too.

"I'm sorry," he said. "I was..." He waved his hand, unable express the depressed, hyperproductive fugue state he'd entered to finish his art in words. "Working." He shrugged. "But I'm here now. Let's have some fun." The E was helping. He could hear the dreamy distance of his voice, and it was like welcoming back an old friend.

"What about you and..." She trailed off. Nathan fidgeted, ready to end the conversation. If she noticed, she didn't care. "What going on with you and Rachel?"

"I said it's done." Nathan moved past her to join Dillon, who had already ordered a pitcher. Bobbi could read the slightest shift in his expression like tarot cards, and he wasn't ready to discuss Rachel with her yet. Maybe he never would be. He was embarrassed by the way he'd lost her— by what she'd chosen over him. His friends didn't have to know how naive he'd been about their relationship. Joe's guilt trip had been bad enough.

Dillon poured a frosty mug and slid it toward Nathan. Bobbi sat in the booth on his right. "You should have let me order," she griped.

"You always take forever," Dillon said. "And these people don't know what grain of hops each brand uses or whatever."

"Grain of hops? I'm a chef, not a brewmaster. I just wanted to see what they had on tap."

"Spoiler, it's beer." Dillon pointed to the pitcher.

Nathan slumped into the booth and took a long drink. He could feel Bobbi watching him, but he refused to look at her. Dillon looked back and forth between them, picking up on the tension, and pointed to the jukebox. "We should play 'Cha Cha Slide.'"

Nathan grinned and said, "Are you still testing out your theory?"

"It's the only song that every white person on the planet will dance to. It comes with instructions!"

"What do you think, Nathan?" Bobbi caught his eyes. "You up for 'Cha Cha'? Or would you prefer Portishead? Something somber and broody to match your new artisanal asshole vibe."

Nathan huffed a breath. "So now I'm an asshole?"

"You have been kinda dickish lately, Nate," Dillon said.

Nathan was stunned. Dillon faltered briefly and then cleared his throat. "You've been moody. And impatient. Like that night at the drive-in. Then you completely disappeared for weeks—"

"That wasn't about you guys," Nathan interrupted. He was kicking himself for being so careless with their friendship. He just lost Rachel. He couldn't lose them too. "I'm...I'm sorry I did that. Really."

"Sure, man," Dillon said, his face creased with concern. "Apology accepted. But tonight you seem stoned or something. You're here, but you're not really *here*."

Nathan looked at Bobbi for conformation. She nodded, and embarrassment heated Nathan's neck. He looked away. "Let me make it up to you. I'll open a tab—see if we can get a few flights."

"No. Nope." Dillon shook his head hard enough to dislodge a blond curl from his deep side part. "You did a major art thing and we're celebrating. I'm paying." He waved a hand at the bartender, who picked up another pitcher. "Which means we're stuck with the cheap beer, but it's the thought that counts, right?"

"He's right," Bobbi said. "You're about to show your art, with your real name attached. That's huge!"

Nathan didn't want congratulations or attention. He wanted things to be the way they were before he'd agreed to do the gala. Before he met Rachel. When he could be a neutral bystander to his friends' bickering and add an occasional joke to ease the tension. He wanted to go back to being present but not actually seen. "It's really not a big deal," Nathan said. He nudged Dillon. "It's fine, man. I can get the beer."

"It is a big deal," Bobbi snapped. "And if he wants to pay, let him pay. Your bank account is not a goddamn superpower."

"Fine," he said flatly as he drained the rest of his beer. "I'll be sure to take advantage."

"That's what I'm talking about." Dillon slapped Nathan's back. "See, Bobs? I told you he'd bounce back."

Nathan looked at Bobbi. "Bounce back from what?"

Bobbi's chin lifted. "I told him that you probably disappeared because you were seeing someone, and it was serious. And that it might have ended badly."

Nathan clenched his jaw so tight his teeth ached. It was like Bobbi wanted him to fall apart. Then he'd have to admit that she was right about him all along. *Nathan loves Rachel. Nathan isn't fine. He's a skin sack of grief pretending to have bones.*

"I wasn't seeing anyone," he said. The lie was grit in his mouth, and he reached for water, only to find his glass empty. Nathan waved over the server, a cute and curvy woman with dark brown skin, and long braids laced with purple highlights. He ordered tequila shots and looked at her name tag. "Deja. Nice ink." He pointed to the small tattoo on her wrist.

She smiled. "Thanks, it's from Larry's on Third."

Bobbi groaned and chopped her hand through the air between them. "Enough. You've made your point, so turn it off." She looked at Deja. "Ignore him, please. He's just been dumped and is throwing a very charming tantrum. He's not safe for female consumption right now."

Dillon lifted his hand, doing his best to get Deja's attention. "I'm totally safe. For consuming." Deja rolled her eyes and walked away.

Nathan sighed. "I was just being friendly."

"Oh right," Bobbi said. "I've seen that kind of friendly, and it usually ends with me being Dillon's wingman after you disappear for the rest of the night."

"Don't slut shame him," Dillon said, and slapped Nathan's shoulder. "It's good to see you jumping back in it, Nate. I was getting worried."

Bobbi folded her arms. "I'm still worried."

"No one needs to worry about me. I am fine. I sent the pieces off this afternoon. It's over. Done." He directed the last bit at Bobbi, with a pointed *so shut up about Rachel* look. She returned his gaze with a stony *I've never shut up a day in my life* glare.

"I'm just glad it's all over," Nathan lied. The truth was he would rewind time if he could. He'd go back to that morning at the lake and fight harder. Say all the right things. Something to make her stay. "Rachel's the one who has to like it, not me."

"Rachel?" Dillon wrinkled his nose. "Who's Rachel?"

"Rachel Abbott," Bobbi said, her eyes glued to Nathan's face. "The mayor's wife."

"Could you not—" Nathan sighed. "Why does everyone call her that?"

"I suck at names," Dillon said simply.

Deja brought tequila and shot glasses to their table. She looked up, briefly met his eyes, and flipped her braid behind her shoulder in a clear invitation before walking away. He'd forgotten it could be that easy.

"It's late," Bobbi said. She sounded tired, like the effort of holding a grudge was finally taking a toll. "The gala's tomorrow night. You should rest. I'm sure you'll have to give a speech or something."

"I'm not going." Nathan poured a drink. "Like I said, it's done. I promised art, not a public appearance." He slammed the shot and welcomed its fiery trail down his throat. If he couldn't fuck the memory of Rachel away, maybe he could let it drown.

"Why do you always do this?" Bobbi grabbed her purse and slid to the end of the booth. "I'm so stupid for wanting more for you. Why should I when you clearly don't want it for yourself?"

"You don't want more for *me*," Nathan said, desperate for her to finally get it. She needed to accept that this was all he was, some basic guy in a bar. Not some brilliant artist "squandering his potential." "You want it for some other guy, with goals and ambition...and I tried, but—"

"Stop. I am sick of you pretending that no one loves you because you're too afraid to love them back. Well, that's life. Love, pain, and expectations. Welcome to it." Bobbi grabbed her purse and spat, "Grow up," over her shoulder before she marched to the door.

Nathan leaned back against the booth, staring at his empty glass with her words heavy on his mind. His phone vibrated.

**Joe:** I know you don't own a tux. I got you. Hit me back in the morning.

He hadn't spoken to Joe in weeks. He'd figured his brother had finally lost faith in him. But here he was, offering the same olive branch he always did.

"Hey, Nate. Are you okay?" Dillon frowned. "Bobbi didn't hurt your feelings, did she? You look like you're about to cry."

"I'm okay," Nathan said. Bobbi was right; he needed to grow up. He needed to appreciate the people who loved him, by doing the one thing they'd ever asked of him: showing up.

---

Rachel knew how to grieve. She had a whole life of loss to draw from. When the pain became too much, she would think about something worse than losing Nathan. Like abandoning Faith again. Or becoming more like her own mother. If someone noticed her red eyes, she blamed exhaustion. If someone mentioned his name, she changed the subject. She woke up each day and reminded herself, like a mantra, that she would eventually move on. These things had stages.

But the strategy kept her in stasis, in a state between despair and numbness that nothing could penetrate, not even Matt's clumsy attempts to be a good husband. She couldn't even get angry. Which was why, the day before the gala, she wasn't surprised to see their marriage counselor sitting in her living room.

Rachel waited for someone else to speak. Matt propped his elbow on a pillow, glanced at Rachel's rigid posture, and sat up straighter. "I'd like to say something that's long overdue."

Shania nodded with a tilted head. "Sounds like progress. Rachel, are you ready to hear it?"

The question was pointless, because they both knew the answer didn't matter. Engaging quietly while smothering a primal scream had always been the cost of her life. But unlike in previous sessions, she couldn't fake the requisite enthusiasm. Her shoulder lifted with a shrug so lackluster that Shania looked concerned.

Matt reached out like he wanted to take her hand. Rachel made a fist. He rubbed the couch cushion between them instead. "I don't know how to say this, so I'll just... say it. I've been unfaithful to Rachel."

She was stunned. After months of hand-wringing and blackmail schemes, the easy slip of the truth from his mouth stole her breath. There had to be a reason, some new strategy she was missing. Shania looked dumbfounded. Matt stared down at his hands.

"I've thought a lot about why I did it," he said. "What I was looking for. And I think... no, I *know* that I was lonely." He looked at Rachel with desolate eyes. Her chest tightened. Without his usual cockiness, Matt was almost unrecognizable. "We stopped talking. I don't know when it happened, but we shared this house without being *together*. You didn't like being around me." Rachel shook her head, but he lifted a hand and said, "It's true. Please, let's be honest for once. You hated being alone with me. And I'm not blaming you, I just... I don't know why."

Rachel's first impulse was to reach for the anger she always kept sharp and ready for attack. But losing Nathan had worn down the edges. Thirteen years of heartache rushed out in its place.

"You stopped listening," she said. "I tried to tell you that this life, your career, was strangling me, but you didn't want to hear it. You couldn't hear that and keep pretending everything was okay. So I stopped trying."

She paused, replaying the last few years of their marriage. How quiet it was unless they argued. How cautious and still. "I've been lonely too," she said. "And jealous. Your life is filled with so much purpose, and I've drained mine of anything real." Each word cracked her open, bit by bit. She dug deep and pulled out more. Maybe it was also healing something. "I don't know why you married me."

Matt looked horrified. "What? That's a ridiculous thing to say."

"No, Matt," Shania interjected, surprising them both by her sudden shift in loyalties. "Don't negate how she feels. There's a question in that statement, and she needs an answer."

Matt sat back with a furrowed brow. He stared at Rachel for a moment, then slowly shook his head. "How could you not know? You *captivated* me. I spent our first year together being rocked by you and it was the best thing that ever happened to me." He retreated into his thoughts, his lips twitching into a smile. "You were beautiful. And funny. I don't think you know that, but you're funny without even trying. You were strong. Creative. And brave." He met her eyes again. "You didn't care about who I was or what anyone else thought about you. That wild whirlwind of *stuff* inside you? I never had that. I was grateful to be invited in. To just hang on and watch."

Rachel recognized the woman Matt described. She'd gotten drunk in the rosebushes and nearly wrecked a vintage Camaro. She'd plunged headfirst into the kind of full-body love that can destroy you. She was the scandal Herman feared and Matt never fought for. The woman she'd been pressured to leave behind.

"You didn't marry her," Rachel said softly.

Matt blinked, confused. "What?"

Rachel met his eyes. "That woman you described. She wasn't someone you could build a life with."

Matt swiveled on the couch to face her. "That's not—"

"You said we were being honest." Her voice trembled, thick with tears. "So don't rewrite our history. We agreed, remember? To be partners. To be what each other needed. And you needed to be *this* man who needed *this* wife at his side." Her eyes blurred, hazing out the details of his face. "And I said yes. *I* was here. Where *the fuck* were you?"

"Okay," Shania said. "I think maybe we should—"

Matt held up his hand to cut her off. "What the hell are you talking about? I was always here for you and Faith. My family has always treated you like one of us. Better! Christmas ski trips and dinners. We didn't have family dinners growing up. And it took years for Dad to set up our trusts, but Faith was only eight years old when he—" He stopped. The red flush leached from his face, and he closed his mouth so quickly it made a popping sound.

Matt was a bad liar, but only if you were paying attention. If she hadn't been ignoring him all these years, maybe she would have caught his cheating sooner. His complexion was a mood stone that would always betray him.

"When he what?" Rachel asked. Matt's shoulders caved, revealing the truth; the trust Herman showed her had nothing to do with her decision to stay. "He opened that account when we got married?"

Shania leaned in again. "We're getting off topic."

Rachel stood. "You lying son of a bitch."

She left the room, grabbed her car keys, and sped out of the garage. Her vision was so clouded by tears she had to pull over. She was done. Whatever war she'd been waging was over.

Once the tears faded, she realized she had nowhere to go. Nathan had been her haven. Years ago, she'd thought it might be Alesha and briefly fantasized about being welcomed into some perfect long-lost family. But real families were messy and flawed. They saw the truth of your horrible marriage even when you didn't want them to. That's what she needed. Something real.

Ten minutes later she knocked on the door of a two-story bungalow with an old, dented Corolla parked out front. Mia opened the door and blinked in surprise. Her face was sweaty like Rachel had interrupted her workout.

"Sorry I didn't call first," Rachel said, her resolve not to cry again crumbling at Mia's worried expression. "My life is a mess and I really need help."

Mia's living room was filled with the type of overstuffed furniture that swallowed you whole. Rachel chose a recliner and sank into its cushions. She explained everything, from Herman's deal to being in love with Nathan. It felt good to finally admit it out loud.

"So, the Abbotts tricked you," Mia said. She'd listened to Rachel's story with the grimness of an undertaker.

"Yes," Rachel said. "And I fell for it. I saw all that money and threw away—" The rest, she swallowed back. She'd learned her lesson about speaking her pain into existence. She couldn't take another bruise. "Now I don't know what to do."

"What do you want to do?"

Rachel laughed. "What I want is not an option."

"Why not?"

"Because it just isn't. It never was." She shucked off her shoes and pulled her legs up to her chest. "Where's Livie?"

Mia turned to look over her shoulder, as if her daughter would appear out of thin air. "She's with Ken in DC," she said. "Her dad got her concert tickets to see that boy with the big glasses and curly hair?" She shrugged. "I never know what to do with myself when she's gone."

Rachel pointed to the treadmill in the corner of the room. "Work out, I guess?"

Mia nodded slowly. "Sure." She paused. "Do you like lions?"

Rachel blinked. "I don't know. I never thought about it."

"Livie used to love them. It was one of her first words. She'd say *la la* instead of *lion* and it was so cute. I got mad when Ken would correct her. Anyway, for a while it was lion everything. Stuffed lions, lion birthday cake, Halloween costumes. As she got older, it was National Geographic documentaries. Her friends were into princesses, and she was obsessed with hunting conditions in the savannah."

"I miss that," Rachel said. "How passionate Faith would get about something. It was so intense."

"We lose that, don't we? Passion. Like it's something you outgrow." She propped her legs up on the coffee table. "So, one day, Livie is talking my ear off about how lionesses abandon the pride when they have cubs. They leave to protect them from predators, moving from place to place to hide their scent. Did you know that?"

"No, I didn't." She also had no idea where the conversation was going. But just listening to Mia's low voice was calming. She sank deeper into the chair. "How long are they gone?"

"According to Livie, six or seven weeks. After that they take the cubs back to the pride. Back to all that danger they were protecting them from. It made no sense to me. I asked Livie, 'Why would a mother uproot her life to keep her children safe, and then take them back to that same danger two months later?' And Livie gave me that bored look I hate, you know the one, and said, 'Because she's not a mother. She's a lion.' "

Mia extended her arms overhead and stretched. "It really is hard to remember who we were sometimes. Or who we are."

Rachel used to believe that dissatisfaction was her nature. That abandoning Faith was in the blood her mother gave her, and that she'd never truly be satisfied standing still. But then she thought of Nathan, and how content she'd been with him. At the drive-in. At the lake. Maybe the real problem was where she'd been standing.

"I get it," Rachel said. "But my situation's not that simple."

"Who said love was simple?" Mia leaned forward. "Love made me flunk out of law school. I ditched all my classes to help my fiancé through a mental health crisis, and he still chose work over me." She shrugged. "Doesn't mean I shouldn't have loved him, or that I don't deserve to be happy. Mistakes aren't debts we owe to other people. They're just part of living."

Rachel had considered telling Faith the truth a dozen times. She'd rehearsed the conversation like a script, parsing the best way to explain that while she and Matt were over, nothing else would change. She would have a home. A life that her mother had cemented into place. So even as Faith made her way in the world, Rachel would always be her anchor.

That's what she would have been for the rest of her life. A constant. A fixed point on a compass. But Nathan had found her. And he said she was the sun.

# CHAPTER TWENTY

B y the time Rachel arrived at the National Portrait Gallery, its court-yard had almost been completely transformed by the crew setting up for the gala. Slender walls with donated art had been erected throughout the space. Round tables covered with white linens were positioned to make room for dancing. A section of chairs near the front had been set up for a jazz ensemble.

Rachel was still working up the courage to open the wrapped can-vases that had been delivered that morning. She'd decided it was safer to open them here, mere hours before the gala, when she'd be too busy to be tormented by Nathan's work. She'd imagined seeing the pieces for the first time in a room bustling with harried catering staff and flo-rists. But she'd underestimated the efficiency of the people working for Sofia—aside from Nathan's collection, everything was done. Instead of being surrounded by strangers, she was alone with the covered paintings and Hailey Dearwood, who smiled while gripping her clipboard hard enough to turn her pale knuckles even whiter.

Matt had probably sent her to spy. She hovered close and deemed everything "interesting." It was *interesting* that the media couldn't take pictures before the gala. Rachel's decision to keep Nathan's work hidden until the auction closed was also an *interesting choice*. "I wonder if such an unusual approach is a good idea."

"These people don't need art," Rachel said. "Some of them don't even want it. But they will pay millions to screw over someone else, regard-less of what the paintings look like." She pointed to Nathan's covered art. "The minute someone sees it and decides it's not for them, we lose leverage. I want to max out the bidding before that happens."

Rachel ran a finger along the edge of the canvas. Her nail snagged the paper and caused a small rip. Hailey stared and asked, "Can I see it? I can't afford to bid anyway."

Rachel had thought she wanted an audience when she did this. Now, in the moment, she wanted to gather up the paintings and find a dark, empty room to hide in. But the clock was ticking. And the longer she waited, the more suspicious Hailey became. Rachel ripped away the wrapping and stepped back to take it in.

It was a charcoal drawing of a young woman with brown skin and large eyes with wisps of black hair floating around her shoulders. A lace veil covered half her face. Rachel crouched to look more closely and saw that the veil was made of pressed white flowers that he'd crushed and twisted to create an intricate pattern. *Abuelita* was written in light script at the bottom.

"This is lovely," Hailey whispered, awestruck.

It was more than lovely. On the way to New York, Nathan told her how devastating it was to lose his grandmother, how she'd always been his fiercest champion. It was a heartbreaking tribute. Rachel hid the tears clouding her eyes by pretending to study his signature. "It's brilliant."

She opened the next one more quickly. But when she pulled the paper away, her heart bottomed into her stomach. It was a self-portrait. Nathan's head was bowed and most of his face was hidden behind a harsh shadow, but the charcoal drawing was unmistakably him. It was black and white except for his tattoos, which he'd re-created in vivid color. The phoenix on his arm had been formed with red and yellow pressed leaves, layered to create the illusion of real feathers. He'd burned the bottom right half of the canvas, forming a jagged black void that encroached upward, threatening to consume him.

Rachel glanced at Hailey. "What do you think?"

"Me?" Her face was flushed. "That's him, isn't it? Nathan?"

"Yes."

"Beautiful." Her face reddened even more. "*It's* beautiful, I mean. He's very talented." She opened her mouth, closed it, and then spoke in a breathless rush. "What is he doing?"

Rachel studied his figure, the clenched muscles along his neck and shoulders, the bulging biceps, the intense expression that could be pain, pleasure, frustration—the euphoric torture of being pulled to the edge of release, but not allowed to reach it. She'd made him beg for it at the lake house, a gradual destruction with his heart thundering beneath her hand.

The sound of paper being ripped brought her back to the present. Rachel started to protest, but Hailey had already torn the last of it away. "Oh my god," Hailey whispered, shock replacing her earlier reverence.

At first, Rachel thought it was another woman. She didn't look at her own naked body often enough to recognize it instantly. She usually saw herself in pieces. A dimpled thigh. An old scar across her stomach. Only flaws. But it was her hair that finally made it register. She knew those mixed-pattern curls from countless years of wrestling them into submission.

He'd drawn her at the lake house, during that late golden hour, when the sky was glowing and her limbs were liquid. She had reclined on a window seat surrounded by white pillows as he sketched on a notepad with a ballpoint pin. Everything had stopped. The lake was still, and the sun hung forever in that perfect spot in the sky. For Rachel, it seemed that the world had held its breath for one long, flawless moment and Nathan had re-created it all on his canvas.

It was mixed media like the others, but less precise, a chaotic mass of charcoal, ash, and oil paint, with her image pulled from the wreckage. The lines were hazy, as if her nude body were made of smoke. Except her eyes. They were drawn with such accuracy that it almost looked like a photograph cut and pasted in. They were also the darkest part of the work, midnight pools dotted with light that looked like stars. Rachel was so mesmerized by her own gaze that she didn't hear Hailey speak at first. "I'm sorry, what?"

"Is that you?" Hailey pointed to the portrait. Rachel thought about Mia's lioness and smiled.

"Yes. That's me."

"But it's not *you* you, right? This is him guessing. Or maybe he found an old photograph?" Hailey's voice lifted slightly. She sounded like Matt, begging for another lie. Or Herman, waving that envelope around. Their voices cascaded together, tempting her to take the convenient excuse Hailey was offering. *Just one more. One more lie to make it easier.*

But it would never be just one more. There would be another lie each time Faith wrote a check from that trust. Or in every moment Rachel pretended there was anything in her life with Matt worth saving. It was in every second she didn't tell Nathan how she felt.

Love would be so much easier if it were perfect, if it came to you at just the right time from exactly the right person. But love was rushing to capture dawn with brushstrokes. It was an untouched photograph slightly overexposed and gorgeously flawed in all the ways that made it real. Staring at her portrait, Rachel could finally appreciate it in herself. The messy mistakes that had molded her. The chaotic passion that made her human.

"He's my lover." Just saying it, *finally*, soothed so much pain. "Or he was. He left me because I wasn't brave enough to turn down the fifteen million dollars Herman Abbott offered so I wouldn't leave his cheating son."

Hailey swallowed hard. "*What?*"

Rachel told her about Matt's affair and how he'd changed his mind about wanting a divorce. Each confession felt like medicine. Hailey inched farther back as she spoke. "He must be bored by his mistress," Rachel said. "Girlfriend. Whatever the hell she was."

"You don't know her name?"

"No. And I don't care. She can have him."

Hailey's face had paled to a sickly gray color. "Matt wouldn't do something like that. He's a good, honorable man."

Hailey wasn't a friend, but Rachel respected her enough to be sympathetic. She used to be the same, enabling Matt's obliviousness with unquestioning loyalty and trust. "Your boss isn't honorable, Hailey. He's just a politician."

Hailey's face crumpled, and she let her clipboard fall to the floor. Rachel touched her arm. "Hey, I'm not looking to derail anyone's career, including yours. I just want a divorce. No one has to find out about any of this."

"I'm so sorry, Rachel." Hailey shook her head. "I didn't know. I'm so sorry he did that to you."

"No, I'm sorry. This whole thing is a mess, and you got dragged into it."

Rachel's mind went back to the gala, her panic increasing. They had only a few hours before people would start arriving. She hurriedly opened Nathan's final piece, a landscape of Oasis Springs. He'd drawn the business district that housed Vasquez Industries in charcoal on parchment that he'd torn down the middle. Beneath the jagged rip was an oil painting of a coffee farm, rendered in vivid color, and dotted with the dark silhouettes of farm workers, the city's original citizens.

*Abuelita*, his self-portrait, and the landscape could be a series honoring his family and their role in the town. The nude would twist everything into a sex scandal. "I need to put this somewhere," Rachel said, grabbing her portrait.

Hailey ran a shaky hand over her face. "Let me take care of it." Rachel started to protest, but Hailey insisted. "This is what I do, remember? Control the narrative." She touched the frame with light fingers and a tight smile. "Trust me. I'll put it somewhere Matt will never find it."

---

Elaborate private parties at public institutions chafed at Nathan in a way that excess for the sake of excess always did. The same people who spent thousands on dinner tickets would also feel entitled to take selfies in front of priceless paintings with *No photography* signs prominently displayed.

He was forced to endure four awkward conversations about his art before he even reached the courtyard. Since the paintings were hidden,

Nathan didn't know how much he was supposed to tell them. He was relieved when a waiter passed by with champagne. It wasn't really his thing, but he gulped the fizzy liquid down like a shot.

He grabbed another glass and drained it just as quickly while he moved into the larger, open-air space. A tall, thin white man shook his hand and introduced himself as a friend of Lyric's. "I can't wait to see what you've done for us," the man said, gesturing toward the stage. Being fawned over before anyone had seen his art made it feel even more hollow. Rachel's portrait was his best work, and while he'd never meant to send it, a selfish part of him was disappointed there were only three canvases onstage, covered in sheets. She'd probably buried it in the back of her studio.

Sofia found him with another empty glass in his hand. She pried it from his fingers and stroked his arm. "You look nervous."

"You look great," Nathan said. She wore a green strapless evening gown with huge emeralds dangling from her ears.

"I don't know why she insists on hiding your work until later," Sofia huffed. "And what is this?" She gestured toward the band. A few couples had migrated onto the floor and swayed slowly to the music. "Dancing before dinner? I never should have added her to the planning committee."

"She's good at this," he said. "Let her do her job."

She gave him a long look, a little too intense for comfort. "So, you two are friends now." It wasn't a question, but an irritated accusation. "I should have known. A woman like that—"

"A woman like what?" He sounded possessive and it made him feel pathetic. "Whatever. If you don't like her, why'd you ask her to host?"

"Because of her husband," Sofia said quickly. "But marrying into that family has gone to her head. This secret bidding gambit feels cheap and amateurish." She gestured at his paintings. "Rachel Abbott makes grandiose promises, but it's just a sad little performance. I pray she doesn't drag you down as well."

He scanned the room, searching for a distraction. The crowd had swelled, making it harder to tell one tuxedoed man from another. "Is Beto here?"

"He had to finish up something for work," Sofia said. "But he'll arrive before the program starts."

He wanted to believe her. That last conversation with his father had given him hope. There was no reason to doubt that Beto would walk in at any moment, and his whole family would be there when someone pulled that sheet away from *Abuelita*. But with every minute that ticked by, more of the old skepticism crept in. Beto had never chosen any of them over work before.

Nathan had emptied two more champagne glasses while he spoke to his mother. Now his mind was racing, while the alcohol caused a slow-limbed, frantic feeling that made him stumble as he moved to the bar. He'd nearly reached it when Joe grabbed his arm. "Have you seen Beto yet? Mom said he got a work call, and they took separate cars."

"I think she left to call him." Nathan shook off his hand and took a step toward the bar. Joe grabbed him again.

"What's up with you?"

"Nothing. I'm fine." Nathan ordered bourbon while Joe hovered. The bartender passed him a drink, and Nathan tossed a twenty into his tip jar. The man nodded his appreciation. "See. This guy thinks I'm fine." He drained the glass in one swallow.

"Oh yeah, man. And doing shots in black tie isn't a huge red flag." Joe grabbed Nathan's glass and pointed to the entrance. "She's here."

Nathan's plan had been to fake cool ambivalence when he saw her, but his body didn't listen, flashing hot as his lungs abandoned any attempt to breathe. He saw a bit of gold fabric quickly obscured by the crowd. A second glimpse confirmed it was Rachel. Her dress was a literal work of art. It was made of small pieces of gold leather that looked like someone had poured tiny, molten scales over her body to form a low-cut evening gown. She'd styled her hair in a waist-length goddess braid, threaded with matching gold highlights. Her eyes were rimmed with smoky metallics, and her lips painted a soft nude that made them look plush and erotically bare.

Nathan caught the bartender's eye and was about to order another drink when Joe handed the man a hundred-dollar bill and said, "Stop serving him."

Nathan glared. "Seriously?"

"I'm not watching you get wasted tonight." Joe waved his hand at the crowd. "Everyone in this room is rooting for you. Including her."

Nathan's eyes were drawn to Rachel again. "How do you do it?" he asked Joe.

"Do what?"

"How can you stand to be so close to someone you love, and not tell her." He looked at Joe. "You don't even mention Mia, and she lives ten minutes away."

The champagne had slowed his brain, and the reality of what he'd implied hit him too late. Joe was too practical and honest to pine after one woman while married to someone else. Nathan was the piece of shit who always did the wrong thing.

"God." Nathan rubbed hard at his eyes, trying to will himself sober. "I'm sorry. Please forget I said that."

Joe blocked his view of the crowd and stared him down. "I know you love this woman, and it probably feels like you discovered that feeling—no one else could possibly have loved the way you do because if they had, nothing else would matter. But, Nate, being in love is selfish. It's all about how good you feel, and what you want. Giving love is selfless. So no one cares if you want to say the words or not. What matters is whether that person needs to hear them."

Nathan thought about his reaction to Rachel's deal with Matt. He'd dismissed her reasons like a kid screaming, "So what," over and over because he thought his love was more important. And now Joe was telling him the exact same thing she did: he may have heard her reasons, but he didn't bother to listen.

"I wanted to take care of her." It sounded so naive when he said it out loud. "I thought it was what she needed." Nathan scanned the crowd, searching for a glimpse of gold. "But maybe it was what I needed. Sometimes I feel so goddamn useless."

Joe grabbed his shoulder and squeezed. "You don't have to prove yourself to the people who love you, Nate. Just let us do it."

Nathan had been clinging to the hope of a *someday* that deep down he'd never believed would come. Someday he'd make Beto proud. Someday his mother would choose him over his father. Someday he and Joe could be just brothers instead of burdens to each other. But the man he imagined in all those somedays wasn't really him. That's what Joe had been trying to say. That the man he was, *this* man, the weird afterthought with blurry non-dragons and too many feelings, this was the man they were all supporting tonight. Because they loved him, and because he was enough.

Joe's gaze drifted past his shoulder, and Nathan turned to see Rachel standing a few feet away. She extended a tentative hand.

"Will you dance with me?"

Nathan didn't move. He looked at the dance floor, which was dotted with older couples, swaying to the last notes of the saxophonist's solo. Rachel had to know they would attract attention. Her fingers curled back slightly, like she was losing her nerve. But then she met his eyes and whispered, "Please."

The word cut through him, even after everything.

The band started playing again. He ignored her hand and reached for her waist instead, pulling her into his arms. A dozen eyes swung their way, but he wouldn't allow himself to care. What if this was his last chance to hold her like this? After tonight there were no more excuses— no galas to force them into each other's lives.

"I wasn't sure you would come," Rachel said. She slid both hands up to his shoulders. "I'm glad you did."

He looked around. The sly looks had turned to staring and whispering. Her fingers grazed the nape of his neck. Nathan met her eyes again. "Where's your husband?"

He was trying to shock her into realizing they were making a scene, but she didn't blink. "I miss you, Nathan."

His throat tightened and every messy, lovesick feeling he'd tried to ignore over the last three weeks flooded him at once. "Don't. It doesn't matter."

"Yes, it does. It *does*." She gripped him tighter. "Please listen—"

"I don't even know why I'm here." He shook his head. "To see you, that's why. I'm a goddamn masochist. How many ways can you break my heart before I stop giving it to you?" He lowered his mouth to her ear and spoke in a harsh whisper. "I'd be inside you right now if you said you wanted me." She tightened her hand on his neck. The buzzing chatter swirling around them was rising. He looked up and locked eyes with a short redhead who had stopped dancing to stare. "But they're always watching," he said, staring back. The woman blushed and looked away.

Rachel caught his gaze again. "So let them watch."

---

"May I have your attention?"

Rachel felt Nathan's arm slack around her waist as Hailey's amplified voice pulled his attention to the stage. Rachel wanted to pull it back. She'd rehearsed this moment so many times. How she'd tell him that she was done with the Abbotts. That she was sorry for hurting him and that she'd do whatever it took to earn his forgiveness. She would give him space if he needed it. She could probably use it too, at least until her divorce was final. She had explanations and plans and timelines, but it all evaporated once he took her into his arms.

But she also knew that tonight wasn't about her apologies. It was about Nathan and all the work he'd put into this moment. A moment that had inexplicably been hijacked by Matt's communications director.

Rachel spun around, searching for Sofia. Nathan told her that his mother had left a while ago to call Beto. Hailey said, "Is this on?" and slapped her hand against the microphone. It made a muffled thumping sound, followed by a high-pitched squeal of feedback.

"Welcome to the gala! I'm Hailey Dearwood, communications direc-tor for our esteemed Mayor Abbott, who's hosting the event with…"

She scanned the room until she spotted Rachel. "There she is! Rachel Abbott. Please applaud her. She deserves it."

Servers froze in the middle of placing salads on the tables. The program wasn't supposed to start until after they'd served dessert. The room broke into a slow, confused applause.

"Rachel is amazing," Hailey continued. "She makes me feel inadequate in every way." The microphone flopped to one side. She looked flushed and unsteady, eyeing the crowd like a rock singer about to launch herself into a mosh pit.

"Is she drunk?" Rachel whispered.

Nathan touched her arm. "Do you want me to do something?"

A group of men in navy blazers were poised to rush the stage if someone signaled. It would cause a huge scene. So far, the damage was minor. "I'll handle it." She started to move closer but stopped when Hailey pointed to her again.

"Would you look at her? God, that dress! She looks like a supermodel." She peered into the crowd and yelled, "Chime in whenever you want, Mayor."

A tense chuckle filled the room. Matt sat at a table near the front. He didn't laugh. He stared at Hailey as though he didn't recognize her.

"Rachel was supposed to do this part of the evening. But she works so hard, I thought she deserved a break. She also deserves our gratitude. As of thirty minutes ago, this is officially the biggest fundraiser that the Vasquez Foundation has ever held. This woman has outraised every single prior event."

The crowd went from confused to appreciative, their applause louder, peppered with a few excited shouts. Hailey spoke into the microphone as their claps faded. "You all sound so surprised. I don't blame you. I'm shocked too." She snorted. "That sounds so mean. But seriously, how would we know? Did *you* know she was brilliant?" She pointed to someone in the crowd. "How about you? Did *you* know?"

Hailey strolled across the stage. "She's just so *pretty*." She spat the last word like a curse. "You all know what I mean. Everyone in this town is pretty and perfect, but really, no one is. Deep down we're all ugly inside. Selfish. And greedy. But we keep pretending because we all want…" She stopped walking when she reached Matt and stared down at him with watery eyes. "We all just want the fairy tale."

Rachel gasped. "Oh my god," she breathed. "It's her."

"What?" Nathan grabbed her arm.

"Matt's mistress." Rachel closed her eyes. "I am so stupid. Of course she is."

"Hailey." Matt moved to the stage with the forced smile of a maniacal Cheshire cat. He gestured for her to come down. "I think that's enough."

Hailey glared. "I already know what you think. I know everything about you." She pointed to Rachel. "And you don't deserve her. She's put up with so much from you without one fucking word of complaint." Hailey laughed, a harsh chuckle that echoed through the stunned ballroom. She looked at Rachel. "I admire you for being the bigger woman." Her eyes glazed with tears. She looked at Matt, and her anguish flattened into bitter loathing. "But I'm not."

Hailey grabbed the sheet covering one of Nathan's pieces and pulled it away. Rachel closed her eyes. She knew what was coming. The shocked murmur that rippled through the crowd confirmed it. Hailey had switched the portraits before the gala. It was her. Naked.

Someone gasped. Rachel opened her eyes and saw Matt rushing to the stage. Hailey planted herself in his path and he froze, hands outstretched like he wanted to grab her. But he shouldered past and snatched up the frame.

Rachel didn't realize that Nathan was gone until she saw him next to Matt, trying to yank the portrait away. She rushed to the stage, but Joe beat her there. He grabbed Nathan's arm and pulled hard, breaking his grip on the canvas. Matt stumbled back, and it clattered to the floor.

"That's enough!" Joe shoved Matt toward the stairs and jabbed his finger in Nathan's direction. "Both of you. *Go.*"

The room had become a sea of iPhones, backed by a discordant symphony of high-pitched outrage and gleeful shock. Rachel was numb.

Hailey confronted her with tears still sliding down her cheeks. "Tell Matt I quit." She walked away with the regal posture of someone who'd been crowned prom queen instead of revealed as a jilted lover.

Rachel spoke into the microphone. "I apologize for the disruption, everyone. Thank you for coming, and for your generous donations." She looked out at the crowd. Half of them were ignoring her. The other half were trying to get another glimpse of her naked portrait. "There are donation cards at your table, and I hope you'll consider additional gifts to a worthy cause."

There was still no sign of Sofia. Rachel rushed offstage. She intercepted security and somehow managed to convince them to focus on crowd control rather than the earlier drama. A few minutes later, she found Nathan, Matt, and Joe facing off in the darkened special collections area. Matt flung curses over Joe's shoulder, while Nathan glowered, a silent, impenetrable wall.

"You need to calm down," Joe said.

Matt sputtered something about calling security, but froze when he saw Rachel. His long glare felt endless, and she floundered beneath it, trying and failing to summon actual words. She remembered how ashamed he'd looked when she pushed his birthday cake to the floor. Was there a right thing to say in moments like this? *Sorry I hurt you, but I wanted him more.*

"How long have you been fucking my wife?" Matt refused to look at Nathan, trying to provoke them both.

"She's not your wife," Nathan answered, giving him nothing but stoic contempt.

"Not my—" Matt's eyes narrowed on Rachel. "You *told* him?"

She stepped back, putting distance between herself and his rage. "Yes, but—"

"Is this what you've been doing? All those times you disappeared. You were off fucking this kid?"

Rachel grabbed his arm. "Would you stop and listen to me? We can't do this here!"

"She's right," Joe said. "There's press hanging around the lobby. One of them could walk through that door any minute."

"Thirteen years," Matt muttered as he shook Rachel off. "I gave you everything. I pulled you out of the damn gutter and for what? So you could humiliate me in front of the whole world?" His lips curled into a disgusted sneer. "You were going to take my money. Make me beg you to stay while you were slutting around town with some—"

Nathan's fist slammed into his jaw and sent him skidding to the ground. The dull thud made Rachel gasp. She stumbled back to avoid being hit by the wild sprawl of Matt's legs.

Nathan crouched to meet his eyes. "I told you not to talk to her that way."

Matt stood and shuffled back. "You stupid son of a bitch. I could have you arrested."

"*No.*" Rachel stood between them. "Matt, please. Don't do this. You're mad at me, not him."

He shouldered past her. "You can both go to hell."

# CHAPTER TWENTY-ONE

The fallout started as a slow trickle. Mia called while Rachel was driving home. She'd read about what happened in a PTA group chat, and the story had already changed multiple times. In the latest version, Nathan had punched Matt onstage and damaged an exhibit while Rachel cowered in the corner, sobbing. "I muted that shit," Mia said. "But I thought you'd want to know what people were saying."

Walking into an empty house was a relief. Matt was probably already discussing divorce strategies with Herman in some Abbott war room. Rachel closed all the blinds and poured a glass of wine before she looked at her phone again. There were fifteen voicemails. One from Faith that she barely understood because of a bad connection. One from Ben asking if she was okay and another from Julia demanding a call. The rest were from reporters. Her social media apps had so many notifications that they'd defaulted to a plus sign instead of updating the number.

Rachel FaceTimed Faith. It took her daughter longer than normal to answer, and when she did, she looked mussed and bleary, like she'd been startled awake.

"Mom, what the hell?" Faith was on her laptop and held her phone in one hand. "My DMs are blowing up. I think a reporter called me. How did they get my number?"

"Block them. I'll get your number changed."

"Just tell me what's going on. Matt called an hour ago, but I wanted to talk to you first. Did he really cheat on you? Did you both...cheat? Are you getting divorced?"

Rachel heard the lingering hope in Faith's questions, that somehow a dozen news outlets had gotten the story wrong. It reminded her of Matt's birthday party, and how she'd clung to her denial despite the clear evidence of his lies on her phone. She took a deep breath and confessed the truth. "We haven't been happy for a long time. I should have told you what was happening, but I knew it would hurt you." It was such a weak excuse. Rachel covered her face, giving in to the urge to hide. "I was a coward. You deserved better and I'm so sorry."

Faith rubbed her eyes until they were red. "I knew something was wrong. I should have said something. I should have—"

"It's not your job to fix us." Rachel paused. "Or to fix me. I know you worry about me."

"Because I love you," Faith said. "And you're always beating yourself up for stuff that doesn't matter. Like folding the napkins wrong or forgetting my shoe size. And I know you still feel guilty, but I barely remember all that stuff with Grandpa. All I know is that you sacrificed everything to take care of me." Her eyes filled. "But no one takes care of you."

Rachel thought about Matt's loneliness and Nathan's desperate attempts to help her. "It's because I won't let them," she admitted. All these years, she'd been atoning for her sins in full view of her daughter, and that was the real damage she'd caused, making Faith feel helpless in the face of her mother's misery. "I never believed I deserved it. But I'm working on that. I promise to take better care of myself from now on."

After they hung up, Rachel slept soundly for the first time in weeks. She woke up the next morning and immediately called Mia, asking if she could use her spare bedroom. Mia agreed, but made it clear that her "guestroom" was a pullout sofa over the garage.

"It sounds perfect," Rachel said, and meant it. The media coverage was growing savage and relentless. It was the last place anyone would look for her.

She'd just rolled her suitcase down the stairs when someone rang the doorbell. Alesha was the last person Rachel expected to see on her front porch. It took Rachel a while to commit to doing more than glaring through the peephole. Alesha jammed her thumb against the bell until the annoyance of that constant ringing compelled Rachel to open it.

"Took you long enough." Alesha smoothed the lapels of her white blazer and glanced up at the house. "I'm kind of surprised you're still here. I was sure he would have tossed your stuff out on the lawn by now." Rachel stepped back and tried to close the door in her face, but Alesha wedged her foot against it. "Let me in."

"I can't handle one of your lectures right now."

"I spoke to Mia. She told me you're planning to stay in that storage room, but I have more space. I want you at my house instead."

Rachel huffed a laugh. "No. Absolutely not." She tightened her grip on the door handle, fully prepared to put her entire weight into slamming it again. Alesha raised her hand, softened her voice, and used a word Rachel had been sure wasn't part of her vocabulary.

"Please. Hear me out."

Rachel relented, and led her to the formal sitting room. Alesha sat on the sofa. "I haven't seen the inside of this place in a while." She surveyed the room and sucked her teeth. "Still boring."

Rachel laughed and groaned, "Why are you here?" She slumped into the opposite chair.

"Did you know that your husband's out there playing the victim? He pitched the *Post* an exclusive last night. He's also milking that bruise your little boyfriend gave him for the cameras."

"I'm not surprised," Rachel said. "Matt has a lot more to lose than I do."

"Really? You think so? Mia told me about the prenup. Do you plan on letting them get away with that?"

"I hired a lawyer," Rachel said. "Julia Beaumont."

Alesha raised her eyebrows. "That girl is practically a criminal. Do you trust her?" Rachel nodded, and she shrugged. "Then maybe it's what you need."

Rachel ran a nervous hand over her legs. Matt would probably be home soon. If he saw Alesha there, it would make things worse. "Was there something else you wanted to say?"

Alesha swallowed hard and seemed to shrink on the couch. "Can I have a cup of tea? Chamomile if you have it. To settle my nerves." Rachel was so stunned by the admission of weakness that she immediately went to the kitchen and made a cup. When she returned, Alesha was looking out the window.

"Vultures," Alesha muttered, tapping a finger on the glass. "That's not journalism out there. It's hunting." A row of photographers lined the street. They stirred at the movement in the window, and Rachel stepped back. She handed Alesha her tea and returned to her chair.

"Ramona used to love having her picture taken," Alesha said.

Rachel was thrown by the sudden change in topic. "I had no idea you knew my mother."

Alesha nodded and kept her eyes downcast, focused on the cup. "We met in college." She looked up, and finally made eye contact. "We dated in college. That's also how she met my brother."

Rachel's mouth dropped. "You *dated* my mother?"

Alesha took a deep, fortifying breath. "She was a year older and was assigned as my upper-class mentor. We were the only Black English majors in the dorm." She tapped nervously against her teacup. "I wasn't out then," she said. "I was barely out to myself. Being bisexual wasn't something most people talked about. There was gay or straight, and I spent a chunk of my life thinking I was both or neither." She paused. "It's nice that Faith can be herself with the people she loves. I never really had that."

Rachel's throat tightened. It was the first time Alesha had ever implied she was a good mother.

"Ramona was beautiful," Alesha continued. "People were always telling her that. It's why she quit writing and got into theater. I think maybe if she didn't hear about it so much, she might have been a novelist, or a journalist like me." She sipped her tea and swallowed hard. "Instead, she got close to Peter. They both had stars in their eyes, while I just wanted to make enough to pay the bills. A few months later, they eloped. I never saw her or my brother again."

She looked at Rachel. "When you showed up fifteen years ago, looking just like her, something in me snapped. All those things I said to you, those horrible things? I was saying them to a ghost." She shook her head. "By the time I realized the damage I'd caused, you were dating Matt Abbott. And I thought, well, if she wants that, let her have it." Alesha hunched her shoulders and sank into the cushions, like the story had drained her. "But it wasn't what you needed. And I'm sorry I wasn't there for you."

If Alesha had told her this fifteen years ago, Rachel might not have believed her. But now she knew what betrayal looked like. It came from the place you least expected and fed on insecurity like a parasite. She thought back to their worst arguments, and how unhinged Alesha had seemed. Now, she could see her aunt more clearly. Alesha was like her, struggling to put a painful mistake behind her, where it belonged. And like Rachel, she'd finally found the strength to seek forgiveness.

"Does anyone else know about this?" Rachel asked.

Alesha shook her head. "My kids have no idea. They think your father and I fell out over money. Everyone else is gone." She leaned forward. "But I need you to believe me when I say I'm trying to help. That I won't throw stones at you, because my whole damn house is made of glass."

Rachel couldn't speak. Relief engulfed her, so intense and smothering, she could only nod or risk bursting into tears.

"Good." Alesha sat up straighter and crossed her legs. "Now let's get you out of this house and into my guest room. Then we'll call that shady lawyer and get to work."

---

Nathan had to close the laundromat. The day after the gala, people with cameras were lined up at the door, shouting his name when he tried to service a washer. The customer he was helping had gathered his dirty clothes and fled the scene like he'd witnessed a Mafia hit.

He wasn't entirely surprised when Mia stopped by. He'd seen the look in Matt's eyes after that punch. The bruise on his jaw had spread to his ego, so he'd used the one weapon he had left, threatening to call the police. When it came to drunken midnight fistfights, guys like Matt would always win in the harsh light of day.

Mia greeted him at the door with a steaming paper cup. "Brought you coffee."

Nathan winced as his right hand closed around it. His bruised knuckles had swollen during the night. "Thanks."

She briefly fussed over his hand before sitting next to him. "Matt's making some noise, so I wanted to check in and see what happened last night."

"He was being a dick. So I hit him."

She sighed. "Nathan—"

"Is Rachel okay?"

Mia stiffened, and for a second, he thought she would ignore the question. "You could call her and find out."

"My phone went dead last night and I just put it on the charger." He'd also been drunk and humiliated, his phone exploding with so many notifications on the way home that the dying battery had been a relief. "I doubt she'd want to speak to me after last night." If she did reach out, what could he say? *Sorry I mailed the portrait, but I was too high to know what I was doing*?

"I ruined the gala and her reputation in front of the entire country," Nathan said. "Have you seen what they're saying about her online?" *BuzzFeed* was having a field day. He had muted their names, but the gala story kept popping up in unexpected places. While some people mentioned Matt's affair, Rachel's nude was the biggest headline. She was the duplicitous gold digger and Nathan was the oblivious artist, too young and naive to know he was being used for revenge.

"I'm sure it's not the *entire* country." Mia looked at him over her coffee. "Those tickets are expensive. So it was probably a quarter, at most."

Nathan groaned. "All these years, and you're still not funny, Mia."

She grinned. "You just don't like my jokes."

"Because they're *not* funny."

Her laugh was cut short by the door being shoved open and Joe stalking into his apartment, still dressed in last night's tuxedo. Nathan glanced at Mia. He should have told Joe about her visits a long time ago. Now, in addition to hiding his relationship with Rachel, he had another poorly kept secret his brother could hold against him.

"Why the hell aren't you answering your phone?"

Nathan stood, and his coffee spilled, burning his hand. "I just woke up a little while ago." He set down his cup. "My phone went dead last night, and I lost my charger. I had a spare, but I think I might have left it at the—" Nathan paused, and decided it was a bad time to remind Joe of the lake house. "Somewhere. It'll turn up."

Joe looked disoriented when he finally focused on Mia. "What are you doing here?" His voice cooled. "Did Abbott call you?"

Mia stood slowly. "No." She was staring at Joe like she saw something Nathan didn't. "Joseph," she said, her voice soft and measured. "Did something happen?"

"You should go," Joe said, and ran a trembling hand through his hair. "I need to talk to my brother."

Joe's eyes were red, and Nathan wasn't sure how to read his expression. He'd never seen it before. Mia stood and Nathan grabbed her arm. He suddenly didn't want to be alone with his brother. "Wait," he mumbled, "Just wait."

Joe squeezed his shoulder. "Nathan," he whispered, and his eyes glazed with tears. "Why didn't you answer the goddamn phone?"

Nathan stopped breathing. He braced himself for what Joe would say next. But he already knew.

He knew.

"I thought—" Nathan finally exhaled, gasping. "I thought I had more time."

Joe pulled him into a hard embrace. It was the only thing that kept him standing.

———

Beto used to say that memories couldn't be trusted. Every recall distorted the truth like a filter. Nathan now knew he'd used bad memories of Beto to justify his anger. He'd focused on the pain, letting everything else blur and fade. Now, too late, he told himself different stories. He unfolded memories he'd repressed for years and saw his father's love hidden in the creases.

Now he remembered Beto standing and clapping loudly during his graduation, even though none of the other parents had done the same. He remembered test-driving his first car with Beto in the passenger seat, bemoaning the death of manual transmissions. He remembered being four years old and watching his father crouch low to fit inside the fort they'd built in Nathan's bedroom—Beto's large hands weaving delicate Christmas lights between the sheets. He remembered falling asleep with his ear to his father's heart and trying to will his own to match its steady rhythm. Because even then, he knew that was how you loved someone. Like an extension of your soul in someone else.

It was their chef, Arianna, who found Beto and called Sofia away from the gala. Beto had stayed after everyone left to make arrangements for a surprise celebration. "I think he was nervous," Arianna said. "He said that he never knew how much work Señora Cárdenas put into those things."

Nathan had made plans to meet with Bobbi and Dillon after the gala. It would be nice to think he would have made the right choice and accepted his father's invitation to join them at home. But he was done lying to himself, and he realized now that he had no instincts when it came to Beto. If he did, maybe he would have known the day with the photo album would be the last time they saw each other. If Nathan knew his father better, he would have seen Beto's anger for what it was—self-loathing and fear, the knowledge that every second that ticked by was a lost chance to change things. If Nathan knew, he wouldn't have gotten drunk at the gala while Beto had a stroke, and maybe his father wouldn't have died alone.

The paramedics said it was painless. The doctors told them that strokes were a common risk for people with brain tumors, and that Beto had probably been experiencing symptoms for a while but hadn't told anyone. "That's just like Beto," Sofia had said, huffing out a laugh that sounded nothing like her.

Nathan didn't answer his phone all week. Bobbi and Dillon had tried to stop by, but he ignored the knocks on his door. He ordered pizza when he got too hungry to sleep; he only went outside to take out the trash so it wouldn't attract flies. The first few times, some photographer took his picture, but that stopped eventually. The news cycle had moved on, and photos of a grieving son tossing beer bottles in the dumpster could only be sold so many times.

That's how Rachel found him, carrying a trash bag and empty pizza box to the back of the building. She was dressed in jeans and a T-shirt, and her hair was curly, the way it had looked when they got caught in the rain. As soon as they locked eyes, she stopped walking and wrapped her arms around her waist, like she needed comfort.

"Hi," she said.

He moved the trash bag to the opposite hand. "Hey."

"I was in the neighborhood—" She stopped and shook her head. "No, I wasn't. You won't answer the phone, so I've been sitting in the parking lot watching Netflix, waiting for you to come out."

"I put it on silent for the wake, and now I'm not sure where it is." That was three days ago. Which meant he probably had seventy-two hours of messages from complete strangers poking at his grief.

"It's okay," she said quickly, and moved closer. "You have a lot going on."

The funeral mass was yesterday. He'd been forced to listen to eulogies about the man everyone thought his father was. Beto Vasquez was a business leader. A compassionate philanthropist. But Nathan knew that he also loved old cars. He made homemade marshmallows for hot chocolate, and only used cocoa from Oaxaca, because, as he put it, "We're not animals, mijo."

"Yesterday was hard," Nathan said. "Long. Mom was pretty out of it by the end."

"I wanted to be there."

"I'm glad you weren't."

She nodded. "You're right. It would have been a distraction."

"That's not what I meant. It's just that people are terrible. I could hear them talking about us during the service." He took a deep breath. "Before the gala, I couldn't handle us not being together. I don't even remember sending you that portrait. It was reckless and selfish, and I'm so sorry."

"Please don't be," she said. "I wasn't angry when I saw it. I thought it was gorgeous." She paused and slipped away for a moment, remembering. "You made me look beautiful," she said, so hushed and intimate that it shrank the parking lot, the town, the whole world down to the distance between them.

He wasn't angry with her anymore. Clinging to pride in a sea of grief was just a faster way to drown. He wanted to explain that he finally understood her choices, but being this close made it hard to say anything that wasn't a confession. *You're always beautiful. You also broke my heart and it's useless without you.*

Instead, he asked, "Why are you here?"

She walked up the steps and sat on the cement landing. "To listen." She patted the spot to her right. He wanted to invite her upstairs but was embarrassed by the state of his apartment. She'd probably start cleaning and offer to cook for him. And he'd let her do it. That's how weak he was. He'd take anything from her right now, including pity.

Nathan sat and started confessing the shameful truths he hadn't told anyone. Selfish things, like how he resented his father for refusing chemo and keeping his symptoms a secret. "I blame him," he said. "He was stubborn his whole life and he died that way. None of us got to say goodbye." He shook his head. "Or maybe they did. Mom and Joe were saying goodbye this whole time, while I was pretending I didn't need to. Now all I can think about is how he never saw it. That's selfish, right? My father's dead and all I care about is that he missed my fucking show."

"It's not selfish. He lost that too. You all did. That's what hurts the most when someone's gone." She grabbed his hand. "And you'll want to keep clinging to that hurt because it feels like all you have left. Eventually you'll realize that you have better things to hold on to, and you'll cling to that instead."

He thought about what Beto had said to him, that Nathan was a moving target he could never pin down. "We barely knew each other. What if there's nothing to hold on to?"

"Did you love him?"

Nathan thought about Beto's fort and listening to his father's heartbeat. Those feelings were real, no matter how hard he'd tried to ignore them. He nodded and swallowed against the tears gathering in his throat.

"Then it's enough."

Nathan's tears broke free. Rachel grabbed his shoulders as he reached for her waist. He buried his face in her hair and inhaled, breathing freely for the first time in days.

"Get away from my son."

Rachel jerked back. Sofia stood over them, gripping her purse like a weapon. Joe stood behind her looking defeated, like he'd tried and failed to stop this from happening.

Rachel rose so quickly she nearly tipped over. Nathan steadied her and Sofia tensed, ready to pounce. Nathan lifted a hand to snap her out of it. "Calm down, Mom. Rachel was just—"

"I know what she's doing." Her chin hitched up and she kept her eyes on Nathan. "I'm surprised it took this long. Has her husband filed for divorce yet?"

Rachel folded her arms. "Sofia, I'm—"

"*Ms. Cárdenas.* Don't address me like a friend. We are *not* friends."

Joe touched Sofia's arm and scanned their surroundings. "Mom, can we not do this here?"

Sofia jabbed a finger at Rachel. "She's the one groping my son in public. Haven't you humiliated us enough?"

Nathan nudged her hand down. "If you want to blame someone for that, blame me. I painted the damn thing."

Rachel touched his arm. "Your mother's right. This is my fault."

Joe sighed. "Actually, it's Hailey Dearwood's fault."

"Either way." Rachel turned to Sofia. "I am so sorry for what happened at the gala. And for any additional pain I've caused your family." She glanced at Nathan. "I came here because I care about your son. Very much."

"Then stay away from him." Sofia stepped closer. "You and your husband are salacious tabloid garbage. Stop dragging him down with you." She turned to Nathan. "Can we go inside, please? Or are you just going to stand there and look at her?"

Nathan didn't move. He took a step toward Rachel, but Joe touched his shoulder. His brother gave him a pleading look, begging Nathan to do the right thing.

"Your mother needs you," Rachel said softly. "I'll be fine."

When Sofia argued with Beto, she was always eerily calm, as though she was waiting for him to figure out that she'd already won. Once, after a huge blowout, Nathan discovered Beto grumbling to himself as he picked up pieces of a broken vase.

"That *woman*. Sometimes she makes it hard to...*breathe*."

Now he understood what Beto meant. Nathan went upstairs and found Sofia gliding around his apartment, straightening pillows, and making decorating suggestions as if the fight outside had never happened. Even Joe looked uneasy.

"We came over to deliver the good news in person," Joe said, eyes still on Sofia. "About *Abuelita*, right, Mom?"

Sofia moved a stack of coasters to the coffee table. "You have multiple offers from private collectors. Large offers, particularly for your grandmother's portrait and..." Her jaw tightened. "*Rachel*. The nude is very popular."

"It belongs to Rachel," Nathan said. "And it's not for sale."

"Well, you may want to ask her first," Sofia said. "With her current financial situation, she might disagree."

Joe's eyes flew wide. "Mom! Can you give it a rest? Let Nate celebrate his success without you—" Joe stopped when Nathan shot him a *let me handle this* look. "You know what," he said. "This is between you two. I'm going to grab something from that taqueria I saw on the way over."

"They use manteca, Joseph," Sofia sighed. "Even in the beans."

"I'm sure I can get some shredded lettuce or something. I'll be right back."

They watched Joe rush out in silence. Nathan folded his arms and looked down at his mother, who was perched on the edge of his couch. "You're looming," she said. "Sit."

"You've got to stop ordering people around."

"No, I don't. I'm still your mother, Nathaniel."

"You are. But I'm not a little kid anymore. You can stop pretending I'm not the one who caused all this in the first place."

Sofia stiffened. "She lied to me."

"No, she didn't."

"It was humiliating," Sofia snapped. "Our foundation auctioned a naked portrait of my son's cougar lover. And I was the one who chose her as host!"

Nathan sat next to her. "How much money did she make for the foundation that night? I could have a career because of her."

Sofia pursed her lips, like she'd tasted something sour. "It's embarrassing."

"Do you see how everyone's treating her? Like some predator who lured me into her art studio." He could hear the irritation in his voice and tried to pull it back. His mother was grieving, and hurt people spread their pain around so they wouldn't suffer alone. But he couldn't let her cause more damage.

Sofia averted her eyes. "She's an adult. She knew the risks."

"So am I," he said. "I knew the risks too, and I fell in love with her anyway."

She cut her eyes and huffed. "*Love?*"

"Yes, love," he said. "For a while now."

She flicked a dismissive hand. "But how long have you known each other?"

"How long did you know Beto?"

They hadn't said his name since he died. Sofia would leave the room when anyone talked about him outside of planning the funeral arrangements. But here, in Nathan's apartment, there was nowhere for her to go. She glared at him. "That was different," she said with a finality that tried to end the conversation.

"Not the way he told it," Nathan said. He wasn't going to let her escape this time. Too many years had gone by with all of them tiptoeing around their own stories. He'd wasted his chance to connect with Beto. He refused to do the same with his mother. "He said you two met on set and things were so intense you could barely look at him."

Her voice softened. "Well, he just kept staring at me." She touched her face, sliding back into the moment. "It wasn't love at first sight, but it was...something."

"You were always so quick to forgive him. For everything."

"Because I loved him. And he needed it. He never would have survived without his family. And I needed to forgive him too. Hating someone you love only makes you smaller. Those feelings take up so much room." She was silent for a few seconds and then looked up at him with a tired smile. "Is this my lesson? To not give Rachel Abbott my precious space?"

"Maybe," Nathan said. "Also, show some compassion? You two are not that different."

She ran a finger around the rim of her glass. "So, what exactly do you want from me?"

Nathan took a deep breath to shore up his resolve. Sofia watched him with growing apprehension. "Is there some other secret I don't know about?" Her eyes widened. "Oh my god. You did *not* get her pregnant. Nathaniel! How could you be so—"

He touched her hand. "Rachel's not pregnant." He paused and let her catch her breath. "But even if she was, it's my life. I don't need you to agree with my choices, but I do need you to respect them."

"I've always respected you." She sat up straighter. "But I knew you were capable of so much more—"

"There you go again," Nathan groaned. "Why does *but* come after every compliment? I need you to support me without so many *buts*."

Her brow knitted and she sighed. "Okay. You're right. I want the best for you boys, but I should think more about what you want for yourselves." She made the sour face again. "Even if it is Rachel Abbott."

"Go easy on her, please. She's been through a lot."

Sofia's lips thinned. "For you, I will try. But be patient with me. I know you're a man now, but—" Her chin trembled, and she covered her mouth. "Both of you. You're still my little boys."

Nathan scooted closer and she leaned into his embrace, covering him with the smell of jasmine that made him feel so safe as a child. Now she felt fragile. He wrapped his arms around her shoulders and held on tighter.

---

The chilly air circulating through the Abbott and Associates conference room seemed excessive for this time of year. Rachel tried not to show her discomfort. She wore a different version of the T-shirt and jeans she'd recently adopted as her new uniform. Across from her, all three Abbott men sat comfortably in their dark wool suits. She thought of the woman in the pencil skirt she'd seen on the way in. What did it feel like to work in an office so hostile to your gender that it literally froze you out?

"Is she still coming?" Ben glanced at his watch. He was the only one who seemed concerned by Julia's absence. Matt was more preoccupied with the notifications on his phone. Herman wasn't concerned about anything. He sat with a foot crossed over one thigh, and his hand resting next to a blank legal pad that he probably wouldn't use.

Rachel folded her arms and did her best not to shiver. "She'll be here."

Ben sat back in his chair and exchanged a quick glance with Herman.

His father's face was impassive, but Ben was visibly tense. He had waffled between kindness to her and loyalty to the men beside him since she'd arrived. But ultimately, he was on the opposite side of the table.

Julia burst through the door carrying her purse, a briefcase, and a stack of brown accordion files under her arm. She set everything down with a thud. The files spilled their contents across the table, obscuring Herman's legal pad. He eyed the mess but didn't move to help. Julia sighed as she surveyed the room. "Well, this doesn't feel fair. Three against one?" She smirked at Ben, who was staring at the empty sandwich wrapper that had landed near his hand. "Good to see you Benji. Been a while."

Matt pushed her things away from him. "We've been waiting for half an hour. Don't you have an assistant? Or a calendar?"

Herman didn't speak until Julia repeated her complaint about the number of lawyers in the room. "It's actually only two," he pointed out. "Matt is the client here. Not counsel."

"Lucky him," Julia said. They were forced to wait again as she shoved the files around, searching for the right one. "Ah. Here we go. I really do need an assistant. Do you guys know anyone who's looking for a job?"

Herman smiled. "We pay pretty well here. I doubt you can afford them." His head tilted slightly. "But you should know that, right? Your mother was one of our best employees."

Julia's bemused mask turned to ice before she pasted on a huge, carefree smile. "I'll tell her you said hello. Now, let's talk money."

Matt laughed. "What money? She's not getting a dime from me. Not a fucking penny."

Ben lifted his hand. "Hold on, Matt—"

"No, *you* hold on." Matt glared at his brother and then focused on Herman. "Why is he here? You know he's on her side—"

"Enough," Herman said. He looked at Rachel. "You can understand where Matt's coming from. You made a deal and didn't follow through."

"No." Matt leaned across the table. "She ran around town, screwing that tattooed meathead instead of doing what she promised. Supporting me and my campaign."

"You had a mistress," Rachel said. "Who you sent dick pics in the middle of your birthday party. I'm not sure you should be talking to me about broken promises."

Matt's eyes shifted to his father. Herman didn't meet his gaze, but his shoulders were stiffer than when they started. Julia cleared her throat and slid a piece of paper across the table. "Let's discuss this trust."

"That's Faith's," Matt said quickly. "It's with a trustee, so you can't touch it. She'll get full control when she turns twenty-five."

Rachel looked at Herman. "You have an excellent poker face."

He gave a half shrug. "I don't play poker. Gambling's for people who never win."

"How insightful," Julia said flatly. "And also unethical. But who am I to throw stones, right?" She winked at Ben, who looked annoyed. Apparently, his professional respect only extended so far outside the courtroom.

"This is a waste of time," Matt groaned. "You signed the prenup. You broke our deal. What are we even talking about?"

"Our marriage," Rachel said. "Which we ruined with the selfish choices that brought us here. But we don't have to keep making the same mistakes."

Matt shifted in his chair. "What do you mean?"

"I don't want to fight you," she said. "We raised Faith together, and that should be the only thing that still connects us. The *good* thing. Not this. Not you robbing me of the chance to build a life without you."

"I'm not doing that. You can get a job, or go back to school—"

"I could have done those things years ago," she said. "But I was too busy being your wife."

Matt blinked and his brow furrowed. She knew him well enough to know when something finally resonated. She'd been there when he drafted his first platform. Her inbox was still filled with all the blog posts and articles she'd written in support of his campaign. She could open her calendar and show them an hour-by-hour accounting of how she'd prioritized his life over hers.

Rachel stared across the table and watched the truth slowly register on his face. Herman drummed his fingers, his unnatural calm finally caving to the long silence between them.

"My son is right," Herman said. "Unless you plan to challenge the prenup—"

"We do." Julia licked her thumb and slid the prenup across the table, to Herman this time. "See that signature there? That's Ben as Rachel's attorney of record."

Herman's jaw clenched and he gave Matt a sharp glare. "Goddamn it, son."

Matt frowned. "What? What is it?"

"Good thing he's a politician," Julia said. "He's not a very good lawyer. If Benji is *here*"—she tapped the contract—"then he shouldn't be *here*." She pointed across the table to Ben. "That's a conflict of interest."

"It's a weak argument," Herman said. "Rachel consented, and Ben doesn't have to be part of the legal team."

"Sure, maybe." Julia nodded. "A judge might go for that. Or, they might see it as two self-interested rich, powerful white men railroading a Black single mother into an unconscionable contract without adequate assistance of counsel." She nodded. "So maybe not so weak."

"You're right," Herman said. "We do have money. Enough to drag this out until it bankrupts both of you." He looked at Rachel. "Is she working on a contingency?"

"You don't talk to my client," Julia snapped. "You talk to me."

Herman leaned forward and met her eyes. "*You* can't win this."

Julia pulled out another sheet of paper from her bottomless folder and placed it in front of Matt. Rachel looked on in awe, though she had been expecting this. Julia had explained every tactic she planned to use during their strategy meeting. "Men like Herman aren't used to waiting. He won't show it, but it'll set his teeth on edge. That's how we'll start this off," she'd said.

Matt picked up the paper and started reading, while Herman waited. Julia lifted a finger and said, "Give him a minute."

Matt paled. "What the hell is that?"

"It's Alesha's next op-ed in the *Post*," Rachel said. "Written by me."

"Summarizes the whole scandal," Julia said. "I might have added a few choice details. Like that part about you having sex in the bathroom with your girlfriend at the Vasquez anniversary party."

"You can't print that!" He slammed his hand on the table. "It's defamation."

"No, it isn't," Rachel said. "Read it again, Matt. It's all true." She paused. "Except for the bathroom part. Was it in the study?"

"This is blackmail." He glanced at Herman, who kept his eyes on the op-ed. "You fucking shark. You can't *blackmail* people to win a case."

"But paying someone off to win a federal election is fine?" Julia looked at Herman. "You're right," she said. "I don't have the money you do. I could last eight, nine months in litigation, tops." She tapped the op-ed. "But this? Costs nothing. And we can do it for years."

Herman crumpled the article in one hand. "Don't underestimate me, Julia."

"You shouldn't underestimate *me*." The look she gave him was so lethal that if someone told Rachel that Julia put a hit out on Herman Abbott, she might actually believe them.

Ben lifted a hand. "Swords down. This is supposed to be a negotiation, so let's negotiate." Ben focused on Julia. "How about a monthly allowance until she gets back on her feet?"

"No allowance," Rachel said. "I want the money I was promised. And the house."

Matt shook his head. "That house is worth—"

"It's *my* house." She paused. "I also want the building on Broad Street."

Matt's confusion confirmed her suspicions. He didn't remember that it was her idea to buy the building in the first place. Two years into their marriage she'd approached him about starting a nonprofit for young artists. She'd done the legwork, found the commercial space, and celebrated with champagne when they'd closed. Six months later, she was told the space was being used for his mayoral campaign headquarters. His staff had rotated in and out of the building ever since.

"I need that building," he said. "For the campaign."

"Based on the latest polls, I don't think you'll be needing it much longer." Rachel crossed her legs and swiveled in her chair. "Find another place for your dying career prospects."

"Just give it to her," Ben said. "You can find another building."

The room fell silent. Rachel's demands sat next to Alesha's article. Matt stared at them like someone had discovered the dead bodies he'd buried.

He finally conceded. "Okay."

Ben grabbed his briefcase and stood. Matt didn't move. He clasped his hands on the table and looked at Rachel with begrudging respect. "My campaign headquarters. Really? The money wasn't enough?"

Rachel looked at Herman, who watched them with his dead, gray eyes. "When it's for your dignity, it never is."

# CHAPTER TWENTY-TWO

I saw that naked picture you drew of the mayor's wife."

Nathan kept sweeping the floor next to Ruby Miller's laundry basket. Her clothes had been dry for fifteen minutes now. Instead of shoving them in the basket and leaving like she'd done every other Saturday morning, she'd spread them out over a folding table and moved them from side to side like a shell game. She was barely five feet tall and had recently started using a walker. Her limited range of motion was the perfect excuse to linger.

Ruby usually spoke to him like the grandmother she was—blunt and maternal, but also slightly patronizing. But she had greeted him that morning with gentle condolences about his father. It had been two months since the funeral, and thanks to his weekly bereavement counseling sessions, he'd gotten better at accepting them graciously. Now that she knew he was okay, Ruby felt comfortable getting to the reason she'd decided to linger.

"You can't do that, you know. Not these days." She snatched a T-shirt from the pile and took her time balling it into a sloppy square. "People post all your business online. That's why my sister Eunice uses that site with the little blue key to share her pictures."

Nathan paused midsweep. "OnlyFans?"

"She said it's more private."

Nathan ducked his head to hide a grin. "I don't mind people seeing it," he said. "But it belongs to her. That should have been her decision."

Ruby unwrapped a stick of Juicy Fruit. "I didn't know you liked Black women."

Nathan bit back a laugh. "Was it ever a question?"

She waved her hand. "I saw your last girlfriend. The one who was always taking pictures of herself. Personality of low-sodium chips. And the other one. Tall and mean."

As if conjured by Ruby's description, Bobbi parked out front and pulled a large grocery bag from the passenger seat. "Bobbi isn't my girlfriend," Nathan said. Ruby started gathering up her things. "You don't have to leave."

"I'm done washing clothes." She stuffed the shirts she'd folded into a laundry bag. "And I'm too old to bite my tongue around that snitch. She told that hippie at the community center that I only go to PETA meetings for the cookies. Which is true, but that girl's got too many opinions about grown folks' business."

Nathan grabbed the last pair of pants and folded them neatly for her. "What are you, thirty? Thirty-five?"

"Don't flirt," Ruby said, and winked. "I know you like 'em older too."

Bobbi leaned into the door with a grocery sack in each arm. Nathan rushed to open it for her.

"Why are you so picky?" she huffed. "Do you have any idea how hard it is to make you a birthday meal? There's stuff for three different dishes in here."

Nathan smiled. "I'm not picky. I'm—"

"Discerning. Yeah, right." She set the bags on the folding table and looked at Ruby. They faced off like hostile cowboys. "I'm not making cookies."

"I'm leaving." Ruby snatched her bag and left with her chin in the air. Bobbi rolled her eyes.

"So, what do you have a taste for? Waffles, French toast, or croissants?" Bobbi rubbed her hands together like a villain. "I plan to ply you with pastries."

The door swung open again before Nathan could respond. Joe entered in workout clothes, holding two green smoothies. "Happy birthday, little—" He saw Bobbi and frowned. "Is it a breakfast day?"

"It's Saturday," she said. "You two don't work out on Saturday."

"Well, it's my brother's birthday," Joe said, with a possessive tone that implied a superior claim on Nathan's time. "I thought we could spend the day together."

Over the last two months, they'd abandoned their rigid schedule for something more frequent and spontaneous. Most days, Nathan had lunch with Joe at his office. After work, Joe would stop by the laundromat to chat before he went home. They both attended Sunday dinners with Sofia.

Nathan lifted a hand to stop the debate that was brewing. "I can do both. Have breakfast and go work out. I've got no other plans today."

"Really?" Bobbi said. "I thought you might go to—"

"That sounds great," Joe interrupted. He gave Bobbi a pointed look.

Nathan caught her eye. "What were you going to say?"

"Nothing, apparently." She gathered her groceries and looked at Joe. "My food isn't vegan."

He lifted his smoothie. "I'm good."

"We'll meet you upstairs," Nathan said. He waited until she was gone before turning to Joe. "Mom said Zara filed for divorce. How are you holding up?"

Joe sat on the folding table. "Depends on the day. Numb right now. Probably angry tomorrow. She wants full custody of Angel, even though she's never in the same city for more than a few months. That's not a way to raise a kid."

Nathan didn't say what he was thinking, that Joe's busy work schedule wasn't ideal for raising a kid either. "What are you going to do?"

"Only thing I can do. Fight for my son." He looked at his hands. "Don't ask me if it's the right thing, because I don't know. But I can't lose someone else I love."

Nathan squeezed his shoulder. "Let me know what I can do to help. Babysitting. Moral support. Anything you need. I'm here."

Joe batted Nathan's hand away. "Okay, but you've got your own shit going on. Mom told me you've booked another art show?"

It would have been nice to share his own news once it was official. But his mother was desperate to replace the gossip swirling around town with something more positive. Nathan explained that he hadn't booked anything yet, but there was interest. He'd set up meetings with a few gallery owners and art dealers for next week. In the meantime, he'd started doing research. "They mentioned career goals, and I've never thought about any of that. Now I'm working on a portfolio."

"A *portfolio*?" Joe raised his brows and emphasized every syllable. "Look at you, little brother. Can I see it?"

Upstairs, Nathan's apartment smelled like sugar and cinnamon from Bobbi's skillet. He didn't recognize the heavy cast iron but didn't say anything to avoid a thirty-minute lecture on why he should know what was in his own kitchen. Nathan pulled out the new leather sleeve he'd purchased and flipped it open to show Joe the sketches he'd put together. Rachel had told him once that a portfolio should tell the story of who he was as an artist. He decided to show the evolution of his drawing, from the fantasy creatures he'd loved as a child, to the fan art that helped him channel his anger, to the portraits he'd done while working with Rachel. Putting it together, he couldn't help but think of how much of her was in his art now. His first love. His first broken heart. He'd done some of his best work with all of it bleeding into the lines.

"So, are you going to her art show or not?" Bobbi side-eyed Joe with a bowl of batter on one hip. She stirred slowly, waiting for Nathan's answer.

Joe groaned and sat on the couch. "You have always had the biggest mouth."

She snorted. "I've seen your high school yearbook. Your nickname was literally The Mouth, so stop projecting."

They traded exaggerated glares before Joe turned back to Nathan. "You don't have to go, if you don't want to, Nate."

"*She* clearly wants him to."

Nathan held up a hand. "What the hell are you two talking about? Go to what?"

They exchanged another look. Joe stood with his phone in hand. "You really haven't read about what Rachel's doing?"

"Or spoken to her at all?" Bobbi added, in a way that meant she had opinions on the subject.

Nathan knew that Rachel was giving him space to work through his issues, and he was trying to do the same for her. She'd kept in touch, but he wouldn't call their brief texts an actual conversation. It was more like checking for signs of life. They all started the same way, with her asking, How are you feeling today? instead of the typical "Are you okay," or "Do you need anything" he got from others. Rachel seemed to get that being okay was impossible and that what he needed was for each day to hurt less. But his feelings seemed to shift by the hour. He'd answer—angry or tired or good, but I feel guilty for it—and was always a little lighter afterward, like she'd lifted some of the weight he was carrying.

He wanted to do the same for her but had no idea how. She was being put through a very public ringer, and a huge part of that was his fault. When he would ask the same thing, How are you feeling? it didn't seem to work the same magic on her. She'd say, Like myself, without much elaboration, and he didn't feel like it was right to push for anything more.

"I've spoken to her a little," Nathan said. "And the press keeps writing sexist bullshit about her divorce, so I stopped paying attention." He paused. "Did something happen?"

Joe reluctantly showed him an article on his phone. It was Rachel standing next to the collage that got her in trouble all those years ago. The website had blurred it out, but she stared into the camera with a look that dared whoever was reading to think she should be ashamed.

"It's some kind of pop-up exhibit," Joe said. "She's showing her photography." He motioned for Nathan to scroll down. There was a picture of a large, open room with photos on the wall. He recognized some of the pictures from when he'd scanned them into files for her.

Nathan looked at Joe. "I can't believe she did this."

"Neither can I. They kicked her off three nonprofit boards last week.

I had to sit through a rant about how no respectable buyer would put an offer on her house during my last lunch meeting."

"She sold the house?"

"She's trying to." Joe paused. "You really didn't know any of this?"

"No!" Nathan shoved a hand through his hair. "I was giving her space. She's in the middle of a divorce, and I was...I was trying not to be a selfish asshole like you told me."

Bobbi snorted. "You're taking love advice from this guy? That's like getting directions from a fish in the desert." Joe made a half-hearted grunt of protest. Bobbi waved him off and gave Nathan a pointed look. "Read that profile. It's obvious she wants you there. You should go."

"Hang on." Joe blocked Nathan's view of Bobbi. "Think about this. Your career is just getting started. I know you care about her—"

"I love her," Nathan said. "I can't lose someone else either."

And that's when Joe faltered. Despite the gaps that would always exist between them, this would be where they connected. The place where they'd both let something slip away and vowed to hold on tighter from now on.

Joe slapped his arm and said, "I'm proud of you," with the weight of that promise in his voice. Nathan hugged him.

"I'm proud of you too."

"Fuck." Bobbi sniffed and dropped her spatula on the counter. Her eyes were damp and red. "Don't look at me. Breakfast is ready, so just shut up and eat."

---

### How Rachel Thomas Mastered the Art of Scandal

*By Carlos Fitzpatrick*

You've probably never heard of Rachel Thomas. That's perfectly fine with the woman herself. "I prefer it. The exhibit is a different experience without all the noise coloring your reaction." The noise Thomas is referring to is a cascade of tabloid headlines and trending hashtags under her married name, Rachel Abbott. We won't go into the details of the scandal here (a quick Google search will produce the entire sordid tale, including rumors of an upcoming tell-all memoir penned by Matt Abbott's mistress) and Thomas doesn't have much to say about the end of her very public marriage. "People make mistakes. Sometimes painful ones. That doesn't mean they should be public." But as we toured the empty office space that houses her debut photography exhibition, it was hard to ignore the optics of the building's history as Matt Abbott's campaign headquarters. I asked whether the location was an intentional dig at her ex. "I don't bully people through my work. But I can't control what someone takes away from it either. As soon as you hang art on the wall, it isn't yours anymore. You can't shape the emotions or assumptions it elicits. That's pointless and dishonest."

Thomas invited me to draw my own conclusions about her work, so here are a few reflections: The collection is stunning. And offensive. And uncomfortable. And heartbreaking. It's confronting in the ways that good art should be. They're primarily black-and-white pieces of an unfiltered life that she's kept private until now. A large self-portrait of a sixteen-year-old Thomas, heavily pregnant in a messy, adolescent bedroom greets the patrons when they walk through the doors. Her affection for cigars is prominently on display in photos of her college years. Unedited photographs in both suffocating shapewear and lacy lingerie are framed and displayed next to collages of nude models in borderline pornographic positions. This isn't the polished figure that frustrated the paparazzi with her inhuman ability to hide the smallest blemish from their cameras. This is the timeline of a life. It's a conversation about the burden we place on the sexuality of Black women. It forces us to see Thomas, and her other subjects, as authors of their own narrative, rather than objects for lust or ridicule.

My second takeaway is that while Thomas may shy away from discussing her marriage, her affair with Nathan Vasquez, the son of recently deceased billionaire Beto Vasquez, is openly referenced in her work. In one of the few pieces that has been rendered in bright, saturated color, Thomas has created a dizzying spiral of newspaper clippings about the gala and photographs of Vasquez's work, including the nude portrait that sparked her divorce. Up close, the piece is easy to dismiss as a chaotic collection of provocative news headlines and overexposed photos. But step back far enough, and you'll see that the oversaturated yellows, red, and oranges are arranged into a shape and pattern mimicking sun stars. The piece is called *Photosynthesis*, a love letter amid a swirl of scandal that requires a change of perspective to truly comprehend.

As a journalist, I felt compelled to ask the questions that are on everyone's mind. Yes, she has been approached by publishers about selling her story, but no, she isn't interested in doing so. According to industry sources, the offers have been substantial. But whether Thomas is taking the high road or has signed an NDA along with her divorce settlement is, again, open for interpretation. One thing she will say is that she's ready to move on from her public life as an Abbott. Just don't call this a second act. "I'm not onstage anymore," she says definitively. As with art, I'll let you draw your own conclusions.

COMMENTS:

**@peepmyfishnets:** Ew. SLUT.

**@tokenblackknight REPLY TO: @peepmyfishnets:** That's not how you spell QUEEN. Stay mad bitch.

---

Rachel had laughed when Faith suggested creating a velvet-roped VIP section for the opening. Now, with a line wrapped around the building, she was grateful for her daughter's foresight. There were no velvet ropes, but Rachel did exclude a few feet of space from the exhibit. She stood near Faith with enough room to move her arms comfortably, which was more than she could say for everyone else.

"So, obviously I have questions," Faith said as she examined the *Fast Girls* collage. "*Lots* of questions."

"I'm happy to answer all of them," Rachel said, but paused, remembering that first wild night of the photoshoot, before she had forbidden the models from pregaming before a session. "Well, most of them." Faith gave her a sharp look, and Rachel shrugged. "Some things you don't want to know, sweetie."

"There she is!" Kat's squeal was loud enough to be heard over the dull roar of a hundred voices. She tugged Niles through the swarm of bodies with surprising ease for someone so small. Her daughter was swaddled against her chest with the wrap Rachel had given her. "Oh my god! Look at this. Look!" She waved her hand at the crowd. "Are you charging an entrance fee?"

"No," Faith said, with clear disapproval. "Mom has this thing about being accessible to the masses."

Niles chuckled. "I think we've all had plenty of access already."

Kat slapped his arm. "Stop."

"I'm just playing." Niles rubbed his bicep, and grinned at Rachel. "You know I'm joking, right? Nathan's portrait was fire. All of this…" He pointed to a photograph of Rachel, sitting on a classic Mustang at the beach. "Is amazing. Really beautiful. I'm proud of you."

Rachel's lingering doubts about the show faded. Maybe it was arrogant to center herself, but it was also her truth. It was shouting down her shame, loud enough so that anyone with a similar story could hear.

"Soooo," Kat purred, sidling up to Rachel. "Would you be willing to do our Christmas card this year? I want something glamorous but authentic. Like disco Diana Ross meets *Black Is King*."

Niles looked skeptical. "So is the baby Simba or Blue Ivy?"

"Mom doesn't do domestic photo shoots." Faith hitched her chin, and said, "Now that she's a famous *artiste*." Rachel nudged her daughter's side, and Faith giggled.

"I think I can make an exception." Rachel looked at Niles. "For family." His answering smile warmed her insides. For years, family was the burden of deserving the Abbott name. Now, it was blood. It was the comfort of her father's eyes mirrored in the open admiration on Niles's face.

"Speaking of family." Niles scanned the crowd. "Where's Mom and Mia?"

Rachel pointed to the far-right corner of the room. Alesha was surrounded by a group of art critics she'd invited to the show. "Your mother is over there trying to bully her friends into writing favorable reviews. And Mia is..." Rachel looked at a series of all-caps messages on her phone, "ten minutes away. I'm getting live, road rage updates."

"Is there an after-party? Where are we celebrating?" Kat asked, bouncing to soothe the squirming newborn on her chest.

"Alesha mentioned her house," Rachel said.

Niles nixed the idea with a dramatic, slow-motion headshake. "Hell no. It'll just be me and Mia picking up after everybody and being assigned chores. I still don't know how I ended up scrubbing toilets last Thanksgiving."

"What about your restaurant?" Faith turned to Niles. He smiled and started suggesting protein options and wine pairings. Rachel half listened, while keeping her eyes on the crowd. It seemed to have doubled in size, despite how close they were to the end of the night.

Niles suddenly paused midsentence. "Looks like the guest of honor has arrived."

Rachel frowned. "There is no—" Her breath caught at the sight of a tall, dark-haired figure staring up at *Photosynthesis*. She had imagined seeing Nathan so many times over the last two months that at first, she refused to believe it was him. But then she caught a glimpse of the familiar swirl of red-and-gold feathers on his arm.

Rachel tried not to react even though her heart seemed determined to escape her rib cage. Faith looked uncomfortable, while Kat's excitement bubbled and sparkled like glitter. She grabbed Rachel's arm and leaned close. "I think he's here for you. What are you going to do?"

"Okay." Niles gently pried Kat's fingers from her arm. "Let's not narrate Rachel's love life."

Rachel looked at Faith. "I don't have to do this now."

"Yes, you do." Faith's smile was small but genuine. "It's fine, really." She glanced at Nathan, who'd been pulled into a conversation with a patron. "Kat's right. He's here for you."

Rachel grabbed her hand and squeezed. Faith squeezed back and said, "It's okay," with the same confidence she'd had all those years ago. *It's okay to feel this.*

Nathan spotted Rachel when she was a few feet away. She stopped, suddenly at a loss for what to say. All those mental rehearsals of what she'd do when she finally saw him again were useless. They hadn't prepared her for the way his eyes drank her in, or how every possible greeting dissolved on her tongue when he smiled.

Nathan approached her and leaned in close to be heard over the noise. "Congratulations."

The crowd jostled them even closer, and Nathan's hand darted out to keep her steady. Only his touch had the opposite effect, a disorienting shift that left her spinning.

"I brought you something." He lifted a brown paper bag. "A gift to celebrate." The curious eyes that turned their way made him lower it just as quickly. "Is there somewhere we can talk?"

The building was filled with glass walls. The only room with any real privacy was Matt's old office. Nathan put the paper bag on a desk, next to a large bouquet of flowers. He stared at them a moment and then turned around, arms folded. "Lots of people out there."

"I know." She took a breath and kept her hands against her sides. No more armor. "I should have asked for RSVPs. It's probably a building code violation."

His eyes lifted briefly to the ceiling. "So, this place is yours?"

"Yes. I plan to repurpose it as affordable art studios for people just starting out."

He grinned. "You mean people like me?"

She rolled her eyes. "Every dealer in the Western Hemisphere wants to work with you right now, so no. But you're welcome to fill out a donation card."

He laughed. God, she'd missed that. Making him laugh.

"I'd be happy to donate," he said. His smile faded, and he studied her. "So, I guess you've been keeping tabs on me."

Heat flared across her cheeks, but she didn't bother denying it. "I might have set up a Google Alert or five. A lot of people misspell your name."

He moved closer. "I bet you're in the comments, setting them straight."

"Of course. Someone has to protect your search algorithm."

Their laughter interlaced, and she wanted to bottle the sound for safe-keeping. Nathan cleared his throat. "None of it would have happened if it wasn't for you," he said, staring at her in a way that used to unnerve her, like he was picking apart her thoughts. Any minute now he'd realize how desperate she was to touch him again. The space between them was the only thing keeping her emotions in check.

Her new therapist, Diane, had told her to focus on living in the present. That she'd spent so much time in that hovering, floating headspace that she was disconnected from her own feelings. "It's hard to trust someone you don't know," Diane had said, in that patient and firm way that Rachel knew she needed. "You're so alienated from who you really are that being in your body is like living with a stranger."

Facing Nathan, she did her best to remain flat-footed. She looked for something tangible to focus on and pointed to the brown paper bag. "Are you going to show me what's inside?"

"Right." He hesitated and gripped it tighter. "I thought maybe you could use it."

He pulled out a bottle of Pappy Van Winkle, and her eyes filled when she saw it. This was classic Nathan, doing something thoughtful in those barely visible ways that seeped through the cracks in her heart. It was how he'd always loved her.

"Fuck." He put the whiskey down. "Okay. Please don't cry."

She bowed her head so he couldn't see her face. "I'm sorry. This wasn't what I wanted. I wasn't trying to lure you here for *this*." She gestured at her tears with disgust. "The exhibit is about working on forgiving myself and not being ashamed of who I am. I know that's why I hurt you. And I have no right to ask you for a second chance, so I won't, but I miss you." Her eyes watered again, and she rubbed them hard, hoping to stop the flood. "I *really* miss you, so maybe we can start over. As actual friends this time? And I can work on earning back your trust."

He looked down, like he was gathering courage to do something hard. She held herself still and prepared to be gutted. "Rachel, can I ask you something?"

She nodded.

"What were you going to say when we were dancing at the gala? Before we were interrupted?"

So much had happened since that night that her mind blanked for a moment. And then she remembered how desperate she'd been to tell him everything. That he was right to walk away from her and deserved so much more than what she had offered. And that she had wanted to give him that. Love with no strings attached. But now it all stuck like glue inside her throat.

"Don't you already know?"

Nathan gently opened her arms and pulled her closer, until she was pressed against his body. "I do," he said, and brought his lips so close to hers that they were almost touching. "But I want to hear you say it."

Her "I love you" was smothered by his kiss. He leaned back and touched her cheek, tracing her bottom lip with his thumb. "I don't want to start over. Or be friends. I just want you."

"I want you too," she said, the words still tumbling out as he kissed her again. Slower. Savoring it, even as his heart hammered against her palm.

"Guess what?" he asked as his mouth moved lower to her neck.

"What?"

He nuzzled her and mumbled, "Today's my birthday."

"Oh, happy birthday," she whispered as he trailed kisses up to her ear. "Can we celebrate? Is there anything special you want?"

Nathan cradled her face in both hands. "I have a very long list."

He moved to kiss her again, but the door swung open. Faith yelped, and Rachel spun around to find her daughter staring pointedly at the floor.

"Mom, I am so, so sorry. Sorrier than you'll ever know."

"It's okay," Rachel said. She glanced at Nathan, who was red-faced with embarrassment. "Nathan, this is my daughter. Faith."

He offered a stiff outstretched hand, realized how odd that was, and switched to a mildly less awkward wave. "I've heard a lot about you."

"Same," Faith said. "Mostly from my class group chat. You're very popular with the pastry chefs. They spend all day airbrushing ombré frosting, so they probably overidentify with you or something."

Nathan laughed. "Well, I'm just grateful it's all about icing and not shit-talking my clothes."

Faith gave him a half smile. "We're taking Mom out to celebrate after. You're welcome to come along." She lifted her hand. "But please try to keep the PDA to a minimum. This is still the woman who used to reenact *Blue's Clues* to help me fall asleep."

He smiled. "I'd love to come."

"So." Faith clasped her hands and nodded at the door. "You two ready to face the world?"

Nathan looked at Rachel. "What do you think? Are we done hiding?"

Rachel wrapped her arms around him and said, "Yes," so quickly, it made him laugh. Nathan kissed her temple and pulled her in closer. Faith opened the door, and the world rushed in: loud and bright, with dozens of phones aimed in their direction. But Rachel barely noticed the stir they caused by walking out together, so obviously a couple. Because she didn't have to. Not anymore.

# ACKNOWLEDGMENTS

I have a confession to make. I can't tell you where the idea for this book came from. The first words of the first draft were written over a decade ago, before I stopped writing to focus on my legal career and starting a family. For a while, I'd given up on my dream of publishing a novel someday. But then the pandemic happened. And we all realized just how much of our lives we'd been taking for granted. I stopped thinking of writing as something I'd return to "someday" and combed through my old Dropbox files for unfinished stories I could use to remind myself how to write a book. So much of that journey of rediscovery spilled over into parts of Rachel and Nathan's story. Like Rachel, I had to figure out how to balance being a wife and mother with excavating an old passion. Nathan's fan art was a way to honor the role fandom played in my writing journey and discovering my voice. So, while I can't pinpoint the exact moment *The Art of Scandal* was formed, I can easily tell you what this story is about. This is a book about all the different shapes of love. It's about how passion creates us, hurts us, and heals us, but also shows us who we really are.

I'm so grateful to my agent, Sharon Pelletier, for believing in this book and being a champion for me and my work. To my editor, Seema Mahanian, who helped me find the beating heart of Rachel and Nathan's story. I have learned so much from working with you, and I'm eternally grateful for your wisdom and encouragement. Kirsiah McNamara, thank you for playing a huge part in whipping this book into shape. Angelina Krahn, Tareth Mitch, and Lauren Bello: I couldn't have asked for a better editorial team. To Lila Selle for designing the cover of my dreams.

To Tiffany Porcelli, Alana Spendley, and Kamrun Nesa for working so hard to make sure this book reached the readers it was meant for.

A huge thank-you to my Pitch Wars mentors Denise Williams and Charish Reid, for plucking me out of the submission pile and teaching me how to revise a novel. To everyone behind the Pitch Wars program that basically changed my life. To my Pitch Wars Romance family, Courtney, Nikki, Sarah, Ella, and Amy, I don't think I could have survived all this without you. Vanessa, Alicia, and Jessica, your support has meant the world to me. To Monica and Adrianna, for helping me depict Nathan's identity and heritage with respect and care. To Kristen and Rebecca, for cheering me on and making the day job bearable when juggling it all felt overwhelming.

Thank you to my parents, for your unconditional love and wisdom. To Vivian, for sharing your love of books. If you were still with us, I know you'd be proud. To James and Finley, for being the loves of my life. You are and will always be my reason. To Karen, for always believing I could do this, and loving all my characters as much (if not more) than I do. To Angel, for being the best twin sister I could ever ask for. All those summer library trips hauling heavy backpacks stuffed with books were worth it.

And finally, a huge thanks to you, my readers. Time is a gift and I'm honored to have been the recipient of yours.

# READING GROUP GUIDE

# DISCUSSION QUESTIONS

1. After Rachel learns of Matt's affair, she demands one million dollars and the house. Matt pushes back, but Rachel tells him that if he respects her, he'll give her what she's owed. Discuss what Rachel means by this.

2. Rachel feels like an outsider in Oasis Springs, while Nathan feels like an outsider in his family. How do their communities contribute to their feelings of isolation? Have you ever felt like an outsider in your community?

3. When Nathan lets Rachel drive his '69 Camaro, she tells him, "Nathan, that was amazing. It made me feel so... *alive.*" Being in a relationship with Matt has forced Rachel to give up many of the things she used to enjoy. Discuss how Nathan helps Rachel rekindle her passions and find her true self. Did this inspire you to revisit any passions in your own life?

4. Matt campaigns on a progressive platform, but his words don't always match his actions. Discuss how Matt uses his relationship with Rachel to support his political career. How does race affect their relationship? What are some of the ways in which Rachel takes control of her narrative?

5. When Rachel first learns that Nathan's last name is Vasquez, she asks if he is related to Beto Vasquez. He brushes it off, saying, "I mean, in this town, isn't everybody?" Why do you think Nathan hides who his family is from Rachel?

6. After Beto reveals to his family that he has been diagnosed with a late-stage brain tumor, Joe and Sofia urge Nathan to reconcile with his father. Why is Nathan reluctant to reconnect, even in the face of Beto's terminal illness? Should Nathan change his mind about his father, even if Beto doesn't change his mind about Nathan?

7. Nathan doesn't think his art is serious enough to be in the art show because it is based on a children's novel. Fan art and similar works, like fanfiction, are often not considered "real art" or "real writing." Why do you think some creative works are taken less seriously than others?

8. Rachel is called the "DC Meghan Markle," "the Ice Queen," and other names by the media. Discuss the ways in which the media shapes our perception of public figures. How are Matt's and Rachel's affairs portrayed at the end of the novel? How does race play into these characterizations?

9. When Matt and Rachel get engaged, Herman Abbott tells Rachel that she's a "scandal waiting to happen" and that he's not "talking about race" but rather "pedigree." Discuss what Herman means by this. Does race still play a part in his judgment of Rachel? Given the scandal caused by Rachel's relationship with Nathan, was Herman right?

10. While Faith is away at school, Matt and Rachel decide not to tell her about the affair and their plan to get a divorce. Why do they decide to do this? Does Faith have a right to know what her parents are going through?

# AUTHOR Q&A

**What inspired you to write *The Art of Scandal*?**

I wanted to write a book about a woman in the public eye who was privately dealing with a betrayal that caused her to question everything about her life and identity. I started thinking about high-profile scandals involving women who stood by their powerful husbands while the world questioned their motives for doing so. A common question is "Why would someone stay married after being publicly humiliated?" I wanted to answer that in an interesting but also very human way. Deciding to leave someone you planned to build a life with is difficult, regardless of how big the betrayal might be. And, of course, I made that decision even more complicated with an unexpected romance at the worst possible time.

**Art and artists play a big role in the novel. What importance does art hold in your life? Do you make art of your own in a medium other than writing?**

Art has always been how I could express myself in ways I didn't feel comfortable doing in real life. I grew up in a single-parent household with limited access to museums, plays, or concerts because we couldn't afford to invest in them. But I've always found ways to make it a part of my life. I'm not a musician, but I love music, so when I was a kid, I made mixtapes, memorized song lyrics, and performed concerts for my family instead. I dreamed of writing books, but buying them was cost-prohibitive, so I practically lived in the public library. I don't draw, but I do graphic design as a hobby. I love art and try to engage with it in small ways as often as I can.

**The Art of Scandal takes place in the political world of Washington, DC. Do you have a personal connection to this space?**

I grew up in a fairly homogenous small town and rarely traveled until I went to college. Washington, DC, was one of the first major cities I visited regularly. It's a large, diverse cultural hub that buzzes with power-hungry energy, and it imprinted on me in those early years. I absolutely love everything about it. When I started brainstorming settings for *The Art of Scandal*, I immediately thought of DC—it's the perfect place for a story about political intrigue.

**Were any of your characters inspired by people you know or public figures?**

I used bits and pieces from various public figures to develop my characters. Matt is a combination of Pete Buttigieg's "Mayor Pete" persona and Bill DeBlasio's progressive brand, which leaned heavily on the optics of his interracial marriage during his mayoral campaign. Anthony Weiner's accidental tweets inspired the reveal of Matt's affair. And I used the media attention that Michelle Obama and Megan Markle received for being Black women married to powerful public figures to inspire some of the pressure Rachel faces for being Matt's wife.

**The characters and community of Oasis Springs are all intertwined in numerous, messy relationships. How did you come up with all these conflicts?**

I was a latchkey kid raised on daytime soap operas like *The Young and the Restless* and *Days of Our Lives*. Those shows always featured large families living in tight-knit communities with small degrees of separation between the characters. I wanted to replicate those messy connections that kept me tuning in daily to see what would happen next in the pages of a book. To do that, I created detailed family histories and biographies for every character, regardless of whether the information ultimately ended up in the final novel. This allowed me to spot opportunities to weave their lives together in tense, tantalizing ways that are slowly revealed as you read.

**Were there any characters or sections of the book that you found challenging to write?**

Nathan was the most challenging character to write for many reasons, but primarily because he starts the book very privileged and aimless in a way I've never experienced. Finding Nathan's voice and figuring out why he failed to launch after high school took several revisions. Once I started to dive deep into his history with his family, many things fell into place, particularly all the reasons he would fall so hard and fast for a woman like Rachel.

**Were there any parts of the novel that evolved significantly between your first and final drafts?**

Aside from Nathan evolving as a character, Rachel was much more passive in earlier drafts, and Matt was more of a two-dimensional villain with no redeeming qualities. I was initially very sensitive to how complicated their situation was and hesitant to write inside the gray areas I ultimately explored in the final version. But once I decided to make Rachel the instigator of their million-dollar deal, everything started getting more interesting and real. I focused more on Rachel's anger and grief over the loss of the life she'd invested so much time in. I also made her culpable in the slow erosion of her marriage. I developed Matt more as a person, into someone who could look in a mirror and still be the hero of his own story. I made him a loving stepfather who was genuinely clueless about how his marriage fell apart. I think it made the whole situation more heartbreaking.

**Did you learn anything about yourself through writing this novel?**

It forced me to examine many of my feelings surrounding the loss of my identity after marriage and motherhood. I stopped writing when I started a family because I thought it required a mental and emotional investment that should be reserved for my husband and daughter. I missed writing but felt guilty for grieving that part of my life when I had been blessed with this amazing husband and daughter. Writing about Rachel's journey of returning to her art while still being a good mother and loving partner to Nathan helped me embrace the idea that pursuing my passion didn't make me less of a wife and mother. It made me a better one.

**Who are some of your favorite authors, and did they influence the way you wrote *The Art of Scandal*?**

*On Writing* by Stephen King was the first writing craft book I ever read, and it made a huge impression on me. It taught me how important it is to write honestly, regardless of how messy or uncomfortable it may be. That's what I tried to remember while I wrote *The Art of Scandal* and what I try to do in all my writing—no matter what the premise might be, it has to feel honest and true.

My entry point into romance novels was primarily 1990s historicals by authors like Catherine Coulter and Jude Deveraux. They have definitely influenced the type of romances I love to read and write. *Waiting to Exhale* and *How Stella Got Her Groove Back* by Terry McMillian taught me that characters could have fully realized inner and outer lives in addition to existing within the romance plot. *Range of Motion* and *The Pull of the Moon* by Elizabeth Berg were two of the first books I read that focused on the inner lives of more mature, married women while featuring love stories. They expanded my idea of what a romance could be.

## ABOUT THE AUTHOR

**Regina Black** is a former civil litigator, current law school administrator, and lifelong romance reader who has always been passionate about the depiction of Black women in popular culture. She currently resides in Little Rock, Arkansas, with her husband and daughter.